The Scent of
Jasmine

BOOKS BY JUDE DEVERAUX

The Velvet Promise
Highland Velvet
Velvet Song
Velvet Angel
Sweetbriar
Counterfeit Lady
Lost Lady
River Lady
Twin of Fire
Twin of Ice
The Temptress
The Raider
The Princess
The Awakening
The Maiden
The Taming
The Conquest
A Knight in Shining Armor
Holly
Wishes
The Mountain Laurel
The Duchess
Eternity

Sweet Liar
The Invitation
Remembrance
The Heiress
Legend
An Angel for Emily
The Blessing
High Tide
Temptation
The Summerhouse
The Mulberry Tree
Forever . . .
Wild Orchids
Forever and Always
Always
First Impressions
Carolina Isle
Someone to Love
Secrets
Return to Summerhouse
Lavender Morning
Days of Gold
Scarlet Nights

JUDE DEVERAUX

The Scent of Jasmine

A NOVEL

DOUBLEDAY LARGE PRINT HOME LIBRARY EDITION

Pocket Books

New York   London   Toronto   Sydney

Pocket Books
A Division of Simon & Schuster, Inc.
1230 Avenue of the Americas
New York, NY 10020

First Pocket Books paperback edition January 2011

POCKET and colophon are registered trademarks of Simon & Schuster, Inc.

Cover illustration by Melody Cassen

Manufactured in the United States of America

ISBN 978-1-61129-028-8

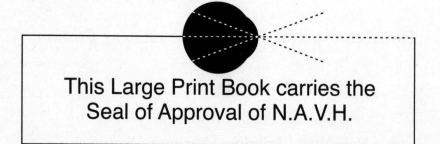

This Large Print Book carries the
Seal of Approval of N.A.V.H.

One

🍀

Charleston, South Carolina, 1799

"Think about the Highlands," T.C. Connor said to his goddaughter, Cay. "Think about your father's homeland, of the people there. He was the laird, so that means you're the laird's daughter, which means—"

"Do you think my father would want me to do what you're asking of me?" Cay asked, her thick-lashed eyes smiling at him.

T.C. lay on his bed with a splint from his knee to his hip. He'd broken his leg just hours before and grimaced from pain at the slightest movement, but he gave Cay a weak smile. "If your father knew what I was asking of his precious daughter, he'd tie me to a wagon and drag me across a couple of mountains."

"I'll go," Hope said from the other side of the bed. "I'll take a carriage and—"

T.C. put his hand over hers and looked at her fondly. Hope was the only child of Bathsheba and Isaac Chapman. Her beautiful young mother had died years before, while her grumpy, unpleaseable old father lingered on. T.C. Connor claimed he was just "a friend of the family," but Cay had heard whispers among the women that there had been more between Bathsheba and T.C. than just friendship. It was even whispered that T.C. could possibly be Hope's father.

"That's very kind of you to offer, dear, but . . ." He trailed off, not wanting to state the obvious. Hope had been raised in a city and she'd never been on the back of a horse. She traveled only in carriages. And, also, she'd fallen down a staircase when she was three and her left leg had healed incorrectly. Under her long skirts she wore a shoe with a two-inch-thick sole.

"Uncle T.C.," Hope said patiently,

"what you're asking of Cay is impossible. Look at her. She's dressed for a ball. She can't very well ride a horse wearing that gown."

T.C. and Hope looked at Cay and the sparkling splendor of her nearly lit up the room. Cay was just twenty years old and, while she'd never be the classical beauty her mother was, she was very pretty. Her dark blue eyes peered out from under extraordinarily long lashes, but her best feature was her thick auburn hair that was now pinned up, with curls escaping and softening the strong jaw line she'd inherited from her father.

"I want her to go directly from the meeting place to the ball." When he tried to sit up, T.C. had to suppress a groan. "Maybe I can—"

Hope gave him a gentle push on the shoulder, and he fell back against the mattress. She wiped his sweat-covered forehead with a cool cloth.

Winded, he looked back at Cay. The gown she had on was exquisite. A white satin overlaid with gauze, it was covered with hundreds of little crystal beads set in intricate patterns. It clung to her slim figure perfectly, and if he knew her father, Angus McTern Harcourt, the dress cost more than T.C. had earned last year. "Hope is right," T.C. said. "You can't possibly go in my place. It's much too dangerous for anyone, especially for a young girl. If only Nate were here. Or Ethan or Tally."

At the mention of three of her four older brothers, Cay sat down on the chair by the side of the bed. "I can outride Tally," she said of her brother who was less than a year older than she was. "And I can shoot as well as Nate."

"Adam," T.C. said. "If only Adam were here."

Cay gave a sigh. She couldn't do anything as well as her oldest brother Adam could. But then, only her father was a match for Adam.

"Uncle T.C.," Hope said and there was warning in her voice, "what you're doing isn't right. You're trying to goad Cay into doing something that is absolutely and utterly *impossible* for her to do. She—"

"Maybe not impossible," Cay said. "I

mean, all I'm to do is to ride to a specified place leading a pack horse, and pay a couple of men. That's all there is to it, isn't it?"

"That's all," T.C. said as he again tried to sit up. "When you meet the men, you hand the bag of coins to them, and give Alex the reins to the packed horse. The men will go away, then you'll ride your mare on to the ball. The whole thing is really quite simple."

"Maybe I could—" Cay began, but Hope cut her off.

Hope had stood up, with her hands on her hips, and she was glaring down at T.C. on the bed. "T.C. Connor, what you're doing to this poor child's mind is nothing short of evil. You are twisting her thoughts around until she can't even remember the facts of all this—if she ever knew them."

Hope was nearly thirty, a full nine years older than Cay, and she often treated Cay as though she were barely past the age of rope jumping.

"I *do* understand what he's asking," Cay said.

"No, you don't." Hope's voice was

growing louder. "All of them are criminals. Every one of them. Those two men
you're to pay—" She glared at T.C. "Tell
her where you got them."

"Jayz," T.C. mumbled, but at Hope's
look he said more clearly, "Jail. I got
them as they were being released from
prison. But where else was I going to
get men to do what I needed done?
From church? Hope, you're forgetting
that it's Alex who matters in all this. It's
Alex who—"

"Alex!" Hope put her hands to the
side of her head, and for a moment she
turned away. When she looked back at
the man on the bed, her face was red
with anger. She wasn't an especially
pretty woman and the color didn't make
her more so. "You know nothing about
this Alexander McDowell. You never
even met him until you went to see him
in prison."

Cay's eyes widened. "But I thought—"

"You thought our dear uncle T.C. knew
him, didn't you? Well, he doesn't. Our
godfather served in the army with this
Alex's father and your father, and—"

"And the man saved my life more than

once." T.C.'s tone was angry. "He protected us when we were so green we
didn't even know to duck when people
started shooting at us. Mac was like
a father, or a big brother, to all of us.
He—"

"Mac?" Cay said as she was finally
beginning to put the story together.
"The man you're helping to escape from
prison is the son of the Mac who my father speaks of?"

"Yes," T.C. said as he turned toward
Cay. "I don't think your father would be
alive today if it weren't for Mac."

"Tell her what the son did," Hope
said, her face still as red as a sunburn.
"Tell Cay what the man did to get himself put in jail."

When T.C. was silent, Cay said, "I
thought he was—"

"What? Arrested for drunkenness? For
falling on his face into a horse trough?"

"Hope!" T.C. said sternly, and Cay
could see that his face was also red—
and in exactly the same way as Hope's.
"I really think that—"

"That you could bamboozle Cay into

doing what you want her to do without telling her the facts?"

"What did he do?" Cay asked.

"He murdered his wife!" Hope nearly shouted.

"Oh." Cay was unable to think of anything else to say. Her eyes were so wide she looked like a doll in her beautiful dress. There were three stars covered in diamonds in her hair and they sparkled in the candlelight.

Hope sat down on the chair by the bed and looked at T.C. "Should I tell her or will you?"

"You seem to be set on telling all the gory details so *you* tell her."

"You weren't here," Hope began, "so you didn't see all the nasty stories in the newspapers. Alexander Lachlan McDowell came to Charleston three months ago, met the very beautiful and talented Miss Lilith Grey, and married her right away. The day after the wedding, he slit her throat."

Cay put her hand to her neck in horror.

Hope looked at T.C., who glared back

at her. "Have I said anything wrong? Exaggerated anything?"

"Every word is straight out of the newspapers," T.C. said tightly.

Hope looked back at Cay. "This man Alex was only found out by accident. Someone threw a rock with a note attached to it through the window of Judge Arnold's bedroom. The note said that Alex McDowell's new bride was dead and she could be found beside her husband in the suite at the top of the best hotel in town. At first the judge thought it was a horrible joke, but when Dr. Nickerson started pounding on the door, saying he had received the same note, the judge went with him to investigate." Hope looked at T.C. "Should I go on?"

"Can I stop you?"

Cay looked from one to the other and saw two jaws set in exactly the same way, two pairs of eyes flashing anger in the same way. She imagined how when she got home she and her mother would giggle together over every word, every gesture, of what had gone on tonight. She'd tell her father, too, but she'd have to edit the story carefully and leave out any mention of "jail" and "murder."

"The judge and the doctor burst in on this Alexander McDowell before it was even daylight, and beside him on the bed was his new wife. She was lying there with her throat cut!"

Again Cay gasped, her hand at her neck.

"I'd be willing to stake my life on it that Mac's son did not commit the murder," T.C. said calmly.

"That would be all right but you're risking *Cay's* life, not yours!" Hope shot back at him.

Cay looked from one to the other and wasn't sure they were ever going to speak to each other again. "So you're breaking him out of jail and sending him away?"

"That was my plan, except that I was going with him."

"On another of his long, dangerous treks," Hope said, her voice still angry. "Where were you planning to go this time?"

"Into the wilds of Florida."

Hope gave a shiver of revulsion.

All her life, Cay had heard about Uncle T.C.'s travels. He'd gone with exploration teams into the far west and seen things no other white man had. He loved plants, seemed to know the Latin names of all of them, and he'd spent three years learning to draw what he saw. However, while others praised his drawings, Cay and her mother had kept their opinions to themselves, for they shared a talent for art and they found his paintings too simple, too unschooled. One of Cay's drawing masters—she'd had them since she was four—had been the English artist Russell Johns. The man was a tyrant in the studio, and Cay'd had to work hard to keep up with his demands, but she'd done it. "If only you were a boy," he'd said to her many times, his voice wistful.

Cay didn't realize she'd said the words aloud until she saw T.C. and Hope staring at her. "I was thinking about—"

"Mr. Johns," T.C. said. "Your latest teacher." He was looking at her with envy. "How I wish I had your talent, Cay. If I could draw as well and as quickly as you, I'd produce three times as much,

and all of it would be good. Foreshort-
ening drives me mad!"

Hope didn't know much about Cay
or her family. Their shared interest was
T.C., as he was godfather to both of
them. All Hope had been told was that
Cay had "a decision to make" and she'd
come to stay in Charleston while she
made it. "Do you paint?"

T.C. gave a little laugh that sent pain
shooting through his body. He rubbed
his knee under the bandages while he
tried to catch his breath. "Michelangelo
would be jealous of her talent."

"I hardly think so," Cay said, but she
was smiling. Modestly, she looked down
at her hands on her lap.

"And you want to risk this lovely
young woman to rescue a murderer?"
Hope was glaring at T.C.

"No. I just want her to do something
for a man who has lost everything! If
you'd visited him in jail with me, as I
begged you to do, you would have seen
his grief. He was more concerned about
what he'd lost than what was going to
happen to *him.*"

Hope was unmoved and Cay guessed

that this was an argument they'd had many times before. "And after this man is rescued, then what does he do?" Hope asked. "Spend the rest of his life running from the law?"

"As I said, the original plan was for Alex to travel with me into Florida with Mr. Grady." He glanced at Cay. "Mr. Grady is the leader of this expedition and we've been planning this trip since the spring. I was to be the recorder, to draw and paint all that we see. Mr. Grady was kind to hire me, as he knows I can't draw a person or an animal. Only plants interest me. Cay can—"

Cay didn't want to hear more praise of her artist skills; they seemed superfluous when someone's life was in danger. "If no one is there to meet him, what will this man do?"

"Get caught, returned to jail, and hanged tomorrow morning," T.C. said.

Cay looked at Hope for confirmation, but she refused to make a comment. "So you want me to take a horse to him?"

"Yes!" T.C. said before Hope could speak. "That's all. Pay the men who are to break him out of jail, give the horse to Alex, then leave."

"And where will he go if I do this?"

"To Mr. Grady. I've drawn a map of where Alex is to meet the expedition." He gave Cay a look of speculation. "I guess that now Mr. Grady will have to get someone else to do the recording as I can't go. Too bad . . ."

Cay smiled, knowing what he meant. "Even if I were male, that's not something I'd like to do. I'm quite happy living near my family in Virginia, and I want to stay there. I leave the adventuring to my brothers."

"As is right and proper," Hope said. "Women aren't supposed to run all over the country doing what men do. And they are most certainly *not* supposed to straddle a horse and ride out to meet a murderer."

T.C. was looking at Cay with serious eyes. "I've known you all your life and you know I'd never ask you to do anything dangerous. You can cover your dress with Hope's big hooded cloak, and I know you can ride. I've seen you jump fences that scare most men."

"If I didn't, my brothers would laugh at me," Cay said. "They'd . . ." As she thought of them, she asked herself what they would do if faced with this situation. Tally would already be saddled, Nate would ask a hundred questions before he left, Ethan would be packing because he'd take T.C.'s place on the expedition, and Adam would . . .

"They would what?" T.C. asked.

"They'd help any friend of our father's," Cay said as she stood up.

"You can*not* do this." Hope was looking at Cay from across the bed.

"Didn't I hear you say that *you* would go if you could?" Cay asked.

"Yes," Hope said, "but that's different. You're so young and . . . and . . ."

"Childish? Spoiled? Rich?" Cay asked, her eyes narrowing with every word she spoke. Ever since she'd met Hope she'd felt as though Hope dismissed Cay as too young, too frivolous, too pampered, to ever be able to actually accomplish anything. While it was true that Cay hadn't had the misfortunes that Hope had had in her life, of an accident that had left her with a limp, the death of her mother, and a lifetime of caring for a ceaselessly complaining old father, Cay'd had some setbacks in her life. In her opinion, being the only girl with four older brothers was enough to qualify her for battle pay.

"I'll do it," Cay said as she gave Hope the look she used to stop Tally from putting a second frog down her collar.

"Thank you," T.C. said, and there were tears in his eyes. He grabbed her small hand and kissed the back of it. "Thank you, thank you. And you'll be fine. Alex is a very pleasant young man and—"

"I doubt if his wife's family would agree with that," Hope said.

When T.C. gave her a look, she sat down on her chair. She knew when she'd been defeated.

"Perhaps I should change," Cay said.

"No, no, I want you like that. Go from the meeting place directly to the ball."

"That will give you an alibi," Hope said, some of the anger in her voice gone.

"Yes, it will. Not that you'll be asked

where you were, but . . ." T.C. trailed off.

Hope let out a sigh of defeat. "And keep your face covered. Don't let anyone see you. Not even *that man.*"

"Will people be chasing him?" Cay asked as she began to understand what she was volunteering to do.

"I've been planning this for the many weeks he's been in jail," T.C. said, "and I think I have every possibility covered. There will be three sets of men escaping, and only you will know where to meet the correct one."

"This must have cost you a lot," Hope said.

T.C. waved his hand in dismissal. This rescue had cost him everything he owned, but he wasn't going to tell them that.

"When should I leave?" Cay asked, swallowing as she thought of the coming night.

"About twenty minutes ago."

"He doesn't want to give you time to think about this," Hope said.

"My maid—"

"I'll keep her busy," Hope said. "She'll

not even notice that you've escaped her."

"I . . . I, uh . . ." Cay stuttered.

"Go!" T.C. said. "Don't think any more, just *go!* Keep covered, let no one see your face, not even Alex, then ride to the ball. Leave your horse at the back of the ballroom, so there'll be no talk about how you arrived. Hope will take care of that."

Cay looked at Hope, who gave her a curt nod. "All right, then, I guess I'll leave. I don't know how I'm going to ride in this dress, but—"

"The cloak will cover every inch of you," T.C. said, his eyes pleading with her to take no more time in discussion. "Tomorrow we'll have chocolate for breakfast and laugh about all this."

"Promise?" Cay said, smiling.

"I swear it."

After hesitating long enough to give him another smile, she grabbed her skirt and ran down the stairs. Her heart was racing, but she knew this was something that *needed* to be done. Tonight she was going to save a man's life. That he may or may not be a murderer was not something she wanted to worry about. No, it was better to just do the job, and think about what she'd done later.

Two

♣

Cay sat on her horse in the dark and wished she were in Virginia with her family. It was autumn, so it would be cooler there. Would they have a fire blazing in the parlor? Would her brothers be home or would they be out doing . . . whatever it was that boys did all the time? Ethan had been seeing one of the Woodlock girls, but Cay didn't think much would come of it. The girl wasn't pretty enough or smart enough for Ethan.

When her mare began to prance about, Cay shifted in her saddle and calmed it down. Hidden in the trees behind her was the heavily laden horse that Alexander McDowell was to take with him when he finally arrived with the men who'd broken him out of jail.

She looked around but could see little in the night sky. It had been difficult finding the place where her uncle told her she was to meet Mac's son, which was the only way Cay could think of him. He was the son of the man who'd helped her father, and that was her reason for being there. If she didn't concentrate on that, she knew she'd start looking about the dark countryside and thinking about how she was to meet a man who had probably committed murder.

Hope had gone downstairs with Cay, helped her cover her gown with the big wool cloak, and given her the map T.C. had drawn that showed where Cay was to go.

"It's not too late to say no," Hope said as she fastened the hood around Cay's head.

Cay put on the bravest face she could manage. "I'm sure I'll be all right. Besides, I doubt if this man is actually a murderer."

Hope lowered her voice. "You didn't read the newspaper accounts. The doctor and the judge found her locked inside the room with him, and he was sound asleep. He had no conscience about what he'd done. He is pure evil."

Cay swallowed. "What did he have to say about it all?"

"That he'd had a glass of wine then fallen asleep."

"Maybe he was telling the truth."

"You are so very young," Hope said in a patronizing way. "No man falls asleep on his wedding night."

"But maybe—" Cay tried to say, but Hope interrupted her.

"The sooner you go, the quicker you can get back. I'll be waiting for you at the ball. I won't be dressed as richly as you are, but I'll have on my rose-colored silk, so look for me at the back." Hope put her hands on Cay's shoulders and looked at her for a moment. "May God go with you," she said, and quickly she kissed Cay's cheek. In the next minute the two of them were running for the stables where the horses awaited them. Hope helped Cay adjust the voluminous cloak over her dress and the lower part of her legs, which were exposed in their silk stockings. The ball gown was narrow, and when she was on the horse, it rode up on her legs.

"No matter what our godfather says, please be very cautious with this man," Hope said when Cay was at last in the saddle and covered.

Trying to lighten the serious mood of the moment, Cay said, "Can I bring you back anything?"

"Your safety will be enough," Hope said without a smile, but when she saw Cay's disappointed look, she said, "A husband. Not too tall, not too short, not rich, not poor. I just want a man who can stand up to my father." She gave a little smile. "And I want a man who won't fall asleep on our wedding night."

"Which father?" Cay quipped and instantly realized she was more nervous than she'd thought. She started to apologize, but Hope laughed.

"The complaining one, of course. The other one, I have no trouble with—except that he won't obey me. Now go!"

Cay kicked the horse forward and rode west toward the place where she was to meet the murderer.

Now, she sat on the horse and

waited. They should have been there by now, but she heard or saw nothing. Had something gone wrong? Had the escape attempt failed? She was aware that she knew remarkably little about what Uncle T.C. had done to make this plan and she should have asked more questions. She should have been more like her brother Nate, who loved to solve puzzles. He liked to figure out who did what and why. In the dark silence, she thought about the first time Nate had solved a dilemma that had put her entire family and all the people who worked for them in a tizzy. The flour in the kitchen was disappearing at an alarming rate, but no one would admit to taking it.

Smiling, Cay's mind began to wander back to that time, but a sound to her right made her pull back on the reins to her mare. She'd securely tied the other horse to a tree about fifty yards away, and when she glanced that way, she could see nothing.

But her senses told her that something was different. "Who's there?" she called out.

Out of the darkness slipped a tall,

bearded, older-looking man, who stood so close to her that she jerked the reins and started to flee, but he caught her by the calf—and when he did, her silk-clad leg and a bit of her gown were revealed. The crystal beads sparkled even in the blackness of the night.

"Bludy heel," the man said as he looked up at her. "Th' glaikit cheil sent a vemen childe tae dae a mon's job. A wee, dreich hen ay nae use 'at Ah main troost wi' mah life. Ah main an aw shet myself noo." He paused, then said in American English, "Are you on your way to a party, Miss?"

Cay kicked his hand away from her leg and looked down at him with all the contempt she could express. "As suin as Ah gie rid ay ye, Ah am. Kin ye keep up wi' me?" She'd spent several summers in Scotland with her cousins and she understood the insult he'd given her, and all she could think was that he was an ungrateful lout.

She didn't bother pointing out where the other horse was. If he was so sure that a "vemen childe"—a woman child—was so useless that he "might as well shoot himself now" then he could "bludy" well find the horse by himself.

He was just standing there, staring at her in open-mouthed astonishment, and she thought he was probably shocked that she understood his thick brogue. He said something under his breath that sounded like "You're a McTern," but she wasn't sure what he'd said.

When a shot rang out, she wasn't surprised. Obviously, T.C.'s plan had gone awry. The men she was to pay hadn't shown up, and the foul mouthed Scotsman had come alone. He was certainly on his own now, she thought as she kicked her mare to run faster.

As she rode, she could feel her dress riding up higher on her hips. At this rate, she'd look awful when she arrived at the ball. The hood of the cloak had blown off her head and she could feel her carefully dressed hair coming out of its pins. She was glad she'd thought to pin the diamond stars inside her bodice. Her father had given her those for her eighteenth birthday and she'd hate to lose them, especially in so unworthy a cause.

Behind her, she could hear another horse coming up fast. Turning, she saw that it was the Scotsman. Even though he had a lot of hair on his head and face, she could still see that his eyes were blazing with anger.

"Cover yerself, you daft girl," he shouted at her.

"Now's not the time for modesty." She stood up in the saddle and the horse took on more speed. She'd always loved riding and she'd spent a lot of her life on horseback. Racing with her brothers—and beating them—was one of her favorite pastimes.

"So they won't see you're a lass," he yelled as he tried to keep up with her. But his horse was so laden with what he was to take on the expedition it couldn't. Still, the man kept urging it forward until Cay felt sorry for the animal.

"We must part," she said as she quickly reined her horse to the left. She didn't know her way around the outside of Charleston very well, but she had a good sense of direction, and besides, she could see lights in the distance. She was going to go to T.C.'s house where she planned to pack her clothes and go home in the morning. She'd had all the excitement she could stand for one visit.

When the man turned with her and nearly made her run off the road, it took all her years of experience in riding to keep the horse on track.

"What do you think you're doing?" she shouted at him.

"Saving your wee life," he yelled back. "If you go back into the city they'll arrest you."

"No one knows I've ever even met you." She glanced over her shoulder. She'd heard a shot, but she'd seen no one.

"They saw you."

"They did not!" she shouted at him.

To her astonishment, he grabbed the bridle of her horse and pulled so hard she almost fell off. If she'd had a whip in her hands, she would have used it on him.

"You must come with me."

"I will not! You're a criminal!"

"So are you now. Either you follow

me or I'll pull you off that horse and put you across my saddle."

She was tempted to test him to do that. She could see that he was thin under his raggedy clothes, and she was much younger than he was, but he still might be strong enough to pull her. "All right," she said at last, and in the next second he took off, seeming to expect her to follow wherever he led. She wanted to turn and ride away, but she heard another shot in the distance, so she went after him. Maybe he knew of a safe place to hide. Didn't all people who were put into jail know such things?

She rode behind him for what must have been a mile, then he seemed to disappear in the darkness. As she pulled her horse to a halt, she looked around her, but she didn't see him. She heard a bird whistle, but there were few other sounds. In the next moment, she heard a horse's hooves pounding on the road, and when the man appeared, even with all the hair on his face, she could see that he was angry.

Marveling at his ingratitude, she

moved her horse into the bushes at the side of the road, and dismounted.

"Ah thooght 'at coz ye coods kin me, ye micht hae a wee bit ay sense tae ye, but nae, yoo're as dumb as a bairn."

"I can understand every word you say," she said, "and I don't like any of it. When I get back—"

"Quiet, girl," he growled as he pushed her to the ground, his arm across her back.

Cay was about to protest when she heard the horses approaching. As she lowered her head, she felt the man's arm slide up over her. He smelled vile, and she wondered if he had lice and other vermin on him. If he did, she'd never get them out of her hair.

Four horses and riders stopped not far from them, and she held her breath as she waited for them to go on.

"I tell you, it was that red-haired girl staying with T.C. Connor. I saw her face when she looked back," one of the men said loudly, and Cay gasped.

The Scotsman put his hand over her mouth. He was very close to her, his long body pressed against hers, one of his shoulders over hers, holding her to the ground.

She moved her head to get his hand off her mouth. He removed it, but he gave her a warning look to be quiet.

"A girl?" one of the men said. "Why would a girl help a murderer escape?"

"She's probably the reason he killed his wife, and now they're runnin' off together. Everyone knows he married Miss Grey for her money."

"What a fool to have killed a beauty like her."

"You two sound like old hens discussin' the gossip. I think we should go back to Connor's and see if the girl is there. If she ain't, then I say we should ask him some questions."

With that, they turned their horses and left.

Instantly, Cay moved toward her horse, but the man grabbed the bottom of her cloak and pulled her back down.

"Where do you think you're going?"

"Back to my godfather's house to warn him."

"And that means T.C.'s house?"

"Of course."

"You do that and they'll catch you and put you in jail for helping a murderer escape."

She glared at him as he got up. "I guess that means you're not planning to give yourself up to protect your benefactor?"

After giving a snort, as though to say she was the dumbest person alive, he got up and went to his horse. "Connor can take care of himself. From what I've heard of the man, he's outrun Indians, bears, and a shipload of pirates. I think he can handle a few locals looking for a pretty girl to terrorize."

"Yes, but . . ." Cay didn't want to take the time to argue with him. "All right, then I'll go home."

"And that means . . . ?"

"Edilean, Virginia."

"Does anyone in Charleston know that's where you live?" He was checking the packs on his horse.

"Several people here know my family. My parents have been here often, and my brothers—"

"Spare me the family history. You can't

go home because that's the first place they'll go after they question Connor."

"Can't go home?" Cay smiled as she got up and went to her horse. "You have no idea who my father is, do you?"

"He can't help you now. Get on your horse, and try to keep your legs covered. They distract me from my purpose."

Cay wasn't sure that was a compliment, but if it was, she didn't like it. The images Hope had given her about what this man had done to his wife were vivid in her mind.

"Where are we going?" she asked. "My father knows a lot of people and he could—"

He reined his horse in tightly to stop beside her. "Your father was raised to be the laird of the McTern clan, wasn't he?"

"Yes, he was," she said proudly.

"Then he'll be a man who protects his family?"

"Of course. He's the best—"

"If you know that about him, then is it your intention to start a war between your father and the city of Charleston?"

"Of course not."

"If you go home and hide with your father, he'll no doubt fight to the death to protect you. Is it your aim to see your family dead?"

"No," she said, her breath held because she knew that's exactly what her father and brothers would do. "I don't want that, and when my father hears of this—"

"I'm sure T.C. Connor will keep your father from hearing of it. What we must do is find you a safe place to hide until I can prove my innocence. When I'm free, so will you be."

"But—" She stopped herself from saying that she wasn't so sure he was innocent. "How can you prove you're not guilty if you're traipsing around in the jungles of Florida?"

"I need to give these people time to calm down. I found out at my trial that no one would listen to me. Too many people liked . . ." He looked as though he was about to choke.

"Your wife?" she asked. "People liked her?"

"Did you think I'd marry a woman no one liked?" he snapped.

"Your ingratitude astonishes me. After all I've risked for you, you—" She took a breath. Saying what she wanted to wasn't going to help the situation. "What did the doctor say?"

"The bastard died of a heart attack the day after Lilith . . . left. She was buried before I saw her again."

"If she was well liked, then the doctor died from shock of it all, it's no wonder people want to hang you for murdering her."

He seemed unperturbed by her accusation. "I will do more than hang the man who killed her," he muttered. "Now follow me and don't give me any more of your sass."

As Cay followed him, she tried to think of a way out of this predicament. If she couldn't return to her godfather, couldn't go to other family friends, and she couldn't go *home,* where could she go? How long did being a fugitive from justice last? Maybe she should take a ship to Scotland and stay with her father's family for a while. But how long would that be? Six months? A year? The Scotsman said he wanted to let the authorities in Charleston "calm down"— or as he said it, "caum doon"—then he planned to find his wife's real murderer. Would that take long? What if he really was the murderer? That would mean he'd never be cleared. He'd always be a wanted man—which would mean that Cay would also be wanted by the law forever.

She was still following him, but she was tempted to turn and head back to Charleston. But the memory of the men on the road looking for her, knowing who she was and where they could find her, stopped her. Also, the Scotsman's words about her family's reaction to all this kept her going forward. If she returned to Charleston, went to T.C.'s house, and gave herself up, she would no doubt be put in jail. She couldn't imagine the anger that would engender in her family. She could almost see her father and her four brothers shooting their way in and out of the prison. Would one of them be *killed*?

When tears started rolling down her

cheeks, she didn't bother to wipe them away. She tried to think of something good, but all that came to mind was how stupid she'd been. This was the first time she'd ever traveled alone— by herself except for her maid and her footman, Cuddy—and she'd had to argue for the privilege.

"You'll get into trouble without us there," Tally had said.

"You'll meet other men, so you'll have more than three marriage proposals to think about," Ethan said, his eyes full of merriment.

Nate gave her a list of books he wanted her to buy for him and said, "You'll take care, won't you?"

Adam had been the worst. He'd kissed her forehead and told her he trusted her, believed in her, and knew that she had enough wisdom to conduct herself with propriety at all times.

Cay glanced down the side of the horse and saw that one of her legs was exposed to above the knee. She tried to pull the cloak over it, but it was caught beneath her.

As for her father, when she asked his

permission to travel alone, he'd said, "No." Just that. "No." Her mother said, "Don't worry, I'll persuade him"—and she did.

So now Cay had betrayed the trust of all of them—except for Tally, who thought his sister was a scatterbrained nincompoop.

"Here!" the Scotsman said and handed her a dirty handkerchief. When she hesitated in taking it, he said, "Your nose will dirty it more so why does it need to start out being clean?"

When she began to answer his question, he rolled his eyes skyward and urged his horse ahead of her.

Cay blew her nose, then held the filthy cloth at arm's length, not sure what to do with it.

"Don't drop it," the Scotsman said quickly. "They'll have dogs after us."

Cay was so shocked by that thought that she did drop the cloth, but the Scotsman pulled back on the reins of his horse and grabbed the handkerchief before it hit the ground.

"You may not like me but we're in this together," he said angrily as he shoved the dirty cloth into a saddlebag. Then his voice softened. "I'm sorry, lass. I never meant to drag you into this, but then, *I* wouldn't have sent a girl—"

"If you say 'to do a man's job' again I'll turn you in myself."

She wasn't sure, but she thought she saw a tiny smile under all the hair on his face.

"Come on, lass," he said, "cheer up. If they catch me, you'll get to see me hang."

As he urged his horse forward, she said, "But will I hang next to you?"

"No. Tell them I kidnapped you. They'll believe that."

"*I* believe that," she muttered as she kicked her horse and went after him.

Three

❧

Cay's legs hurt, her back ached, and she was so sleepy she could hardly hold on to the reins of the horse. They'd been riding all through the night and most of the day, and the poor horse was more tired than she was.

But she didn't complain to the man she was following. She looked at his back, at the way he sat straight up in the saddle, with no signs of fatigue, and she wondered if he was human.

Abruptly, he turned back and was soon beside her. "We must rest the horses."

She started to say that he could ask about *her*, but she didn't. "Yes, my horse is quite exhausted," she said in her haughtiest tone. She wasn't sure, but she thought she saw a bit of a smile in his blue eyes. With all the hair on his face, it was difficult to tell.

"I want you to wait here for me." He motioned to a big oak tree with branches that hung down to the ground. "Stay on the horse or you'll never get back on."

"I think I'm fully capable of dismounting and remounting," she said.

"Dis and re." He shook his head at her. "Had some schooling, did you?"

"I majored in good manners. Ever heard of them?"

"Not in *this* country," he said, but there seemed to be a smile under his untrimmed whiskers.

She followed him under the tree, ducking to miss the low-hanging branches.

"Do you have the money you were to pay the men?"

Cay's face showed her alarm. Was he going to take what little money she had and leave her there alone to face the law?

The humor left his face and his eyes blazed fire. "I'm not a thief! I need a few coins to buy us a place to stay the night, and some food. You can keep the rest."

She reached into the satchel by her

leg and pulled out the bag of money that Uncle T.C. had given her. She couldn't help pausing for a moment as she remembered when he'd put it in her hand. He and Hope were so far away now.

"Do you mean to keep it all night?" the Scotsman snapped at her.

She wanted to throw the coins in his ungrateful face, but she held back. "How much do you need?"

"A dollar or two should do it. Now, will you stay here and wait or will you run to the authorities? I need to know what to expect when I return."

Part of her wanted to go to the local sheriff and say she'd been kidnapped by this man, but the larger part of her knew she couldn't do that. She'd never be able to face Uncle T.C. again. "I need a pen and paper and ink," she said. "I must send a letter to my family letting them know I'm all right."

"Do you plan to lie then?"

"I beg your pardon."

"You're under the care of a man who was one day from being hanged. I don't think your family will see that as 'all right.'"

Cay didn't want to think about her father's anger or her mother's tears. She especially didn't want to imagine what her brothers would do to search for her.

"If you mean to weep again I'll have to get the hanky."

Cay sat up straight in the saddle. "I am *not* going to cry and I'd rather blow my nose on my sleeve than use that filthy rag *you* gave me."

"Wise choice," he said, his eyes again crinkling at the corners. "Now stay here, be quiet, and wait."

"I will if I feel like it," she said defiantly but knowing that she just wanted to stop moving.

Again she saw the corner of his mouth twitch, as though he was holding in laughter, and he turned his horse and headed east.

When she was alone, Cay thought that she should get down, if for no other reason than to show him that she wasn't going to be ruled by him. But she didn't have the energy. Instead, she let her head drop forward, and she fell asleep instantly.

When Alex returned, that's how he found her, sitting on her horse, still holding the reins, and sound asleep. Leaning forward, he peered into her face. She was a pretty little thing. The beads on her fancy dress reflected onto her small chin, and she looked no more than twelve years old. What in the world had T.C. Connor been thinking when he'd sent this child into the middle of the hell that Alex's life had become?

There was a part of him that wanted to turn himself in and be done with it—done with life. There wasn't one moment when he didn't remember the vision of seeing the woman he loved lying beside him, her beautiful throat one bloody cut.

Everything that happened after that, the way he'd been treated in jail, the trial, all of it, had seemed to be what he deserved, not because he'd harmed her, but because he'd failed to protect her.

So now, T.C. Connor, the only man who'd been his friend during the ordeal, had put another woman under Alex's care—and he was ill equipped to shield her from the dangers that were all around them.

Carefully, he took the reins from her tired hands and led her horse forward. He watched to make sure she didn't fall out of the saddle, but she held steady as they rode the distance to the barn where he'd bought them shelter for the night. The old man who owned the place, Yates, had driven a hard bargain, so Alex was glad he'd had little money with him. If the old man had seen the girl in her expensive dress, he would have demanded everything they had. Or worse, he would have put two and two together and gone to the sheriff.

Alex knew that the two of them were such an incongruous pair that they'd arouse suspicion wherever they went. The girl was young, and there was an air about her that proclaimed that she was rich. From her hair, which fell about her shoulders in thick, lustrous curls, to her tiny feet encased in silver slippers, she shouted "money." She reeked of wealth and class, education and refinement. He wondered if she'd ever drunk tea from a homemade mug. Or did she only use porcelain?

As for him, he was the opposite. His clothes were torn and filthy, his body emaciated from the weeks he'd spent in prison. When T.C. came to visit he brought a box of food every time, but the guards had so delighted in "searching" the contents that by the time it reached Alex, the food was almost inedible.

He'd been allowed no shaving materials, no washing water. The people of Charleston hated him for what they thought he'd done and had responded accordingly. He'd been treated worse than any animal.

So now Alex had the care of this innocent young girl, and he had no idea what to do with her. Should he coach her in a lie that she could tell her family? She could say that she'd been kidnapped by an accused murderer and he wouldn't let her go. But he doubted if she could carry that story off. If T.C. had somehow tricked her into going to meet an escaped prisoner, that meant she had a good heart but no sense of self-preservation.

Besides, how was she to get back to her family on her own? How could he release a girl like her to her own protection? One glimpse of her fancy dress under that huge cloak and every thief from here to Charleston would be after her.

No, he liked T.C.'s plan, where he was to join an exploration group and travel down into the wilds of Florida. The plan had been for T.C. to draw what they saw, while Alex was to be a wrangler. He was to handle the horses, to bring in game, and to help in any way he was needed.

Today, on the way south, when he'd asked the girl why T.C. hadn't shown up, she'd told Alex that T.C. had broken his leg. Just that morning, T.C. had climbed a ladder to the roof and fallen backward. Alex had muttered to himself about the stupidity of doing that on the day he was to help an escaped prisoner—but he'd kept his voice low. That the girl could understand him even in his heaviest accent had shocked him.

When Alex first arrived in America, no one could comprehend a word he said. For the first six months, he'd had to pantomime everything. But he'd begun to learn the American way of speech and how every word was pronounced exactly as it was written. Personally, Alex thought that was boring and totally uncreative, but he managed it.

By the time he met Lilith, the woman he was to marry, he spoke as clearly as most Americans. It was only in times of great stress, like when he escaped from prison and found a wee girl waiting for him, that his heaviest accent returned.

It took just minutes to reach the dilapidated barn of the man Yates, and when Alex saw the old man's face peering out of a dirty window, he placed his body in front of the girl's and was glad he'd thought to cover all her hair with the hood. From this angle, no one would be able to tell if she was a girl or a boy—which he wanted, as Alex had said he was traveling with his young brother.

Alex led the horses into the barn and dropped the crossbar over the door behind him. The old man had a cow and an ancient horse in there, and a few chickens roosting in the rafters. It was a dirty old building and Alex hoped it didn't rain or they'd be soaked, for he could see the fading daylight through the holes in the roof. They'd been riding hard for nearly twenty-four hours.

He left the girl, still asleep, on the horse as he checked that all he'd paid for was there. A bale of straw was in the corner, there were some oats for the horses, and a bowl of thin, watery soup and a hard hunk of bread was on an old table. Meager as it was, Alex felt that the old man had given as much as he could spare.

After spreading the straw in an empty stall, Alex went for the girl. She was falling into a deeper sleep and beginning to weave about on the horse. He put his hand up to her waist to steady her and carefully pulled her toward him. She was a sturdy little thing, heavier than he'd thought, but then again, he was weaker than he usually was. Still asleep, she snuggled against him, as though she was used to being carried by a man—and he knew she was. One of the reasons he knew who she was and about her life was because when he was small, his mother had read the letters from her mother, Edilean Harcourt, aloud to Alex and his father.

It was after his mother's death, when he was just nine years old, that he started exchanging letters with Cay's brother Nate. They were born in the same year, and Mrs. Harcourt thought that corresponding with someone his own age would help with Alex's grief. It had, and he and Nate had never stopped writing each other.

In the fifteen years or so that he'd been corresponding with her brother, he'd learned a lot about the Harcourt family. When he and Nate were ten, they decided to keep their letters secret. For Alex that meant he'd not read Nate's letters aloud to his father—but he'd told his father everything. But for Nate, living with his large family and sharing everything, that meant he kept Alex for himself. Only his parents knew of the correspondence between the boys.

Alex remembered every word Nate had written about his young sister, and while he was in prison, T.C. had said the daughter was visiting him in Charleston.

"But he didn't have to send her to me," Alex muttered.

The girl stirred in his arms, and as he lifted her higher, her arms went about his neck. The cloak fell away, revealing her iridescent white dress, her bare arm, and the upper part of her bosom.

When he tried to cover her, he almost dropped her. Weeks of little food and no exercise had taken a toll on him.

Carefully, he laid her down on the straw in the stall, then stood up and stretched his back. He couldn't help looking at her. Her dark red hair was spread out around her like a halo, and the beautiful dress sparkled in the fading sunlight coming through the roof. She lay on the big cloak, which spread under her like a blanket. She was indeed a vision of loveliness—and the sight made him groan.

What the *hell* was he to *do* with her?

To send someone as fragile and innocent as her into the world alone was not something he could fathom.

He left her lying there, sound asleep, while he took care of the horses. He removed their saddles and the packs, rubbed them down with handfuls of straw, and gave them food and water.

When he went back to the girl, she hadn't moved, so he sat down at the rickety old table and chairs by the end of the stall and looked at her as he ate half of the meager meal Yates had set out for them. It took him only minutes to finish, and all he wanted to do was sleep. He wished he had his plaid with him so he could roll in it and cover his thin, torn clothing, but he didn't.

He was considering where to sleep when the girl moved to her side, leaving part of her big wool cloak uncovered. He knew he shouldn't, but the comfort she offered was irresistible. He lifted one side of the cloak, stretched out beside her, and pulled the heavy wool over him. If he weren't so dirty, he would have snuggled beside her, but he knew the filth of him would soil her dress. As he fell asleep, he wondered how she could ride a horse for so many hours and stay so clean. But then, in his opinion, an ability to remain clean was one of the mysteries of women.

Four

❧

Alex awoke with a start, but he lay still, his eyes closed, and listened. When he heard nothing, he got up and looked about him. On the surface, the barn was just as he'd left it, but he could feel that something had changed—or was about to change. His father said that Alex had inherited a wee bit of the Second Sight from his mother. She always knew when someone was coming. By the time Alex was six and he saw his mother scurrying about to clean the house, his heart began to race with anticipation because he knew something was about to happen. She was *never* wrong.

Alex glanced down at the girl, still on her side, and still sound asleep. He stood there quietly, listening to the soft sounds of the few animals in the barn;

nothing was amiss. But Alex couldn't rid himself of the feeling that something bad was about to happen.

When he glanced up at the holes in the roof, he saw that it was hours before daylight, which meant he'd had little rest. Something inside him said that he needed to get the horses out. When the danger came, he knew that he and the girl would have to leave quickly, so he needed to have their horses ready.

Quietly, Alex went to the stall where his horse was and ran his hands over the back of the animal. It wasn't one of the racehorses he was used to, nor the sturdy Highland ponies of his youth, but the animal was a good choice for carrying the equipment that T.C. knew Alex would need.

In a soft voice, Alex apologized to the horse as he began to put the gear back on him. The animal had not had enough time free of its burdens, but under Alex's gentle, knowledgeable hands, the horse didn't protest.

Next, he moved to the girl's mare and ran his hands down its flanks. He had an idea that this animal was probably the best T.C. had in his stables. The mare fidgeted, but Alex quietened her with his whispered words and his gentle hands. She was young, and he had an idea that she could run fast enough to leave others behind. As he checked the mare's hooves, he couldn't help smiling as he remembered the girl's riding. She'd been taught well and was as at ease on horseback as if she'd been raised in the Highlands. At that thought he smiled broader. No doubt she'd tell him that any Virginian could ride as well as any Scotsman.

Slowly, silently, Alex began to saddle the mare with the pretty English saddle the girl used. It had no bags for carrying things and was therefore useless, but it was certainly lovely. Alex was glad to see that the girl hadn't ridden sidesaddle—even though he knew she probably usually did.

When the horses were saddled, Alex went to the big barn door and cautiously opened it. He heard nothing, saw no one. Silently, he led the animals out, then walked them the half mile or so to the big oak tree and securely tied them there. If it didn't rain, they'd be all right, but he knew they'd miss the comfort of the barn. After an apology to them, he made his way back to the barn.

He bolted the door behind him and went to the girl. She was still asleep, still in the same position he'd left her. Obviously, she'd had a lifetime of safety where there was never a need to stay alert even during the night. Alex moved about the barn, his hands running over the dark walls and searching. The only door was the one in front, but Alex felt that they might need another way to escape. There were four loose, rotten boards toward the back, and it was easy to remove them. He closed the wide gap by leaning the boards over it.

When he at last felt safe again, he went back to the girl. She rubbed her nose in her sleep, making him smile. Nate had once sent a tiny sketch of his little sister, drawn by their mother, and Alex had kept it by his bed for years. When Lilith saw it, she'd almost been jealous.

At the thought of his wife, his smile left him. Now all he seemed to have in his mind was the image of her in a pool of blood. Her death, her leaving, had at first taken away his will to live. It was T.C. who'd given him the idea of clearing his name.

"Go to Florida with Grady," T.C. had said, his voice low so the guards wouldn't hear him. "A few months on a flatboat in such splendor will give you time to think and to remember."

"I don't *want* to remember," Alex had said.

"I know what it's like to lose the person you love most in the world. I lost mine twice, first when her father made her marry someone else, then again when she died. I know it doesn't seem like it's possible, but time does heal wounds. Go to Florida, and give this town time to calm down. Let yourself gain some peace. Alex, you *need* to let people know that you're innocent."

Now, Alex glanced up at the roof. He could get another two hours of sleep before they needed to leave. As yet, he wasn't sure what he should do with the girl, but a plan was beginning to form in his head. All he had to do was keep

her safe until they reached the place
where he was to meet James Grady.
If Alex could get her safely there, he
could leave her with T.C.'s friends. She
could wait there for a few weeks, then
pay someone to escort her home. Her
story would be that the murderer—he
drew in his breath at the thought—had
kidnapped her, but she'd managed to
escape him.

As Alex lay down on the straw beside her, he withdrew his big knife from
the sheath hidden under his torn, dirty
shirt, and put it beside him. There was
a pistol and a rifle on his horse, but Alex
well knew how firearms could jam, that
powder could get wet. For right now, a
knife was his best defense.

⚜

Cay awoke slowly, and for several long
seconds she didn't know where she
was. Her eyelashes were matted together and there was something lumpy
in her back. Blinking and rubbing her
eyes, she turned her head. When she
saw *him* beside her, she had to work

to keep from gasping. His hair-covered face was inches from hers, and the stench of him was nearly overwhelming.

Her only thought was how to get away from him. Now that there'd been some time since the escape, surely she and Uncle T.C. could figure out a way to prove her innocence. Since he looked to be soundly asleep, she thought of rolling away and tiptoeing out, but since the big cloak was entangled around them, to move more than her arms would wake him.

As her eyes adjusted to the dull light in the barn, she saw the knife by his side. If she could reach it, she could hold it at his throat and force him to . . . to release her. Yes, that was it.

As she stretched her bare right arm over his face, she watched him to see any signs of his waking, but he didn't move. She was so sure he was asleep that when he spoke, she gasped.

"Lass, what are you up to?" he asked softly, his eyes still closed.

Cay's thoughts spun as she imagined rolling away from him and running. Could she reach the barn door before he did? Would whoever owned the barn help her get away?

With his eyes still closed, Alex reached for the knife beside him, and offered it to her, handle first. "Is this what you're after?"

In one swift movement, Cay took the knife and held it to his throat. "Release me or I'll take your life," she said in her most threatening tone.

"Lass," he said patiently, "if you need to get away from a man, you can't give him warning."

She pressed the knife deeper on his throat. "Out of respect for my godfather I won't kill you. All I want is to get away from you."

Alex still hadn't opened his eyes but lay there quietly, the knife against his neck. "You're free to go, but I warn you that there hasn't been enough time. If they can't find me to hang, they might decide to stretch your wee neck."

"But I'm innocent."

Opening his eyes, Alex looked at her. Their faces were just inches apart. "Helping a condemned man to escape is innocent?"

"I was helping my godfather, not *you*!"

"Ah, then they can hang him beside you."

She put the knife closer on his throat. "If I had any sense, I'd kill you now and let people see—"

She broke off because Alex brushed the knife away with his arm, and quickly rolled to his feet. "Someone is out there," he whispered as he pulled Cay to stand up, but her feet got entangled in the bottom of the voluminous cloak and she fell against him.

"Ah ne'er saw a lassie as useless as ye," he muttered as he pushed her away.

Cay nearly fell against the barn wall, but she got herself untangled and stood upright to see the man run to the door and look out a crack. In the next instant he was beside her. "Old man Yates is coming and he has someone with him. We must go."

Cay had just seen the food on the table and her stomach rumbled in response.

"No time to eat now, lass," Alex said as he pushed her toward the back of the barn. When she nearly tripped again, Alex grabbed the piece of bread and shoved it inside his dirty shirt. In the next second he was in front of her and he set the wall boards to one side. Someone started pounding on the big double doors. Sounding angry and sleepy, Alex called out, "Whit dae ye want?"

"Say it in English," Cay hissed at him. She was already outside, and it occurred to her to run to the front of the barn and give herself up, but she thought of the Scotsman's words of a double, or triple, hanging, and she hesitated.

"What do you want?" Alex shouted as he slipped through the open place in the wall. But the seam of his trousers got caught and he couldn't pull free.

It was only then that Cay realized she was still holding his knife in her hand. She raised it and for a moment Alex's eyes met hers—and Cay knew he thought she was going to stab him.

Swiftly, she brought the knife down by his side, cut the seam to his trousers, and released him. The look of thanks in his eyes almost made her blush.

"The horses are under the oak tree.

It's just a short distance down the road, but we can't go that way. We need to go through the fields and quickly. Can you run, lass?"

"I can escape brothers," she said, as though that was an answer to his question. Hitching up the cloak and the bottom of her gown, she flung them over her arm.

Puzzled by what she'd said, Alex began to hurry across the fields, and Cay stayed with him. After they'd been running in a zigzag pattern for nearly twenty minutes, Cay was tempted to remove the cloak and her gown and run in her underwear. And if she did that, she'd use the Scotsman's knife to cut her corset strings. Right now she needed to breathe deeply more than she needed a tiny waist.

Once, they had to cross a wooden fence. Alex went first, then lifted his arms to help her down, but when she nearly fell on him, he staggered backward.

"You are a very weak man. I've leaped on my brothers from tree branches and not taken them down."

Alex opened his mouth, as though he meant to defend himself, but he closed it again, and began running, Cay close behind him. But she heard him muttering to himself and saw him shake his head a few times. That she'd managed to annoy him made her smile. It was the least she could do when he was causing her so much discomfort.

When they finally reached the horses, she halted in surprise. He'd told her they were under the big oak tree, but hearing that and seeing them were two different things. She stopped, her clothes bunched over her arms, her drawers damp and clinging, her stockings torn and filthy. "When did you do this?"

"No time for questions now, lass," Alex said. "We must leave here." When she didn't move, he took her hand and pulled her forward. "Must I throw you into the saddle?"

"You?" she said, coming out of her shock. "My youngest brother is stronger than you are."

"Tally?" Alex held his hands together, she put her foot into them, and vaulted into the saddle. "That boy is more likely

to throw mud at his enemy than hit him."
The instant he said it, he regretted his
words. He was referring to something
Nate had written about his younger
siblings when Nate and Alex were just
boys.

Cay stared at him with her eyes wide.
"How do you know that?" Her father still
laughed over the huge mud fight she'd
had with her youngest brother when
they were three and four.

Reining his horse around, Alex tapped
his temple. "Have you no heard of the
Second Sight, lass? I can read minds."
He gave her a smile, showing even,
white teeth, then ducked and led his
horse out from under the overhanging
branches. In the next moment, he kicked
his horse forward and began galloping.

"And I guess he assumes I'll follow
him," Cay said as she patted her mare's
neck. She glanced back the way they'd
come. It wasn't quite daylight yet, but
she could see enough to know that no
one was coming after them. Maybe she
should go back to the barn and get that
man to help her return to her family.

Cay even turned her horse that way,

but something stopped her. Maybe it was the way the Scotsman had let her keep his knife when he could easily have taken it, or maybe it was his mention of Tally. Or it could have been her uncle T.C.'s belief in him, but she didn't run away from him.

"I think I'm going to regret this," she said aloud as she turned her horse toward the Scotsman and went after him. It took a while to catch up, and if his horse weren't so laden with supplies she didn't think she would have. He could ride as well as her Scottish cousins.

When she rode up beside him, his look showed his relief. "I came because you have the bread," she said loudly. He reached inside his tattered shirt and withdrew the hunk of coarse, stale bread, and handed it to her.

It was no easy task to reach across the two running horses and take it, but Cay had run relay races with her brothers, so she knew how to grab something while going full speed. She snatched the bread and for a moment she thought, Am I supposed to *eat* this dirty thing? If she hadn't been so hungry and if he hadn't been watching her, she would have thrown it down, but she wasn't going to give him that satisfaction. She tore off a hunk of the bread with her teeth and chewed it with gusto.

"Well, Catherine Edilean Harcourt, maybe you aren't useless after all," he said in a clear American accent, then kicked his horse forward.

For a moment, Cay was so stunned that he knew her name that her horse slowed down.

"Come on, lass!" he called to her. "We haven't got all day for you to lay about."

"Lay about!" she muttered as she ate the last of the bread. "Come on, girl," she said to her horse, "let's go get him."

Five minutes later, she passed him, and ten minutes after that she was so far ahead that when she looked back she couldn't see him. For a moment she thought she'd lost him, but when she turned a·curve in the road, there he stood—and he was angry.

"Do not do that again," he said softly, but his tone was almost frightening. "I can't protect you if I don't know where you are. It's one thing to tease a man, but to endanger your mare is another. You could have hurt her forelegs on this hard road."

"Me?" Cay said, her mare going in circles around him while he and his horse stood perfectly still. "You beat me here, so you must have run faster than me. Didn't you use the road?"

"How *I* went is of no concern to you. If I'm to protect you, you *must* obey me."

Anger ran through her. "The only man I 'obey' is my father—and sometimes Adam," she said as an afterthought. "As for you, if you can't keep up, then I suggest you sit down and wait for the sheriff to find you." With that, she reined her horse around, and took off down the road as fast as the mare would go.

It took over three miles of riding as hard as she could before her anger began to calm down. Of all the overbearing, arrogant things that had ever been said to her, his was the worst.

She slowed her horse and looked behind her. There was no sign of the man. Well, maybe, truthfully, what he'd said hadn't been the worst of the worst. One by one her brothers had all told her she was to "obey" them. And the truth was that she had. They wouldn't let her, so much younger and a girl, tag along with them if she hadn't. But she'd *never* obeyed Tally!

When her horse gave a little limp, Cay got down and walked her to the shade of a tree. The poor animal needed to rest—as did Cay. She listened but heard nothing. There was no one else on the road. As soon as she stopped, she realized how very hungry and thirsty she was. Her mare had only the pretty leather saddle she'd brought from home on it. There was no canteen as the Scotsman had.

She was leaning against the tree when she heard voices. She stood up quickly, ready to greet whoever it was, but in the next second she realized that a group of men was approaching. She glanced down at herself. Her ballgown had once been beautiful but was now dirty, with beads hanging off of it in strings. Still, it could be seen that the dress had been expensive. And there was her mare, a lovely animal, with the handmade saddle on her back. All in all, Cay thought it would be wiser to not allow a group of strange men to see that she was a woman alone. Until she saw them and assessed who and what they were, she thought she should hide.

Leading her horse into the dense trees beside the road, she waited. When the men came into view, she was glad she'd had the sense to conceal herself. There were four of them, all dirty, and from the way they sat their horses, they didn't look fully sober.

"They've been drinking all night," said a voice in her ear. Cay couldn't help but gasp when she saw the Scotsman beside her.

"What was that?" one of the half-drunk men said as he jerked on the reins, halted his horse, and got down.

"Nothin'," one of the other men said. "Let's go home."

"I tell you, I heard somethin'."

The first man moved closer to the trees and stared into the dense shade.

Alex put his arm around Cay's shoulders, threw the hood of the cloak over her head, and pulled her down to the ground beside him.

"Yates said—"

"That ol' liar? You believed that he had two murderers in his barn last night?"

"Why not? That killer from Charleston escaped with his lady friend, so why not hide in Yates's barn?"

"Because a match would burn it down. If they're murderers, why didn't they kill Yates? I know I've wanted to many a time."

"He had those coins, so where did he get them?"

"I've always thought he has money. He's just too cheap to buy his own beer. Come on, let's go home. You probably heard a cat."

Alex and Cay watched as the first man reluctantly turned away, mounted his horse, and they all left.

When Alex moved away from Cay, she rolled on to her back, and looked up at him.

"You are free to go," he said, anger in

his voice. "I'm no jailer and I won't be thought of as one. You may leave whenever you want, but if you stay with me, you have to—" He broke off and looked as though he was trying to figure out how to arrange his words. "At least *listen* to what I say and give it some consideration."

Cay wanted to be defiant and tell him she was going to leave, but the words of the men rang in her ears. That the news of the Scotsman's escape had spread this far south was frightening. Even worse was that she was still being considered as his accomplice.

"You must not have sisters or you'd know not to tell them to 'obey' you." She was still lying on the ground and looking up at him.

He shook his head. "No sisters nor brothers. I am my father's only child."

"And your mother?"

"Died when I was nine."

"I'm sorry," she said. He was looking down at her, his blue eyes with no humor in them, and waiting for her answer.

Cay didn't want to give it. She didn't

want to plight her course with this man. She wanted to go home, to be with her family, to take a hot bath and put on clean clothes. She just wanted all of this to be over with!

Alex's eyes softened as he sat down beside her, his legs drawn up and his arms around them. "Lass, I know how you feel. I didn't ask for any of this either. One minute I was racing my horses and winning money from those lazy, rich boys in Charleston, I was to marry the most beautiful woman alive, and the next thing I knew, I was in a filthy prison and about to be hanged." His voice lowered. "And the woman I loved was dead."

His face was in profile and she could see the sadness—no, the *grief*—in his eyes. She hadn't really had time to think of the situation from his point of view.

When she said nothing, Alex went to his horse and tightened the cinch. "I'll take you back," he said. "You don't deserve to be part of this."

Getting up, she went to stand beside him. "You mean to Virginia?"

"Aye, to Virginia, or to wherever you want to go."

"But what about the danger to my family?"

"Better that than you have to stay with a murderer." He untied his horse and was about to get into the saddle, but Cay blocked him.

"We need to talk about this."

"Nothing to talk about," he said as he swung up into the saddle. "I think we should leave, but then saying that might make you think you have to *obey* me, so do what you want."

She didn't move. "Maybe we should take the time to make a plan."

He was on his horse while she was standing on the ground—and she looked so very small. Her glorious hair was down about her shoulders and there were sticks and leaves in it, but they didn't take away from her beauty. Nate had never mentioned his sister's hair, except to say it was red and her brothers teased her about it. Tally once dyed an old wig red and pranced around the house pretending to be Cay. She stopped him by dropping one of her mother's prized Chinese vases over the balcony and barely missing his head. Alex had laughed at how both children had been punished by spending a week doing the household laundry.

"That's a good idea," Alex said. "You have any thoughts about what we should do?"

She blinked at him a few times, taken off guard by his honesty, but the truth was that she had no idea how to escape when being hunted. As she usually did in her life, she fell back on humor to cover herself. "We'll put you in a dress and we'll go back to Virginia together as two old women." Her eyes were laughing. "Of course that would mean you'd have to shave and even take a bath." She moved her horse close to a tree stump, climbed on it, and mounted.

"If it means a bath, then I can't do that," he said, and his tone was so serious that Cay wasn't sure if he was teasing or not. "And I willna wear a dress." He looked at her, his eyes very serious. "Do we go north or south?"

Cay swallowed. Never in her life had

she had to make such a decision. It was the thought of what might possibly be done to her family that decided her. If her brothers were in this situation, they'd never hesitate in protecting their loved ones. "South," she whispered at last.

She started to say more, but he gave a quick nod and reined his horse away, and they started riding at a rapid pace. They stopped twice to water themselves and the horses, then went on.

At one break, Cay asked how far he thought they'd have to go before they were out of the gossip area. She'd not so much as seen T.C.'s map. All she knew was that they were going south, with the sun always in her face.

"People love horror stories, and my guess is that we'll have to reach Florida before we escape the talk."

Florida, she thought, and couldn't repress her shiver. Swamps and alligators and plants that eat people. At least that's one of the stories Uncle T.C. used to tell her and Tally when they were little. Adam said it wasn't true, and he'd been the one who held her that night when she screamed in a nightmare.

"Don't worry," Alex said. "You won't go with me into the swamps. I'll leave you with T.C.'s friends." He went to his horse, checked the pack, and handed Cay a piece of beef jerky.

"I hate this," she said as she reluctantly chewed it. "I thought you said you didn't have a plan."

"I didn't if you meant to have me take you to Virginia."

When he said nothing more, she said, "So? Do you intend to share it or not?"

He held out his hands to help her mount her horse. "Not."

Annoyed, Cay put her hand on his shoulder and moved her foot to his thigh. It was a move she'd often done to her brothers and it was guaranteed to throw them off balance. But Alex was ready for her, and he stepped back in a way that made Cay nearly fall backward. He caught her hand before she hit the ground.

She started to bawl him out, but what she could see of his face looked so pleased with himself that she couldn't help smiling. "Are you *sure* you don't have sisters?"

"None, but I'm learning that I just think of the most devious thing you can do and that's what you will do."

Cay opened her mouth and closed it a few times, meaning to defend herself, but then she laughed. "You may be weaker and older than my brothers, but you might be smarter. Except for Adam, of course."

He held out his cupped hands, she stepped into them, and mounted her horse. "Except for Adam," he said as he got back into the saddle. As he turned away, he said, "How old is Adam?"

"Twenty-eight."

"That's what I remembered," Alex said thoughtfully as he glanced up at the sun. "I don't know about you, lass, but I could use a bite to eat."

"I've been looking at the rump of your horse ravenously."

"Have you now?" Alex said. "Perhaps I should be glad it wasn't *my* rump you covet."

"The dirt would poison me," she said

without a hint of a smile. "The horse is cleaner. And smells better."

Alex couldn't help smiling as she tossed her beautiful hair back, put her chin up, and moved ahead of him.

Five

❦

"Are you *sure* you'll be all right?" Alex asked Cay for the third time.

"You're worse than my father," she said, but she was faking her bravado. The truth was that she was scared to death to be left alone in the forest. She glanced back at the spooky old ruins where he'd set up a canvas roof. Since the front was open, there wouldn't be any protection from . . . from whatever was lurking in the trees. "I'm fine," she said. "I'll just wait here until you return."

"You have the pistol and you know how to use it, don't you?" He'd already wasted a lot of time reassuring her that bears were unlikely to attack the camp.

"I can shoot quite well." She rubbed her arms against the chill in the air as she glanced at the sky. "It looks like it might rain soon so maybe you should go." She wanted to beg him not to leave her alone there, but she would die before she told him that.

Alex wasn't fooled by her act of bravery. He knew she was frightened, and since they were wanted by the law and being hunted by every reward seeker in three states, she was right to be afraid. But he needed to get them food, and he couldn't go into public with her with him. Too many people were looking for a man and a woman traveling on horseback together.

"I'll take your mare," he said, watching to see how upset she'd be by this. When a look of panic crossed her pretty face, he almost relented. There were bags of dried food in his saddlebags but they'd need them later. Right now, they both needed a hot meal, and if possible, Alex was going to get it for them.

"Go!" Cay said as she stepped back toward the canvas covering. "Stop worrying about me. I can take care of myself."

Alex thought she could barely walk by herself, but he wasn't about to say that. His real fear was that she'd again decide this was her chance to escape and she'd leave as soon as he did. He hated to think what a bunch of vigilantes would do to a young girl they thought was a criminal.

Reluctantly, he saddled the mare and, with one more backward glance, left her alone in the woods, sheltered by a few falling-down brick walls of a burned-out house.

He rode as quickly as possible along the narrow path through the trees, and for the thousandth time he cursed T.C. Connor. On the one hand, Alex owed his life to the man, but on the other, it was T.C.'s fault that he was stuck with the care—and feeding—of a girl who didn't know how to do *anything.* She refused to obey orders and went where she wanted when she wanted to. And when Alex so much as made a suggestion of how she should do something, she told him he was the most ungrateful, smelliest man she'd ever met.

As Alex came to the road, he couldn't

suppress a smile. She could ride, he'd give her that, and the memory of her on her horse with her hair flying, the huge cloak billowing behind her, and that white dress sparkling on her trim little body made him chuckle out loud.

Immediately, he stopped and looked about to see if anyone had heard him, but no one was on the road.

The truth was that the girl was good company, which was something he desperately needed after the last months of his life. The trial had been a farce. There wasn't a person in the courtroom—including his own lawyer— who didn't think he was guilty. Every day he was half dragged from the jail to the courtroom, and people hissed at him, spat on him, even threw rocks. By the time the guilty verdict came in, Alex had begun to doubt his own inno- cence. But then, a defense of "I don't know what happened" wasn't a very convincing one.

Only T.C. had shown him any kind- ness, and when the man told of his plan to free Alex, he'd been skeptical. That on the day of the breakout T.C. broke his leg and couldn't supervise, and that one of the men paid to help Alex escape had been shot and the other captured, seemed to fit the whole situation. When Alex finally made his way on foot to the rendezvous site and there sat a pretty girl wearing a sparkling ball gown, it had seemed like the end of the world. He was sure he'd be dead within minutes—and she with him.

When she'd understood his brogue— which most Americans couldn't—he'd realized with horror that she was the daughter of Angus McTern Harcourt. She was the beloved, precious sister of Alex's best friend, and she'd been put under the care of Alex when he couldn't even protect himself. If he'd had time to think, he was sure he'd have turned himself in rather than risk her life. But the bullets flying past hadn't allowed them to do anything but run.

But the girl had proven to be made of sterner stuff than she'd first seemed. He'd seen how frightened she was, but she'd gathered her courage and made the best of a very bad situation.

He urged the mare forward. T.C.'s

map had shown that there was a tavern nearby, and he meant to do what he could to get them some proper food. It had been weeks since he'd had a hot meal and he could feel his ribs sticking out. Again he chuckled at the way the girl had told him he was weak—and old. Alex ran his hand over his beard. He needed that now to hide his face, which so many people in and around Charleston had seen. But the beard seemed to make the girl think he was an old man, certainly older than her adored brother Adam.

Alex ducked his head as he passed a man and a woman in an open buckboard, then breathed a sigh of relief when they passed without recognizing him as an escaped convict.

As he kept riding, Alex tried to remember what Nate had told him about his sister, but there hadn't been much. Nate was interested in solving puzzles, and he and Alex had exchanged letters about things they considered mysterious. Nate had only written about his little sister when she did something that got her punished—and that usually meant a fight with her brother Arthur Talbot Harcourt, "Tally." Many times, Alex had made his father laugh when he retold the antics of Cay and her brother Tally.

"She sounds like her mother," Alex's father would say. "Did I ever tell you about the time she shot at Angus?" Alex would say yes but that he wanted to hear it again. It had been Malcolm, Cay's great-uncle, who'd first told them the story. Three times Alex and his father had visited the McTerns where they lived just north of Glasgow. Alex had met all six of Cay's first cousins, all of them older, richer, and better educated than Alex was. It was only when it came to horses, to any animal for that matter, that Alex was considered the leader. It was the oldest boy, Derek, eleven years Alex's senior, who had recognized Alex's gift. Derek had been adopted by Malcolm, who was now the laird of the McTern clan, and his wife, Harriet, and someday Derek would be the laird, so others listened to him. He said Alex was a "magician" with animals, able to make them do whatever he wanted them to. When Alex wrote Nate this, he started calling Alex "Merlin"—and to explain the name, Nate sent Alex a book about the ancient wizard. The name stuck, and forever after Nate called Alex "Merlin."

Alex's mind returned to the present when he saw the tavern in the distance. It was larger and much busier than he'd like for it to be. His hope had been that he could walk in and order food, but with that many people there, they were bound to have heard the news from Charleston. If Alex were clean and in good clothes, with his face hidden behind his beard, he could probably walk in unnoticed. But as he was, he looked like someone who'd just escaped prison.

"Damnation!" he muttered and thought of going back to Cay. They could live on the beef jerky and dried fruit for another few days. The farther south they went, the less likely that they'd be recognized.

But his stomach growled, reminding him of the need for food. Alex dismounted and led his horse into the trees where he could watch the activity at the tavern. He could see that the kitchen was at the back of the house and there was even a big kettle outside. He saw cooks and butchers in bloody aprons moving about.

In the front, the double doors opened frequently as people went in and out. No, there was no way he would be able to get in there without someone knowing who he was.

An idea came to him. If he couldn't go in, then he'd just have to make *all* of them come out. He checked the supply of gunpowder he'd brought with him. With that and some pinecones, he'd be able to make a great deal of noise.

❧❧

Cay ran along the path until the Scotsman was no longer in sight, then she went back to the dreary little campsite and sat down on a log. She had the pistol he'd left her in her hand, and she began to wonder if the powder was dry. If it was wet and she shot it, the pistol could blow up in her face. Even if it didn't explode, it would take her at least three minutes to reload. But what if the powder was on the other side of whatever she was shooting at? If it were, say, a bear coming at her and she missed her first shot, how did she get around the huge thing to get the powder and reload? On the other hand, if she didn't kill the bear with the first shot, it would kill her, so getting more powder wouldn't matter because she'd be dead.

When a branch behind her broke, she jumped up and aimed her pistol, but it was only a squirrel.

"You *must* calm down," she said aloud and looked to see if anything had heard her. It was daylight, but the overhead canopy of trees made it seem like twilight.

Cay wasn't used to being alone. Whether she was at home in Virginia or with her relatives in Scotland, someone male was *always* nearby. For a moment she closed her eyes and wished to see one of her brothers or her cousins or her father. "Even Tally," she whispered. If Tally came riding up right now she'd be so glad to see him that she'd endure all his taunting and teasing with a smile.

She opened her eyes and sat back down on the log. None of the many males in her life was going to show up to rescue her, to hug her, and tell her that everything was going to be just fine. Nor was she going to be able to run to her mother and pour out all her troubles to her. The truth was that if Cay went to any of them right now they could be arrested for having helped a murderer escape.

Tears came to her eyes, but she brushed them away and glanced down the old pathway. The man hadn't been gone long, so there was no hope that he would return soon.

She jumped again when she heard something behind her, but she didn't see anything, at least not a bear running down the hill intent on eating her and the horse. That the horse was quietly chomping on grass and seemed not to hear anything reassured Cay enough that she sat back down.

She would like to have a fire, but he'd told her no, fearful that someone would see it. It was cool and dank and very lonely in the forest, and the fire would give warmth and light and cheer—and she could use burning branches to keep the wild animals away.

Again she told herself to calm down, but her mind kept wandering. Maybe the Scotsman wouldn't return. He could move more easily and faster without her. She'd not seen Uncle T.C.'s map, so she had no idea where he was to meet the explorers—not that it mattered to *her.* She was to stay somewhere else and wait, or to send someone to her family to come and get her.

Getting up, she went under the canvas cloth he'd set up for her and wondered if he'd meant it as a campsite just for her.

She wrapped Hope's big cloak about her, put the hood over her head, and drew her knees up. Feeling the wool about her made her remember the last night at Uncle T.C.'s house. Cay knew she'd been so very brave, but then, she'd been angered by the way Hope had treated her, as though Cay were too young and frivolous to be able to do something as simple as what T.C. was asking of her.

"And she was right," Cay said aloud as she sniffed away the tears that threatened to come. She needed to think of something good. She could think of . . . of . . . Of Hope's request for a husband, she thought. That was good for a laugh. Hope was bossy, controlling, not always nice, and she sometimes said hurtful things. No wonder she wasn't married.

Maybe Hope and the Scotsman should marry, Cay thought, and that idea made her relax, even warmed her inside. Since he seemed to expect women to blindly obey him, she imagined the arguments the two of them would have. Hope would demand that her husband take a bath once a year, and he'd tell her that she had to do whatever he told her to, even if it made no sense.

The images made Cay chuckle aloud. Stretching out on the leaf-covered ground, she worked to keep the amusing thoughts in her mind. The Scotsman was older than Hope—she guessed him to be in his early forties—but that was all right. At almost thirty, Hope couldn't be too choosey about whom she found to marry her.

Gradually Cay began to relax enough that she drifted into much-needed sleep.

Six

♣

When Alex returned with a big bag of hot food, he didn't go directly to the campsite but went around it. He wanted to see what was there without blundering into something. When he saw the ruins, but no horse and no girl, he nearly panicked. It took time to calm his heart, which seemed to have leaped into his throat. She had taken the horse and left. Or no! Maybe she'd been found and abducted. Would he have to break her out of jail?

When the horse, tethered on a long rope, wandered back into sight, Alex was so relieved that he was embarrassed. He didn't want to admit it, but he was going to be glad to see her for herself, not just because she was his responsibility. She was a link to his father, to Scotland, and to Nate, who was his best friend even though they'd never met in person.

Alex slowly walked his horse down the hill, holding the big bag out, and anticipating her joy when she saw the food he'd brought.

He dismounted, removed the horse's saddle, and set the mare out to graze before he went into the little makeshift shelter he'd built for her. Lying on the leaves was the girl, and she didn't wake when he stepped closer to her. From her tear-stained cheeks, he could tell that she'd been crying.

It looked as though, while he was away, her bravery had given out. He opened the bag and silently began to pull out the contents. First there was a loaf of bread still warm from the oven, then a thick gooseberry pie in a ceramic dish. Under it was a huge wooden bowl filled nearly to the top with beef stew with big chunks of meat, potatoes, and carrots, all swimming in a fragrant gravy. On the bottom was a single wooden spoon.

Alex dipped the spoon into the stew,

and held it by Cay's nose. It took a moment before she moved, but she seemed to come out from under the hood nose first, her eyes still closed.

He drew the spoon back and she followed it.

"Ooooh," she said as she opened her eyes and reached for the spoon—but Alex pulled it back. Cay just sat there, looking at him in astonishment.

"Give me that!" She made a lunge, grabbed the spoon from him, and ate the stew. As she chewed, she closed her eyes in ecstasy. "Heaven. Pure Heaven."

Alex reached to take the spoon from her, but she drew it away.

"Get your own."

"I did get my own and that's it. We have to share it."

"Share a spoon?" She was aghast.

His long arm reached behind her and took the spoon while tossing her the loaf of bread. "Use that, and now who's the ungrateful one? I guess you think I should have risked getting caught just to steal *two* spoons."

Cay tore off a chunk of bread and

dipped it in the bowl. It soaked up gravy, but it was difficult to get the meat; it kept falling off.

Alex watched her make several unsuccessful attempts at getting meat, then held out the spoon he'd used.

When she realized it was share or go hungry, she snatched it from him. "You have the manners of a barbarian."

"And you have the appetite of a lumberjack. Give that back to me or I won't tell you how I got this. I was nearly killed."

"Did anyone follow you?" Cay asked, spoon halfway to her mouth.

He took the utensil from her. "I tell you I was nearly killed and your only concern is if *you* might get caught?"

Cay started to defend herself, but she saw that his eyes were teasing. "If someone followed you, I'd have to share the spoon with more people. You're bad enough."

"I guess a convicted murderer sleeping next to you is as much as you can take."

Cay didn't like his joke. It was too real—and too frightening. "I think you should tell me your side of what happened in Charleston." She used her most sympathetic tone to encourage him to talk, but he barely looked at her.

"Hmph!" he said as he again took the spoon from her.

"What does that mean?"

"It means that it's none of your business."

"I think that if I can risk my life for you, and if you—"

"Was that a bear?" he asked, a piece of bread halfway to his mouth.

Cay half rolled, half leaped, to move closer to him as she gave a little squeal of alarm.

"Naw, just the wind," he said and continued to eat.

She realized he'd made it up about the bear just to get her to stop talking about the murder. "I don't think you're a very nice person."

"All of Charleston would agree with you on that one."

"A whole town that's a good judge of character." She had meant the words to sound light, but she could see by his face that she hadn't succeeded. They ate in silence for a while, then she said, "Did you love her very much?"

"Aye, I did."

Encouraged by his words, she went further. "How did you meet?"

"At a race." They'd finished the stew and Alex reached behind him for the pie—which Cay hadn't seen.

"Gooseberry? My favorite."

"And what food wouldn't be your favorite right now?" His eyes had lost their sad, faraway look, and she was glad.

"Beef jerky, dried apples, and creek water with little bits of moss floating in it."

With a chuckle, he used his big knife to cut the pie into quarters. "We'll save some for breakfast. If you leave us any food, that is. Where do you put all that you eat, lass?" He looked at her, mostly hidden under the cloak, but there wasn't much of her.

"Muscle," she said, her mouth full as she licked juice off her wrist. "I am pure muscle."

He laughed at that, and she liked the sound.

"How long did you know her?"

"Who?" he asked.

"Your wife. How long did you know her before you got married?"

"Three weeks."

With her mouth open in shock, she stared at him. "But that's not long enough to get to know a person before you commit yourself to marriage."

"And who told you that? Your mother?"

"And my father."

"And the pastor, too, I'm sure."

She ate another bite of pie. "So I guess you're an expert on love, too, as well as on how to hide from the law." She thought maybe her remark would make him clam up again, but it didn't seem to bother him.

"I know when I feel love, yes. So what did your mother tell you to do? Get to know a man before you marry him?"

"Of course."

"As she did your father?"

"She knew him for years before she married him," Cay said, narrowing her eyes at him. "You seem to know a lot about my family. Did Uncle T.C. tell you about us?"

"Some, yes. Do you think you're finished now, or should I make another raid on the tavern? They might have a pound or two of beef left."

"That's enough, but I hope you plan to protect that half of the pie."

"With my life." She watched as he put the pie in its plate back into the bag, tied a rope around it, and hoisted it into a tree.

When he came back to the little tent, she asked him how he knew to do that.

"Always protect your food, lass. I'm surprised your Scots relatives didn't teach you that."

"When I visit them, I stay in a castle, not outside." As she spoke, it began to rain and the air cooled. She pulled the cloak around her and drew her knees up. It had grown dark while they ate, and now she was isolated with this man she hardly knew.

"Are you going back to being afraid of me, lass?" he asked softly.

She straightened her spine. "Why would I be afraid of a weak old man like you? What were we talking about?"

"Your experience of courting," he said quickly, his voice full of laughter.

"I'm glad I can entertain you, but, as a matter of fact, I went to Charleston to consider three marriage proposals." She was pleased when he looked at her in astonishment.

"Three?"

"Did you think that men don't want me? Just because you think I'm useless doesn't mean—"

"Are you telling me that you can't make up your mind which of three men you want to marry?"

His tone told her he thought this was an odd thing, maybe even that it was wrong, but she had no idea why. "Yes," she said hesitantly. "They're all good men, and—"

"But what about *passion*?" he asked vehemently.

Cay was glad the darkness covered her blush. "If you're talking about what a man and a woman do when they're alone, I can assure you that I know all about that. I've spent my life around animals and boys. They're a dirty bunch of creatures, and by that I mean the boys, not the animals." He was staring at her with his eyes wide. "Why are you look-ing at me like that?"

Turning away for a moment, Alex shook his head as though to clear it. "Do any of the three men make your blood boil?"

"My blood boil? What a ridiculous thing to say. No, they don't make my blood do anything except what it nor-mally does. You know, I think we should get some sleep." She stretched out her legs in the torn stockings and tried to compose her mind to go to sleep, but she'd had hours of napping and was restless. Besides, he still seemed to be waiting for an answer. "They're all good men, and they can provide for my fu-ture and that of our children. I don't see what's wrong—" She broke off because he gave a snort of such derision that she raised up on an elbow to look at him. He had stretched out on the damp grass, with no covering over his thin clothing, his back to her. "And what does that mean?"

"Nothing, lass. Go to sleep."

She sat up. "No, I want to know what you meant by your hateful little snort."

"Snort?" he murmured, seeming to be amused by what she'd said. "It was no 'snort,' just a sound I make when I hear something so unbelievable that I can't even understand it."

"If you don't tell me what you mean I'll . . ."

"You'll what, lass?"

She leaned toward him. "I'll make your life miserable," she said softly.

Alex turned to look at her, and she could see he was imagining ways she could use to carry out her threat. "I guess that means you'll talk me to death tonight."

"That would be the starting place."

He rolled onto his back and put his hands behind his head. "From what I've seen of marriage, it's not easy, and the only way to get through it is if you love the other person."

"I agree with that," she said hesitantly, not understanding what his complaint was.

"So you love all three men?" He was looking up at her, as she was sitting and he was lying down.

"I could love them. For your information, I've had eight proposals of marriage since I was sixteen years old, and I've narrowed them down to three men who I would consider. It's not like all I've had are three proposals and I'd take any one of them. The man who first offered for me was . . . Well, he was *very* unsuitable, and I didn't include him."

"Ah, so you chose three of them who you think you can love, and you went all the way to Charleston to decide which one it's to be?"

"Yes," she said, glancing at him, but not understanding what he was laughing at her about. "*What* is so funny?"

He seemed about to answer, but then he sat up and looked at her. "Lass, you need to feel passion." When she started to speak, he put his hand up. "You should look at a man and feel that you'll die if you don't spend the rest of your life with him. Your heart needs to leap into your throat and stay there."

"I think you *learn* to love someone. I know you believe I'm little more than a child, but I've seen some of your 'passion' marriages, and they never work out. One of my mother's friends ran off with a man much younger than she is, and . . . Well, now they argue all the time. Their daughter is my friend and she spends half her life at my house rather than go home to be with her arguing parents."

"How many children do they have?"

"Eleven."

"They have eleven children but they argue *all* the time?"

Cay willed her face not to blush, but she couldn't control it and hoped he wouldn't see it. "They are not a happy couple."

"Sounds to me like they do all right. It's the ones who are polite to each other that are so unhappy."

"That's ridiculous. My parents are very polite to each other."

He looked at her hard.

"Perhaps not all the time," she conceded. "My mother is a bit headstrong, and my father gets a tad out of sorts about it sometimes, and there have been a few times when my brothers and I said we were going to leave home if they didn't make up. But they love each other very much."

"And they chose each other because they were a sensible match, did they?"

"My father was the laird of a clan and my mother was an heiress. Yes, I think they were very well matched."

With another little snort, he stretched out on the ground, his arms across his chest and looking as though he meant to go to sleep. "They were the most ill-matched couple in all of Christendom," he mumbled.

"I want to know how you know so much about my family."

"T.C.—"

"I don't believe that Uncle T.C. told you so much about us. Did he tell you about Bathsheba and him?"

"He mentioned her," Alex said, but he didn't turn over. "Was he passionately in love with her?"

"Insanely. My mother said that when Bathsheba married another man, Uncle T.C. nearly killed himself in grief."

"I know that feeling," Alex said softly. "I know it very well."

Cay wanted to say more, even wanted to argue with him. She wasn't especially sleepy, and the night around them, with the rain coming down, made her nervous. "And you loved your wife very much?" she asked softly.

"With all my heart and soul."

"And you knew that in just three weeks?"

"I knew it in the first moment. Her eyes met mine and I was hers."

"But you knew nothing about her, not her personality, not what she liked or disliked, what her hopes for the future were, nothing?"

"And I guess you know all about the men you're considering marrying."

"Of course."

"Make lists, do you?"

Cay thought of her notebook full of her comparisons of the men she might possibly marry. She had compared ages, houses, backgrounds, whatever she could think of. She knew that marriage was a serious matter and she didn't want to make a mistake. She wanted a marriage as good as her parents'. "Of course I didn't do any such thing," she lied. "I'm going to let my heart make the decision for me. Isn't that what a bride should do?"

"If you're asking me what I think *you* should do, I think you should lie down and go to sleep. We'll leave early tomorrow, before light, so you need to get as much rest as you can."

Reluctantly, Cay lay down on the hard ground and tried to still her mind, but it kept working. "Have you finished making a plan for me yet?"

"Aye, I have, but I'm not going to tell you what's in my mind, so there's no use in nagging me now."

"I don't nag," she said.

"You could give lessons in it. You could open a school that teaches how to nag a man until he's crying for relief from your tongue."

She truly hated the way he treated her like a child! "Micah Bassett didn't want relief from my tongue. In fact—"

"Lass, you're alone in the forest with a convicted murderer. Tell me you're not going to talk to him about what a girl can do with her tongue."

"I, uh . . ." Cay couldn't think of what to say to explain herself, but then there was no explanation she could give. Instead, she rolled to one side of the cloak and, after a moment's hesitation, she threw the other side over him. He grunted his thanks, and when he moved closer to her, she could feel his body heat on her back. Maybe it was the comfort or maybe it was the soft sounds of the rain, but she closed her eyes and went to sleep.

Seven

"I am *not* going to dress as a boy," Cay said. "Absolutely, positively no! That's the end of it, and I won't discuss it anymore."

"Good!" Alex said. "Then I won't have to hear more of your complaining. When you get dressed—as a boy—you can keep your mouth shut—unless you meet some man you think you should marry, then you can do other things with your mouth."

"You are disgusting. You're worse than *any* of my brothers."

"Does that include Adam?" he asked. "Or is he too perfect for unchurchlike thoughts?"

She was pulling the cinch on her mare and she looked under the horse's neck to glare at him. He didn't look at her, but she could see that he was pleased with himself, thinking that he'd bested her in a duel of words. "My brother Adam doesn't have any thoughts that he couldn't repeat in front of a congregation in church. Are you ready to go or do you need help?"

"I don't need any help, and your brother sounds like a bore," Alex said as he walked around her horse, bent, grabbed Cay by the calf, and nearly threw her up into the saddle.

Only years of experience and very strong thigh muscles kept her from going over the other side. But she refused to give him the satisfaction of complaining.

"Look at that, you're half male already." He looked up at her. "The truth is, lass, if you didn't have all that hair, you could pass for a boy."

In that one sentence, he said everything she'd ever feared. Her mother was so beautiful that men had written poems about her. One young man composed a song about her beauty. But Cay, the only daughter, didn't look so much like her mother as she did her father and brothers. In fact, when they were growing up, what with only ten months difference in the ages between her and Tally, sometimes people thought they were twins—male twins.

Alex, standing by her feet and looking up at her, saw that he'd hurt her feelings and she was trying hard not to cry. He hadn't meant to. The truth was that after a good meal and a full night's sleep, he'd awoken this morning to see a very pretty girl in a beautiful gown reaching up over her head to try to get a bag down from a tree. At first, he hadn't remembered where he was and all that had happened in the past few months. He was in the moment and he thought he'd never seen a prettier sight in his life—and therein lay the problem.

The idea of dressing her in boy's clothes had come to him when he'd told old man Yates that he was traveling with his young brother, but Alex hadn't told her his thoughts for fear that she'd react just as she had. What was it with women that they thought they didn't exist if they weren't wearing ribbons every minute of the day?

"It's just for a while," he said gently as he looked up at her. "There's a town near here and today's Sunday. I figure we can get inside a store while it's closed and get what we need. And leave money to pay for it all," he added because he already knew her well enough to know that she'd want to do that. "After you're kitted out, we can go down to Florida. I'll leave you with T.C.'s friends and you can wait there until I've been gone a couple of weeks, then you can go home. People won't notice a boy traveling alone, but a pretty girl by herself will cause nothing but problems."

"Not according to you. *You* think I look like a boy as it is. I guess you want me to hide my hair under a wig."

When he didn't answer, she saw that he was studiously working on packing his horse. She drew in her breath. "You want me to cut my hair, don't you?"

Alex mounted his horse and after a cowardly moment, he met her eyes. "I've thought of that and your hair would ruin the disguise. You look very young as it is, and in boy's clothes you'll look even younger. If you wear a powdered wig, you'll draw attention to yourself. Besides, with the way you ride, the wig would come off, then all that hair of yours would show."

Cay put her hand on her hair, which was hanging down past her shoulders. As a child, it was her hair that had finally stopped her from being compared to her brother. "I won't cut it." She moved her horse forward. "I might consider the clothes," she said. "But I *will not* cut my hair."

"All right," he said softly. "We won't do any cutting." Even as he said it, he knew he was lying. He wasn't going to risk her life and his because of her vanity.

"Why don't you lead for a while?" he said in a conciliatory tone. It was the least he could do when he thought of what he might have to do to her. If she wouldn't do it voluntarily, he'd have to do it without her permission—and that thought scared him. If he cut her hair while she was asleep, he'd better never close his eyes while around her or she'd cut something on him—and it wouldn't be his hair.

They rode for three hours in the early morning dark, staying off the major roads and making their way through fields whenever they could. As they went farther south, there was more distance between the towns, and they began see plantations. The plantations were like small towns, with everything that was needed by the family and the workers grown or made on their land.

Cay was quiet for most of the ride, and Alex knew her silence was because she didn't want to dress as a boy, but he could see no other way of keeping her safe. Thanks to her arriving wearing a dress that looked as though it was made of starlight, the men chasing him had easily seen that she was female. So now they were looking for a man and a woman together. If Alex could change even one aspect of that description, they'd be safer.

He wasn't about to tell her, but he figured that by now there were handbills out about them both, and her hair was the most recognizable feature of the two of them. He could almost see the words on the handbills. "Flaming red hair." Or "three feet of thick, lustrous, dark red hair" and "porcelain skin that looks as though it's never been exposed to the sun."

As for him, he'd like to shave, but the woodcut in the newspapers during the trial had been of him shaved. If he was going to be recognized, it would be with a clean face. Also, as Cay had told him many times—too many for his liking—the beard made him look much older than he really was.

Cay glanced back at him, then reined in her horse so she could move beside him. "What's that look for?"

"Nothing. It's the way I look," he said grumpily.

"I don't know why I have to put up with your bad temper. I'm the innocent one, and I'm only in this mess because I volunteered to help you out."

"Now who's in a bad temper?"

"I have a right to be. You should be grateful."

"I thank you for saving my life, but I don't thank you for nearly getting us caught."

"When did I—?" she began, but then

closed her mouth. In the next moment she'd turned her horse and was heading back the way they came at full speed.

Alex had a difficult time catching up with her, and he cursed the fact that his horse was so weighted down with equipment and supplies that the poor animal had difficulty moving. When he did reach her, he nearly pulled his arm from the socket as he tried to get the reins from her so he could slow her down. But she was very good on the horse, and try as he might, he couldn't overtake her. "I'm sorry," he shouted at her as she rode away. "I apologize. With all my heart, lass, I'm sorry for what I said."

Alex was sure he'd lost her, but to his disbelief, she slowed down, and turned toward him.

"Say it again."

It went against him to grovel. His father had always told him that they may not have a title or money, but they had their pride, and a man never gave that up. But now he was looking at this bit of a girl and he felt that if he had to, he'd kiss her feet to make her forgive him. And that thought, of kissing her feet, made the bad humor and the self-pity leave him.

"I'm sorry, lass," he said, but there was a bit of a smile about his lips. "You were a person of courage and strength to take on what T.C. Connor had mucked up, and I ask you to forgive me for saying otherwise."

"Do you mean that, or are you just saying it so I'll not leave you out here alone?"

He nearly choked on her words. He'd be much better off without her, but he'd not say that. Right now he wondered what Angus McTern Harcourt was thinking in teaching his daughter to be able to ride as she did. But then, she was half Scots, so maybe it was in her blood.

"You're still looking at me oddly."

"I was thinking that with a set of racing silks you could win any race. If I had my horses and we weren't in this mess, you and I could make a fortune on the track."

Cay couldn't help but smile. "Is that what's made you so bad tempered this morning? That you miss your race-horses?"

He started to tell her the truth, that he was afraid of the future and what would happen if they were caught, but he didn't. Instead, he lowered his eyes and said, "I was thinking about how awful it will be to have to cut hair like yours. But, lass, you're much too pretty with that great halo swirling about your head."

Alex was sure that she'd tell him he was full of horse manure and ride off, never to see him again, but she didn't. Instead she touched her hair and smiled sweetly. "Do you really think so?"

"Aye, I do," he said, and he was sincere.

"I guess I got too angry too fast," she said. "It's always been a problem of mine. Adam says it's my biggest fault."

"And of course Adam is always right," he murmured.

She looked at him hard, trying to see if he was teasing or being honest.

Alex worked to keep his eyes calm and not let the laughter inside him escape. "Will you no come with me now, lass?"

"Only if you call me by my name," she said. "I know you were told my full name, but I'm called—"

"Cay," he said. "For your initials of *C-E-H*. It's what your brother Nate thought your name was because your mother embroidered everything with your initials before you were born. She was determined that you were going to be a girl. Now . . . . Cay, are you ready to go? We should be at the town very soon."

When he turned his horse around and headed south, obviously hoping she would follow him, Cay couldn't move. What a great lot of information Uncle T.C. had told him! In her opinion, he'd told too much family business to a stranger. Frowning, she at last began to follow him.

When Alex heard the clip-clop of her horse, he smiled to himself and thought that maybe he'd just learned something about women. He knew he'd tarnished his pride by apologizing and begging her to go with him, but he'd also won because she was now following him.

Maybe pride and women didn't go together. Whatever the truth was, he was glad she was doing the sensible thing and allowing him to protect her.

❧❦❧

"I don't like this," Cay whispered as Alex jiggled the nail he'd pulled out of the side of the building in the door lock.

"Do you think I do?" he whispered back. "I'd like to be at home with my wife right now, not here."

"I'm sorry," she said contritely. "I sometimes forget about your loss."

Alex pulled up on the lock and pushed down on the nail, and the door finally came open. "Quickly," he said as he let her go inside before him. He stayed outside for a moment as he looked around to see if they'd been seen. But it appeared that every person in the small town was in church on this Sunday morning, so they were safe for a while.

"It's a nice store," Cay said as she looked around at the well-stocked shelves on the walls. Toward the back were cabinets full of clothes. "It's not

Charleston or New York, but for where it is, it's not bad."

Alex didn't care how good the store was as long as they could get what they needed and get out of there before they were discovered. "We need to get out of here and go," he said, his voice low. "And be quiet."

"You always think that I know nothing," she said as she walked to the back of the large store. In the front was a long counter, with boxes and bottles behind it. There were barrels of hard crackers and one of pickles.

Alex took a big canvas bag from behind the counter and began to fill it with crackers and dried apples. He hadn't told Cay he was worried that news about T.C.'s involvement in the jail break had reached Mr. Grady and he would be looking for a man of Alex's description. He hated to think that they could travel all that distance only to reach a trap.

When Alex heard nothing from Cay, he assumed she was changing her clothes, so he didn't want to bother her. He set the bag down by the door and walked quietly to the back of the store. There were cabinets full of clothing there, none of it of the quality he was sure she was used to, but of sturdy, serviceable cloth and well made. It took him only moments to strip off his torn, dirty clothing and put on new fawn-colored breeches that hugged his thighs, a white shirt with a cravat that tied about his neck, and a long vest of dark green. When he saw a shelf full of wide-brimmed straw hats, he took one. It would protect him from the Florida sun. As he looked down at himself, he fancied that he looked like a rich plantation owner, certainly not an escaped convict recently from the Highlands of Scotland.

Smiling, he stepped out to show Cay and to see what she'd found to wear, but when he saw her, he halted.

There was a tall mirror on a stand in the back, and she was standing before it, a brush in her hand, and quietly stroking her hair. He would have said that he was used to the sight of her by now, but he'd never seen her without the covering of the cloak. Her dress was tattered along the hem and he saw places that weren't in the best repair, but it was still a beautiful gown. The neckline was low and her breasts rounded over the top. Short sleeves exposed her long, bare arms, and he could see they were well shaped by years of dealing with stubborn horses. The white gown was tight over her breasts, tied with a ribbon just below, then fell loose to the floor.

He stood still for a moment, watching her, and thought of how she'd dressed to go to a ball in Charleston. She'd probably imagined moonlight trysts with young men, maybe even adding another marriage proposal to her repertoire that she'd tell her grandchildren about.

But because of her good nature, she'd agreed to do something that few wealthy—or poor, for that matter— young women would do. She'd risked her life to save a man she'd never met, a man she had reason to believe was guilty of murder.

He kept watching as she brushed her hair, and he figured she was thinking that it would be the last time. And he knew by the look of loss on her face that she was going to agree to cut it.

How he wished he could turn the clock

back! If he could, he'd go back . . . He couldn't think of that because he knew he'd go back to the time when he'd been the happiest in his life, when he'd married Lilith.

Taking a deep breath, Alex stepped out from between the shelves full of goods and went to her. "May I have this dance, Miss Cay?"

He held out his arms for her and hoped that she didn't mind about his dirty hair, and the stench of the prison that was still on his body.

But she had been taught her manners well. She smiled graciously at him, held up her skirt, and put her other hand in his. As Alex put his fingertips at her waist, he wished he had music, but the best he could do was hum an old, slow Scottish ballad that his mother used to sing to him. It wasn't a proper dance, with the intricate changing of partners, but a private one, just between the two of them.

When she began to hum with him, showing that she knew the song, his smile broadened, and he swirled her about the room, between tables and shelves, in front of the counter and behind it. When she reached out and took a dark brown bottle and set in on the counter, he laughed out loud. She wasn't forgetting the business side of why they were there.

It was several minutes before he took her back to the mirror, then bowed as he stepped away from her. "I must say, Miss Cay, that I have never enjoyed a dance as much as I did that one."

"Nor have I." She curtseyed to him, holding her skirt out to its full width.

Stepping away, he looked at her, thinking that she was so very pretty in her long white dress—and he wanted to remember her like this. She was the girl who'd saved his life.

"You'll have to help me," she said.

Alex was still staring at her. In all the years he'd spent writing her brother, Nate hadn't mentioned that his little sister was so beautiful. "Help you do what?"

"Undress."

It took Alex a moment to realize what she'd said. "You want me to help you . . . undress?"

She smiled sweetly at him. "If we're going to travel together, then you have to act as one of my brothers." She turned her back to him and lifted her hair. "You can start by unfastening the buttons down the back."

"There must be a thousand of them. We'll be here all day."

"You're a married man, so you must know how to unfasten the back of a gown."

"I was married for just a few hours," Alex said as he struggled with the fourth button. They were tiny and the little loops were slippery.

Cay glanced at him over her shoulder. "A few hours? Then you didn't . . . ?"

"Not that it's any of your business, but no, we didn't." He was frowning at the buttons.

"Hope said that you fell asleep on your wedding night, but I didn't believe her."

"I did not 'fall asleep.' I was drugged."

"Ah, yes, glass of wine, then sleep. Who drugged you?"

"If I knew that, I could have saved

myself at the trial." He was two-thirds of the way through the buttons.

"Hope said the door was locked from the inside and that only you and your wife were in her room."

"That's about the only thing the lawyers got right." Alex pulled on the last button. "There, now, get out of that dress and let's get going. Someone may come in here."

"On a Sunday? Surely not. Not even my father works on Sundays."

"So I guess that means that no man does," Alex said in a derisive way. He was looking at the back of her dress as though he'd just climbed a mountain and was proud of what he'd done.

"Turn around," she said. "I'm still a girl and you're a man and . . ." Breaking off, she stared at him as though she was just realizing that he was in new clothes.

"You like this?" he asked, holding out his arms.

"You look like a planter," she said softly. "Those clothes suit you." She turned back around to face the mirror but kept looking at him in its reflection.

"Of course the fact that you're the dirt-iest man in the country, and that you have nits in your hair takes away from the overall effect."

He ran his hand over his hair. He used to keep it neatly trimmed and tied back at the nape of his neck with a black ribbon, but now it had grown wild and long, and she was right that it was very dirty. "Maybe I can wash it when we get to where we're going."

"No. You're going to take a whole bath today or I'm not going to put on boy's clothes."

Alex smiled at her. "Too late for that. You'll never get those buttons done up without my help."

Cay grabbed a dress from a shelf near her and held it up. It was a plain thing, made of brown plaid, with black braid around the collar. There was a look of threat in her eyes.

He wasn't going to tell her, but if she was going to continue wearing a dress, he much preferred the white one she had on. He'd grown used to the way it flashed in the sunlight. The surprise was that she'd seemed to know, through some mysterious female way, that he wouldn't like for her to wear the plain brown dress.

"You have to take a bath."

"I promise that I'll wash." He was smiling at her. "I'm not a barbarian, even if you think I am."

Cay looked back at the mirror. She was holding her beautiful dress about her, and she took one last, long look, glanced at Alex as he turned his back to her, then she let the dress fall and stepped out of it. She looked at herself in the long corset, her pantaloons going down to her knees, and at her torn stockings above the worn and dirty slippers. This was her last glimpse of herself as a girl.

Worse, she knew that she was going to have to get his help in removing the corset. Her maid had tied it for her days ago, and she hadn't had it off since then.

"You have to untie me," she said.

"I'll have to turn around to do that. Or should I wear a blindfold?"

"You wear a blindfold when you get shot for untying a woman's corset strings when she doesn't want you to, but I'm asking you to do this, so it's all right."

Laughing, Alex turned around, and Cay was pleased when he drew in his breath. He was the only man to have ever seen her in her underwear. Except for her father and brothers, she thought, but they didn't count. Tally had once put itching powder in her corset just before she was to meet her mother's old friend, Thomas Jefferson, who had become the governor of Virginia. At the memory of what she did to Tally afterward, she couldn't help smiling.

"Where do I start?" Alex asked, keeping his eyes on the back of the boned garment.

"Pretend it's a horse harness and untie it."

"I could use my knife and—"

"No!" she said. "No cutting."

He almost made a joke about "not yet," meaning that he wouldn't do any cutting until he took his knife to her hair, but he thought better of it. The strings had been tied in a way that had hardened into a knot over the last few days, and it took a while to get them loose. As he began to pull the strings out, he could feel her take deep breaths.

"My maid pulled it in tighter than usual because of the ball," Cay said as she let out another breath.

"Isn't that painful?" He had hit a snag and he dearly wanted to pull out his knife and slash the blasted thing.

"Of course it is, but you men love a small waist."

Bending, he put his face closer to the laces. It looked like the maid had tied a knot in the middle as well as at the top. "But those dresses you women wear today hide your waist."

"Do they really?" she asked, her voice all sweet innocence.

He pulled the laces loose, stepped back from her, and smiled. She had him there. The high-waisted fashions concealed little. "No, they don't hide much of anything. When a woman stands in front of a candle you can see—" He cleared his throat. "It's done."

Cay was already shrugging out of the corset. He'd left the bottom of it fastened, so she had to step out of it. Alex meant to turn away, but she started twisting about in such a manner that he couldn't stop looking at her—and laughing.

"I can breathe!" She ran her hands up her back and scratched through her long cotton shift, and when that wasn't enough, she went to the wall and rubbed up against it, her face showing her utter delight.

"You shouldn't have been afraid of the bear, he would have thought you were one of his tribe."

"Do shut up," she said amiably. "If *you* had spent days in a corset, without even taking it off at night, you'd—" She turned her back to him. "Make yourself useful and come over her and scratch my back. It itches until I could go mad."

Alex hesitated, but he did as she said, gently scratching her back through the fabric.

"I know you're a weak man, but surely you can do better than that."

He began to scratch harder and when his nails weren't enough, he took out his knife and used the handle of it to

rub her back until he was sure he'd remove the skin.

At last she stepped away. "Better.
Much better." She was still twisting
about, shrugging her shoulders, and
moving her arms in circles.

Again, he marveled at how pretty she
was. Why hadn't Nate thought to mention that in all his letters? "Do you think
you could get dressed now, lass?"

"Sure. What should I put on?"

"Anything that covers you," he muttered, and went back to searching the
store to see if there was anything else
that they would need. On the counter
was the bottle she'd put there while they
were dancing. It was labeled "jasmine
oil." It looked like, even if she was going
to wear boy's clothes, she planned to
smell good. He would, of course, have
to tell her that she couldn't wear it, but
he wouldn't ruin her good mood now.
He put the oil back on the shelf.

In the back of the store, Cay was having trouble with the clothes. She left her
shift on, but when she put a boy's shirt
on over it, her breasts were still promi-
nent. And they tended to move when

she walked. She wasn't about to tell the Scotsman about this problem and ask his opinion. Instead, she had to look around the store to find cloth she could use to bind her breasts. In a back corner were rolls of fabric and scissors, so she cut a bit of white muslin and made a big bandage of it. She didn't pull too hard, just enough to stop the movement and make her chest into a lump, and she put the shirt back on. If she kept it loose, she thought it would work.

It didn't take long to put on the other clothes. She traded her torn silk stockings for a boy's thick white ones, and breeches went easily over her slim legs. She had a great deal of trouble fastening them at the waist, what with all the buttons and ties, but she figured it out. She tucked the shirt into the trousers, slipped her arms through a vest, found a lightweight wool coat, and put it on. As she started for the front of the store, she grabbed a big straw hat off the shelf, and went to the front counter.

"Well?" she said to Alex's back.

Turning, he gave her a long look, but said nothing.

"You don't like it? Did I do something wrong? I'm not used to breeches, but I think I fastened them properly."

Silently, he went behind her, put his hands on her shoulders, and pushed her toward the mirror. Her reflection showed a girl in boy's clothing. Her hair hung past her shoulders in thick curls, and she was still wearing her pearl earrings. It was amazing that they'd stayed on as long as they had—but then she'd tightened them often.

Without a word, Alex held out his hand, and she knew what he meant. She unscrewed the earrings and put them in his palm.

"I'll put these with your other clothes and take them with us."

"Of course we're going to take my dress. Maybe it can be repaired. I don't plan to wear these hideous clothes forever. Once you've left on your travels with the other men, maybe I can go back to being a girl."

"And travel all the way back to Virginia as a lone female? No, you will not." The moment the words were out of his mouth, he regretted them, but she didn't say anything. Instead, she was again twisting about.

"What are you doing now?"

"Moving. It feels odd not to have on a corset. I've worn one every day of my life since I was twelve."

"Twelve?" Alex said. "You've been tied into that thing since you were little more than a babe?"

"Of course. How else does a grown woman get a small waist? You don't think a mother would wait until her daughter was an adult, then try to pull her waist in, do you?"

"I can honestly say that I never wondered how a woman got a small waist. I guess I thought they were born with them."

Cay shook her head at him. "Next you'll be telling me that you think women naturally have a shine to their hair and roses in their cheeks."

Since that was true, Alex could only stare at her in silence.

"I think you missed out on a lot in life by having no mother or sisters."

"I think I was a babe in the woods until I met you," Alex said under his breath, then louder, "Are you ready to go, lass?"

"You'll have to stop calling me that, now that I'm supposed to be a boy."

"When we do something with your hair so you don't look like one, I will."

All humor left Cay's face. "I think that if I wash it and comb it back when it's wet, it might be manageable just as it is."

He didn't like the sadness in her eyes. "Might as well say that about a lion's mane," he said and was glad when she smiled.

"Truly?"

"Completely. You know, I don't think I've ever before seen so much hair on one person. And the color is truly magnificent." As he talked he was walking toward the door and Cay was following him.

"You don't think it's too red?" she asked, her eyes wide in innocence. She wanted to distract him enough so that he didn't see the things she was putting into the bag.

With his eyes on her, he picked up the big bag of goods and held the door open for her. "I wouldn't change a strand of it." He glanced back into the store, saw the money he'd left on the counter, and closed the door behind her. "I once had a pony with a mane the color of your hair and it was my favorite of all of them."

Cay looked at the closed door behind her. "Are you just saying these things to get me to do what you want?"

"Aye, I am, but I'm also telling you the truth, lass," he said softly. "You have beautiful hair."

Smiling, she went down the stairs.

In the store, she'd felt the looseness of the boy's clothing, but it wasn't until she mounted her mare that she really saw how different they were. Instead of having to rely on people or things to help her mount, without a skirt holding her legs together, she put her foot high up into the stirrup and hoisted herself up. She looked down at her legs in the dark breeches and knew that if her elegant mother saw her now she'd faint. Edilean Harcourt would *never* wear boy's clothing, no matter what the circumstances. But Cay couldn't help feeling just a bit more free. She saw that the Scotsman was watching her in curiosity. "I want to see the map to where we're going," she said in the firmest voice she could manage.

She had no idea what she'd said that made him laugh so loud, but she reminded him that they had to be quiet or someone would hear them.

"I think I've made my lot worse," he said as he reined his horse away and started going south, Cay right behind him.

Eight

❦

Cay had been careful not to say another word about the Scotsman's hair or the state of his body until they stopped to camp that night. When she'd lowered her lashes and asked sweetly that they camp by a stream or a river, he'd squinted his eyes, as though to ask what she was up to, but he said nothing, and that's where they'd stopped. All through their dinner of dried fruit, crackers, and pickles, she'd said nothing.

It was only after they'd finished eating that she stood up and stared down at him. "It's time for you to take a bath."

"Too cold," he said without looking up.

"It must be eighty degrees and you're a Scot, so how can anything be too cold?"

"The river current is too strong."

She didn't have to look at the stream to see how gently it was flowing. "I have soft soap for your hair."

"I don't need it." He still hadn't looked up at her. "As for you, lass, I'm afraid it's time to trim your hair. I brought scissors so I won't need to use my knife, but I think we should get started on it."

She knew he was trying to distract her, but it wasn't working. "You smell so bad that I have to hold my hand over my nose and breathe through my mouth. Your hair is so dirty that I've seen cow tails that are cleaner. You stink, and I can't stand it any longer."

Alex kept his eyes straight ahead, looking at the water and the sun low in the sky, and not looking at her. The truth was that he didn't want to remove the stench of the prison from his body. He knew he was being foolish, but he hadn't been allowed to bathe since the day he'd married Lilith, and if he washed, he knew it would remove his last connection to her.

And then there was the fact that he was alone with a young woman whom he was beginning to see as being quite desirable. All in all, he thought it would be better to make her stay away from him. "I like the smell of me."

"Well, I don't. If we're going to make it to Florida together, then there are going to be times when you need my help, and if you want me to give it to you, then you are going to be *clean.*"

When he just sat there, she turned away from him, went to her horse, and began to saddle it. He took longer than she'd thought he would before he stopped her, but he did.

"Why didn't your father turn you over his knee and teach you to obey your elders?"

"My father would never strike a child, but my mother . . ." She glared at him. "Don't get me started on my family! There's the water and the soap is in the bag. And when you get through, I'm going to coat your hair in jasmine oil."

Alex took a step back from her, his face filled with horror. "Nay, you will not."

"The oil will kill whatever is living in there. Smother it."

"But the smell, lass . . . I couldn't bear the stench." When he saw that she wasn't going to give in, he looked back at the water. "No, I won't do it."

"Fine," Cay said as nicely as she could manage. "But *I* am going to take a bath." Turning, she slipped into the surrounding forest and removed her shoes, cursing him with every breath. "I guess he wants turpentine," she muttered. "Make him smell more like a *man.* Good. Then he can stay as filthy as he wants to and I won't care. But he's not going to share *my* cloak again, and he's not going to sleep beside me ever again. He's not going to—"

She stopped her tirade when she heard a big splash. It was either a huge fish, a bear coming to eat them, or . . . She stepped closer to the stream and looked to see the Scotsman's head just above the water.

"It may be warm on land but this water is cold," he said, and even in the fading light she could see that his face was already red.

"The water in Scotland is colder," she said, laughing.

"Aye, but I don't get into it naked. I have my plaid."

Cay kept the smile on her face and stepped back into the trees. She was alone in the forest with a naked man who might be a murderer, but she was smiling. Even to her, that seemed odd.

"Will you no come in, lass?" He sounded like a old man calling to a young girl—which was what was happening, but she knew he was doing it as a joke.

His jest removed the awkwardness of the moment. "Use the soap. I just hope it's strong enough to remove some of the dirt."

"Could you not come in and show me how?" he called in a teasing way.

Cay stayed out of sight, but she was laughing. When he said nothing more and she heard a lot of splashing, she cautiously peeped around a tree and looked out at the water. He was standing chest deep, lather on his head, and he was shivering. As she watched, he dove into the water and she saw his naked behind above the surface. Turning back, she giggled and began removing the rest of her own clothing.

What would he do if she did get into the water with him? she wondered. In her group of female friends, it was Jessica Welsch who was the flirt. One time Cay's mother said that it was a wonder Jess hadn't run off with a man when she was thirteen, considering what her mother Tabitha's past was like. Cay had wanted to know all the story behind that remark, but her mother wouldn't elaborate on it.

"What would I do if I were Jessica?" she wondered aloud. It came to her that she'd remove all her clothing and walk naked into the river. The pale evening light, the warm air, being alone with a man . . . It all seemed to be right.

But Cay leaned against a tree and sighed. What was wrong was that this wasn't the right man. This was a man she hardly knew, he was much too old for her, and he wasn't the sort of man her family would be proud that she'd chosen. Even if he were proven innocent of murder, there would always be the stigma of the accusation and the trial attached to him.

No, she thought, and gave another sigh. Maybe the circumstances were right, but the man wasn't.

She waited until she heard him leave the water, then she went in. She stayed a good distance from where he had been, and even though she wanted to swim and play in the water—which was colder than it looked—she didn't. She soaped and washed her hair, rinsed, then used one of the two towels that had been in Uncle T.C.'s supplies to dry off.

When she went back to their camp, he had built a fire and was sitting there in his clean clothes, and he looked and smelled much better. In fact, maybe it was the light, but he looked younger and maybe even a little bit handsome.

"Better?" he asked.

"Much. Except that now I'll not be able to find you by smell alone."

He was leaning over the fire and seemed taller than he had when she first met him, and now his hair was wet and clean and no longer standing out from his head.

Cay held up the brown bottle of jasmine oil. She'd seen the bottle of oil, probably made by the storekeeper's wife, and known that it would work on nits and lice and all manner of vermin. But then, so would several other oils. The object was to smother the creatures so they couldn't breathe. She'd chosen jasmine over the other oils that the storekeeper had because she liked its smell so much. She'd had to retrieve it after Alex had tried to hide it. He'd been so involved in his flattery of her that he'd not seen her slip the bottle into the bag.

Alex didn't say anything, just nodded that she could pour the oil on him. When she sat down behind him, a comb in her hand, his eyes widened.

"What do you mean to do to me, lass?" he asked in a soft voice.

"Not what you're hoping. Bend down so I can see your hair."

Smiling, he sat in front of her, but when she did nothing, he looked back at her.

"You're too tall for me to reach." She spread her damp towel across her lap. "Stretch out and put your head on my lap."

"Lass, I don't think—"

"That you can control your 'passion' for me?" she asked without a smile. "Are you afraid you'll touch me and fall in love instantly?"

He knew she was making fun of him and he didn't like it, but on the other hand, she had a knack for making him laugh. "I'll save myself for someone older and let Michael have you."

"Micah," she said as he put his head on her lap and she began to comb his hair. When she had the tangles out, she poured the oil on it, and began to work it through. The heavenly fragrance of jasmine filled the air around them.

"I did this once to my brother Ethan when he got honey and beeswax in his hair. My father wanted to shave his head, but I couldn't bear that, so I said I'd get it out."

"How old were you?"

"Eleven, I guess."

"So that means he was . . . ?"

"Fourteen."

"Were you always like a mother to them?"

"Not at all." She massaged the oil into his scalp. For all that she'd complained often about his having lice, she didn't feel anything, just his scalp and his too-long hair. "Maybe I was a bit of a mother to Ethan, but he's the sweetest of my brothers, and the most gentle and the prettiest."

"Pretty? Like a girl?"

"No. At least no girl thinks he's pretty in that way. Women old and young make such a fuss over him."

"That must be pleasant."

"He takes it well. It's my mother who has the hard time. She says that girls of my generation have no restraint and no shame at all. She says that girls today throw themselves at men."

"Like you and your young man?"

"I never—"

"Didn't he teach you about using your . . . ?" He waved his hand about in the general area of his mouth.

"No," Cay said hesitantly, reluctant to admit that she'd lied. "Jessica told me about that. She's had more experience with boys than my other friends and I've had."

"So you didn't do anything you shouldn't have with the boy Micah?"

Cay didn't like the way he sounded like her father. "He's hardly a boy. He's thirty years old, has never been married, and conducts services on Sundays."

Twisting about, Alex looked up at her. "He's a minister? You're thinking about marrying a pastor?"

"And what's so wrong with that?"

"You agreed to help a convicted murderer escape from prison. Don't you think that's a wee bit against what the good wife of a holy man would do?"

"I told you that I didn't do it for you but for Uncle T.C."

"And this is the man who was passionately in love with a woman named Bathsheba?"

"Yes," Cay said, not understanding what he was getting at.

"Tell me, child, did T.C. ever do anything about his passion?"

When she didn't say anything, he looked up at her.

"Come on, lass, I can see it on your face. What did he do?"

"Hope."

"He *hoped* he'd find the woman he loved alone someday?"

"No!" she said as she put her hands on his scalp and turned his head back around. "Bathsheba had a daughter named Hope and she looks a lot like Uncle T.C." She glared down at him. "If you keep looking at me like that I'll pour this oil into your smirking mouth."

Alex closed his eyes, but he was still grinning. "All I'm saying, lass, is that if you marry the pastor and people find out what you did, it won't make life easy for your husband. But then, he might be an understanding man and forgive you for your sins."

"I haven't . . ." She trailed off, not sure what to say. What *would* Micah do when he was told what she'd done? How could she explain that she'd spent days alone with this man, had even had his head on her lap, but nothing sinful had happened? When she saw the way Alex was smiling at her, as though he actually could read her mind, she was tempted to make good her threat and pour the oil in his mouth. "Are you forgetting that you're a convicted murderer and we're alone out here? I know you don't want me to talk to you about . . . about men."

"And rightly so. I just wanted to know that you haven't done something you shouldn't have."

"The more I know you, the more you sound like one of my brothers."

"Which one?"

"Part Nate and part Tally."

"But not the beautiful Ethan?"

"Definitely not Ethan."

"What about the perfect Adam?"

"Adam is unique. No one is like Adam."

For a while they were quiet and Alex closed his eyes as the smell wafted about him and Cay's small hands worked on his scalp. "I swear, lass, that you have put me in a trance."

As she stroked his hair, pulling it out across her legs, she began to think more about her family, and where she was, and the fact that she didn't know where she was going or what was going to happen. All her life had been well planned, and she'd always known what she wanted to do with her life. She could have drawn pictures of herself at thirty. She would have two boys and a girl by then. All she had to do was decide which man was to be her husband. Now she wondered if one of her prospects would even want her after her time of running from the law.

Suddenly, tears began to form, and one of them dropped on Alex's forehead.

He had his eyes closed, his mind and body given over to the first comfort he'd felt in a very long time, but he knew what she was feeling. He didn't like to think that he'd made a girl cry, especially such a sweet and innocent one as she was. "Did you know that I came here to this country to race horses?" he asked, his voice so soft she could barely hear him.

"No. I . . . ." She hiccuped and sniffed as she drew back her tears. "Actually, I know very little about you."

"Except what you read in the papers," he said, and she felt his body stiffen.

"Actually, I didn't read them. All I know is what Hope told me." When her words had no effect on him, she did what she would have with one of her brothers and began to stroke his hair in a way that she knew would calm him. "Do you like any other animals besides racehorses?"

"I like all of them," he said. "Birds, horses, raccoons, I like them."

"What about spiders?"

He smiled. "Less so, but yes. I did a very bad thing back in Scotland. I did it twice."

She continued combing. His hair was spread out over her lap and it was coated with the fragrant oil. "My brothers have done some things that my father didn't like. One time, I'm not sure what Nate did, but my father was angry at him for an entire week."

Alex couldn't help grinning. He knew exactly what Nate had done, why he'd done it, and what his father had thought his son had done. But he wasn't going to tell Cay that. "I secretly mated my mare to Lord Brockinghurst's great stallion. Twice."

Cay laughed. "Did you?"

"Aye, I did. I had a lovely little mare, as feisty as can be. A bit like you, really. And I took her down south to England and waited until the man's fastest stallion was put in the pasture at night. He charged a lot to mate a mare with the great beast, but I couldn't afford it."

"So you stole what didn't belong to you."

"I like to think that I gave the horse the pleasure of my pretty mare for the night."

"So you were a philanthropist."

"More or less." He was smiling.

"And what was the result of your generosity?"

"The first colt was female, and as you know, mares can't run as fast as males."

"Maybe they don't want to," Cay said. "Maybe they want to stay in one place and be with their families."

Alex opened one eye to look up at her. "I'll get you home, lass, don't worry about it."

"Looking like a boy? Maybe I should take up chewing tobacco."

He was still looking at her. "Mayhaps

you should, lass, for you don't look like a boy now. Your hair is—"

When he started to reach up to touch it, she pushed his hand away. "We were talking about horses."

"Ah, yes." Turning back around, he closed his eyes. He well knew that whatever had been in his hair had long since been combed out, but he was glad she wasn't pushing him away. "The second colt was a beauty, perfect in every way."

"Meaning that it was male."

"Of course. What else could be perfect?" When she started to push his head out of her lap, he laughed and caught her hand. "I'm only teasing, lass. Do you not know that?"

She relented and continued combing. "So what did you do?"

"I had a plan, you see."

"And what was that?"

He wanted to tell her, but he couldn't, for the plan involved her family. He knew that about ten years ago, Nate's father, Cay's father, had purchased a horse farm not far from Edilean. There was a house and a barn, a stream, a pond, everything a man could need to raise a family and horses. Nate had written about the place and said that his father had too much to do to take proper care of it, so the farm was losing money. When Alex wrote back that it sounded like his dream farm, Nate had begged his father not to sell it, hinting that he might someday want the place for his own.

It had been the possibility of someday owning a farm near his friend that had spurred Alex on in his life. His father had told him about the opportunities to be found in America, and Alex had long dreamed of going there. His plan had been to win enough money from racing his horses to buy the farm, then his father would come to America and live with him. Everything had gone a little off track when he'd met Lilith and married her before he had enough money to purchase the farm, but he knew enough to take love when he found it. Of course Lilith hadn't exactly been what a man thought of as a farm wife, but he'd been sure all that could have been worked out.

"What was your plan?" Cay asked when he was silent.

"To make a lot of money. Isn't that why everyone comes to America?"

"And did you?"

"Yes." He opened his eyes to stare into the darkness. There was light from the fire, but the sun had gone down and evening had come quickly. "I boarded a ship with my three horses, the mother and her two children. My plan was to breed the mares and race the son. Tarka was a fast—"

"Tarka? That was the name of my father's fastest pony when he lived in Scotland. I rode him when I was a girl."

Alex almost said that Nate had written the story to him, and it's why Alex had named his horse that, but he didn't. "It's a common enough name."

"Is it? I thought it was rather unusual. So you brought your horses to America and you raced them? Or just Tarka?"

"My little mare could beat most of their horses. I saved Tarka for when I wanted to win a big purse."

"I see. You made them think that they might be able to beat you, but then you brought out another horse. Did you keep him hidden?"

"You have a devious mind," he said, but he was smiling.

"Is that what you did?"

"Aye, it's exactly what I did. I kept Tarka hidden so far out in the country that not one of those rich boys could find him. I won races and lost them, but then I brought out Tarka." His smile broadened. "You should have seen him. Tall and black and as beautiful as the sunrise. He was a magnificent animal, and he knew it. He walked with his head high and his tail up, and he wouldn't so much as look at the other horses. And run! On a racetrack, he took off as though the other horses were there to graze. He beat them by lengths. There was nothing in America that could touch him."

Cay was frowning. "You sound as though he's . . ." She hesitated. "As though he's no longer alive. What happened to him?"

"I don't know," Alex said, and the joy went out of his voice. "When I was accused of murder, everything I had was taken from me. I asked T.C. what happened to my horses, but he knew nothing and could find out nothing."

"You should have told Uncle T.C. you'd found a plant that no one had ever seen before and he would have moved the earth to find it."

Alex smiled, his good humor back. "You always make me laugh, lass." He turned over on his side and looked up at her. "When I get my name cleared, I'll get Tarka and his mother and sister back."

"And how do you mean to clear your name?"

"I have—" He started to say that he'd already done a lot of work toward clearing his name, but since what he'd done involved her brother, he couldn't tell her of it. When T.C. visited him in prison, Alex had written to Nate about the facts of what had happened to him. Alex knew the guards wouldn't let him keep pen and paper, so he'd had to write the letter over many visits, and T.C. had taken the pages when he left. When Alex had written everything, T.C. hired a rider to take the long, detailed letter to Nate. Alex had thought there'd be enough time for Nate to come to him and they could talk about what had happened, but the judge said that Alex's crime was so heinous that he was to be hanged two days after the verdict came in. There hadn't been time for Nate to receive the letter, then get to Charleston and clear Alex.

"You have what?"

Alex got up and put more wood on the fire. "Nothing, lass. I have nothing at all."

She knew he was lying. She was sure he'd meant to say that he'd figured out something to do, but he wouldn't tell her what it was. She was trusting him with her *life,* but he couldn't so much as tell her what he was going to do to defend himself. She pulled her knees up and wrapped her arms around them. When she put the towel beside her, the scent of jasmine was all around them. "Could you please call me something besides 'lass'?"

His mouth went up on one side in a half smile. "As soon as you call me anything at all."

"That's absurd. I call you . . ."

"Aye, what do you call me?"

"Mr. McDowell."

"I like that." When he stretched, his damp shirt clung to the muscles in his back. "It shows that you have respect for your elders. Perhaps you could add a 'sir' to it now and then, as is proper in our present situation."

"Present . . . ?" she said. "If it weren't for my rescuing you, you'd be dead by now. When I first saw you, you were on foot and being chased by men who were shooting at you. What happened to the men who broke you free?"

"One was shot and the other turned himself in," Alex said quietly.

"How did you get away?"

"Rolled away in the dark and came up running. I didn't think I'd escape them." Looking at her, he smiled. "But a lovely young girl dressed for a party was waiting there to save me. You looked like an angel."

"That's not what you said at the time. You told me you were doomed."

"You misunderstood me. I said I thought I'd died and gone to Heaven."

"You said—" she began, then realized he was teasing her. "Yes, I do believe that you referred to me as an angel and you were oh, so very glad to see me there waiting for you."

"That's just how I remember it, too." His eyes were twinkling in the firelight, and she couldn't help smiling back.

"Lass, I think . . ." He looked at her. "Cay, I think we should get some sleep. We'll leave early tomorrow morning."

She groaned. "Before daylight again. When I'm at home, my maid wakes me with a pot of hot chocolate, and I lie in bed and sip it while she asks me what I want to wear that day."

"Sounds very boring," he said as he stirred the fire.

"No, it's . . ." She looked around them at the still night. They were far enough south now that the plants were beginning to change. She'd noticed flowers that she'd only seen in Uncle T.C.'s drawings. "I didn't think it was boring then," she said as she looked at the ground. "Alex."

"What did you say?"

"That when I was at home, I didn't think it was boring."

"No, I heard that. What was the last part?"

She smiled. "Alex. Is that what you wanted to hear?"

"No, I like Mr. McDowell better."

She picked up a clod of dirt and threw it at him, and when she hit his arm, he made sounds as though he were truly hurt. "You aren't a gentleman."

"Never wanted to be. I just wanted what a gentleman's stallion had."

Laughing, she stood up. "I think it is time for sleep. I'll just have my maid warm the bed for me and get my chocolate and I'll be ready to turn in." She expected him to laugh, but he was looking at her hard. "What is it?"

"You don't look like a boy."

"I hope not." She glanced down at her clothes. "I must say that these breeches do give a person a great deal of freedom. And the lack of . . . of certain undergarments made riding today much easier."

"No, it's the way you walk, the way you move. Lass—" He held up his hand.

"Cay, I mean, you'll never pass as a boy looking like that."

She put her hand to her hair. She was *not* going to cry! "I know. My hair is—"

"I could shave your head and you'd still look like a girl. It's the way you stand, the way you move your hands."

"What's wrong with the way I move my hands?"

"There's nothing wrong with any of it if you're a lady entering a ballroom. But you look like a girl in boy's clothing."

"Oh," she said, at last understanding what he meant. "You want me to move like Tally does."

"I don't know, but try it."

She walked to the far side of the fire, put her shoulders back, her flattened chest out, and strode past him with a swagger that said she was the best and the greatest. When she stopped, she used her fist to wipe her nose, and looked at him in an insolent way, as though daring him to fight her.

Alex chuckled, then he full out laughed. "Surely you're not telling the truth. The boy couldn't walk like that."

"He does all the time."

"Let's try it again, only this time not as though you're trying to start a brawl. Shoulders back is good, but less swagger to your walk."

"Maybe more like Adam." She walked again, only this time she ate up the ground in just a few long strides, and she had a look that said she was too busy to pay attention to the rest of the world.

Alex cleared his throat to keep from laughing.

"No good? How about Ethan?"

Alex put out his hand to say she could try it.

Cay went back the other way, only this time she went slowly, noticing everything, and when her eyes lit on Alex, she gave him a long look, as though she'd never seen him before but would very much like to get to know him.

"Lord in Heaven!" Alex said. "Surely the boy doesn't do *that.*"

Cay shrugged. "Girls follow him down the street."

"Well, uh, I don't think that you need to do that. We don't want people following us. What about the other brother? What was his name?"

"Nathaniel. Nate."

Cay looked about for something, then picked up a leather satchel lying by her saddle. "Pretend this is a book." She held it close to her face and walked slowly across the space, oblivious to everything but the book. When she came to the end, she kept her head down but walked around a tree.

She returned to the fire and looked at Alex. "Well?"

He couldn't keep from laughing. "I don't think any of them are right. Could you not . . ?"

"Not what?"

"Well, lass . . . Cay, could you not walk like *me*?"

"Oh? You mean like this?" She puffed out her chest, put on a frown, and glared down at an imaginary person. "Can't you come on, lass? I haven't got all day. You're more trouble than you're worth." She hurried off into the darkness, leaving herself behind.

"I don't. . . ," Alex began, then shook his head. "Maybe I do. But if you kept the walk and said nothing, you might do all right."

"Was there a compliment in there?"

"Not from me," he said, but he was smiling under all the hair on his face. "I think we should sleep now. We'll work on your walk some more tomorrow."

"You aren't going to tell me I have to sit with my legs apart, are you?"

"Aye, I am," he said solemnly.

"Maybe that's good. If I committed that big of a sin my mother will find me wherever I am." She picked up Hope's big cloak off the ground and wrapped it around her. She planned to use it as a cover and as protection from the earth, but as she looked down at her breeches, she thought about the reality of their situation. If someone guessed that she was female, and if they saw that she was with Alex, it wouldn't be difficult to figure out who they were. They could both be put in prison.

"I want you to cut my hair now," she said softly, and she didn't dare touch her hair or she'd start crying again.

She saw that he was about to apologize, or maybe make an excuse about

why they should leave it until the morning, but he didn't. He nodded toward a
piece of log nearby, and she sat down
on it, her back rigidly straight.

Alex took the scissors he'd taken
from the store out of the satchel on the
ground and went behind her. Her hair
was still damp from her swim, but as
it was drying, it was fluffing out into
fat curls. To cut such hair was a great
waste of beauty.

Cay glanced up at him, saw his hesitation, and wanted to tell him not to
make this harder for her. Instead, she
decided to goad him on. "Did I tell you
about Benjamin?"

"And who is that?" Alex asked as he
picked up a strand of her hair and held
it. He wanted to put it to his face and
feel it on his skin. Between the time in
jail and the weeks of the trial, it had been
months since he'd felt the softness of a
woman. "You have a fifth brother?"

"Benjamin is the youngest of my
suitors. He's just twenty-two and very
handsome. Not as handsome as Ethan,
of course, but very nice to look at. His
family is quite wealthy, and he loves

to gamble and play games and bet on horses."

"Bet on horses? Surely you aren't thinking of marrying a gambler!" Holding a thick strand of her hair, he made the first cut. As the glorious red hair fell to the ground, he stared down at it.

When Cay felt her hair being cut, she was determined not to cry. "But he makes me laugh and he comes up with wonderful games to play. I think maybe he's the one I should marry. He'd think it was a great adventure that I ran across the country with a convicted murderer."

"What kind of man is he that he cares naught about what you've been through?" Alex cut more of her hair. "What if I were guilty as everyone thinks I am? Do you have any idea what I could have done to you by now?"

"But you haven't, and when I get back, I'll tell Ben all about everything. He'll even laugh about the jasmine oil I put in your hair."

"Will he now?" Alex asked, frowning as he cut more of her hair. "He won't be jealous?"

"Ben says that being jealous is a stupid emotion and when we're married I must never be jealous of him no matter what he does."

"He sounds like he means to run off with other women while you stay home with a passel of brats."

"Isn't that what a wife is supposed to do?"

"No," Alex said. "I think a couple should work together to raise a family."

"So you're saying that a man *should* be jealous?"

"I think—" He stopped because he realized she was teasing him. "You're a bothersome bairn, is what you are. There now, I've finished."

When Cay stood up, the cloak fell from her shoulders, and for a moment she just stood there looking at him, afraid to move her head. What would it feel like to have so little hair? Slowly, tentatively, she moved her head to one side, then the other. Actually, it didn't feel so bad. He'd cut it until it hung just to her shoulders so she could tie it back at the nape of her neck as her brothers did.

She moved her head to one side, but this time faster. With about a foot of her thick hair gone, it was surprisingly light. She began to shake her head, and her hair flew about her face. When she stopped, she looked at Alex. He was watching her with wide eyes, the scissors still in his hand.

"I do believe that I rather like it." She put one foot on the log and held an imaginary pipe in her hand. "So, tell me, sir, what do you think of the price of wheat today? Do you think it will go up again or have the English ruined that for us as well?"

He'd never seen anyone look less like a male than she did. Her hair swirled about her shoulders in thick curls and her long lashes made shadows on her cheeks. "I think you should let me do the talking."

She stood up straight and swung her hair about her some more. It really did feel wonderful.

"Will you stop doing that!" Alex snapped.

"Why?"

"It bothers me, is all. You should go to sleep."

"And what about you?"

"What I do is my own business," he said, knowing he sounded grumpy. He knew he was still in love with Lilith, but it had been a long time since he'd been alone with a woman, and Cay was . . . He searched for the right word. *Enticing.* She was indeed enticing.

She was standing there staring at him, and he knew what she wanted. She wanted to know where he was going, what he was going to do, and when he'd be back. He wanted to again tell her that what he did was his concern, not hers, but he didn't. "I'm going to wash this vile oil out of my hair," he said at last. What he was really going to do was take a long plunge in the icy cold stream.

"You can't do that," she said. "You need to leave the oil in at least until morning to smother whatever's in your hair. You can wash it out before we leave tomorrow." She picked up the cloak and wrapped it around her. "But do what you want. I'm going to sleep now."

She stretched out on the ground near the fire and lay there in silence for a moment, then she flipped one side of the cloak away from her. It was an invitation to him. It wasn't much, but the wool would be separating them, and for her, she felt safer when he was nearby.

For what seemed like a long time, Alex didn't move. It was as though he was making a decision. Finally, she heard his soft chuckle—a sound she was coming to know—and he stretched out on the grass next to her and pulled the side of the cloak over him.

"Good night, Cay," he said.

"Good night, Alex," she answered, and when she felt the heat of his body through the wool, she went to sleep.

Nine

❧

"It still reeks," Alex said as he sat down on the log and lowered his head, his fragrant hair hanging about him. "I can't get rid of the stench of it. I soaped it three times, but all I can smell is . . . is flowers. I smell like a bloody *flower*!"

Cay was behind him with the scissors and trying to cut a few inches off his long hair. Personally, she envied him the smell of his hair, but she knew better than to say that.

She thought his real problem was that when they woke up this morning, they'd been snuggled together like puppies. While it was true that the heavy wool of the cloak was between them, they were still close together. Alex was on his side, facing the fire, and Cay was behind him, her body against his and her arm over his chest. Her face was buried in his fragrant hair, and she was having sweet dreams.

She knew Alex didn't want to admit it, but he must have been having good dreams, too, because he'd picked up her hand and put her palm against his cheek.

But when Alex had awakened more fully, he came to his feet in a roar of anger. But he didn't frighten Cay. She stretched out, smiled up at him, and told him he smelled wonderful. That's when he ran to the stream, stripped off, and did what he could to remove the jasmine oil.

It hadn't worked. His hair still smelled great. Cay got him to sit on the log so she could cut it, and every time she made a remark or, worse, put her nose to his hair, he got even more angry.

"I'll shave my head, that's what I'll do," he muttered. "I'll go bald."

"You'll have to shave your face, too, as I do believe that that beard of yours smells just as heavenly."

Turning, he glared at her.

"Sorry. The smell is very masculine.

However, I can't wait to tell my women friends about it. I wonder if I can get the recipe from the shopkeeper's wife. I've never smelled jasmine oil so strong. I wonder what her jasmine tea is like?"

Alex stood up, still glaring at her, and took the towel off his shoulders. Unfortunately, it was the towel that was coated in jasmine oil, and just moving it made the air around them fragrant.

Cay had to bite her lips to keep from laughing out loud, but then she was tired of trying to placate him. He was being ridiculous. "At least you're not a bank robber," she said.

"And why is that better than being called a murderer?" He was saddling his horse and putting on the packs.

"They could identify you as soon as you walked in the door." When he turned and gave her a look meant to make her stop talking, she just blinked at him. "They'd hire ladies to track you."

Glowering at her, he took a step forward and she went backward. If she'd had on a dress, she would have tripped over some twigs on the ground, but with her breeches and her newfound freedom, she agilely stepped over them. "What would the handbill for your arrest say? 'Smell this criminal.' Maybe they could pass out little samples of the oil on bits of paper. People could compare the smell to the hair of every man they met."

"You—" Alex began, but she could see that the anger was no longer in his eyes.

"The men who use rosewater would be eliminated. No, only jasmine would be guilty. Think what you'd do for the world of criminals. It wouldn't be a man's picture but his smell that would identify him."

"All right, that's enough," Alex said, but he was hiding a smile. "Get on your horse and let's go. If you can stop making fun of me, that is."

"I'll make my best effort, but I have a request. May I ride downwind of you?"

He couldn't keep his laughter in. "Go on, lass, get up or we'll never get to the rendezvous with Mr. Grady."

She climbed into the saddle, and when she reined her horse past him, she ostentatiously took a deep breath and closed her eyes, as though in ecstasy.

Ignoring her gesture, he led the way out of the little clearing and back onto the road. "Remember, now. When we see people, keep your head down and say nothing. It wouldn't take much for them to know you're a girl."

"But I don't smell like one," she said, grinning. "I leave that to you."

He shook his head at her and they started moving.

Ten

♣

Where is she? Alex asked himself again. Cay should be in the tavern beside him but she wasn't. It had been her idea to give her disguise a test, and earlier, they'd had an argument about it.

"You will not!" he'd said in a way that was meant to be an order.

"I'm going to have to appear in public sometime, so why not now?"

"We're still too close to Charleston." He was sitting on his horse rigidly, his eyes straight ahead, not looking at her.

"I know we're south of Savannah. Not that I've been allowed to look at the map, and not that you've told me anything about where we are, where we're going, or how long it will take us to get there. In fact, you've still not told me what your plan for me is. I saved you from death, I've put my own life in jeopardy, but you don't so much as inform me where and when, and when I ask you—"

"All right," Alex said loudly. "If you'll stop your chatter I'll let you go into the tavern in your boy's clothes. But you have to behave yourself. And stop fiddling with your hair!" As he looked at her on the horse next to him, he felt as though they might as well turn themselves in to the local sheriff now. To him, Cay didn't look like a boy at all. And her absurd posturing that she said was like one or other of her brothers was laughable. No one in the world was going to believe she was male.

Cay's smile was brilliant. "Do stop looking like you're facing your doom. Only you think I look like a girl. By the way, is my dress packed away carefully?" She didn't tell him, but she was concerned about the diamond pins in the bodice.

"Aye, lass, it is." He couldn't help looking like he was near to death because that's how he felt when he saw her. He was sure they'd be caught as soon as she showed herself.

Glancing at him, she smiled and pulled her horse back so she was behind him. It was minutes later that he saw her lifting herself up on her right foot while removing her left from the stirrup. "What is that you're trying to do?" he asked as calmly as he could muster.

"It's a trick that Tally does that I couldn't do because I always had on a dress. My cousin Derek taught it to him. He's—"

"To be the laird," Alex said quickly and he couldn't help his feeling of . . . well, it was a feeling very much like jealousy. Alex was the one who'd shown her cousin, Derek Moncrief, how to put both feet into one stirrup and hide at the side of the horse. Alex had often used the trick when he wanted to sneak away from his father after he'd been forbidden to ride in the heather during the night.

"Not like that," Alex said with more anger than he meant. "Put all your weight on your right foot, then slide your left leg back around. There, lass, now crouch down. No one can see you from that side of the horse."

Cay grinned at him with such thanks that he looked away. "I guess it's a Scottish trick."

"Actually, I learned it from my father, who learned it from your American Indians. I would imagine that it was your father who taught it to your brothers."

"He . . . ?" Cay couldn't suppress her feeling of hurt that her father had taught such a useful movement to her brothers but not to her. What other things had he shown them but not her? "What else do you know how to do?" she asked Alex.

"Do you think I'm going to show you how to do tricks that would let you run away from me?"

"You said I wasn't a prisoner and that I could leave at any time. Besides, now that my ribs are no longer tied down, I'm beginning to . . ."

"To what? Enjoy yourself?"

"No, of course not. But I—" She narrowed her eyes at him. "Do stop looking at me like I'm a great bother to you and show me something else. When I see Tally next time I want to be able to do something that will impress him grandly."

"Ah, then if you want to impress him *grandly,* you might want to try this." He knew he shouldn't take the time to show her a horse trick, but he couldn't bear for all the credit to be given elsewhere. He had her exchange horses with him, and told her to stand to the side of the road with his. He dropped the dirty handkerchief he'd offered her the first night, then walked her mare down the road. While Cay watched, he rode toward her at a blinding speed and when he came to the handkerchief, he bent down and picked it up. It was almost the same thing he'd done when she'd dropped the cloth days before, but this time he went lower, and Cay had no idea how he held himself in the saddle without falling off.

Halting, he turned and walked the horse back to her.

"I want to learn how to do that."

He got down and handed her the reins to her mare. "I'll teach you, but not now. We don't have time." When he saw her face, he leaned toward her. "And if you try that alone and break your neck, you'll answer to me."

"When will you teach me?"

"When—" He wanted to say that he'd show her as soon as they got to Florida, but he knew that he was to leave with the exploration team and she was to stay behind. It was possible that he'd never see her after the two more days it would take them to get to the rendezvous place. But he wasn't going to tell her that. "When we have time," was all he'd say.

For the rest of the day, Alex watched her practicing the first trick. He made her ride in front of him so he could see what she was doing wrong and correct her—and to save her if she was about to break any of her body parts. But having her in front of him turned out to be a mistake, as he watched her moving all over her horse in her too-tight breeches and her thin shirt.

By the time they reached the tavern, he was in a bad mood. It made sense that she wanted to test her disguise, but he couldn't make himself admit that. Or maybe it was that he wanted to spend the night on the trail with her again. He'd grown to like being close to another human being. During his hideous weeks in prison, for all his grief, there were times when he'd longed to be near people. To talk to someone past the few minutes he was allowed with T.C. To listen to a person other than a lawyer!

"I can make people think I'm male," Cay said when she was trying to persuade him to let her appear in public as a boy. He couldn't bear to disappoint her.

"All right," he'd at last agreed. "But you have to do exactly what I say."

"I always do, don't I?"

Alex groaned. "You're as obedient as a chicken."

"A what?" she said. "A chicken? Of all the animals you could have chosen, why did you have to compare me to a chicken?"

"Maybe it's the hair. Red rooster. Red hen." Once again, she had restored his good humor.

Now, he was in the tavern and waiting for her to appear. He'd ordered two dinners and two mugs of malt, then wondered if she'd ever drunk an alcoholic beverage. But he couldn't keep the myth that she was male if he ordered her a pot of tea.

Again he glanced at the door. She'd gone to the privy, but that was half an hour ago, so where was she, and what was she doing? Had she been recognized already?

There were three men at the table next to him, and one of them said, "Come join us. You can't be alone on such a fine night."

"I'm waiting for my, uh, my brother."

"Then both of you can join us," the second man said.

"No, but thank you," Alex answered, doing his best to remember his American English. He hadn't used it since he'd met Cay. When the three men kept looking at him, he said, "My brother is shy. He doesn't do well with strangers."

"Is he a pretty boy?" asked the third man. "Thin as a reed?"

Alex tried not to gasp or let the man see how his words had startled him. Alex fully expected the next sentence to be that the man knew she was a girl. But Alex managed to nod.

"Then he's not so shy," the first man said, smiling. "I saw him with the barman's daughter, and they were anything but shy with each other. They were laughing and talking."

Alex could do nothing but look at the men in horror. What in the world had Cay done now? She was going to give them away! He was half out of his chair when the front door opened and in she came. She'd left her coat on her horse so her slight figure was well outlined by the big white shirt and the breeches that slid over her slim hips. What in the world had made him think that she could ever look like a male?

"Here he is now. So, boy, did you make any progress with the girl?"

Cay grinned and said, "Aye, I did. But I'll not tell you old men about it, so you can stop hoping."

Laughing hard, the three men went back to their mugs of ale.

"What do you think you're doing?" Alex said, his teeth clenched, as soon as she took a seat next to him.

"I'll tell you later," she said under her breath as she raised her pewter mug to the men at the next table, who were still chuckling. She drank deeply of it.

"Put that down!"

"I'm thirsty."

"All I need is for you to get drunk and start dancing about the place and show everyone what you really are."

"So what if I did dance?" Cay asked. "No one would think I was a girl. It's only you who sees me that way." She reached for a pickled egg from the bowl in the center of the table and took a bite. "Do you want to hear what I was doing? This is good. Maybe I could get the recipe."

"Males do not ask people for receipts."

"I could say that my mother . . . No! That I want my fiancée to make them for me after we're married."

He took the uneaten half of the egg from her and ate it. "Say as little as possible to anyone and do not ask for any receipts. Understand me?"

"I understand that you're fretting

about things that don't need to be worried about. Ah, here's our food."

"At least that's one place where you're as good as a man: your appetite." Alex was so worried about what was going on that he hardly noticed the girl who delivered their two heaping plates full of food. There were thick slices of ham, green beans, buttered potatoes, cornbread, and apple butter. When Alex saw that Cay had been given almost twice as much on her plate as was on his, he looked up at the waitress in question.

She was a pretty girl, with blonde hair and blue eyes, and a bosom that took up all the space from her neck to her waist—and a good deal of her was exposed by her low-cut blouse. When he glanced at the men at the next table, they were staring at the girl with their mouths hanging open.

"Your bodice isn't straight," Cay said as she put both her hands on the girl's prodigious bosom and proceeded to straighten the entire front of her blouse. If Alex had taken a bite, he would have choked. As it was, all he could do was stare in speechless shock.

"There now," Cay said, "much better."

"Thank you, sir," the girl said as she dropped a curtsey to Cay, who turned her attention to the food.

Every other eye in the tavern—all of them male—watched the girl leave the room to go back to the kitchen.

When she was gone, all the men started to laugh, and their good humor was directed toward Cay. Two of the men walked over and slapped her on the shoulder.

"Good for you, boy!"

"Well done!"

Cay's head almost hit her plate after the second slap, but she stole a look at Alex, who was glaring at her in anger.

When the laughter and attention had finally calmed down, she said quietly, "See? They all think I'm a boy."

"You drew attention to yourself," Alex said under his breath, then smiled at a man who congratulated Cay as he walked by. "That was a truly disgusting display! And that the girl allowed you to do such a thing to her is beyond belief!"

"You're sounding more prim than

Adam," Cay said, her mouth full. "Could you please pass me that mustard? They have Apple Brown Betty for dessert."

"And what do you plan to do with *her*?"

After a moment's look of confusion, Cay smiled. "Tickle her under her petticoats?"

Alex drew in his breath in shock.

"Would you please calm down?" Cay said as she smiled as another man hit her on the shoulder. "I knew what I was doing. I need to tell you what happened in the stables. I talked to—"

"Please tell me I didn't hear you correctly. You did not say that you *talked* to someone, did you?"

"You're not going to listen to me now, are you? I think I should just wait until we're in bed together, then I'll tell you."

That statement was so outrageous that Alex couldn't think of another word to say. He finished his dinner, and when a hush came over the tavern, he knew without looking up that the barman's daughter was back. "Touch her and I'll—"

"You'll what?" she asked, glaring at him.

"I'll make you spend the night outside and I won't sleep anywhere near you."

Cay started to protest, but the prospect of being alone at a campsite made her close her mouth. She murmured "thank you" to the waitress when she served their dessert, but Cay didn't touch her. When the girl was gone, the men in the tavern let their disappointment be known, but the lack of further display made them quieten down.

"That's better," Alex said.

Cay moved her apple slices about in the earthenware bowl. "I was trying to help, but you won't listen to what I have to say."

Alex lowered his head so it was near hers. "I'm just worried that someone will recognize you."

"I know, but I did some good. I got a letter to Nate."

"You what?" Alex had to pause to nod at a man walking by. "You did what?"

"I got some people to deliver a letter to my brother. I asked Nate to go to Charleston and figure out what really happened."

Since Alex had sent exactly the same request to the same person, he could make no reply.

Cay misunderstood his silence and started to defend herself. "If you'd just listen to me, I can explain everything."

"All right," Alex said. "What's this about our room?"

"Eliza—that's the waitress's name— gave us one of the private rooms. You and I have to share a bed, but—"

"That's not good."

"All right, then, I'll tell her that you'd rather we stayed in one of the big rooms with eight beds in it. If I don't sleep with you, then it'll have to be with another man. This place is too full for anyone to have a separate bed."

Alex glared at her. "Are you finished with that?"

Cay shoved three huge bites of apples and syrup in her mouth and stood up. "I am now." She had to wipe her lips with the back of her hand as the juices overflowed on to her chin.

"Upstairs," he said. "Unless you want to fiddle with some more petticoats."

"No, I'll leave that to Josiah."

"Don't tell me he's another one of your suitors."

"Keep your voice down!" Cay hissed at him. "Josiah is the man Eliza loves and they're eloping tomorrow, and they're going to live on the farm my father owns, the one I told you about."

Alex's eyes widened. He almost asked if she meant *his* farm, the one that Nate had worked hard to save from being sold, the farm that Alex had been saving money to buy, where he planned to live with his wife and their children. Instead, he followed Cay up the stairs to the small room that had been prepared for them. He was glad to see that a long bolster pillow had been tossed onto the bed. It was used to separate strangers when they shared beds in the inns along the roads.

"All right," he said, "I'm ready to listen." He sat down on the only chair in the room and waited.

"I was on my way back from the privy when I heard some sounds, so I—"

"What kind of sounds?"

"Uh . . ." She hesitated. How could she say that she heard kissing sounds, the rustle of fabric, and heavy breathing without sounding like she was spying? Which, in a way, was what she'd been doing. But wouldn't anyone be curious in such an instance?

"Out with it," Alex said. "And don't take the time to make up some story you think I'll like. What did you hear and what did you do?"

"I heard some sounds in one of the stalls in the barn and since I was being very cautious, of course I wanted to in-vestigate." She glanced at him to see if he was buying that story, and she was glad he was looking at her in that pa-tronizing, avuncular way that she was coming to know well. He looked much better now that his hair was trimmed and pulled back, but his face was still covered with whiskers. However, there seemed to be fewer lines at his eyes, and he looked younger than she'd first supposed. Maybe it was the dim light in the room.

As she sat down on the end of the

bed, she asked herself why she was bothering to sugarcoat the truth. After all, this man wasn't related to her, so why did she have to protect him from the realities of life? "I heard sounds of lovemaking."

"Lovemaking?"

"Yes. Kissing, that sort of thing. I went toward it and I saw Eliza and Josiah in the stall and they were kissing and . . . and . . ." She waved her hand. He could fill in the rest for himself. "I started to tiptoe away, but then Eliza began to cry."

"So you went back," Alex said. "Don't you realize that that's just what a female would do? How can you keep your disguise if you always act like a girl?"

"Might I remind you that on that first night when I cried, you handed me a handkerchief? Does that make *you* a girl?"

Alex turned his head away to hide his smile, but she saw it.

"So what was Eliza's problem?" Alex asked, and she could tell that the anger was gone. She knew that the cause of his bad temper was that he'd been worried about her.

"Her father wants her to marry a rich old man."

"And I take it that she wants to marry a young and poor one."

"Yes. She's in love with Josiah, but he hasn't a penny." Cay was looking at Alex and thinking how familiar he'd become to her in the last few days. When she thought of being in Charleston with Hope and Uncle T.C., it seemed like a very long time ago.

"So what did you do? Give them a farm?" He couldn't keep the bitterness out of his voice. After all he and Nate had done, it now looked as though Cay was blithely going to give the farm to someone else. Never before had he resented her sense of entitlement, but he did now.

"I told them that if they'd take my letters to my family I'd see that my father gave them jobs. Josiah likes to grow things, and since my father has a farm that needs a manager, I suggested that place in my letter to my father. What is wrong with you? You're acting like I did something I shouldn't have. I thought you'd be pleased that I was able to get letters out, one to Nate telling him the truth, and one to my father telling him I'm having a great time in Charleston. They'll be delivered in person."

Alex was concerned that the Charleston paper would have included Cay's name in their stories of the prison break and that by now her father and brothers were in town. But he wasn't going to tell her that.

"Did the barmaid know you were female? Is that why she let you . . . ?" He made a gesture in front of his chest.

"No, she thinks I'm a boy who is making it possible for her to elope with the man she loves. As for the . . ." Cay made the same gesture he had. "Her shirt was out of place from the . . . you know, in the stables with Josiah, and I was fixing it for her. I'm afraid I forgot that I'm supposed to be a boy. For a minute. I only forgot for one minute, and I won't forget again. Those men certainly made a fuss over that, didn't they?"

"Yes, they did. Much too much of a fuss, and because of it, they'll remember us well." Alex got up, went to the narrow window, and looked out. He needed to get himself under control. She'd done a good job and he had no right to be angry at her. If T.C. had managed to keep her name out of the papers, and if for some reason Alex's letter had never reached Nate, Cay had done a *very* good thing. And she wasn't the one who'd stolen a dream from him. That had been done when Lilith had been . . . taken from the earth.

Cay knew nothing of Alex's worries. She was thinking that it was odd being in the small room with him, as they'd mostly been out of doors together. But with walls that confined the space, it was much more intimate than being outside. Cay went to stand beside him. "Are you thinking about your wife?" she asked softly.

"Yes. I wanted to raise horses, and we were going to—" Breaking off, he turned to look at her. Her thick hair was loose from the tie at the back, and her long eyelashes looked up at him in in-nocence.

Cay could feel the awkwardness between them and she didn't like it. She liked the easy camaraderie they'd developed and she wanted to keep it. "You sure do smell good," she said.

Smiling, Alex turned away from the window, and the uncomfortable moment was gone. "I want this side of the bed, the one near the door."

"So in case someone bursts in you can protect me?" She'd meant the words to be a jest, but the moment she said them, she wished she hadn't. It sounded like she was referring to the night his wife died. "I didn't mean—"

He had his back to her, and she couldn't see his face, but he drew his shoulders up for a moment but then released them. "I will do all that I can to protect you." Turning, he looked at her, and for just a second she saw the deep pain that was inside him.

I must make him laugh, she thought. His sense of humor was what drew him out of himself. She began to unbutton her shirt.

"What the hell do you think you're doing?" he snapped.

"I've ordered a bath to be brought up

and I'm going to get into a tub full of hot water."

Alex looked shocked for a moment, then his face relaxed. Yet again, the pain was hidden. "And I'm going to wash your back for you."

"Eliza's going to do that."

"Then I'll wash *her* chest."

Cay laughed, as he'd bested her. She couldn't top that one. "Turn around. I have to remove this binding strip before I go to bed."

"You slept in a corset, so why can't you sleep in that?" he asked as he turned his back to her.

"A corset enhances what's on top, but this thing . . . Oh, there. Yes, that's wonderful. True heaven. You can turn back around now."

Turning, Alex looked at her and wished he hadn't. She had the shirt on and it was buttoned, but it left little to the imagination. "Why in the world those men thought you were a boy is beyond me."

"Thank you," Cay said as she sat on the end of the bed and removed her shoes and her stockings.

"That's it. Not one more thing are you to take off."

Cay couldn't help smiling. She'd been paid many compliments in her life, but what Alex said seemed more real. He wasn't saying nice things to her because he knew her family was rich or that she stood to inherit a lot, but because she was, well, desirable. For all the comfort of boy's clothes, she liked being a girl better.

Still smiling, still mostly dressed, she got into the bed on the side by the window, pulled the light covers over her, and watched Alex as he moved about the room. She thought how someday she'd be married and alone in a bedroom with a man she loved and they'd be a true husband and wife.

Alex removed his boots and his vest, but as he started to unbutton his shirt, he looked at her and stopped. As she did, he slipped into bed wearing most of his clothes, blew out the candle, and pulled the cover over him.

Cay lay in the darkness, listening to him breathe. They'd spent several nights together, but, somehow, being alone in this small room seemed more intimate. Between them was the long, heavy round pillow, but she knew he was near her.

She was tired from a long day on horseback and wanted to go to sleep, but she could hear Alex's breath coming on fast and strong and she knew that something was upsetting him. It took her a moment to figure it out, but then she realized that this was probably the first time he'd slept in a bed and a room since the night his wife had been murdered.

Had been murdered, she thought and realized she'd remembered it in terms that said Alex didn't do it. "What was she like?" Cay asked softly.

"Quiet," he said, and at first she thought he was saying he wanted her, Cay, to stop talking. But she could hear his breath and she knew she'd been right in guessing what he was thinking about.

"Not like me then?" she asked.

"No, not like you. She was quiet and gentle and refined."

"She didn't spend her days jumping back and forth on a horse, did she?"

"No. But I will say that I enjoyed some of your jumping quite a bit."

Cay could hear and feel the uneasiness beginning to leave him. Her strategy was working. Turning on her side, she put her head on her hand and looked at him across the big pillow. He was on his back and she could see his profile in the moonlight that came in through the window. "Tell me about her."

"What do you want to know?"

"Anything. Where did she grow up? What was her family like? Where did she go to school? How many brothers and sisters did she have?"

"I don't know," Alex said, and there was wonder in his voice. "I don't know the answer to any of those questions."

"You don't know where she grew up?"

"No." Turning, Alex looked at her. "I never asked and she never told me. But then, we were together for such a short time."

Cay lay back on the pillow. "That's odd. I told you about my family ten minutes after we met."

"Aye, you did, lass. You've told me so much about your life and your family that I feel I know them. But Lilith wasn't like you. She said little, just what was important."

"But family *is* important. Family is everything. I know your father means a lot to you. Did you tell your wife about him?"

"I did. I told her a great deal about my life in Scotland and about my dad. She liked to listen to the stories. She couldn't understand me when I didn't speak with the American accent, but I couldn't blame her for that, now could I?"

Cay was glad to hear the humor in his voice and she was pleased to hear his breathing slow down. She'd done what she intended and calmed him. Of course it did cross her mind that if she had any sense at all she'd not spend the night locked in a room with a man who'd been convicted for cutting the throat of the woman lying beside him.

Just as she felt his change in mood, he knew when there was a difference in her breathing. "If you'd rather I went into another room, I will."

"No," she said. "I feel safer with you here."

He didn't say anything for a while, then he reached across the big pillow and took her small hand in his. "Thank you for that. You're only the second person who has believed in me."

Cay liked his big, warm hand on hers—liked it too much. She removed her hand and turned on her side, facing away from him. "If you go off into Florida without showing me how to do that handkerchief trick, I'll take it all back." She smiled when she heard him chuckle, and his breathing eased and she heard him go to sleep. His soft, quiet breathing relaxed her, but she looked at the moon out the window and thought about what was going to happen in the next few days.

Thanks to her many questions, she'd been able to piece together his "plan" for her. His intent was to dump her on some friends of Uncle T.C. while Alex went exploring. After a week or two, still dressed as a boy, Cay was to travel back to her parents' home in Virginia and hope that nothing ever came about because of her escapade of helping a criminal escape. There was no more talk of trying to prove Alex's innocence as there had been at first. Somewhere along the way, he seemed to have dropped that idea. For the last couple of days he'd spoken only of Cay returning to her family and safety.

Had he given up his thoughts of justice? she wondered. And if he had, had he done it because of her? The way he spoke now, he meant to go into the jungles of wild Florida and maybe never return.

But she'd heard the difference in his voice when he spoke of the past. When he talked about his horses, he was full of energy, even excitement. He'd left his homeland and his father with hope for his future life.

Just as I have a plan for mine, Cay thought. She knew what she wanted out of life, and so did he. He'd even started working on it while he still lived in Scotland. She smiled at the memory of his story about illegally mating his mare with a "great beast" of a stallion. He'd done it so he could get to America and someday have his own farm, with his own wife and children.

He wants exactly what I do, she thought, and sadness nearly overwhelmed her as she realized that it was possible that she'd get the future she wanted, but Alex never would. For all his life, he'd be haunted by the fact that he'd been convicted of murder and had escaped hanging by just one day.

But what if Nate got her letter and went to Charleston and found out the truth about who killed Alex's wife? Knowing who killed someone wouldn't bring that person back to life. While it was true that Alex could possibly be cleared of the murder charges, he'd *never* get back the woman he loved. Such a tragic happening would take years to recover from—if he ever did.

"Stop thinking so hard," Alex said. "It's keeping me awake."

"All right," she said. "It's just that I don't think that going to Florida will solve anything."

"Nor do I," he said, "but right now

it's the only thing I can do. We need to sleep, as I plan to leave very early."

"Maybe if I bury my face in your hair and smell the jasmine, I'll be able to fall asleep."

"Don't even think of touching me."

"Yes, Mr. McDowell," she said as she closed her eyes.

Eleven

❧

The next morning, well before daylight, Alex told Cay to get out of bed, but she couldn't seem to wake up. "We need to go, so put that thing on your chest and let's leave."

"I want my chocolate," Cay mumbled as she tried to stand up. "And I want to take a bath."

"You had a bath two days ago. Now get dressed."

As soon as Alex went to the other side of the room, she fell across the bed and was asleep instantly.

"Up!" he said as he grabbed the waistband of her breeches and pulled. "Fall down like that again and I'll give you a smack across that round little bottom of yours."

"You're cruel." She couldn't seem to

get her eyes open and she was standing, but she swayed on her feet.

"Cay!" he said sharply. "Get dressed."

"Am dressed," she mumbled.

He picked up the binding cloth and tossed it on to her shoulder, but she just stood there. When she didn't move, he said, "So help me, I'm tempted to leave you here! I've already been downstairs and the barman's found out his daughter ran off with the stable lad. The man knows someone here helped them. If I left you here, there's no way you'd keep your mouth closed and not brag that *you* arranged everything. He'd probably have you put in jail."

Cay opened one eye. "You wouldn't actually leave without me, would you?"

Alex, fully dressed, paused at the door. "Five minutes. If you aren't at the horses in five minutes you won't see me again." With that, he left the room, closing the door behind him.

Cay stood still for a full minute. He was, of course, lying, but on the other hand, maybe he wasn't. Four and a half minutes after Alex left the room, Cay was outside the barn, standing beside

her mare and yawning. Alex was no-
where to be seen. When he walked out
of the tavern, two steaming mugs in his
hands, she said, "You took long enough.
I've been waiting for hours." She saw a
hint of a smile under his whiskers, but
he just handed her a mug. "Where's
breakfast?"

"This is it. The barman's too angry to
cook. The man he wanted his daughter
to marry is in there."

When he said nothing else, she said,
"So what's he like?"

Alex's eyes showed his merriment.
"Very old, very ugly."

She drained her mug and headed toward the tavern, but he caught her arm.
"Where do you think you're going?"

"To tell the man about jasmine oil. It
makes even old, ugly men look good."

"Get on your horse," Alex said, laughing. "If we ride hard for the next two
days we can be there by tomorrow evening."

"Tomorrow?" she asked, and that
word woke her up. Just one more day.

Alex looked at her from atop his horse.
"Will you miss me, lass?"

She wanted to say that she'd be glad to see her family, but the words wouldn't come out of her mouth. When she saw Alex's frown, she knew he was starting to worry again. "Did I tell you about Ephraim?" she asked as she got on her horse.

"Is he the third suitor?"

She followed him out of the courtyard and on to the road. "Yes. He's forty-two, a widower, and he has three nearly grown children."

"Lass, please tell me you're making a jest."

"No. He's quite wealthy, has a beautiful house, and—"

"But does he makes your heart dance with joy at the very sight of him?"

"I do believe, Alex McDowell, that you're the most romantic man I've ever met."

"Except, of course, for Adam."

"On long winter evenings, Adam writes poetry."

Alex groaned. "I hope I never meet your perfect brother."

When Cay looked at Alex, it occurred

to her that he might never meet any of her family.

He saw her face change, saw the gleam leave her eyes. "Are you ready to ride? Can you keep up with me?"

"I can outride you any day of the week."

"That's better. No more sadness, now. You'll be rid of me soon enough." Turning, he started down the road at a rapid pace, Cay close behind him.

As they traveled deeper south, they began to run out of towns and even roads. They passed huge, magnificent plantations that were more like villages than houses. Acres of fields full of indigo, cotton, and rice bordered the rutted, weed-infested roads they rode on.

Where there weren't plantations, there were tiny, falling-down houses that all seemed to have a dozen children running around them. It was a marked contrast between the very wealthy and the very poor.

Cay looked at everything the best she could while keeping up with the grueling pace Alex set. Once in a while, he'd turn and ask if she was all right and she always nodded.

The sun became brighter, the sky more blue, the people and buildings more sparse. She pulled her straw hat down over her head to shade her eyes from the glare and kept riding.

At noon they stopped by a stream and ate and drank.

"Still wishing you were home?" Alex asked.

She looked about her at the tall, narrow-trunked palm trees and the huge ferns. "No, I don't think I do."

"Not even for your two men?"

"Three men."

"You aren't really serious about the one with grown children, are you? How old is the oldest child?"

"A son, eighteen."

Alex put the stopper back in the canteen. "He'll climb into bed with you."

"He would never do such a thing. He's a very nice boy. He's studying law."

"Oh, then, if he's a lawyer he must be of sterling character."

"You're horrible."

"Never said I wasn't." He mounted

his horse and looked down at her. "If you eliminate the old man, that leaves you with a preacher and a gambler. Lass, you need to think hard about who you're going to marry." Chuckling, he led his horse back to the narrow road.

As Cay mounted her mare, she stuck her tongue out at Alex's back. But he turned and saw her—and he laughed in a way that made her want to hit him.

They rode for hours more, and the roads narrowed until they were little more than pathways. Twice they stopped at houses so Alex could ask directions. Each time the people invited them inside, as the owners were hungry for company and news of the outside world. Cay wanted to stay, wanted to get off the horse and walk around, but Alex always said no. At one house, a pretty girl, about sixteen, looked at Cay from under her lashes and gave her a big piece of cornbread. But the girl offered nothing to Alex.

When they were back on their horses, Cay ate the cornbread with gusto. "I do believe this is the very *best* cornbread I've ever had. Mmmm. So delicious."

She didn't offer Alex even a bite. "You do know why she gave this to me, don't you?" she asked.

Alex said nothing.

"She was flirting with me, that's why. And she was flirting because she thought I was a boy."

Alex looked her up and down. Her breeches clung to her thighs, her hair was about her shoulders, and her big hat made a shade like a veil over her face. He thought she couldn't look more feminine. "You have just proven that people are stupid."

"They see what they're supposed to. When are we going to stop for the night? Are there any taverns around here?"

"Not on this road. Are you going to share that or not?"

Cay had a big chunk of uneaten corn-bread in her hand. "I'll sell it to you."

"You have the money."

"I don't want money. I want you to tell me what the plan for me is."

He narrowed his eyes at her. "As if you haven't already figured that out."

"You mean you saw behind all my subtle questions?"

"You don't know the meaning of sub-tle."

"All right, so tell me a story about when you were a little boy."

"How about if I tell you that when I was in prison I shared the cell with rats? Or maybe you'd like to hear about the townspeople throwing rocks at me when I was dragged into the courtroom?"

Cay's face lost its smile and she handed the cornbread to him.

He ate it in two bites. "That soft heart of yours is going to get you in trouble one day. I win!" He kicked his horse forward.

"You—" she called as he raced ahead of her. Blast it! Why hadn't she listened when Tally wanted to teach her curse words? "You're a very bad person, Alexander McDowell!" she called out, and his laughter floated back to her, but by then she was smiling, too.

Twelve

❧

"What if those people at the boarding-house don't like me?" Cay asked.

Alex was kicking the remains of the fire out. "How could they not like you?" he asked softly.

"What?"

"I said that you're not going to live with them forever, just a few weeks, so you'll be fine."

"How many weeks?"

"I don't know." He stepped on a branch that was still smoldering. When he glanced up at Cay, she was looking at him as though she thought he knew the answers to all her questions. "Lass, I really don't know what to expect. I can't very well ask someone what they've heard about the escaped murderer from Charleston, now can I?"

Cay sat down on a log and thought she might stay there. According to Uncle T.C.'s map—which she'd just seen—they were a mere three hours from the tiny town on the St. Johns River where Alex was to meet Mr. Grady. The town had a dozen or so houses, a trading post, and a few other stores. One of the houses took in paying customers, and that's where she was to stay. She'd thought she was to be the guest of "friends" of T.C.'s, but it was just a boardinghouse.

Alex sat down beside her. "Come on, lass, buck up. It's only for a while, then you'll be back with your family."

"And how am I to get there by myself? What if robbers attack me?"

"You can outrun them. Or maybe just slip to the side of your horse and hide, as I taught you to do."

She heard the laughter in his voice. Standing up, she glared down at him. "While *you* go running into the wilds of Florida enjoying yourself!"

Late last night they'd made camp amid a thicket of spiny plants, and as had become the way between them, they slept near each other. It was too warm to need the cloak or a fire, so there was no real need to sleep just a foot from each other, but they were too tired to make up excuses of why they shouldn't be together. Alex put a blanket on the moist ground and started to put a second one several feet away, but after a glance at Cay, he put the other blanket next to hers. After all, it was their last night together.

They were too tired to do much talking, but this morning Alex showed her T.C.'s map and she saw how close they were. All morning they'd ridden hard, and Cay hadn't so much as cracked a smile.

"Come now, lass, surely you have a joke in you," Alex said as he rode beside her.

"No, not one."

"What if I poured more oil on my hair?"

She tried to think of something funny to reply, but couldn't.

In the early afternoon, Alex pulled off the rough road into a clearing among the fierce shrubs that threatened to overtake them, and built a fire. He knew he was wasting time, but like Cay, he was well aware of how much longer they had before they would part forever. He was going to miss her. He didn't tell her, but he was deeply worried about what they'd find waiting for them.

Now, sitting on the log, he looked at her. "I wouldn't do this if I didn't have to. You know that, don't you? If I had my way I'd . . ." He smiled. "I'd go back with you and meet your brothers."

She sat back down on the log beside him. "If you didn't need to hide in the jungle, you'd be a married man and you wouldn't even have met me."

"True," he said. "But maybe if I can find out the truth of what has been done to me, I can visit you one day."

"You won't." She sighed. "I think my entire life is ruined."

"I'm sorry for that, lass. I never meant to make you into a fugitive, to have gunmen chasing you, or—"

"But that's just it," she said, standing up again. "I think I *like* all this. Before this happened I was a very happy person. I have a wonderful family, nice friends, and I live in a great little town. I had everything. But now—" She stretched out her arms. "Now I have nothing but the clothes on my back and—"

"And the dress in my saddlebag," he added, "plus three diamond pins." He was so glad to see her energetic again that he wanted to dance about with her, as he'd done in the store.

"Did you know that my mother ran a company?"

Alex had to stop himself from saying that he knew all about it, but he didn't want to interrupt her. "What kind of company?"

"It was in Boston, before she was married, and she hired a lot of women to sell fruit. She was very successful, and when she sold the business, she made a great deal of money, which she gave to her employees. My mother did some truly wonderful things. But what have *I* done?"

"Driven three men insane with your indecision?" he offered.

She knew he'd meant it as a joke, but she didn't take it as such. "That's just it!

The truth is that I'm having trouble re-membering what those men look like."

"Ugly, handsome, and in between."

She nodded. "More or less."

"So what are you saying, lass? Would you like to stay in Florida and wait for me to return? I don't know how long I'll be gone." He wanted to give Nate plenty of time to investigate.

"Wait," Cay said. "I'm to *wait*." To her, the word sounded awful, but at the same time she thought maybe she could sketch what she saw. Her teacher, Mr. Johns, had often said it was a shame she couldn't go out west and paint the magnificent landscapes he'd heard were there. Maybe while she waited for Alex to return, she could go to the big plantations they'd passed and paint portraits of the inhabitants.

"Maybe it won't be so long," Alex said, and he couldn't keep the hope out of his voice. Maybe by the time he returned, Nate would have found out the truth. In the last few days he'd been asking himself *why* someone had wanted Lilith dead. Why her but not him? And, also, a couple of times, he'd asked himself if it was possible that what had been suggested at the trial could be true, that Lilith had drugged the wine and given it to Alex. But, always, he came back to the question of *why*.

"You're thinking about your wife, aren't you? You have that faraway, sad look in your eyes again."

"You've come to know me well." He put his hand on the log beside him, and Cay sat down. "I won't stay long on the trip. What if I stay a month or so, then tell Grady that I have to leave? I'll help him find someone else to take care of the horses, and I'll return and escort you back to Virginia."

Cay grimaced. "Doing that would defeat the whole purpose of your escape. No, we need to part from each other. Your plan of leaving me behind is good, it's just that I don't like it."

He was pleased at her logic—and at her self-sacrifice. "I hope to prove my innocence."

"If you don't, you'll be hiding all your life."

"I know, lass," he said softly, "but I

can assure you that I'll do whatever I can to clear *your* name."

"I'm sure my father and brothers will prevent anything from happening to me. It's you I'm concerned about. You're a nice man and—"

"Am I now?" he said as he mounted his horse.

"Sometimes you are," she said tightly as she put her foot in the stirrup. She was giving him a compliment, but he was, as always, laughing at her.

"Will you invite me to dinner at your big house? You and I will recall the days we slept together on our wild ride south, and it'll make your husband insane with jealousy."

His teasing was infectious. "Then he and I will argue, but my husband and I will reconcile lovingly and that will make *you* jealous." She reined her horse away, her nose in the air.

"Ha!" Alex said as he pulled up beside her. "By that time I'll have two women on my arms—no! three of them—and I'll own the biggest horse farm in all of Virginia."

"You'll lose your shirt in gambling, and

what woman is going to want a smelly old man like you?" She was glad to see him smiling, and she was especially pleased to hear him talk about women other than the wife he'd lost.

"The scent of jasmine will become all the rage in men's clothes," he said, sounding like a man who cared about fashion. "Even the traders will be wearing it with their buckskins."

"They'll attract butterflies, and that'll start a new trend for women. Our bonnets will be covered in butterfly wings."

"And your husband will hate them because they make him sneeze."

"I'm going to marry someone who is so manly that he never even sneezes," she said as she urged her horse forward.

Her good humor lasted another hour, but when she began to think about what was going to happen when they got there, Cay felt more gloomy with every step they took. She was to stay in a boardinghouse alone for a few weeks after Alex left, then she was to proceed, as he'd told her repeatedly, cautiously toward home. She couldn't

think of anything more boring, lonely—
or frightening. She couldn't help but
think of a hundred things that could go
wrong. Even though she'd told Alex that
she was certain her family would clear
her name, she still worried about the
timing. What if the Charleston police
realized that their prisoner had probably gone south? Many people knew
of Uncle T.C.'s explorations, so surely
they knew of his next trip. She knew
that T.C. and Mr. Grady had been planning the journey since the spring, so it
wouldn't take much detective work to
figure out that the escaped fugitive—
and his accomplice—had probably
gone to Florida to meet the exploration team.

If this were true, what would Cay do if
the authorities showed up in Florida after Alex left? Cay would be there alone.
All by herself.

As often happened, Alex seemed to
read her thoughts. "Before you leave
for home, you must ask people for the
news and find out if you're still being
hunted. But I feel sure that T.C. has already taken care of that."

"How could he do that?"

"There are a lot of ways. He could have told them you were meeting someone and got caught in the chaos caused by a prison break. When your family gets to Charleston, they'll verify that you weren't there when I was with Lilith. In fact, you'd never met me."

"So they'll think it was just a coincidence that Uncle T.C. visited you in jail, and that I, his goddaughter, was with you when you escaped?"

"Maybe he could say that you were riding out to secretly meet one of the many men who asks you to marry him. I don't know. I'm sure T.C. could come up with a hundred stories." Alex had to take a breath to calm himself because his voice was betraying his worry. "What I do know is that they'll have fixed it and it'll be safe for you to return home. If I wasn't *sure* of that I'd not let you go."

"But *you* aren't safe."

"I don't have a home anyway," he said softly, but he managed to smile at her. "Think of the good, lass. You'll get to see your family again, and you'll get to see the men you love."

"Oh. Them," Cay said without much interest. "I've been thinking and I believe I should look around some more. Maybe I should look outside Edilean."

"That's a good idea," Alex said. "Maybe you could even look outside Williamsburg."

"What am I going to do without you to make fun of me?"

"You'll find out soon," he said cheerfully.

She gave him a sharp look. "You're looking forward to traveling into this jungle, aren't you?" It was beautiful around them, with palm trees, shrubs bright with blooms, and large birds such as she'd never seen before.

"I do believe I am," Alex said. "When T.C. first told me his idea, I was in a jail cell, and I couldn't imagine being on a boat and floating through what he said was a paradise. But now that I see this land, I think I would like to see more."

"Who's going to take Uncle T.C.'s place as recorder?"

"I don't know."

Cay's mind began to form an idea. "Has Mr. Grady been told that Uncle T.C. won't be going?"

"I don't know. I assume T.C. wrote Grady a letter telling him he'd need a new recorder, so maybe Grady will arrive with one."

"But we came too fast. If Mr. Grady was also traveling here, no letter could have reached him."

"That's not my concern. I'm sure he can find someone else to draw the plants and animals. How hard could it be?"

Cay nearly launched into a long explanation of what went into preparing to be an artist, but she didn't. Instead, she was quiet as she began to think of another possibility. It was an idea much too far-fetched to be possible, but still, she liked what was in her head.

An hour later, they rode into the settlement, and Cay looked around her. The few houses were plastered over with what looked to be whitewashed mud, and the roofs were covered with dried palm fronds. Cay thought that the structures were enchanting. To the right was a long, low building that she assumed was the boardinghouse. Two adolescent girls were outside in the shade, one shucking dried corn, the other using a big mortar and pestle to pound the corn into meal. They paused in their work and looked at Alex and Cay with interest.

Alex nodded toward the house. "Let's get you settled first."

"No!" When he looked at her, she said, "I mean, let's see where you're to meet Mr. Grady. He might be waiting for you and wondering if you're going to show up."

"We're here a day early, so I doubt if he's hired someone else yet."

"But we don't know that, do we?"

Alex tried to repress a smile. "What's frightening you the most, lass? The thought of being alone, or the fear of how much you'll miss me?"

"How will I get out of bed in the morning without you pulling me up by my breeches? And how will I live without the scent of jasmine around me at night?" She'd meant her words as a joke, but they fell flat, for she really would miss those things.

Alex smiled sympathetically at her. "All right then, lass, let's go find where I'm to meet Mr. Grady." He reined his horse away to the left and Cay was glad to follow him. She didn't want to be stuck inside some boardinghouse. The air was balmy and warm and fragrant, and she wanted to stay outside as long as possible.

It was easy to find the rendezvous site, as there was a wharf projecting into a calm, placid river. There were piles of wooden boxes, and two men were looking through them. One man looked to be in his forties, and was short, stout, and had neatly trimmed salt and pepper hair. The other was a boy, tall, thin, with straw-colored hair, a big nose, and freckles. He'd never be handsome, but he was appealing in a way. And he had a swagger about him that reminded her of Tally.

"Are you T.C.'s friend?" asked the

older man, looking up at Alex. "The one who works magic on animals?"

"I don't think I can live up to that," Alex said as he got off his horse. Or that's what he thought he said. What they heard was, "Ah dornt think Ah can bide up tae 'at," so the two men just stared at him.

Cay dismounted and went to stand beside Alex. "What my brother meant to say is that he's not sure he can live up to such an accolade as T.C. Connor has given him." She put out her hand to shake. "I'm Cay. I—" As soon as she said the name, she halted. People usually thought her name was short for Kesia, a girl's name.

Alex put his arm around her shoulders in a brotherly way. "It's an abbreviation for Charles Albert . . ." He hesitated for a moment. "Yates."

Cay gave him a sharp glance. She didn't like being named for the man who'd called the sheriff on them. "And this is my brother . . ." She hesitated over his first name, but "Alex" was common enough. "Alex Yates."

Obviously, Alex didn't like the last

name either, since he tightened his fingers on her shoulder, but she moved away from him. "All this belongs to Mr. Grady?"

"It does," the older man said as he shook Cay's hand. "I'm Elijah Payson, and everyone calls me Eli. And this young rascal is Tim Dawson. Where's T.C.?"

"He fell and broke his leg," Alex said. "He won't be coming." He spoke slowly as he tried to enunciate his words carefully so Eli could understand them.

"Mr. Grady won't like that," Eli said. "He wants us to go some places white people have never been before, and he wants it all recorded."

"If we see plants that eat people, he'll certainly want drawings of them," Alex said.

Eli laughed. "I can tell you've heard some of T.C.'s yarns. If we do see any of those, we'll have to throw young Tim in, so we need someone to draw a picture of him being eaten alive."

Tim didn't seem to like being the object of a joke. His face turned red with

anger. "*He's* smaller than me!" He nodded toward Cay.

"True enough," Alex said, "but my
brother isn't going with us. He's staying here while I'm away." Alex turned
back to Eli. "So show me what's in the
boxes."

"Glad to," Eli said, and the two of
them walked away to start looking inside the crates.

Cay went down the pier toward the
river and admired the beauty of it. When
she was a child, she'd spent a lot of
time sailing and rowing on the James
River with her brothers. She hadn't realized the expedition would be traveling by water, but that made sense. Over
the last few days the roads had become
more and more impenetrable, and what
surrounded the settlement looked to be
nothing but jungle.

"So you aren't going with us?"

Turning, she saw the boy Tim. He was
taller than she was, but younger, and he
was so thin it was as though his body
hadn't caught up with his height. "No,"
she said, smiling at him.

"Afraid, are you?"

"Why no, that's not why I'm not going."

"They have alligators. Ever hear of them?"

"Yes, I have." She was still smiling, but his attitude was making it difficult. He was almost belligerent.

"Seen any?"

"No. If you'll excuse me—"

He blocked her from leaving. "You gonna go cry to your big brother that I called you a scaredy cat?"

Cay drew herself up straight and stared at the boy. "I have no intention of mentioning you to my brother or to anyone else on this earth." Her eyes let him know she didn't consider him important enough to speak of.

"You think you won't remember *me*?" he said, then in the flash of a second, he hit her hard on the shoulder.

Cay fell backward, tried to regain her balance, but couldn't, and the next second she went into the river. She went down under the water, into the plants and rubbish people had thrown out. She saw several animal skulls as she fought her way up to the top. Alex was kneeling on the dock, his hand extended to pull her up, and she could tell that he was on the verge of jumping in after her. He was frowning deeply.

"What the bludy heel waur ye daein'?" His voice was angry and fearful. "Ah dornt hae enaw tae fash yerse abit withit ye drownin'?"

She answered him in the same dialect. "'At worthless wee stumph gae me a stoatin skelp."

"Did he noo?" Alex said, a smile twitching at the corners of his lips.

"He fell," Tim said loudly. "The boy tripped over a box and went right in the water. I tried to catch him, but I couldn't."

"Is that right, lad?" Eli asked, looking at Cay's wet form in sympathy.

The three of them were watching her, waiting for her answer, and Cay was tempted to tell the truth—but she knew that was the female way. She'd seen her brothers do awful things to one another, but they'd die before they told. It seemed to be some misdirected code of male honor to hide the truth.

She had to bite her tongue but she said, "Yes, I fell."

"There now," Eli said kindly. "At least you weren't hurt."

Alex put his arm around her shoulders protectively. "Come on, let's get you into some dry clothes." He looked at Eli. "We'll see you both early tomorrow morning."

"Mr. Grady should be here by noon," Eli said. "I'll let *you* tell him we have no recorder."

"I will," Alex said and started to lead Cay away.

But she turned back. "I forgot my hat." When she'd fallen into the water, her hat had come off and landed on the wharf. As she picked it up, the boy Tim was standing there, smirking at her in triumph. Water was running down Cay's hair and dripping onto her nose. She knew she shouldn't be so childish and she certainly shouldn't stoop to that hateful boy's level, but she couldn't help herself. Maybe the male clothes she was wearing were turning her into Tally. As she came up from getting her hat, she stuck out her leg and hooked her foot around his ankle. His feet flew out from under him and he fell forward, his face hitting the side of a wooden crate.

Cay put her straw hat firmly on her head and walked past him with her chin in the air.

"He gave me a bloody nose!" Tim yelled from behind her.

Eli gave the boy a hard look. "But it was your own fault, wasn't it, lad? Just as you said it was young Cay's fault that he fell in the river, so was your mishap an accident. Wasn't it?"

Cay kept her back turned and her breath held.

"Yeah, I tripped," Tim said with reluctance.

Smiling, Cay looked up at Alex. "Are you ready to go?"

"I am unless you want to do something else. Maybe you'd like to run the boy over with a wagon."

"No. A bloody nose is enough." She was smiling sweetly up at him. "Do you think we could buy me some new clothes? Otherwise I'll have to run around naked until these dry."

"Cay, lass, after what you did to that boy, I'll obey whatever you say."

"If only that were so," she said with a sigh, making Alex laugh.

Thirteen

❧

Cay held her wet clothes at arm's length and straightened her pretty new waist-coat. The owner of the trading post said he'd purchased it from a young gentle-man who needed money for supplies before he set off into the wilderness.

"He never came back," the man said, his eyes wide as he tried to frighten Cay. "He probably got eaten by something."

"My brother isn't going on the trip," Alex said with no humor in his voice. The last thing he wanted was for Cay to be more afraid than she was already. "How much is the waistcoat?"

Now, Alex frowned at the way Cay kept looking at the embroidery around the edge of the vest. It was of honey-bees buzzing about a border of wild-flowers. His personal opinion was that she looked so feminine already that she should have put on the old, nearly worn out garments that he'd chosen for her. But nothing would do for her but to buy the decorated waistcoat. "Stop that or people will know you're a girl," he said under his breath.

"That man thought I was a boy. And that hideous Tim thought so, and Eli didn't doubt that I was male. It's only you who thinks I look like a girl."

"They're all blind."

Moving ahead of him, she turned around and walked backward. "Are you telling me that if you saw me now, if you didn't know me that is, and had never seen me before, that you'd somehow know that I was a girl?"

"Yes," Alex said. "You walk like a girl, talk like one, and you nag like a girl. I've never seen anyone more feminine than you are."

"I think there's a compliment in there."

"No, there isn't." Alex was frowning. "If I leave you here, you're going to be found out, and when someone realizes that you're hiding your true identity, they're going to ask why."

"So take me with you." The idea had been playing in her mind all day, but she'd meant to slowly ease Alex into it, not drop it on him like a blacksmith's anvil. "I can—" She'd started to tell him that she could draw, but he cut her off.

"Absolutely not! Under no circumstances. No, no, and no." He strode ahead of her toward the boardinghouse.

"But—" She caught up with him. "Maybe going with you would be better than staying here alone and unprotected."

"No. Going into uncharted territory where every corner reveals a new danger is *not* better than staying here in safety. And I don't want to hear another word about it." As he opened the door to the boardinghouse, he gave Cay a look that said he wasn't going to listen to anything she had to say.

Cay put her shoulders back and walked inside ahead of him. She wanted to make a sharp retort, but she was instantly overwhelmed by the two girls they'd seen outside when they rode into town.

"We knew it was you," one said, her

eyes wide as she looked at Cay. "I told Alice that you'd be staying with us."

They were twins, looking to be identical, and not especially attractive. They wore dresses that had been washed many times and were faded. Next to them, Cay, in her beautifully embroidered waistcoat, looked resplendent.

"You're the prettiest boy I've ever seen," the second girl said as she slipped her arm through Cay's.

The first girl took Cay's other arm. "Come into the dining room and we'll feed you. You're very thin."

"Is it true that you're going to be staying with us for months and months?"

Cay looked over her shoulder at Alex, her eyes begging him to rescue her, but he was smiling in a way that she'd come to know well. He was thoroughly enjoying her discomfort—and glad she'd be occupied for a while.

"I have some things that I need to take care of," he said, his voice full of laughter. "I'll see you later, little brother. Have a good evening."

Cay sent him a look that said she'd get him back for leaving her, but he just smiled broader as he left, closing the door behind him.

The second she was alone with the two young girls, they bombarded her with questions.

"How old are you?"

"Where does your family live?"

"Are you married? Engaged?"

"What's your favorite food? I'm an excellent cook."

"I saw you riding a horse. I like horses, too. I think we have a lot in common."

"Are you really going to stay for months? We can go riding together every day. Just the two of us. Alone. I'll take a picnic lunch, and if we get lost we can stay out all night."

When the girl who'd made this offer started caressing Cay's hand, she snatched it back and sat down at the dining table.

"Out!" came a voice from behind her. "Both of you get out of here this minute and leave this young man alone."

Turning, Cay say a woman standing in the doorway, a plate of food and a mug in her hands. She was tall and handsome, but she was a bit old to be considered pretty. Cay guessed her to be in her early thirties, but there was a look in her eyes that made her seem older, as though she'd seen and done too much in her short life.

As she set the food in front of Cay, she gave the girls a threatening look, and reluctantly, they left the room.

"I apologize for them," the woman said. "We don't get too many young men staying here, and I'm afraid they went a bit overboard. I'll do my best to keep them away from you while you're here."

On Cay's plate was a roast bird that didn't look like a chicken or any other flying creature that she'd ever seen, and she wondered what they hunted in this country. Tentatively, she picked up the knife and fork that the woman had handed her and began to eat. It was good.

"I'm Thankfull," the woman said as she sat down across from Cay.

Cay almost said, Thankful for what? but she didn't. She'd been around Alex for so long that she almost made jokes about everything. "How did you know I was staying here?"

Thankfull's mouth twitched in humor. "The boy Tim came here to have his nose seen to. It's a good thing you aren't going with them or he'd give you trouble."

"He took a dislike to me right away." Cay was eating some vegetable she'd never seen before, but it was delicious. She wondered if it would grow in Virginia. Maybe in her mother's orangery.

"I think he was jealous," Thankfull said. "He was to be the youngest one on the journey, but there you were with your youth and handsomeness and your education, and—"

"Education?" Cay didn't like for this woman to guess too much about her.

Thankfull smiled. "According to young Tim you sound like an English professor. Not that he's ever met one, but he had a lot to say about your 'uppity ways.'"

Cay was pleased that the woman seemed to understand the boy so well, and she was beginning to think she liked her. That was a good thing if she was going to have to spend a lot of time with her. "Have you lived here long?"

Thankfull went to the sideboard to get a pottery bowl. From the little Cay had seen, the house was sparsely furnished with what looked to be locally made furniture, and it was clean and neat.

"A lifetime," Thankfull said as she spooned sliced fruit into the bowl and put it before Cay. "Not really, but it seems like it's been a very long time."

Cay knew that she shouldn't ask for more of the woman's story because that was a female trait. Her father had often said that he could know a man for twenty years and not find out as much about him as his wife learned in twenty minutes.

But Cay couldn't help it. She was in a strange place among strangers and she wanted to hear about the woman's life. "And why is that?" she asked.

Thankfull didn't say anything for a while, but Cay's expression encouraged her. Thankfull didn't say so, but nearly all their boarders were older men, and all they wanted to talk about was business of one sort or another. They didn't take

the time to sit and talk with a woman
who ran a boardinghouse. "My mother
died when I was born, so for many years
it was just my father and me. He liked
to move around, so I never got to really
know many people, but there was one
young man . . ." She waved her hand
in dismissal. "Anyway, my father heard
that there were better jobs and better,
well, everything farther down south, so
we moved again and again. He remarried when I was seventeen, and his new
wife had the twins, Jane and Alice. She
wasn't a woman who took easily to
motherhood and the domestic life."

"You mean she took advantage of
having an older stepdaughter and gave
the children and the house to you to
take care of?"

Thankfull smiled, and when she did,
Cay thought she looked much younger
and prettier. "More or less. After all, she
was only six months older than I was.
She wanted to enjoy her life."

"But you . . ."

Thankfull shrugged. "She died when
the girls were ten, and my father died
the next year, so it was a good thing

that I was still at home to take care of them."

"So you were a mother without being a wife."

"A person does what she has to."

"Yes, she does," Cay said as she picked up the bowl of fruit and looked at it. She was thinking about all that had happened with her and Alex. She'd indeed done what she'd had to.

"So you're going to stay here and wait for your brother to return from Mr. Grady's expedition?"

"Actually, my brother wants me to stay here a few weeks, then return home."

"By yourself?"

"Yes," Cay said. "Is there something wrong with that?"

"You're awfully young to travel alone."

"I'm twenty."

Thankfull's mouth dropped open in disbelief. "Please don't tell my half sisters that. I told them you were only sixteen. If they know you're twenty, they'll have you married to one of them in two weeks."

Cay smiled. "I hardly think so."

"Yes, they will," Thankfull said seriously. "You don't know how bad they want to get out of here. Alice says she's going to become an actress, but Jane wants to get married and have children."

"But they couldn't be more than . . . What?"

"Fourteen, almost fifteen. But they've been exposed to a lot in their short lives, so it makes them think they're older. I was hoping that maybe you'd like one of them and . . . and . . ."

"Take her off your hands?"

"Yes," Thankfull said, smiling.

"So you'd like to get out of here, too?"

"More than anything."

"But you haven't found a man among all of them who must come and go here?" Cay asked.

"I've been asked, yes, but, no, I haven't found a man I want to keep. If you know what I mean."

Cay started to say that she knew exactly what Thankfull meant, but she thought better of it. If she was going to have to spend weeks in her company as a male, she'd better start putting on the act now.

When Thankfull said, "I have a letter

for you," the news so startled Cay that she nearly choked.

"From whom?"

Thankfull smiled at the "whom" and glanced at the doorway to make sure no eyes were prying. "It's from Mr. Connor."

The way she said the name made Cay look at her sharply. It was almost as though Thankfull had a soft spot for the man. Or, as Alex would probably put it, "a blazing hot lust." But then, he seemed to see romance in everything.

"Do you?" Cay said at last. "And you're sure it's for me?"

Thankfull pulled a folded piece of paper out of her pocket and for a moment she held it, as though she were reluctant to let it go. "It just says 'to Cay' and it's addressed in care of me. It was delivered yesterday by a man on horseback. I think he must have traveled night and day to get here before your brother left."

"He must have," Cay murmured as she took the letter. She wanted to break the wax seal immediately and see what Uncle T.C. had written, but one look at Thankfull and she knew she couldn't.

It was obvious that the woman would want to hear the contents of the letter, but Cay would be able to tell her nothing.

"Have you finished eating?" one of the twins said from the doorway.

Thankfull sighed. "He has," she said as she took Cay's empty plate and bowl away. "But maybe he wants to rest now."

"But I have things I want to show him," one girl said.

"And so do I," the other twin said. "Please come outside with us. We have lots of things we'd like for you to see."

Cay was torn between wanting to run from the girls and wanting to keep her disguise of being a boy who'd probably like two young girls fussing over him. "Will you show me some of the oddities of this country?" she asked as she got up.

"We'll show you anything you want to see," one of the girls said, giggling.

Cay gave them a smile and thought that when she saw her mother she was going to beg her forgiveness. Many times Cay had thought her mother was too strict, too old-fashioned, but now she could see what happened to girls who didn't have a mother to correct them every second of the day. *This* is what they became.

"You don't have to go," Thankfull said, giving her sisters a stern look.

"No, it's all right," Cay said as she allowed the girls to take her hands and pull her out of the room. "I'm interested in this land."

Fourteen

❧

"They tried to *kiss* me!" Cay said in horror to Alex. It was dark out, they were in the barn, and he was rubbing down both of their horses.

"Did they, now?"

"Don't you *dare* start laughing at me. If you do, I'll—" She gave him a half smile. "I'll not let you see Uncle T.C.'s letter."

That stopped him from smiling. Turning, he looked at her. "What did he say?"

"Actually, I haven't opened it yet."

"You haven't read it?"

"For your information, I've been very busy since you dumped me in the middle of those female sharks. Do you know what those two girls wanted from me? Their hands were all over me. And every time I took a step, they were trying to kiss me. One of them tripped me so I'd land on the other one. They—"

"So they're like all the other females on the planet," Alex said in dismissal. "Where is the letter?

"They are *not* like other females. *I* have never—"

"How else is a man to know when a woman wants to be kissed unless she tells him so?" he said impatiently. "Now give me the letter."

"Maybe that's so, but there is such a thing as subtlety. Doctors use leeches that don't stick to a person as close as those two stuck to me. I couldn't take a step that they didn't—" The look Alex gave her made her stop talking about the twins and take the letter out of her pocket, even while she was thinking that she should have read the letter by herself. After all, it was addressed to her alone. But in the last days she'd become so accustomed to sharing everything with Alex that she hadn't even thought of keeping the letter to herself.

She handed the sealed letter to him, but he didn't take it. Instead, he went back to rubbing her mare.

"Read it to me."

Cay broke the seal on the letter. The sight of her uncle's familiar handwriting nearly made her cry, but she took a breath and pulled herself together. "It's dated five days after . . . after I met you." That seemed to be the most polite way of describing the prison break. She began to read.

"My dearest, dearest Cay,

"There is no way I can begin to apologize for all that has happened to you. It was all my fault and I will never forgive myself. But as much as I'd like to tell you in as lengthy detail as I have paper and pen, Adam is here and you know what that means. I am to get on with business.

"First of all, your parents know nothing. On the night of what I can only think of as the Great Error, Hope took a small, fast carriage and Cuddy, your mother's faithful servant, and drove to Edilean to get Nate and as many of your brothers as they could. They were fortunate that Adam was at home and he ar-

ranged everything. He knew that to tell your father would start a war. Angus would be beside himself with fear for your safety—and if he found out that I had caused it, my life would be forfeit, and rightfully so.

"Nate told me that Adam can be an admirable liar when called for, and this time he outdid himself. He gave some outrageous story to your parents to explain their need to leave right away, and he and Nate were here in record time. I think perhaps Adam harnessed an eagle and flew.

"Adam took a day to talk to people here and ask questions, and as soon as I finish this letter, he plans to go away, but he won't tell me where. Nate will stay in Charleston and work on solving the puzzle of how Alex's wife was murdered inside a locked room.

"Cay, your name has been cleared. That was easy enough to do, but if you're reading this letter, then

*you must be in Florida. I wonder if
Alex . . ."*

Cay stopped reading aloud as she
scanned the rest of the letter. She looked
back up at Alex. "You were right when
you said that Uncle T.C. would figure
out a way to clear my name."

"Read the rest of it," Alex said.

"It's not important. Have you had anything to eat? Thankfull—she owns this
place—has cooked some kind of bird
that I've never seen before. She stuffs
it with rice and some spices. It's really
very good, and—"

"Read the letter and don't skip even
a word of it." Alex's tone said that he
wasn't going to be disobeyed.

She picked the letter up again.

*"I wonder if Alex is still with you?
When I visited him in prison, he was
a very angry man, and his grief over
the loss of his wife nearly broke my
heart. Was he any company for you
on the long trip down? My heart
cries for what you must have gone
through with him.*

"Adam told me to say that you're to stay there in Florida and wait for one of your brothers to come and get you. You aren't to leave that place, but to remain there until someone, probably Tally, comes for you. Adam said this over and over. He doesn't seem to believe that you are a very obedient young lady. I told him that you were the opposite, that you readily agreed to help poor Alex in his time of need. Cay, dearest, your eldest brother said some curse words to me that in all my travels among sailors and mountain men, I had never heard!

"I beg of you, please stay there. Thankfull will take care of you, and you're welcome to use my art supplies while you wait. Thankfull will show you where they are. She's a very kind young woman and she helped me assemble it all. ~~Tell her~~

"Cay, dear, I wonder if you got Alex to talk? While he was in the jail, he barely spoke. I'm sworn to secrecy, but let me tell you that he knows more than I thought he did.

Don't tell Alex, but the long letter he wrote while in jail never reached the intended recipient. Nate says that if Alex is still there to tell him that he, Nate, has made a sacred oath that he will find who murdered Alex's wife.

"Now I must go. Adam is giving me looks that frighten me. He is so much like your father!

"I send my love to you and I am sorry for all the pain I've caused you and your family. When we're together again, remember that I owe you chocolate.

"With much love,
"T.C. CONNOR"

Cay folded the letter back together and looked up at Alex, but he kept his face turned away and concentrated on the horse. But she knew him well enough to know that he was thinking hard about what Uncle T.C. had written. "What did he mean that you know more than he thought you did?"

Alex was silent as he rubbed the mare's back with the brush. "I'm glad to hear that they cleared your name," he said at last. "And I agree with your brothers that you must stay here and wait for one of them to come for you. I didn't like the idea of your traveling back alone." He glanced at her. "Even if you're dressed as a boy." His tone said that he thought that was a joke.

"Tally," Cay said, making the word sound heavy and forbidding. "He'll laugh at me."

Alex made a sound as though he thought her being ridiculed would be an appropriate response. "But think how you can best him with stories of your adventure. You rode through the night with an escaped murderer. You can tell him of your fear and the constant danger you were in."

Cay arched an eyebrow at him. "Would that be the danger I was in when we were dancing in the store? Or when you had your head on my lap and I was rubbing jasmine oil into your hair?"

Alex turned his face away so she couldn't see it. "I don't know, lass," he said softly. "That first night you were afraid of me."

"True. I almost cut your throat."

He chuckled. "Did you know that I still have a sore on my side from where you nicked me?"

"I did not!"

"Aye, you did. It was after we went out the side of the barn and you sliced my breeches half off me." He looked back at her. "I'll tell you, lass, that I thought you were going to stab me right then and there, and I didn't know if I'd be able to move out of your reach."

"It wasn't easy for me to choose between you and the man who owned that decrepit old barn."

"Are you glad you chose me?" Alex asked, laughing, but as he looked at her his face became serious. It was easy to see that she was again letting him know that she didn't want to be left behind.

"Yes."

There was an awkward moment as they looked at each other, and the fact that this was their last night together hung in the air.

Alex broke the moment. "So did you kiss them?"

"Who?"

"Did you kiss the girls?"

"You're sick. You're worse than a murderer, you're deranged. You ought to be put away in an asylum."

"What about young Tim? He was mightily taken with you. Did you sneak back and kiss him?"

"I'm going to tell my brother Adam that you weren't very nice to me, and he's going to beat you up."

Alex laughed. "Oh, how I'm going to miss you, lass. You made me laugh after a time when I thought I'd never so much as smile again."

"You wouldn't be alive now if it weren't for me." Her voice was completely serious, her eyes burning into his.

Alex turned back to the horses. "No, you're not going with me, and don't start on me again. Tell me more about the food in this place. After tonight I might be eating alligators for dinner. I wonder what the meat tastes like?"

"I hope it tastes like festering donkey caresses," she said, glaring at his back. "And don't you dare ask me to sleep in the same bed with you tonight, because I won't do it. You, Alexander . . . Yates, are an ungrateful, mean-spirited, bad-tempered numptie. And I wish I knew some of the words my brother knows so I could call you those things." With that, she left the barn and slammed the door behind her.

Turning, Alex looked at the door, and sighed. He was going to miss her very, very much.

❧

It was later that night, when Cay was in bed—alone—that she had to struggle to keep from crying. When she'd left Alex, the twins had been waiting for her with more questions and more attempts to touch her. They were so forward in their advances that she was tempted to tell them the truth, that she was female. But she couldn't do that.

The thought of having to deal with the two of them for even a whole day was enough to make her want to jump in a saddle and head north. She couldn't even imagine a whole week—or more—near them.

And even worse was that at the end

of that horrible time, who was she to see but Tally. Tally! Her brother who liked nothing more than to make her feel as though she were incompetent at everything she tried.

She could hear him now. "So you were in a party dress when you rode out in the middle of the night to rescue a condemned criminal? Weren't you worried that your dress might get soiled? Or your hair come down from whatever you do to make it stay up on top of your head?"

He would go on and on at her while she had to stand there and take it.

But then, maybe she could shoot him, she thought. One bullet to his shoulder. Or maybe to a thigh. He'd recover, but in the meantime, it would shut him up.

She was thinking these lovely thoughts, her mind full of satisfying images, when there was a knock on her door. Since she'd heard Thankfull threaten the girls if they bothered Cay again, she felt sure it was Alex come to apologize. She spread what was left of her hair out on the pillow. "Come in."

When Thankfull put her head inside

the door, Cay frantically began to tuck her hair behind her.

"I don't mean to bother you, but I was wondering if Mr. Connor's letter contained something bad."

"No," Cay said. "Just news from home."

"I couldn't help noticing that when you came in from the stables, you were in a bit of an ill temper, so I thought maybe . . ."

Cay reminded herself that in the future, she had to be more careful. She was used to being on the trail with Alex where they never saw the same people twice. "No, it was just my brother being what he is."

"Oh," Thankfull said. She was looking down at her hands and seemed to have something else to say but didn't know how. "That's good, then. About the letter, I mean. I hope Mr. Connor is well."

When Cay put aside her own annoyance at Alex, she realized what Thankfull wanted: to hear news of Uncle T.C. "He certainly does think highly of you."

"Does he?" Thankfull asked as her head came up and she smiled. "I mean,

I think quite highly of him, too. Did he ever tell you about the time we made his painting chest float?"

"He mentioned it," Cay said, telling a polite lie. T.C. had never said a word about women unless they were of some Indian tribe he'd visited. "But what were the details?"

"Do you mind?" Thankfull asked as she motioned to the chair near the bed.

"No, of course not," Cay said as she sat up straighter in the bed. She'd removed her new vest, but she still had on her big shirt. Her breeches were draped over the end of the bed, and she thought that if she really were a male, this would be a very inappropriate meeting.

"Mr. Connor was here in the spring with Mr. Grady and they made plans for now."

"And they stayed here with you?"

"They did," Thankfull said, again looking at her hands. "Mr. Grady was busy all the time, but Mr. Connor . . ." She looked at Cay. "I guess you know that he's a magnificent artist. Even Mr. Grady said so."

Cay had to work not to reply to that.

In her opinion, Uncle T.C. was a brilliant botanist, but he couldn't draw or paint worth anything.

Thankfull got up and went to the window, glanced out at the moon, and looked back at Cay sitting on the bed. "Usually, I don't pay much attention to the men who come through here, but Mr. Connor was different. He was kind and educated, and we had some wonderful conversations."

"He's a very nice man."

"Isn't he!" Thankfull said enthusiastically as she sat back down on the chair. "He brought boxes of artist's supplies with him. He had great pads of paper that were made in Italy, and he had French crayons and English watercolors. They were all so very beautiful."

Cay could only blink at the woman, for it was obvious that she was giddy in love with T.C. Connor. Cay wondered if the love was returned. According to her mother, Uncle T.C. was incapable of loving anyone but the deceased Bathsheba. "Uncle T.C. said in his letter that you know where his art supplies are and that I could use them while I wait for one of my other brothers to come for me."

"He said that? How kind of him to remember. Yes, I have them in my bedroom."

Cay wanted to ask her if she slept beside them, but she refrained herself. "You said something about a chest?"

"Yes, he'd had a metal trunk made to hold his supplies and his finished art. It was so well constructed that it was waterproof. Mr. Connor and I went to the river and threw it in to make sure that it would float and not leak. Of course we had a rope tied to the chest so it wouldn't end up in Cowford, but it all worked perfectly, just as he'd planned. When we pulled it out hours later, the papers we'd put inside it were as dry as they'd been when we put the box in the river."

"Hours?" Cay asked, and when Thankfull blushed, her face looked years younger. It's amazing what love can do to a person, she thought.

"It took us most of a day to fully ascertain whether the chest was waterproof or not."

"That must have been a pleasant diversion for you," Cay said.

"Very much so." Thankfull stood up again. "The trunk is locked, but Mr. Connor left the key with me. If his letter says you may use the items, I'll gladly give them to you. But I will need proof, of course."

"Yes, proof," Cay said and she had to work to keep from frowning. It looked like Thankfull had come up with an excuse to get to see the letter from T.C.—but of course Cay could never show it to her, as it held too much information that was private. So that would mean she wouldn't be allowed to use Uncle T.C.'s supplies while she was left there by Alex the Ungrateful.

"I'll let you sleep now," Thankfull said as she got up. "Just let me see Mr. Connor's verification and I'll be happy to turn the chest over to you." Smiling, she went to the door.

On impulse, Cay said, "What's Mr. Grady like?"

Thankfull's eyes widened. "I don't think I can describe him. Tim says he'll be here tomorrow, so you can see for yourself."

"Do you think he's a kind man?"

"He's . . . James Grady is in a class all of his own. I think I'd better go now or the girls will get the wrong idea about us." Quickly, she left the room.

It was a full minute before Cay started to bang her fist against the pillow. Worse and worse and worse. Everything was going downhill rapidly. She was facing spending weeks being tortured by three lovesick females. Two of them seemed intent on making Cay their husband, while the third was going to make her show a letter that Cay couldn't reveal before she was allowed to have even a drawing pencil. What was she supposed to *do* during these weeks?

If that weren't bad enough, at the end of the time, Tally was to come and get her.

Yet again, Cay thought about leaping out the window and getting on her horse. Better still, she should dive into the river and swim home. She wondered if the St. Johns joined the James River somewhere. Maybe if she got a boat, she could row herself northward. She couldn't help smiling as she thought of how Alex would worry when he found her gone. It would serve him right! she thought. He deserved to be scared to death after what he'd condemned her to. And after she'd saved his worthless life!

As she began to fall asleep, she wondered where he was sleeping tonight, and she hoped it was someplace uncomfortable and smelly.

Fifteen

❧

Cay pushed the eggs about on her plate. She was so down spirited that she didn't even care what kind of bird the eggs came from. She'd already seen so many strange creatures flying and running about that she couldn't keep track of them. Yesterday she'd tried her best to ask the girls what the huge bird flying overhead was, but they weren't interested in the birds, only in Cay. All they wanted to do was to touch her, to sit close to her, to make her look at them.

"There's no way he's right," Cay mumbled as she thought about Alex saying that *all* girls acted like that. Cay could assure him that she'd never come close to behaving that way with any of her many suitors. She'd always conducted herself in the most respectful, ladylike way possible. The few times when she was alone with one of the three men she was considering marrying, she'd never done anything that she couldn't have done in front of her mother. Maybe not her father, but her mother, yes.

"Did you say something?" Thankfull asked from the doorway as she put another bowl of food on the table.

Cay was the only guest at the boardinghouse, and if she ate even half of what was served to her, she'd get fat. She wondered if being fat would make the girls leave her alone.

"Your brother hasn't been by this morning," Thankfull said. "Do you think he'll want breakfast?"

"I don't know where he spent last night and I don't know if or when he ate."

"I see," Thankfull said tentatively.

"I spent last night under the stars," Alex said from the doorway.

Cay turned to his voice and had to stop herself from running to him. It was wonderful to see someone who wasn't a stranger. Even though she stopped her smile before it could engulf her face, he saw it.

"Mr. Yates," Thankfull said, "please sit down and have breakfast. I'll fix you a plate of eggs."

She left the room and Alex sat down across from Cay. "Miss me?" He picked up a piece of toast from the plate in the center of the table.

"Not at all. I hope you froze last night."

"I only wish summers in Scotland were as warm as the winters here. How long do you plan to stay angry at me, lass?"

"Stop calling me that or Thankfull will hear you."

"What do you think her parents were thankful for when she was born?"

It was nearly the same joke that Cay had thought of when she was introduced, but she wasn't going to give him the satisfaction of hearing her say so. She just glared at him and went back to moving her eggs around on the plate.

"Grady is to arrive today."

"I hope he doesn't." Cay's voice was angry. "I hope *you* have to stay here, too."

"You want me with you that bad, do you?"

"I don't want you with me at all. I just don't want to have to stay in this place and wait for my brother to come and ridicule me."

"Lass," Alex said patiently, "they have mail service out of here, so you can write to your other brothers and ask them to come and get you. What was the pretty one's name?"

"Ethan. No. If Adam said Tally was to come for me, then it will be Tally. No one contradicts Adam."

A quick frown crossed Alex's face, but he got it under control. "Will you come see me off tomorrow?"

"I thought you were leaving today. I was *hoping* you'd leave today."

"Grady is to bring the flatboat with more supplies, and we leave early to-morrow. Will you cry when you wave good-bye to me?"

"I'm going to throw a party."

"And will the girls be there? Will you sneak kisses with them?"

She picked up her fork and lunged across the table at him, but he pulled back, laughing, just as Thankfull re-turned.

"I hope they're cooked to your liking," she said, looking in curiosity from Cay to Alex, then back again.

"Excellent," Alex said, glancing up at Thankfull with a warm smile.

She returned his smile before she went back to the kitchen.

"You were *flirting* with her," Cay said in a voice that was mostly a hiss.

"She's an attractive woman," Alex said.

"And you're a married man."

"Nay, lass," Alex said quietly, "I'm not."

"I didn't mean . . . ," she began, then stopped. She wasn't good at being angry. Even when she was a child and Tally did truly horrible things to her, she couldn't stay mad for long. She put her head on her hands, elbows on the table. "I don't want to stay here alone."

"Thankfull seems like a nice enough person, so maybe she'll turn out to be your friend." There was sympathy in Alex's voice.

"She's in love with Uncle T.C."

"Is she now? Who would have thought of that? Is he in love with her?"

"How would I know that? I'm his god-daughter. He doesn't talk to me of his love life."

"Maybe he should. It would have been better than telling you about the murderers in his life."

Cay couldn't help it, but she smiled. "I agree with you on that."

Reaching across the table, he took her hand, and she looked at him. "I'm truly sorry about all this, lass. I didn't mean for it to happen, and neither did T.C. If he hadn't been so stupid as to climb on that ladder, he'd be here now and not you."

"And he'd be going with you," Cay said, her eyes pleading.

Alex pulled his hand back and took a bite of his eggs. "Don't start on me again. You canna go, and that's final."

"He's here!" one of the twins shouted as she ran into the dining room. Her eyes went directly to Cay. "Oooooh," she said and sat down beside her, but Cay stood up.

"Who's here?" Alex asked.

The girl didn't so much as look at him; her eyes were directly on Cay. "Mr. Grady."

"Oh," Cay said flatly, looking at Alex.

He rapidly took three more bites of egg, grabbed his hat, and said he had to go.

Cay was right on his heels.

At the door, he stopped. "I think you should stay here. I don't know where Grady's been, so he may have heard the news from Charleston. He could be suspicious of you."

"My name was cleared, remember? It's *you* who's in danger, not me."

Alex grimaced.

"But it was a good try," she said. "Really, I almost believed you."

Alex laughed. "Then it was worth it." He put his arm around her shoulders. "Let's go, little brother, and see what awaits me."

"You, not me," Cay said gloomily. "You saw in the dining room what's waiting for me."

"Those girls aren't bad, brother. Maybe when I get back I'll be invited to your wedding."

"You are not funny."

Laughing, Alex tightened his arm around her shoulder, but she twisted away.

"I hope an alligator eats your leg."

"Now, lass, you don't mean that."

"Yes, I do. I—" She broke off because they'd reached the dock and standing amid the many boxes and crates was a tall man wearing a snowy white shirt, with a dark green vest, and fawn-colored breeches. On his head was a big felt hat with a wide brim. His face was turned away from them, but she could see that he was young and had a horseman's muscular thighs.

"Is that him?"

When Alex looked at her, he frowned at her expression. "I guess so. Why?"

"He reminds me of someone I know, that's all."

"I think you should go back to the boardinghouse. If Grady recognizes you, we're sunk. I promise that I'll come to say good-bye to you this afternoon."

She moved away from Alex when he again tried to put his arm around her shoulders. "I'm not going back to that place until I have to. I wish he'd turn around so I could see his face."

Alex stepped in front of her to block her view. "I don't like this. If you think you know this man, then he'll know you. He won't think you're a boy."

"If he's who I think he is, he won't recognize me, since the only time I saw him, I was eight years old."

"I still think—" Alex began.

"Are you Yates?" came a voice from behind them.

Reluctantly, Alex took his eyes off Cay and turned around, and when he heard her gasp from behind him, he realized that this was the man she knew.

James Grady was a very handsome man. He looked to be in his early thirties, was as tall as Alex, but heavier built, as he hadn't spent weeks in near starvation. He had dark hair and gray eyes, and there were long dimples in his cheeks.

As soon as Alex saw the man, he knew things about him. Like Cay, Grady seemed to exude an air of money. When you looked at the man, you saw a drawing room with port in crystal glasses and cigar smoke. You saw women in dresses so elegant they looked to have been created on Mount Olympus.

Without a doubt, Alex knew that James Grady was an older version of the rich plantation boys Alex had beaten in the horse races in Charleston. In other words, he was of the same class and education as Cay. He was of her crowd, her social station in life. He was her equal.

Alex told himself he had no reason to hate the man, but he could feel the emotion coursing through his veins.

"Are you Yates?" the man asked again.

"Yes," Alex finally managed to say. "I'm Alex Yates."

"And you're the friend T.C. wrote me about, the one who can handle any animal?"

"Ah dunnae kinn abit 'at, but I'll dae th' best Ah can.

"I beg your pardon?"

During this exchange, Alex had managed to keep Cay behind him. She'd tried to escape his grasp on her, but he'd held on tight. At last, she dug her elbows into his back and he had to let go.

She slipped around Alex and put herself in front of him to stare up at Mr. Grady with wide eyes. "I'm Charles Albert Yates," she said as she held her shoulders back and her chest out. "This is my brother, and I'm his translator."

Alex realized that, yet again, he'd fallen back into his heavy accent and Grady hadn't been able to understand him.

"What my brother said was that he was appreciative of the compliment from Mr. Connor, and that he'd do his best to live up to expectations."

"Did he now?" Mr. Grady said, smiling down at Cay in merriment. "He said all that in just those few words?"

"He did," Cay said, not seeming to realize that Mr. Grady was teasing her. "He can speak English, but he's not very good at it."

"And why is it that your brother has such a heavy accent, but you have none?"

"Och, but Ah dae when Ah lit myself," she said, her eyes showing her delight.

Mr. Grady laughed. "Well, boy, I can see that you'll be a fine addition to our little team. You can—"

"He's not going," Alex said loudly in American English.

"Oh, excuse me," Mr. Grady said. "I thought he would be going with us."

"He has to stay here and wait for his brother—our brother—to come and get him."

"A fine, healthy lad like this one can't travel around our great country on his own? How old are you, boy?"

Cay started to say she was twenty, but Alex pushed her with his elbow so that she almost fell. While she was trying to regain her balance, Alex said, "Sixteen."

Mr. Grady looked at Cay righting herself and said, "He looks older." He was looking at her as though he was trying to remember something, so Alex stepped between them.

"I'll take care of the horses and do the hunting and whatever else you need," Alex said.

"What I need is someone who can draw and paint the wonders that we'll see." Mr. Grady started walking back to the wharf, Alex beside him, with Cay coming up behind them. She was half the size of either of the men and she had trouble getting around them. Every time she tried to go around Alex, he reached out an arm and stopped her. After two attempts, she ran around the side of Mr. Grady to walk beside him.

"If I'd known about T.C.'s accident, I could have brought someone from home. There's a boy there who can draw a bit. He's not as good as T.C., but few are. Now I'm here, ready to go, but I have no one to record what we see. Have you ever been into the depths of Florida, Mr. Yates?"

Alex glanced across him at Cay and saw that she was wide-eyed as she looked up at Mr. Grady in fascination. Before anything else was done, he *had* to get her back to the boardinghouse.

"By the way, I'm just one generation away from the heather," Mr. Grady said into the silence. "My father came from Scotland when he was just a lad, no older than young Charlie here, and—"

"Cay," she said, and when he looked

down at her, she said louder, "I'm called that for my initials."

"Cay, is it?" For a moment Mr. Grady blinked at her before turning back to Alex. "You two came down from Charleston?"

"We did."

"What is this I heard about an escaped murderer? A cousin of mine lives there, and his letters were full of nothing else. Your name of Alex reminded me of it. Seems the black'ard killed his wife on their wedding night."

Alex opened his mouth to say something, but no sounds came out.

"It was terrible," Cay said quickly, "but there were rumors that the man was innocent, that he was the victim of a plot so evil that they couldn't even write about it in the newspapers."

"Is that so?" Mr. Grady said. "My cousin must not have known about that because he certainly didn't write about it in his letters."

"It was Uncle T.C. who told us all about it."

"Uncle, is it?"

"Yes, sir," Cay said. "He's my godfather."

"Interesting," Mr. Grady said. "I've known T.C. for about ten years, but I've never heard him mention any boys who were his godsons."

"I guess since we lived in Scotland he forgot about us," Cay said. She was careful not to look at Alex on the other side of Mr. Grady because Alex was giving her looks that said she was to keep her mouth shut. The lies she was concocting were piling up on one another. Cay ignored him. "So you don't have an artist for the trip?"

"You aren't going to tell me that you can draw, are you?"

"He can't!" Alex said loudly. "He hardly knows how to hold a pencil, much less a paintbrush. Isn't that true, little brother?" He was glaring at her.

"Actually, in school, I was rather good at drawing. Certainly better than some." She looked across Grady to Alex. "You were away most of the time, so you don't remember."

"Well, then, boy, let's give you a try," Mr. Grady said. "I always carry a portable writing desk with me, so do you think you can make do with stationery and a pen?"

"I can try," Cay said with all the modesty she could muster.

"I don't think—" Alex began, but when both Cay and Mr. Grady turned to look at him, he stopped. "I need to talk to my brother alone."

"Shall we meet back here when you're ready?" Mr. Grady said. "I'll have pen and paper waiting."

Alex lost no time in grabbing Cay's arm and pulling her to the side of one of the buildings. "What the hell do you think you're doing?"

"I want to go with you."

"We talked about this before. This trip is too dangerous, so you can't go, and that's final."

"Walking into the mouth of Hades would be better than staying here and waiting for Tally to come and make fun of me."

Alex ran his hand over his bearded face and tried to count to ten, but he knew that if he counted to a hundred it would make no difference. "You canna go with us," he said as calmly as he could manage. "Even your own brother told you to stay here."

"Adam doesn't know that there are extenuating circumstances. If he knew *who* I was traveling with, he'd tell me to go."

Alex leaned back against the wall to the building and drew in a deep breath. "All right, out with it. Who is he?"

"Who is who?"

He narrowed his eyes at her.

"I just thought I'd add a little levity into this, but you seem to have lost your sense of humor. All right! Stop looking at me like that. Mr. Grady's real name is James Armitage and he—"

Alex groaned.

"So you've heard of the family?"

"I was told of them as soon as I got off the boat from Scotland. The father wanted to buy my horses."

"King."

"What?"

"Jamie's father is called 'King' as in 'King Armitage.'"

"Jamie?"

"That's what his family calls him. It's

my guess that his middle name is Grady. Maybe that was his mother's maiden name. Do you know why Jamie's father is called King?"

"I think he owns Georgia, doesn't he?"

"Only a big part of it. It's South Carolina that he owns most of. Jamie is the third son, and I can see why he's traveling under a made-up name. It's the only way he's going to be treated as a regular person. And he was very nice, wasn't he?"

Alex put his hand over his eyes for a moment. "Please tell me you're not back to trying to find yourself a husband."

She leaned against the wall beside Alex and said in a dreamy way, "When I was eight years old, I went with my parents to Gracewell, South Carolina, to visit the Armitage family. My father worked with Mr. Armitage during the War for Independence, and they're friends. My father doesn't call him King; he calls him Billy, and they spend a lot of time talking about Scotland. When we visited, Jamie was home from William and Mary. That's—"

"I know what it is, and believe it or not, I can read and write, too."

Cay looked at him as though to ask what he was talking about, but then went on with her story. "I was just eight years old, he was twenty-two, and he pushed me on a swing."

Alex waited for a moment, but she said nothing else. "And what happened?"

"Nothing. That's it. He pushed me on the swing for about half an hour, then he went back into the house, and the next morning he left before I was up. I never saw him again."

Alex moved away from the wall to look at her. "Am I missing something here? You made this sound like it was really important."

"It was. That night I told my mother I was going to marry Jamie Armitage, and she said I'd made a good choice."

Alex blinked at her a few times. "Have you always been so obsessed with marriage?"

"I want to get it *right*. What's so wrong with that? I've seen unhappy marriages and I don't want to live like that." She put her arms over her chest and turned away from him.

"Just a few days ago you were talking to me about the three men you were trying to decide about, and now you're after this man."

She turned back to face him. "I'm not after any man. I'm just telling you that I know *this* man. I know his family, his home, and some of the towns that his father owns."

"And you want to travel with me so you can go after him, just as those twins are going after you?"

"You're disgusting."

Alex took a few deep breaths to calm himself so he could try a different approach. "Your brother Adam told you to stay here and wait, and I think that's what you should do."

"I think Adam would want me to spend as much time with an Armitage son as possible. Adam didn't like—" Cutting herself off, she looked away from Alex.

"He didn't like what?"

She didn't want to answer, but Alex kept staring at her. "The men."

"Are you saying that your oldest brother, who you seem to revere, didn't like the three men you were considering marrying?"

"Yes. Are you happy now?"

Alex couldn't resist a smile. "What did Adam say about them?"

"I'm not telling you."

"Was it that bad? Or are you just too cowardly to repeat his words?"

"Adam said those three men weren't good enough to kiss the soles of my shoes. There! Does knowing that make you happy?"

"Pretty much." He was grinning. "You know, every word you've told me about your precious Adam has made me dislike the bas—the man, but now I'm beginning to think we might like each other."

"No you wouldn't. You're too much alike."

"Alike? Are you changing your story and saying that I *am* like your oldest brother?"

"You're getting too much pleasure out of this, so I'm not going to say another word to you about anything, except that

I'm going to go with Jamie whether you like it or not."

"You're not."

"Am."

"Not."

"Am."

Alex made his hands into fists. What he wanted to do was throw her over his shoulder and tie her to a tree. He'd pay someone to free her four hours after they'd sailed away—or maybe it should be six. She could move quickly.

"I don't like the way you're looking at me. I'm going and that's final."

"And do what? Dress the men's hair? Mend their clothes? I heard that you've had some practice in doing laundry. I know! How about if you do the cooking?"

Cay wanted to rattle off the list of credentials of her artistic education, but she made herself keep quiet. His remark about the laundry reminded her that he knew things about her family that must have come from someone who knew them. The logical person was Uncle T.C., but she'd never known him to talk about much of anything except plants. Whatever the source, Alex knew personal, private things about her and her family. However, it was strange that Alex didn't seem to know that Cay could draw and paint. Usually, she had a sketchbook and pencils with her. She rarely went anywhere without the means to draw what she saw, but on the night she met Alex, she'd been going to a ball, so her drawing equipment had been left at home. And since then, everything had been so new and strange that she hadn't thought much about art.

Now, it seemed that Alex's not knowing about her might be a very good thing. "You said that anyone could draw. If I remember correctly, you said, 'How hard can it be?' Can *you* draw?"

"A bit," he said. "Believe it or not, I had a drawing master who trained in London."

"You were meaning to take on the job of recorder for yourself, weren't you?"

"I thought about it." Alex was smiling.

She wanted to kick him! What else had he kept from her? "How about if we both do a few drawings and let Jamie decide which of us will record this trip for posterity?"

Alex kept smiling. "Lass, I should warn you that I was the best in my class at drawing."

"Were you?" she asked, trying to sound impressed.

"Aye, I was. I liked going out into the heather and drawing the animals I saw. If I hadn't been a horseman, I could have . . ." He shrugged. "What training have you had?"

"Mrs. Cooper's Academy for Young Ladies," she said quickly. "We used to paint china teacups." This was true, but she didn't tell him it had been when she was four and she'd painted her family's portraits on the cups—which had made her mother hire the first of several private drawing masters.

"Did you now?" He was smiling so hard it was nearly a smirk. Alex was confident that he'd win any artistic competition. If his sister was good at art, Alex was sure Nate would have told him so, and since he hadn't, Alex figured that she'd had only a little training. Teacups! She had no idea what a journey like this required. She had to be able to draw fast and accurately.

"Is it a deal?" she asked. "We'll have a competition and we'll let Jamie be the judge. If he says that I'm no good, then I'll return to the boardinghouse and stay there until Tally comes for me. Is it a bargain?"

Alex frowned. She was saying all this with such confidence that he thought there was a trick. "What are you up to?"

"Nothing. I just want to go with you and I'm going to do my absolute best to outdraw you. If you'd suggested pistols at dawn I might try to do that, too."

"All this so you can go with this man Armitage?"

"That and other things."

"Tell me, lass, is it the man or his money you want?"

For a moment, she had to fight the urge to slap him, but she refused to sink to his level. "His money, of course, since, according to you, I want to marry men even though I have no love for them. Maybe you think I'm incapable of love. Is *that* what you think? That I'm too coldhearted to love anyone?"

Alex was blinking in confusion. "How did we go from drawing to cold hearts?"

Cay threw up her hands in disgust. "You're an idiot, and worse, you're a *male.*" She moved past him with a gesture that said she was sweeping aside her skirts so they wouldn't touch scum like him.

Alex leaned his head back against the wall of the building and looked upward. He wasn't sure, but he thought that maybe he'd just agreed to let her go on a very dangerous trip into the wilds of a jungle. And the worst of it was that he had no idea how it had happened.

Sixteen

❧

Alex watched Cay walk toward the dock. Her head was up, her chin out, and she walked with the determination of a man about to enter into a fight. In spite of himself, he couldn't help feeling proud of her. It was impossible to believe that this was the same girl he'd first met.

But his pride in her didn't quash his resolve to keep her from going on the trip. He couldn't tell her that the real reason he didn't want her with him was because he knew that if they spent more time together, he wouldn't be able to keep his hands off of her. He couldn't spend more days watching her strut around in her snug little breeches and not touch her. Since they were supposed to be brothers, they'd no doubt be expected to spend the nights together in a tent. How could he do that?

When they'd first started traveling together, Alex had been so angry, so full of rage and hatred, that he could have slept next to a dozen naked women and not taken advantage of what they offered.

But Cay, with her bright outlook on life, her belief that anything could be done, had changed all that. But Charleston and what had been done to him there now seemed something that wasn't real and had never actually happened.

He watched her smiling up at Grady and telling him that she and her brother were to have a competition to see if she would go or not. Alex didn't like to feel smug, but he was sure he'd win. He'd always been good at capturing on paper the likeness of whatever he saw. He hadn't told her, but his father had brought watercolors back from a trip to Edinburgh, and Alex had made many pictures of landscapes. He knew he'd be good at what Grady wanted for the trip, so winning was going to be easy.

What would be difficult was consoling Cay when she didn't get to go with them. He imagined a sweet scene where she was crying and he'd comfort her. He'd be firm but sympathetic, and tell her it was for her own good. He was sure she'd eventually understand that he was right.

Tomorrow morning they'd part, and there'd be tears in her pretty eyes and he'd remember them throughout the perilous journey. His hope was that while he was away, Nate would find some answers, and when Alex returned, maybe he could clear his name.

When he was no longer tainted by injustice, he'd get his horses back, and he'd go north to Virginia to find Cay. If she wasn't already married to some cold, unappreciative boy who would never find out what she was really like, he would . . . He liked to leave that thought to the future.

Cay was waving her hand toward him, wanting him to come forward. It looked like she had the competition set up to begin. Smiling, Alex went toward the dock.

❧❧

"Is this all right?" Mr. Grady asked, nodding toward the two work stations he'd had Eli and Tim set up. Wide boards had been leaned against crates, large pieces of paper on them, pens and ink beside them.

"Young Cay wanted a pan of water," Mr. Grady said to Alex. "Do you need one?"

Alex had no idea why she wanted water along with her ink, but he shrugged it off as he sat down on a crate, put the pen and ink beside him, and picked up his makeshift easel.

"Since, as you know, we'll be traveling," Mr. Grady said, "it's sometimes necessary to record things quickly, therefore, this will be a timed documentation. You will have three minutes to draw what you see. Whether it's the dock, a person, or a bird, is up to you. I just want to see what you can do in a short time."

Cay sat down on the rough wood of the dock, her legs folded, and looked at the blank piece of paper. Everything that her teacher, Russell Johns, had yelled at her ran through her head. When he'd first arrived in America from England, just two years before, he'd been destitute. He knew no one, and her mother said he had a broken heart, but not even she could get him to tell her what had happened to make him so unhappy. Her mother had hired Mr. Johns to teach her daughter, but, truthfully, Cay didn't think she'd ever pleased him. He wanted someone who devoted her life to art, but Cay didn't want to do that. Now, she could hear his voice as he gave her lessons in drawing pictures of movement. "Draw faster!" he'd shout. "Do you expect your brothers to sit still and wait for you?" Cay had learned how to rapidly sketch her brothers playing at ball or riding their horses in just a few strokes. With ink, she'd had to be sure about her lines, with no hesitation, because errors couldn't be fixed. After three months of work on these quick drawings, Mr. Johns had finally grunted. He didn't compliment her, but he didn't complain either. For Cay, it had been the height of praise.

Mr. Grady took out his pocket watch, looked at it, and said, "Go!"

Cay worked with both hands. In her right hand, she had the pen, which she frequently dipped in ink, while she put the fingertips of her left into the water. As she drew in quick, bold strokes, she smeared the wet ink with the water to create shadings of her scene.

When Mr. Grady called time, Cay lifted her pen and stood up. The skinny boy, Tim, smirking at her as though he was looking forward to seeing her fail, swaggered across the deck to see the picture she'd done.

Eli went first to Alex's drawing. "By all that's holy, but that's good. I thought T.C. could draw, but you're far better than he is." He looked at Mr. Grady, who was staring at Cay's picture in silence. "You'll have to hire this man for the job."

Mr. Grady said nothing, just stood beside Tim and looked at Cay's drawing. Curious, Eli went to them.

Alex was watching Cay and trying to repress a grin. After what Eli had said, Alex was sure the contest was over.

"Come on, la—" He caught himself. "Cay, don't be disheartened. We can't all have—"

He broke off when he saw her drawing. In just three minutes she'd captured the wharf, the river, the sky, and Eli with a fishing net on his lap. There were lines and shading, some thick, some thin, some light, some dark. In Alex's opinion, the drawing should be framed and put in a museum.

All the men, Tim, Eli, Grady, and Alex, turned to look at Cay.

"I know it's rough, but I'm out of practice," she said. "I promise I'll do better on the trip."

Alex was the first man to recover himself and turn away. Without a word, he started down the street toward the boardinghouse.

"I think my brother's angry at me," she said and took off running after him.

"You have the job," Mr. Grady called after her, his eyes still on the drawing on the board.

"I've never seen anything like it," Eli said.

"He missed that ugly bird on the

post," Tim said, and the other two men glared at him.

"The pelican wasn't there a minute ago," Eli said.

"I do believe, Tim, you're showing a bit of the green monster." Mr. Grady picked up the drawing and studied it. "I think I'll send this home to my mother. She always wants to know about my forays into the dark unknown. Now I can show her."

Cay caught up with Alex outside the boardinghouse, and she was glad to see that neither Thankfull nor her half sisters were about.

"Did you enjoy yourself?" Alex said under his breath. "Did you feel good about making fun of me?"

"You were the one bragging about your abilities, not me." Cay was bewildered by his attitude. She never would have guessed that he'd be a sore loser. "Are you angry because I can paint better pictures than you can?"

He gave her a look that told her that was an absurd idea.

"Then what's made you so angry?" As soon as she said it, she knew. "You're angry because you don't want me to go with you."

"I haven't made that clear?"

She was glaring at him, her hands on her hips. "You were so sure you were going to win the contest that you made a bet with me, but you had no intention of honoring your wager, did you? You're a vain man who can't admit he was wrong."

"Put your arms down! No male ever stood like you are."

Cay was so angry she could hardly speak. "Try and make me."

Alex grabbed her arm and pulled her to the side of the building, and down a path that led through the palms and shrubs that grew along the edges. Within minutes, they were out of sight of the settlement. Halting in a clearing, he turned back to her. "You don't seem to realize how dangerous this trip is going to be. There are creatures living in this Florida that people have never seen. You could be killed in any number of ways. You could be—"

Cay took a step away from him, her eyes wide as she came to a realization. "You're not afraid for me to go on this journey. There's something else. I traveled with a wanted murderer, with men chasing me, hunting me wherever we went, but you weren't afraid for my safety then. You and I built fires, we broke into a store, and you took time to dance with me. There's another reason you don't want me to go with you, isn't there?"

"No, of course not," he said quickly, but he avoided her eyes.

She stepped closer to him and bent her head so she could look up into his eyes. Sometimes, with his heavy beard, it was difficult to see his expression. "I like to think," she said softly, "that in these last weeks you and I have become close. We've been through a lot together, so aren't we friends?"

Alex started to answer her, but they were in a quiet place, surrounded by lush greenery, with the calls of birds in the background, and the fragrance of flowers around them. He couldn't help himself, but he pulled her into his arms and kissed her. At first, it was a gentle kiss, but Cay leaned back and looked at him in astonishment. She blinked a few times, her long lashes making shadows, and she put her arms around his neck and kissed him back.

He knew that in spite of all her talk, she was very inexperienced, so he was gentle with her, his lips on hers soft, undemanding, but she pressed her body close to his and deepened the kiss. She opened her lips under his, inviting his tongue into her mouth.

It took all his will power, but he thrust her away from him. "That was ill done!" he said, his heart pounding, his breath coming fast.

Cay's heart was also beating hard, and she was looking at him in wide-eyed question. "The other men I've kissed weren't like you."

"Will you put me on your list of suitors?" His remark was more angry than he'd meant it to sound, but he didn't like to think of her kissing other men.

"I'm going to put you at the top of *all* my lists."

She said it with so much enthusiasm that he laughed. She always seemed able to make his ill humor go away.

"Now do you see why I can't take you with me?" he asked.

"You mean because you desire me above all things in life, and because I make your blood boil?"

"More or less," he said. "At least now you see that you and I can't travel together, and we certainly can't stay in the same tent."

"You do have a problem." She turned away for a moment, then looked back at him. "Are you in love with me?"

"I'll be honest with you, lass, I'm not sure I'll ever be able to love again. Maybe a person gets only one true love in his life and I married mine."

Cay tried not to show her disappointment. She wasn't in love with him, either, but a girl liked to think there were at least half a dozen men pining away for her. "So it's just . . . nature that's the hindrance to our traveling together."

"Aye, nature."

She held out the sides of her breeches. "That I'm wearing men's clothes doesn't help dampen your feelings?"

"If anything, that makes it worse. If all women start wearing men's trousers and showing the true form of their legs, I don't know how we men would be able to stand it."

"That's because you haven't seen as many legs of women as I have," Cay said. "I can tell you that there are more unsightly ones than there are nice ones."

"Is that so?"

"Are you laughing at me already?"

"'Fraid so, lass. It seems to have become a habit."

She put her hands on his chest. "What if I promise to do nothing to . . . to stir your blood?" She took a step closer to him. "What if I swear that I'll behave myself every moment of the trip?"

Alex put his hands on her shoulders and pushed her away. "One kiss and you turn into Eve. Get over there and do not touch me."

Cay moved away from him, but she couldn't conceal her smile. Alex was making her feel like a female. After what seemed like weeks of being thought of as a boy, with those awful girls pushing themselves on her, it felt, well, powerful to be considered a woman. It was lovely to feel desired, to be wanted.

She turned back to face him. "Please let me go with you, Alex. I'm sorry for your . . . your male desire, but I promise that I'll do what I can to stop it. I'll be nasty and hateful to you at all times, and I'll kick you if you get within three feet of me. I don't mean to bring up anything bad, but I saved your life. When you needed help, I gave it to you. That night, when neither Uncle T.C. nor Hope could go, it was me or no one else. I was very frightened, but I did it anyway. And except for the time when I tried to cut your throat, I think that, all in all, I've been rather nice to you."

"What you're saying is that I owe you." Alex's face was serious.

"Actually, yes."

"Tell me, do you really want to go or are you that afraid of your brother?"

"Tally? I'm not afraid of him at all, but he will ridicule me, and make me feel truly awful." She threw up her hands in frustration and turned away for a moment. "Don't you see what this means to me? If I were to go home now, my father would never let me out again. He'd be so afraid that something awful would happen to me that he'll lock me in my room and throw the key down the well. My maid would have to send food up a rope through the window."

"Not to mention the chamber pot."

"Ladies don't talk of such things, and you can laugh all you want, but if I have to wait here for Tally to come fetch me, and for Adam and Nate to solve the murder mystery, my father will see me as someone who has to be guarded at all times. He'll think that to protect me he'll have to keep me under permanent house arrest." She sighed in frustration. "In the end, he'll probably marry me off to some Scottish cousin who can slay three dragons before breakfast."

"To marry a Scotsman would be a fate worse than death?"

"You can laugh at me all you want, but I'm *serious.* If I can take your rampant lust for me seriously, I think you should take my problems just as seriously."

"Rampant—" Alex stood up straighter. "All right, lass, tell me how going into the jungle will help you."

"Maybe if I accomplish something, it

will make my family overlook the fact that I ran across several states when men with guns were chasing me."

"And drawing pictures will help you?"

"If they're for a cause. I'd like my father to be proud of me. I'd like my future husband to have something to tell our children about."

"The way you tell people about the fruit company your mother ran?"

"Yes, exactly. Several of the women who worked for her now live in Edilean, and they married men my father knew."

Alex turned away from her. He did owe her, he thought. He might joke about it, but if it weren't for her bravery, he wouldn't be alive now. The real truth of it was that he very much wanted her to go with them. In spite of what they'd heard from her brother Adam— who Cay seemed to think was a saint put on this earth to boss mere mortals around—Alex had never felt safe about leaving her alone. He'd thought about all the bad things that could happen to her. Not everyone could have heard that her name had been cleared. What if someone realized that she wasn't a boy but a red-haired girl? He'd want to know why she was in disguise, and it wouldn't take much to think of the scandalous news that had come down the coast from Charleston. Alex didn't like to think what would happen to Cay if she were confronted by someone who hadn't heard the latest news.

Also, there was the personal side of it. He enjoyed her company. She made him laugh, made him feel good. On the day he married Lilith, he'd sat there with a glass of champagne, watching his beautiful wife moving among their guests and quietly talking to everyone, and he'd thought that he was the luckiest man in the world. Based on the number of guests and their good wishes to him, he thought he'd made a lot of friends since he'd been in America. He smiled as they laughed and drank to his health and future happiness. They'd slapped him on the back and talked about horses, and about investments they'd like to share with him. On that day, Alex had felt part of a world of rich, happy people. He was no longer the man just off the boat with three horses, his clothes dirty and ragged. He'd been Someone, a young man on his way up.

But the next day, Lilith's body had been found next to Alex's, and after that, everything had changed. The rage of the town had rushed the trial through. And while Alex was in that filthy jail, not one of his so-called friends had visited him. Only T.C. had shown up. Right away, Alex had asked for pen, ink, and paper, and T.C. had brought it. Alex had been obsessed with telling the people he'd thought of as his friends that he was innocent, that he would never have killed Lilith. He'd loved her so very much. He'd poured out his heart in the letters and T.C. had personally delivered each of them.

Not one person had answered his letter. In fact, Alex had made T.C. tell him the truth, that all the letters had been returned, unopened. No one wanted anything to do with Alexander McDowell after he'd been arrested. It seemed that no one had even considered the idea that Alex might be innocent.

After three weeks of frantically writing to people he'd met since arriving in America, he wrote to Nate. Maybe it was because they'd been friends since childhood and they'd tried hard to impress each other, but he didn't want to admit to his friend that he'd failed—for that's how Alex viewed it. He'd arrived in America sure that he could do anything, achieve everything. He'd had a lifetime with his father telling him of the opportunities in the new country. After all, it was where his father had made all his money. Many years before, Mac had been awarded a thousand acres of land through the Ohio Company, but Nate's father, Angus, had persuaded Mac to sell the land to a Captain Austin, who was trying to accumulate an estate for the woman he loved. In the end, it proved to be the best thing Mac ever did, because the king of England never signed the papers. None of the thousand-acre plots were given to the people who held certificates of ownership for them. Captain Austin had lost everything.

For Alex, the new country had seemed to be a land of riches—until the morning after his wedding, when everything was taken from him, including, it seemed, the friendship of everyone he'd met. It was only after his new "friends" had shown their true nature that Alex swallowed his pride and wrote to Nate. The letter had taken weeks to write. T.C. was allowed to stay for only minutes at a time, and some days he wasn't allowed to visit at all. He sneaked in pen and ink inside his boot, and lined his coat with paper. Alex would write as much as he could, as fast as possible. He told Nate everything that had happened, in as much detail as possible, hoping that there was a clue somewhere in the story. He knew that Nate's mind would be full of questions. Was there a mysterious person who had asked Lilith questions? Not that Alex had seen. But then, he'd been so in love he noticed little but her. But there must have been someone, because a person had hated her enough to kill her—not Alex but *her.*

"Are you here?" Cay asked.

It took Alex a moment to come back to the present. His mind had been so into the past that he could smell the jail cell that had been his home for so many weeks. More than anything, Alex wanted to pull Cay into his arms and feel her healthy young body against his, to put his face in her hair.

When she seemed to know what he was feeling, to even understand, he made himself step away from her.

"You have your 'wife look' on."

"My what?"

"When you think of her, your eyes scrunch up into lines, and your body seems to droop. If that's what love does to a person, I don't want anything to do with it."

"It's not love that did this. It was—" He broke off because he knew she was trying to get him to stop feeling sorry for himself. "You mean your Abraham doesn't make you feel like this?"

"Ephraim. No, but his son does." With that, she left the clearing and went back toward the settlement.

Alex stayed where he was, but he was smiling. "Be at the boat at five A.M. and have T.C.'s trunk with you," he called after her. When she nodded but didn't turn back to look at him, he smiled broader. Yes, the truth was that he wanted her to go with them because he just plain enjoyed her company.

That he also . . . What had she said? Lusted after her? Something like that. Yes, that was a factor, too, but he knew he could control it. Later, once they got through this, and once his name was cleared, maybe they . . . He couldn't think about the future. Right now, all there was was the present, and he had to live with the here and now.

Seventeen

✣

The next morning, Alex had to work to suppress his amusement when, at 4:30 A.M., before full daylight, he looked up to see Cay sauntering toward them. Behind her came the twin girls carrying T.C.'s heavy trunk full of art supplies, and behind them was Thankfull, holding an old leather satchel and a big basket that he hoped contained food.

Alex looked at Eli and saw that he, too, was about to burst into laughter at the sight of this parade, but Grady was frowning.

"Yates!" Mr. Grady said in the voice of a commander, and Alex didn't know which "Yates" he meant. "Tell your young brother that from now on, he's to carry his own gear. We don't allow parasites on this voyage, and if he can't follow the rules, he's to stay here."

Cay stood by the side of the flatboat and didn't seem to know what to say. "They wanted to help me," she mumbled. "So I, uh . . ."

Alex dropped the ropes he'd finished tying and hurried over to her. "Say nothing," he whispered in his deepest accent. "A boy wouldn't explain."

"Right. Never explain. I'll add that rule to my list." She lowered her voice. "Along with rating kissing."

Alex knew she meant it as a joke, but he didn't smile. "Get the trunk and start working."

"Doing what?"

"Look around. Find what needs to be done, then do it." If she actually were a sixteen-year-old boy, he would have taken the trunk and dumped it in her arms. That Grady had reacted with shock that a boy was allowing women to carry his gear for him, showed Alex that Cay needed to toughen up—and she needed to do some work if she was going to pull off being a boy.

On second thought, Alex went to the

girls, took the metal chest from them, and held it out to Cay. When she didn't move, he said, "Take the bloody thing!"

She did, but she was unprepared for its weight of about fifty pounds. She staggered backward but managed to hold on to it even though she hit the side of the little building that stood at the far end of the flatboat. Alex knew her side must have hurt, but she did nothing more than wince. At last she managed to get her feet under her and stand upright, the chest still in her hands.

When the kid Tim started laughing, as though he'd never seen a funnier sight in his life, Alex wanted to hit him. Instead, he said to Cay, "You need to get some muscle on you if you want to go on this trip." He knew she could hardly hear him over the raucous laughter of Tim, but she understood his meaning and nodded. He saw her put the trunk down on the deck, and Eli showed her how to tie it securely.

Alex stayed busy securing their goods on the boat while Cay said good-bye to the three women. He was glad when he saw Tim muttering as Cay exchanged cheek kisses with all three females. As Alex had told her, Tim was one of those males who very much would have loved the attention of the young girls, but they never so much as looked at him.

At five, they were ready to leave. Alex had given Thankfull more instructions about the care of the two horses that they'd had to leave behind. About a hundred miles downriver was another trading post, where they'd leave the boat and get more horses to begin their inland trek. But for now, they'd be traveling by water during the day and spend the nights on land. If it was too dangerous onshore, either from animals or Indians, they'd stay inside the little structure at the end of the boat.

Grady let Tim untie them from the dock, and the four of them stood there for a while as the women waved to them. Cay started to wave back, but Alex poked her in the side and shook his head.

"How boring men's lives are!" she whispered. "You have to constantly work to keep yourself from doing even simple, pleasant things.

"Nay, lass," he whispered back. "We don't *want* to make fools of ourselves by waving at the girls."

"You're not—"

"Young Yates!" Mr. Grady yelled. "What's that bird?"

"I have no idea, sir," she said, shading her eyes to look up at a bird with a wingspan that looked wide enough to provide shade to a school yard full of children.

"Well, what do your books say?"

"My books?"

"In your trunk, boy! Aren't T.C.'s research books in your trunk?" He was frowning at her, his handsome forehead creased deeply.

"I haven't looked inside, sir, but it's heavy enough to hold Mr. Jefferson's library," she shot back.

Eli laughed but then rubbed his hand over his mouth to cover it.

Mr. Grady's frown didn't change. "I'm sure your mother finds your disrespect amusing, but I don't. Look over there at that pouch and you'll see some plants that I picked because I've never seen them before. Am I right in assuming that since you don't know what the birds are that you don't know what the plants are either?"

"No, sir. I mean, yes, sir, that's right. I don't know anything but the roses in my mother's garden. Oh! Sorry, sir, I wasn't trying to make a joke. I'll get the books out and look up what the plants and birds are."

It was Alex's time to hide his laughter. He exchanged looks with Eli, and they both shook their heads. If Grady and Cay were going to spend the weeks ahead arguing, it was going to be a very interesting trip. Alex thought that if Grady got so angry he sent Cay packing, he, Alex, would, of course, have to go with her.

As they started down the river, Alex felt that a weight was being lifted off his body, and as he glanced down at Cay, seated on the floorboards, her sketchpad in front of her, a dozen plants on her lap and beside her, he smiled. He was glad he'd not left her behind. If he had, he knew he'd be worried about her now. He knew he didn't trust even the supposedly glorious Adam to look after her properly.

"Want me to hold those for you?" She was struggling to keep a plant still in the breeze so she could see exactly how the leaves attached to the stem. T.C.'s drawings were as much science as they were art. She knew that in the best nature drawings, a person could see the fuzz on the leaves, count the nettles, and, most importantly, identify it by its Latin name—or see that it hadn't yet been given one.

Cay grimaced. "If you help, he'll probably say that I'm not working." She motioned her head toward Mr. Grady, who stood at the helm, looking out at the placid water. The St. Johns was well known to be a "lazy" river. It was wide, sometimes even three miles across, and its flow was very slow, and in what had been seen of it by explorers, its elevation varied little.

Alex looked back at Cay. "It's my job to get dinner, so that means birds and fish. How about if I let you draw whatever I shoot or catch before Eli skins it for the pot?"

"That's a wonderful idea."

The gratitude in her eyes made Alex shake his head. She was looking up at him through her thick eyelashes, from under the brim of her straw hat, and he'd never seen a prettier girl—or one more kissable. How could the others not see she was female?

"Mind if I help my little brother with the plants and animals?" Alex called across the deck to Grady.

"Whatever you need to do, do it, but don't neglect your own duties." He was studying his charts and didn't look up at Alex.

"There, now, I told you things would be all right."

"You usually make them so," she said as she looked back at her drawing paper.

Her words made him feel good.

Six hours later, he was beginning to wish he'd never volunteered for the job. At Cay's insistence, but much to Eli's disgust, each bird he shot had been different, and he'd turned them over to her to draw.

At first, she couldn't figure out how to

pose them. She'd leaned the first one against a tied-down crate and, as she'd been taught, she drew exactly what she saw. When she finished, she had a picture of a dead bird against an old board. It wasn't pretty.

Mr. Grady glanced at the drawing and asked her if she meant to paint the cooking pot next to it. Eli looked at her as though asking how she'd take this rough criticism, but Mr. Johns's never-ending complaining had prepared her for anything Mr. Grady said.

"Imagination!" Cay muttered under her breath and quickly sketched the bird as though it were alive and feeding. That she had no idea what the bird ate hindered her. Should she include an insect with the bird or a fish or a plant seed? "What does this bird eat?" she called to Alex.

"The curlew or the snipe?" he asked.

After a moment of staring at his back in disbelief, she used the strongest Scottish accent she could muster and told him in detail what she thought of him for concealing the fact that he knew one exotic Florida creature from another.

"A man must have a few secrets," he said as he brought down another bird for her to draw.

An hour later, she hissed at him, "Just hold it still. How can I draw it if you don't keep it from flapping about?"

"If I could wring the bloody thing's neck, it would stop trying to get away," he said under his breath. On his lap was one of half a dozen birds he'd shot that morning, but he'd only winged this one, and it was very much alive. Who could believe that a bird could be so strong? When it first woke up in Alex's arms and immediately began trying to free itself, taking skin off Alex's hands and arms in the process, he'd started to silence it, but Cay had stopped him.

"It's too beautiful to kill and certainly too lovely to eat. Just let me draw it, then you can release it."

"You wouldn't think it was beautiful if you—Ow! Here, you hold it and I'll draw it."

"I won the contest, remember?" She

had to keep her head down to hide her smile.

When Mr. Grady came over, Alex was sure he'd be on his side. But Grady said to Cay, "I can see that you're an afficionado of Mr. Bartram."

"Yes, sir, I am," she said firmly.

"Carry on, then," Grady said as he went back to his maps and charts.

Cay looked at Alex as he pulled his head back just in time to keep the angry bird from taking a beak to his jaw. "Don't even bother to ask me who Mr. Bartram is. I have no idea. So why do people say you're a magician with animals?"

Narrowing his eyes at her, Alex mumbled about her ingratitude. It was one thing to spend time and effort gentling an animal that was about to run a race, but this was a bird that . . . that was frightened half to death. For a moment he was ashamed that he'd forgotten all he'd learned as a child. With a childhood as lonely as his, he'd had to turn to the animals around him for companionship.

He looked down at the bird he held

firmly in his arms and gave all his attention to it. Long ago, he'd found that if he closed out the external world from his mind, it often did the same thing to whatever animal he was touching. He felt the bird's wildly beating heart begin to quieten, and as it did, Alex touched its head. The feathers were warm and smooth, and he worked with his mind to project peace to the creature. His mother used to say that the gift Alex had inherited from her family extended to what he could make animals feel.

Slowly, the bird began to relax and stop fighting.

When it was still, Alex looked up and saw that the other passengers were watching him.

"How did you do that?" Cay whispered.

Alex shrugged, his hand never stopping as he stroked the wings of the big bird.

She looked at the nearest person, who happened to be Tim, to ask if he'd seen it, but the boy turned away. When she caught Eli's eyes, the older man said, "I guess we won't be eating that bird tonight."

"No, I think he's going to marry her," Cay said with a sigh. She sounded so much like a lovesick female that both Eli and Mr. Grady laughed.

Alex shook his head in warning, but he, too, was smiling. "Would you get on with your drawing now before her mate comes and wakes her up?"

Cay started sketching as quickly as she could. These weren't finished drawings by any means, but she needed to get the details down now. "How do you know it isn't a male?"

"Do you insult me?" Alex asked, and he sounded so genuinely offended that she laughed.

"You two should speak English," Tim said.

"So you can eavesdrop?" Cay asked.

"So the captain will know what to tell you not to do," he shot back at her, then laughed, obviously thinking he'd said something witty.

Cay said a Scottish slang word that made Alex tell her to keep her mouth closed. He sounded shocked.

While she worked, she told him, "I want to do what Uncle T.C. does and show the birds in their natural state. When you hand them to me dead, I draw them so they look lifeless, but if I could put a bug or a plant near them, they'd look more alive."

"Why don't you put down your pen and *look* at where you are?"

"I can't. Mr. Grady will—"

"When he sees how good your drawings are, I'm sure he'll do nothing but praise you," Alex said, but he wasn't sure that was true. From the moment they'd left the dock, Grady had been the stern captain of the ship. You would have thought they were a crew aboard a frigate. And Grady seemed to want everything they saw recorded, and Cay wanted to oblige him. Alex thought that it was a wonder Grady hadn't arrived with half a dozen artists. "He could afford them," Alex said under his breath, and even he realized that some of his bitterness at the rich people he'd thought of as his friends had been transferred to Grady.

"What did you say?"

"Nothing, lass. I—"

She gave him a sharp look. Obviously, she'd heard what he said and knew who he meant.

"Sorry, it was a slip. I promise I won't do it again if you'll come with me and look at this place. It's beautiful."

Cay gave a glance to Mr. Grady, but he seemed to be absorbed in the papers set on a little table and was ignoring all of them. When Cay tried to get up, she found her legs had gone to sleep, and she tumbled against Alex when she stood up. Her hands landed on his chest, and for a moment she left them there. She could feel the muscles under his shirt. "You've gained some weight since I met you."

Alex put his hands on her shoulders and set her a foot away from him. "Now's not the time for that." He looked about quickly, to see if anyone had seen her, but they were all busy with other things.

"I was just concerned for your health. What have you been eating that's made you put on weight?"

"I've been trying to keep up with your

appetite, is all. And Thankfull made a few meals for me."

"Thankfull cooked for you?" They were walking the few steps to the end of the boat.

"Aye, and what's wrong with that? She made meals for you, didn't she?"

"Yes, but I was staying in her boardinghouse, and paying for her services. Did you pay her?"

He smiled down at her. "If I didn't know better, I'd think you were jealous. No, I didn't pay her in money, but I had to pay her in endless stories of T.C. The woman wanted me to tell her everything, down to what the man had for breakfast."

"But of course you didn't know because you were—" His look cut her off from saying the word *jail.*

"Would you please stop talking and look about you? You can't go the whole trip and see nothing but dead birds."

"I . . ." She trailed off because she did look around her. Before them lay a wide, placid river, the surface barely breaking as it flowed toward them. Alex told her they were going "upriver" against the current, as they went south.

"It's like the Nile, in that it flows north," she said, and asked him how he knew so much about this place.

"While you were sneaking into the bushes and kissing the girls, I was in the trading post asking questions. Buy a man a beer and he'll tell you stories all night."

"Is that how you learned the names of the birds?"

"No. I spent the nights awake reading the books in T.C.'s chest. Thankfull lent them to me."

She thought it was interesting that Thankfull had refused to open the chest for a man as young as Cay, but she'd lent the books inside to Alex. Jealousy was a new emotion for her, but she suddenly had an idea what it felt like.

Cay looked back at the water. Along the banks were overhanging trees, their branches draping down into the water. White birds with long, skinny necks stood at the edges. "I want to draw those," she said.

"You'll get your chance."

An eagle flew overhead, then a bird Alex said was called an osprey. "Yes, I know. You want to draw it."

Fish were jumping in the water, and she went onto her hands and knees to see what she could. Alex hadn't brought her any fish yet. She saw something just below the water and put her fingertips down to it as she turned to look up at Alex. "Maybe you can catch us some fish for tonight, so I could—"

Suddenly, Alex grabbed her under the arms and pulled her back. In front of them, the head of a prehistoric-looking creature came out of the water and clamped its long, ugly mouth down on the space where Cay's hand had just been.

For a moment, she sat still, unable to move as Alex held her. When he released her, her fanny hit the deck hard.

"Nearly ate you, didn't it?" Tim said loudly from behind them, his voice pleased by what he'd seen. "If you're dumb enough to put your hand over the side, I think you ought to get it bitten off. If it was your drawin' hand, we'd have to throw you over 'cause what else can you do? Can't lift even the lightest thing." He stood back on his heels and smiled down at her in triumph.

"Well, *I* can lift a great many things," Alex said, glaring at the boy who, tall as he was, was still an inch or two shorter than Alex, and many pounds lighter.

"I was only havin' a bit of fun with him," Tim said. "It's always scary when you see your first gator."

"And how many have you seen, boy?" Eli asked.

"More than he has," Tim muttered, looking at both men, as they seemed to have unfairly ganged up on him.

Cay was still in a stupor, still looking at the end of the boat where the alligator had come up out of the water.

Alex bent down to her ear. "Grady is coming, so get hold of yourself and whatever you do, *don't cry.* Hear me?"

She managed to nod.

"Did he nick you?" Mr. Grady asked, his voice sounding concerned.

Cay drew in her breath and started to stand up. Alex, behind her, managed to conceal that his hand was on her back and he was helping her to stay standing.

"Did he get me?" she asked. "I should think not, sir. Better to ask if I slit his throat with my knife."

"The knife you have in your hand there?"

Cay looked down at her right hand and saw that she hadn't let go of her pen; fear had made her grip it harder. She was holding a long quill pen, feathers intact, the tip covered in ink. It wasn't exactly a weapon that would hold up against an alligator. "Ink in their noses chokes them," she said as she felt Alex's strong hand on her back to keep her from falling down in fear.

Mr. Grady didn't laugh. Instead, he frowned at Alex. "I think you better watch your young brother more closely and make sure we have no more close calls like that one."

"I couldn't agree more," Alex said.

Eighteen

After her bout with the alligator, Cay was more subdued. Adam had once commented that she'd been protected all her life and had no idea what the real world was like. At the time, she'd thought it wasn't very nice of him to have said it, but she was beginning to understand what he meant. Not all the world was like her home, with brothers and a father to take care of her, and a mother who was always there to help her figure out what she should do about any problem.

In a way, the near attack made her feel as though she'd been given a second chance at life. If Alex hadn't been there, if he hadn't reacted so quickly, she would have been bitten by the alligator and pulled down under the water with him. She would never have lived through it.

For the rest of the day, she paid more attention to everything around her, from her fellow travelers to the birds overhead. As they went deeper south, she began to hear noises that she hadn't noticed before. There was an underlying roar beneath the ever-present calls of thousands of birds that were growing louder by the minute. It sounded like a huge stone being slowly pulled over a rock bed. It was eerie and fascinating at the same time.

She glanced up from her drawing of one of the plants Mr. Grady had given her. Eli was cleaning birds for their dinner tonight, which they all looked forward to, as they'd eaten only bread and cheese all day. "What's that sound?"

"The deep one?"

She nodded.

"Alligators. They're settling in for the night."

Cay tried to stamp down the terror she felt growing inside her. "There must be a lot of them to make that much noise."

"Hundreds," Eli said. "Thousands. They climb all over each other. You'll see. But don't worry about them. We'll camp away from them."

Cay could only nod, as words didn't want to come out.

Mr. Grady called a halt to their travel well before sundown, and they poled the flatboat to the shore. Cay could see the remains of what looked to be an old campfire on a little hill up from the shore. "Someone's been here before," she said to Alex as he ran about the boat tying ropes to anchor it.

"People have been here," he said, "but later we'll go places others haven't gone. Are you looking forward to that?"

All Cay seemed able to remember was the alligator's ugly head coming up out of the water at her. Its teeth could be seen clearly, and they looked very sharp.

Alex saw her fear. "Come on. Don't just stand there, pick up those boxes and get them ashore. Do you think you get a free ride just because you can draw pretty pictures?"

"I'll have you know—" Cay began, but

she stopped when she saw Mr. Grady looking at her. She took the heavy box Alex handed her and carried it up the hill to the campsite.

For the next hour, she was too busy to think. Alex and she put up one of the three tents, one for them, one for Eli and Tim, and the last one for Mr. Grady. She carried box after box from the boat up the hill until her legs were aching and the muscles in her arms were so weak they were shaking.

"You'll get used to it," Alex said as he slapped her on the shoulder so hard she nearly fell down.

"Or I'll die," she said after him, but when she saw Tim smirking at her, she picked up the heaviest crate that Eli had set out for them and lugged it up the hill. When all the chests were in place and the tents up, she wanted to lie down and eat half a bushel of food, but no, there was more work to be done. Alex informed her that they had to help Eli prepare dinner.

"But he has the birds. He's been cleaning them for hours."

"See those trees through there?"

Wearily, her hand on the small of her back, she looked through the shrubs toward whatever Alex was pointing at. Looking like something out of a child's drawing, she saw small trees hanging with bright, round fruit. "Oranges!" she said to Alex in wonder. She'd only eaten two in her life, as they were a rare and precious commodity, usually given only as a treat at Christmas. "Are they real?"

"Very. If you hadn't spent so much time kissing the girls back at the boardinghouse, I could have shown you orange trees around there."

"If you hadn't spent so much time rummaging through Thankfull's books and flirting with her, I could have gone with you."

Alex laughed. "Are you coming or not?"

"Where?"

"To pick oranges. Eli wants to cook those birds in the juice of them."

"That sounds wonderful. I think I could eat them all."

When there were several large trees between them and the others in the camp, Alex reached out his hand to her.

"Come on, slowpoke, let's go harvesting in an orange grove."

She took his hand, put her other one to her hat, and they took off running across a field of tall grass to reach the little stand of trees. "They smell heavenly," she said as she released his hand and twirled about.

"Better than jasmine oil?" He was pulling down pieces of fruit and putting them in the big sack he'd brought.

"I'm not sure anything smells that good." She put an orange to her nose and inhaled its fragrance.

"Was it the jasmine or my hair that you liked so much?"

"The fact that you were clean was an olfactory delight."

"I dare you to say that to Tim. He'd probably throw you over the side of the boat."

"Why does that bratty little boy dislike me so much?"

"Because of that."

"Of what?"

"Just what you said. You think of him as a little boy and you treat him as one."

Leaning against a tree trunk, Cay

looked up at the beautiful fruit. "I don't treat him any way at all. I rarely look at him."

"Exactly. He thinks he's older than you, and therefore more experienced, so you should look up to him as being wiser."

"He isn't wiser than my dolls at home."

"No," Alex said as she reached for an orange from a tree. "Not those. Eli said that the ones that grow on the south side of the trees are sweeter. Did you know that oranges aren't native to Florida but were brought here by some Spanish explorer?"

"Let me guess: Ponce de Leon."

"Right. Now that you've had your history lesson for today, how about if we sit down and do nothing for a while? I don't know about you, but it's been a long day."

Cay couldn't help smiling, as she knew he was doing this for her. She couldn't tell that he was tired at all, but she had done more heavy lifting today than she had in the rest of her life total. Alex chose a spot of soft grass under a tree where they could see for a long way over hills and a meadow heavy with flowers.

"Beautiful," she said as he handed her an orange that he'd cut a hole in the top of. "What do I do with it?"

He showed her how to squeeze the fruit, and suck the juice from the hole.

"Delicious," she said, "and I feel downright decadent eating an entire orange by myself. I wish I could take a wagonload of these home to Edilean with me. I'd give them out to all the children and even the adults."

"What about Michael and Abraham? And the other one?"

Cay had to think for a moment. "Benjamin." She had juice running down her chin, and her orange was dry. Alex handed her another one that he'd cut a hole in.

"The gambler?"

"He is, isn't he?" She and Alex were sitting close beside each other, and as she reached for a third orange, her arm crossed his chest. She hadn't been thinking of the kiss they'd exchanged, but when she looked into his eyes, all tiredness left her. One second she was sitting there looking at the scenery and the next, she was in his arms and kissing him. The whiskers on his face annoyed her, as she couldn't touch all of his skin, but she could feel his mouth on hers.

He opened his lips wider and when the tip of his tongue touched hers, she nearly leaped on him. Her body lifted up and she pushed against him, almost knocking him to the ground.

It was Alex who pulled back. "Nay, lass," he said softly. "I canna take too much of that. A kiss is good, but it can lead to other things that I know you don't want."

Cay fell back against the tree, her heart pounding in her throat. "How do you know what I want?"

He said nothing, just sat there, his breath coming fast as he tried to calm himself.

"Alex, you smell so good. There are oranges on your breath and I swear I can still smell the jasmine in your hair. You . . ." Turning, she looked at him with her thick lashes shading her eyes.

He gave a groan that was louder than

any the alligators were making, and stood up. "You are going to drive me insane, lass. Would that I'd never introduced sin between us. But I must say that you've taken to it well."

"Isn't that what the pastor says every Sunday? That we all take easily to sin if given the chance?"

"You have adapted better than most. Now, stop looking at me like that. How can I face T.C. Connor if I take you back to him heart broken and unchaste?"

She stood close to him, her hand on his chest, and looked up at him. "Would you break my heart, Alex?"

"There are other body parts that I'm more worried about breaking. Now go! We need to get this fruit back to Eli."

Smiling, Cay walked ahead of him on the little trail they'd made in the grass as they went back to the camp. Alex said he regretted introducing "sin" into their lives, but, whatever he called it, she was glad for his kisses. She just wished he'd let her finish one of them.

At camp, the others were waiting for them, and Tim had a lot to say about Alex and Cay taking so long to get the oranges. As for Eli and Mr. Grady, they said little, but Cay caught them looking at her in what she thought was an odd way. She sat down by the fire and watched Eli quickly and expertly cut oranges into quarters and throw them in with the birds, peel and all.

Cay was so tired she thought she might fall asleep before the meal was cooked, but she knew that Alex would wake her. As she began to nod off, she thought that Alex always took care of her.

But she awoke five minutes later as a mosquito bit her. It was followed by another, then another. She was slapping at her hands and neck, and even her face, before she jumped up and started waving her arms about to try to get away from them. Eli was calmly cooking and didn't seem to notice the treacherous insects.

"They don't bother me," he said.

"Try this," Mr. Grady said as he handed Cay a round metal container full of a thick salve. "Rub it on your neck and face. It should help."

She put some between her palms,

rubbed them together, and slathered her face, neck, and the back of her hands. Just the smell was enough to help relax her. "What is it?"

"My mother makes it," Mr. Grady said, shrugging. "Some kind of oil, with lavender and something else. If it works, I'll get you the receipt."

"Thank—" she began, but Alex cut her off.

"Our mother would like that, wouldn't she, little brother?"

"Very much," Cay said, looking up at Mr. Grady. The firelight made his eyes sparkle, and the long dimples in his cheeks were shadowed in the dim light. He was a very handsome man, and she couldn't help thinking about his family. He was an Armitage.

"You want something to eat?" Alex asked gruffly.

"Sure." Reluctantly, Cay took her eyes from Mr. Grady's—from Jamie's.

"One sin a day isn't enough for you?" Alex said in her ear when Grady had moved away. "What would your mother say?"

"My mother is a very practical woman.

She'd say that I could crawl into his tent with him if it got me married to an Armitage. It's the *criminal* she'd not want me to kiss."

As soon as she said it, she regretted it. All she could see of Alex's face was his eyes, but there was pain there.

"Well, then," he said as he stepped away from her, "you have my blessing."

Cay watched Alex leave the campsite and head out of sight toward the grove of fruit trees. She looked with longing at the roast birds, their skin dripping with a sauce made of oranges, then back at the pathway. She was tired and hungry, but she'd hurt Alex's feelings and she needed to make amends.

Eli solved her dilemma by handing her a tin plate heaped with two roast birds. "Take these to him," he said softly.

Cay remembered herself just in time to keep from kissing Eli's cheek in gratitude. Taking the plate from him, she headed back into the darkness after Alex.

"Why does he get first choice?" she heard Tim say from behind her.

"Shouldn't he be made to come back here to eat?"

"Sit down, boy," Eli said, "and tend to your own business."

Cay easily found Alex. He was standing under the tree where they'd sat just a while before. "I brought you some food."

"I'd think you'd be sharing it with Armitage."

Cay sat down on the ground at his feet, tore off a bird leg, and began to eat. "This is wonderful. Such an extravagance to eat all the oranges we want. Do you think we'll be sick of them by the end of this journey?" When Alex didn't answer, she said, "What is it that bothers you so much about him?"

"Nothing about *him* bothers me. It's you."

"What did I do?"

Alex sat down across from her and began to eat. "It's the money."

"That he has it?"

"No," Alex said. "It's that you're willing to marry for money."

"You did," she said and braced herself for his anger, but it didn't come.

"No, I didn't. Lilith wasn't rich like everyone thought she was."

"Please tell me about it," Cay said.

"Lilith was the paid companion of a hate-filled, rich, old woman named Annia Underwood. The old hag had run even the greediest of her relatives off, so she had no one. But she didn't want all of Charleston to know that, so she hired Lilith to work for her, but she told the town that Lilith was her grand-niece."

"Was she nice to your wife?"

"Not at all, but Lilith took it until she met me. I said a few things to the old woman that made her stand back a bit. She was angry that Lilith was going to leave her to live with me after the wedding, which, by the way, *I* paid for."

"How angry? Enough to commit murder?"

"If she'd had anyone killed, it would have been me, not Lilith."

Cay looked at him in the darkness, the roar of the alligators around them, and said, "I'm no lawyer, but if Lilith wasn't wealthy as everyone thought she was, doesn't that take away your motive for murder? If you'd told your attorney—"

"Do you think I didn't?" he nearly shouted. "Do you think I didn't tell my lawyer all of this? He went to old lady Underwood, and she kept to her lie. She said that Lilith had been her grand-niece and was her heir and that's why I'd married her. She said I'd killed the poor girl to try to take away Lilith's in-heritance. She even said she'd warned Lilith against me—but at least that part was true."

He took a breath and calmed him-self. "The truth was that the old woman begrudged Lilith every crust of bread she gave her. The expensive clothes Lilith wore were to put on a show for the town, not because the woman was generous."

Cay thought about what he'd told her. "So this is why when I mention the riches of Jamie Armitage you run off into the woods and won't speak to any-one?"

It was dark, but she felt him relax. "Aye, lass, that's what it is."

"Did it ever occur to you that I speak

so sweetly of Jamie because I *want* to make you jealous?"

He paused, a bird wing on the way to his mouth. "No, I canna say that that thought ever entered my mind."

"Sometimes," she said as she wiped her mouth, "a person should look at what—and who—is around him now instead of always dwelling on the past." She looked at the plate full of bones. "I feel much better and I'm going to bed. When you come, would you bring the plates?"

She got only four steps away before he put his hand on her shoulder and pulled her around to face him.

"You always make me feel better," he said as he buried his face in her neck. "You take the worst things in my life and make them something I can bear."

"Alex," she whispered. "Make love to me."

"Lass, I canna do that."

"Today I was a second away from being killed. When I met you, you were one day away from death. Your Lilith didn't live to have her wedding night."

He put his fingertips over her lips. "I'm

not a whole man. What's been done to me has taken away something inside of me. I can't be the man you want."

"And I'll never be the woman you lost, so we're even." Pulling away from him, she took a step back toward the camp, but he caught her.

He took her in his arms, and she stood on tiptoe to kiss him. For a moment he looked into her eyes, searching them to see if she was sure of this. In the next second, his mouth came down on hers in a way that she'd never felt before. She'd had chaste kisses with each of her suitors, and she'd exchanged two kisses with Alex, but she'd never felt anything like what she did now.

His hands slid down her back, and went over her, touching her arms, the back of her neck, her hair. "Do you know how you've driven me crazy since the day I met you?" he murmured as he kissed her neck.

Cay put her head back and her chin up to give him better access. "You hated me."

"You looked like an angel in that dress.

I wasn't sure that I hadn't died and you were there to welcome me to Heaven."

"Alex, that feels so good."

He put little biting kisses along the sensitive cord of her neck, and when he felt her knees begin to give way, he bent and picked her up, his arms under her legs. Carefully, he put her on the soft grass and began to unbutton her shirt. Under it, she had the tight binding cloth over her breasts, but Alex lifted her and soon had removed her shirt and the cloth.

When his lips touched her breast, she gasped. "I had no idea . . . ," she murmured. His hands and his mouth seemed to be everywhere, and her clothes came off her body in one smooth motion. When she was naked, she tried to pull him down to her, but he drew back. "I want to look at you, to see the flesh I've lusted after for so long."

She was small, and her body was firm from her many days of exercise. He ran his hands over her thighs, over her stomach, and up again to her neck.

"I've never seen such a beautiful woman," he said.

"I don't look like a boy?" Her hands were at the back of his neck, clasped, her eyes on his.

Alex merely chuckled in answer.

Tentatively, she ran her hand over his chest. "May I touch you?"

"Yes," he said, his voice husky. "Touch me all you want, wherever you want."

Smiling, she began to unbutton his shirt, and when it was open, she slipped her hand inside. There was much more muscle on him than she'd thought, and it occurred to her that she'd made up her mind about his looks on that first night and hadn't changed it. She'd seen him as a thin old man, and they'd been too busy since then for her to notice that he'd filled out a great deal.

She pushed the shirt off his shoulders, and ran her hands over the hair on his chest, and went down to his waist.

"Ah, lass," he whispered. "You are truly beautiful."

All she could do was smile as he began to unfasten the buttons at the sides of his breeches.

When he was naked and beside her, she kept her eyes on his face and stroked his beard. "Is your face scarred under there?"

"Only my heart bears the scars of my life," he said and began kissing her some more. He nibbled at her ears, and went down her neck again. He kept on, his lips so soft and warm on her skin that she arched against him. "Please," she said. "Please make love to me."

His hand went lower and she gasped when he touched her between her legs. Slowly, he moved on top of her, his hands on her thighs, as he parted them and moved between them.

When he entered her, she instinctively drew back, and he started to move away, but she pulled him back down to her.

"I'm afraid I'll hurt you."

"'But what about *passion*?'" she quoted to him. The words and the tone were exactly what he'd once said to her.

"Is it passion you want, lass?" His eyes were sparkling.

"Yes, oh, yes."

"Then I won't hold myself back any longer." In a second, Alex went from being a kind and thoughtful lover to a man who was nearly overcome with desire for the woman beneath him. His kisses changed to being demanding, and taking from her what he needed. His hands held on to her with a fierceness Cay had never felt before—and she met him in kind.

When his tongue sought hers, she opened to him and she replied thrust for thrust. It was as though something had been trapped inside her all her life, and Alex's hands and lips were releasing it. Somewhere in her mind, she thought, So this is what he meant by passion. And she knew that none of the men she'd ever before met could have made her feel what Alex was sending through her veins. Heaven help her, but it was as though her blood actually was boiling.

When he entered her, he stopped her cry of pain with his lips, and the pain soon gave way to the pleasant feeling of his being inside her. Pleasant soon turned to something different as her body began to feel as though it needed something. She didn't know what it was, but she felt as though she might die if she didn't have it.

"Alex," she whispered. "Alex, Alex, Alex."

His face, with all the hair on it, was buried in her neck. She clasped on to him, her hands at his back, pulling him down and down. His thrusts became faster and deeper until she was nearly screaming with wanting him.

When he came inside her, Cay clasped her legs around him, and she could feel her body pulsating, as though great waves of sensation had taken over her body.

He held her tightly to him, but when he moved off of her, she couldn't bear to release him. He pulled her head onto his shoulder and they lay together, snuggled, their bodies sweaty. They could smell the oranges around them, hear the animals.

It was much too soon when Alex said, "We need to go back."

"In a minute. Now I just want to lie here."

"You want a honeymoon," he said. "It's what a woman deserves."

Raising on one elbow, she glared down at him. "So help me, Alex Mc-Dowell, if you tell me you regret this, I'll . . ."

"You'll what?"

"Make you sorry."

Smiling, he pulled her head down to kiss her lips and put her head back on his shoulder. "Nay, lass, I don't regret a thing. That was what I needed. It was . . ."

"The best you ever had?"

He knew she was teasing him, but he couldn't tease back. "Yes," he said honestly. "You were the best. Now promise me something."

"What's that?" she asked dreamily. Her thoughts went to his asking her to promise eternal love.

"That you won't drive me mad by asking me about all the other women in my life. Now get up, get dressed, and let's get back before they send young Tim after us. I wouldn't like for him to see you like this."

Cay ignored most of what he said as she stood up and began to dress. "Other women? How many women have you done . . . this with?"

Alex groaned. "Not as many as your tone says you think I've had."

"What does that mean?"

"Lass, you have to remember that to the others I'm your brother, so tomorrow please don't make the mistake of asking me about other women. And don't kiss me!"

"You think that *I* will be lusting after *you*? I think it will be the other way around."

"All I'm asking is that you make an effort."

"We'll see who needs a lesson in deportment," she said as she pulled on her shirt over the cloth binding her breasts.

"What a shame," Alex said with a sigh as he watched her button the shirt. "To cover up such beauty is a transgression."

Cay was trying her best to keep her anger, but she couldn't. As she looked at Alex, she thought of what they'd just done, and in the next moment she was in his arms, and they were kissing.

He smoothed back her hair. "It won't

be easy for either of us to keep up the act, but we must. Hands and eyes off of each other. Now give me two more kisses, then we must return."

"Three kisses."

After six more kisses, Alex took her hand and they started back to the campsite and the others. "And nothing can happen in the tent," he whispered. "We can't risk being heard."

"I promise I won't touch you," Cay said. "But I can't vouch for you, as you have murderously wandering hands."

"Do I?"

"Aye, you do," she said seriously.

Alex bent as though to kiss her again, but they heard a voice and he straightened up. With a regretful look, he dropped her hand, and they entered the camp.

Nineteen

❦

It was three days since the first time they'd made love, and Cay was sitting by the side of a little pond, her feet dangling, her legs bare. She was wearing only her shirt, and it was unbuttoned down the front. Alex was just a few feet away, holding long leather bags up to a little stream of fresh water coming from a rock. He was wearing only his underdrawers, so his upper half was naked. She looked at the back of him, at the way his skin played over the muscles of his body, and she wanted to touch him, to put her mouth on his, to do all the things they'd been doing for the last few days.

On the morning after their first night together, he'd had a talk with her about the possibility of conception.

"Then you'll have to marry me," Cay said.

The only sign he gave as to a reaction to this announcement was a flicker of his eyes. "But what if my name isn't cleared? You can't live with a criminal all your life. I may have to go back to Scotland."

Cay decided to display as little emotion as he did, so she made no comment on the fact that they'd just agreed to get married. "Could you bear living with my father's clan, the McTerns?"

He smiled at her. "Have you fallen in love with me, lass?"

She didn't want to say what she felt about him, but then, the truth was that she wasn't sure of her own feelings. All her life she'd known what she wanted and what kind of man would fulfill her dreams, but Alex was far and away from being that sort of man. On the other hand, she deeply enjoyed his company.

But then there was Lilith. As far as Cay could tell, Alex thought the woman was perfect. She'd had no flaws, not even any annoying personality quirks that mortals have. In Alex's eyes, Lilith was the epitome of all that a woman should be. That he didn't know much about her didn't seem to bother him.

Cay knew that if she and Alex did come through all this together, even if they married and had a dozen children, she'd never live up to his memories of his first wife. The wondrous, beautiful, perfect Lilith would always be between them. The woman he'd lost. The great love of his life. The woman he'd fallen in love with at first glance.

Cay drew the name Lilith in the mud by the pond with a stick, then pulled the stick across it, making deep furrows.

"They're full," Alex said, a water skin in each hand.

Looking up, she had to laugh. His beautiful body was nearly naked, but his face was still covered by a bushy, untrimmed beard.

"And what amuses you so much, lass?" He walked across the rocks to get to her, put the sacks down, and began to dress. Around them, the alligators made their deep cries, and the birds were settling into the trees for the evening. By nightfall, all the trees would be so full of birds you'd hardly be able to see the leaves. At the camp, the tents were set up, and Eli, Mr. Grady, and Tim awaited them.

"You and that beard. Don't you think it's time you shaved it off?" When he sat down beside her, she put her hand behind his head and kissed his eyelids. "Or are you hiding something under there? Maybe you don't want me to see how ugly you are. Is that it?"

"How can I compete with Grady?"

Groaning, Cay pulled away from him. "You aren't going to start that again, are you?"

"How can I not?" Alex said. "All day on the boat it's 'Mr. Grady this' and 'Mr. Grady that.' You never stop. And the way you look at him! I swear, lass, that today I nearly shoved the man overboard."

"Did you?" She was smiling. "There's no reason to be jealous. He's my boss, and I have to please him."

"Please him?"

"With my drawings. He likes what I do, don't you think?"

"I think he likes too much about you," Alex muttered.

"If he likes me but thinks I'm a boy, that doesn't say much for his manliness, now does it?"

"As for that, I'm not so sure they do."

"Do what?"

Alex stood up to finish dressing. "Think you're a boy."

"You couldn't think they know I'm . . ."

"I'm not sure. They certainly don't seem to mind when you and I slip away for hours each evening when I do my best to satisfy your insatiable lust."

She started to defend herself but instead laughed and stretched her bare legs out in front of her. "As for that, I think you need to work much harder. And more often. Yes, lots more often."

"I don't think I can," Alex said, looking at her legs. "In fact, lass, you've worn me out. What with the wee, silent ones in the mornings, the quick noisy ones when we slip away during the day, and the long, lazy ones in the evenings, I'm sure I can do no more than that."

"Can you not?" She ran her hand up his leg, curving her fingers around his calf, and going up to caress his thigh muscle that was hard and firm from a lifetime of riding horses.

When she got to the top of his thighs and eased her hand between his legs, he dropped to his knees and kissed her.

"I thought you couldn't do any more."

"Maybe just this once," he said, and Cay giggled.

❧❧

Three weeks, Cay thought as she looked up at Alex from the drawing she was working on. He was at the helm of their little boat, and to her mind, he ran it. At least he was all that she could see.

In the past three weeks, they'd done many things, and a great deal had changed. For one thing, Cay's body had hardened. Mr. Grady nor Alex, or even Eli let up on her physically. At the beginning, she'd had difficulty carrying the cases, but now she practically ran with them as they made their camp. Even the heaviest of the crates was easy for her to lift. At night, when she and Alex lay together in their tent, he'd hold her arms up and admire the muscles she was developing. "Won't be long before you really will be a boy."

"I'll show you who's a boy," she said as she rolled on top of him.

With the noise of the alligators, the birds, and the frogs all around them, they didn't bother to hide the sounds they made. A few times Alex had put his lips over hers to keep her quiet, but for the most part, they talked and laughed without fear of being heard.

At the end of the second week, they'd stopped at a plantation, and she and Alex had slipped away to explore. The big house stood on a hill overlooking the river, and it had been Mr. Grady's duty to spend time with the owner.

"Think his father owns this land?" Alex asked.

"Probably." She gave Alex a sideways look. "When my mother hears that I had time alone with an Armitage and didn't take advantage of it, she's going to skin me alive."

"Oh?" Alex asked. "Do you mean this skin? This skin that you're wearing now?"

She pushed his hand out of her shirt, but her eyes told him that later she'd be more than willing to do whatever he had in mind.

The plantation owner had cleared a wild orange grove of weeds and brush, leaving hundreds of trees behind. There was a big kitchen garden that was flourishing even though it was winter. "The heat and the bugs get everything in the summer," the head gardener told them. "Gardening is backwards here."

All around them were great fields of indigo plants, all tended by slave labor.

"My father agrees with President Adams," Cay said. "There should be no slavery in our new country."

Alex looked out over the fields. "I think that here it's a matter of economics rather than humanity."

After a hearty breakfast the next morning, they left early, and Cay was glad to get back to their boat. She'd come to like their small group—except for Tim. The boy continued to do what he could to make Cay miserable. Every time Mr. Grady praised one of her drawings, she knew she'd bear the brunt of Tim's jealousy. For the first week, she'd had to check her bedding every night to make sure the boy hadn't put something nasty in it. She'd found three plants guaranteed to give her a rash, two snakes (nonpoisonous), and six different kinds of disgusting-looking bugs.

Cay had wanted Alex to step in and make the boy stop, but he'd just shrugged. "It's what boys do to each other."

"Then I think it's time you males stopped it. Here and now. If one man makes the effort to stop boys from torturing one another, then, eventually, it will spread to all of you."

Alex looked at her as though she were crazy. "And girls are better? When girls get angry, they don't hit, they just stop speaking to one another."

"Yes, well . . ." Cay's head came up. "That's better than putting bugs in a person's bed."

"Is it?"

Cay didn't want to argue with him. She just wanted horrible Tim to stop doing mean things to her. She decided to talk to Mr. Grady about it, but he refused to listen.

"I can't get involved in spats between boys," he'd said as he walked away.

Frustrated, Cay decided to take matters into her own hands. She was going to treat Tim like one of her brothers, specifically as she did Tally.

The first time Cay had seen a snake slithering its way into their tent, she'd had to put her fist into her mouth to hold back her scream—and Alex had taken care of the matter. He put his foot on the snake, grabbed it just behind its head, and threw it down the hill away from them. The second time she'd seen a snake making its way into the tent, Alex had also captured it and thrown it out. But the third time, Cay didn't bother him. She just did what he did, held it with her boot, grabbed its head, and carried it down to the river, where she threw it in. It was only when she got back to the camp that she saw that the three men were staring at her.

"What?" she asked.

"That was a cottonmouth," Mr. Grady said.

Even she knew they were extremely poisonous.

Mr. Grady said, "Next time, call one of us."

But Cay didn't call anyone for her next snake, nor the next. But she did consult the books T.C. had in his trunk, and she made drawings of the most poisonous snakes and memorized them.

At the end of the second week, she borrowed a big jar from Eli and filled it with little, nonpoisonous snakes, and one night she dumped them all at the foot of Tim's blanket bed. He wasn't used to Cay retaliating, so he didn't find them until they were crawling up his legs. When she heard his shouts as she lay in the tent beside Alex, she smiled, and he asked her what she'd done to "poor Tim." "Played his own game," she said and began kissing Alex before he could ask more questions.

After that, it was as if a war had been declared. When she saw an alligator head in the water, its body missing, she lugged it up the hill, hid it in the bushes, and the next morning before daylight, she slipped it partially under the tent

Tim shared with Eli. When Alex awoke to screams from Tim, he looked at Cay lying peacefully beside him. "What have you done to that poor boy now?"

She just smiled.

Tim started to be more cautious in the tricks he played on her. He'd learned that there would be retribution for whatever he did to her.

For Cay, what balanced her dislike of Tim was her growing affection for Eli. They were days into the trip before she realized that she'd unjustly made some assumptions about him that were far from true. She'd thought he was a man who'd spent his life cooking for people, but no, as a young man he'd studied to be a lawyer.

"When I was an attorney, I had to deal with too much hatred," he told Cay one evening. "Everybody was screaming and full of hate, so when a client of mine, young Mr. Grady here, said he wanted to go exploring, I shut up my law office and went with him. I've never looked back."

Cay knew that if Eli had worked for the Armitage family he must have been a very good attorney. "So you didn't want a home and family, then?" She saw the light leave his eyes before he looked away and said nothing more.

Later, Cay asked Mr. Grady what that was about.

"He wouldn't like to know I'd told you, but he had a wife and child, but they died of smallpox. He never remarried."

After that, Cay looked at Eli differently, and when she saw him reading a copy of Cicero, she smiled broadly. She knew someone who wanted a husband.

In the third week, they pulled the flatboat half out of the water and began a trek inland to see some ruins that Mr. Grady had heard about. He and Alex carried survey equipment, and Cay put drawing paper and pencils into a bag, while Tim and Eli carried the cooking pots. Alex always kept up with his duty of providing food, so Tim had to carry the big turkey Alex had shot.

Cay couldn't resist telling Tim that the feathers would make a good hat for him. Her hint was that it would be a woman's hat.

When they got to the old fort that Mr.

Grady wanted to map, Cay sat down
to one side and began to sketch. The
fortress had been built by the Spanish,
and even though it was now in ruins,
one tower still had thirty-foot-tall walls.
After Cay had made several drawings,
she and Alex walked around and looked
at the old fort.

"I'd like to make love to you here and
now," he whispered. But as he bent to
kiss her, a big rock fell from the top of
the old wall and landed just inches away
from Cay. Alex looked up just in time
to see a flash of white, which he knew
was Tim's shirt. He took off running, and
minutes later, the forest echoed with
Alex's shouting. "It's one thing to play
tricks and another to try to kill someone," they heard him tell the boy.

Cay, back at her drawing pad, glanced
at Mr. Grady, but he wouldn't look at
her. It was his responsibility to bawl out
Tim for doing something so dangerous,
but Grady was leaving it all to Alex.

For three days after that, Tim was set
to cleaning pots and gathering firewood.

In the evenings, over dinner, Eli,
who'd been down into Florida many

times, would tell them stories from his other visits and ones that he'd heard. One story was about a tribe of Indians that had extremely beautiful women. "Better than anyone has ever seen," he said. "Their hair, their eyes, their bodies were all the most beautiful ever put on this earth. And the women were as kind and as nice as they were heavenly to look at."

He went on to tell about the first explorers who'd stumbled on them. The men had been hunting, got lost, and were on the point of perishing when they saw the women, whom they called the Daughters of the Sun. The women gave the hunters provisions and let them rest, but at sundown, they said the men had to leave. The women said their husbands were fierce warriors and would kill them if they were found. But the men didn't want to leave, so they followed the women back toward their village, which they could see in the distance. But try as they might, the hunters couldn't reach the village. As soon as they thought they were near it, it would reappear in the distance. At long last, the hunters left and went back to their own trading post and told their story.

"Over the years," Eli said, "many men have tried to find the village of the Daughters of the Sun, but no one has."

When Eli finished his story, Cay handed him a drawing of an incredibly beautiful woman. "Do you think the women looked like this?"

Eli puzzled at the drawing with wide eyes. "I would think that they did. Is this anyone you know, or did you make her up?"

"She's my mother," Cay said and there was longing in her voice. She liked where she was, but she missed her home and her family.

The next day they stopped early and Mr. Grady led them to a small Indian village. Cay didn't know what she'd expected, but the clean, orderly little settlement was not it. The children ran to them, and Cay wished she had some candy to give them. There was a big house at one end where the chief and his family lived and where they held meetings. Alex, Mr. Grady, and Eli were welcome inside, but Tim and she were told to stay outside.

The first thing Cay realized was that the Indians knew she was a girl. They had no preconceived ideas based on the clothing rituals of the white man, so they weren't prejudiced by Cay's male apparel. Laughing, the woman pulled her inside a small house with them, but they wouldn't let Tim in. They fed her corn cakes and a bowl of fresh milk. One old woman who could speak a bit of English asked her who her husband was. Cay said, "Alex," without even thinking about it. They nodded approval, but one woman said something and made a motion that imitated Alex's beard.

The first woman said, "She thinks he's a very ugly man and that you'd be better off with the other one. Much more handsome."

Cay couldn't contain her laughter as she nodded in agreement, and told the woman that Alex's hair smelled very good and that's why she liked him. This made the women laugh, and when they left the Indian village, the women followed Alex and kept sniffing his hair.

Alex put up with it with good humor, but he shot Cay looks, as though he was going to murder her. Eli and Mr. Grady said nothing, but when they got back to the boat, they exploded with laughter.

"What's going on?" Tim asked, looking at Cay. "Are they laughing because the women took you in to their house? I thought that was pretty funny, too. They must have seen that you don't even shave." He rubbed his own sparse chin hair with pride.

That statement made Eli and Mr. Grady laugh harder and Alex frown more.

That night when they were alone in their tent, Cay tried to coax Alex out of his bad humor, but she couldn't. "What bothered you so much?" she asked in frustration. "That they were teasing you? Is your pride so inflexible that you can't laugh at yourself? The women liked the smell of your hair. What's so wrong with that?"

"I would never get angry about women liking whatever part of me they care to, it's just that . . ." He didn't finish his sentence because he didn't want to alarm her, but every day he was growing more sure that Eli and Grady knew that Cay was female. Even more, he felt that Grady knew who Cay was. There were small things that Cay didn't see, but Alex did. On the surface, Grady treated Cay just as he did that idiot boy, Tim, but there were little things that Alex noticed. Whereas Tim would drop his spoon into the mud and barely wipe it off before eating with it, Grady always made sure that Cay's plate and utensils were clean. Several times, Alex had seen both Eli and Grady intercept some insect or crawling creature from climbing on Cay while she sat engrossed in her drawings. One time Grady reached out over Cay's head and grabbed a single strand of web that a spider was spinning as it made its way down to the top of Cay's head.

There were other things less physical that Alex noticed. Grady talked to Cay in a way that he didn't use with the others. It was a matter of tone and even vocabulary. What Alex knew from having dealt with the rich plantation boys in Charleston was that Grady treated Cay as one of his own class. Alex had seen that you couldn't enter that class; you had to have been born into it. For all that Americans liked to brag that the new country was a classless one, Alex had seen that it wasn't so.

What Alex wondered was how much Grady knew. To Alex, it wouldn't have been difficult for Grady to guess that Cay was female. She walked, talked, even reacted as a woman would. Even the pranks she pulled on young Tim were done in a female way. Had she been male, by now she would have punched Tim in the face.

What Alex feared was that Grady hadn't so much as guessed the truth about Cay as that he'd been *told*. He seemed to not only know she was female, but also to know she was of his same class, and that made Alex wonder if Grady had received a letter from her family or T.C. telling him of the circumstances. And if Grady had been told about Cay, that meant he knew Alex was an escaped fugitive.

After their visit to the Indian village, Alex became more cautious, and he watched Grady and Eli more closely. As far as Alex could tell, Eli knew only that Cay was a girl, but Grady seemed to know much more. On the personal side, what was worse—to Alex's mind anyway—was that Grady seemed to be making a play for Cay. Alex knew better than to tell his concerns to Cay. She'd laugh and tell him he was jealous, but Alex saw things that bothered him. At night, Eli's stories became longer, so there was less time for him and Cay to slip away. Four times now, Grady had told Alex to go ashore and bring back game and any unusual plants that Cay might draw. That Cay would be alone on the boat with them while Alex was trapped onshore was not something he could protest without telling the truth. It had been extremely difficult to travel on foot through the wilds of Florida, bring down a deer, carry it across his shoulders, and get back to them.

"We thought you weren't going to make it," Eli said the first time Alex came into the camp late at night.

Alex dropped the deer carcass and looked at Grady, but the man wouldn't meet his eyes.

Alex wondered what Grady wanted from Cay. It seemed obvious that he wanted to break the alliance between Alex and Cay, meaning that he wanted to stop their lovemaking. But why? Because Grady knew her family and therefore felt responsible for her? Or was he as interested in an alliance with her family as she was in his?

"You look like you ate something sour," Cay whispered as they went into their little tent together. "Did something happen between you and Mr. Grady?"

"Why do you ask that?"

"I don't know. Maybe it's because you've been frowning at him for two days now, and every time he so much as speaks to me I think you're going to hit him with an oar. It's flattering that you're so jealous, but I think that what you and I do together proves that you don't have a right to dislike him."

"Don't I?" he asked in a loud whisper. "When we leave here, who are you more likely to stay with? Me or Armitage?"

"Quiet, or they'll hear you. Mr. Grady doesn't want anyone to know who he is."

"You think Eli doesn't know? He practically kisses the man's ring."

"Jamie doesn't wear any rings."

"What?" Alex growled, his eyebrows pulled together so they nearly touched in the center.

"Nothing. I was making a joke. I was trying to cheer you up. What has happened to make you suddenly get so angry? I thought you were enjoying yourself." She put her hand on his chest and lowered her voice. "I've been enjoying myself a great deal."

He took her hands in his and held them. "And when this is over, that's all it will be."

"What does that mean?"

"When we get back to a town you'll reveal yourself to Grady, and what will you two do then? Confess that you're in love with each other and post the banns for your marriage?"

Cay gave him a serious look. "Every night after you and I make love, as soon as you're asleep, I sneak away and join

Mr. Grady in his tent. We have wild sex all night long, and by the way, he's a much better lover than *you* are."

Alex drew in his breath so sharply that the canvas walls of the tent moved. "You . . . you . . . ," he began, choking on the words.

"And Eli is the best of all," she said without a hint of a smile. "Tim's not any good, but I've been teaching him what I've learned from you three men. Mostly from Eli, though. Did I tell you that he—"

"Stop talking," Alex said as he pulled her into his arms and kissed her.

It was later, as they were lying together, sweaty and sated, that she again told him that he shouldn't be jealous of Mr. Grady. Cay entwined her fingers in Alex's beard. "Although, he is much more handsome than you are. Even the Indian women said so. Did you get that nest of sandpipers out of this mess?"

He picked up her hand, kissed the palm, and held it on his chest. "It's not looks that worry me. It's that Grady is like a duke, and you're a princess."

Cay laughed, but Alex didn't. "I haven't had a bath in a week and I spend my days hauling big boxes around. I see nothing princesslike in my life."

"I well know that even when you're covered in mud, you act and talk and move like a princess. Even when we share a spoon and a bowl of stew, you're a lady."

Cay knew she should be flattered by his words, but they made her frown. Something big was bothering him, but she couldn't get him to tell her what it was. The only way she could get to sleep was to tell herself that of course he was upset. He'd been unjustly accused of murder and they had no idea what was awaiting him when they left the secrecy of the uncharted territory of Florida. She finally did sleep, but she was restless, and so was Alex.

Twenty

❧

Alex shaved.

The next morning Cay needed the only washbasin they had, and when she saw that Alex was using it, she was too impatient to register what he'd done. "I need that," she said. The flatboat was loaded and she hadn't even washed her face and hands. As always, Eli had saved her some hot water, but she hadn't had time to use it because Tim had played one of his tricks on her that morning, this time involving porcupine quills from the little creature Alex had brought to her the day before. It was only from a month of wariness that Cay managed to escape being impaled on the sharp spikes. Tim had been smirking all morning as Cay pulled quills out of her clothing.

So now, Alex was further agitating her by hogging the washbasin. "Since when do *you* wash?" she snapped at him.

"Go ahead and take it," he said, but she could barely hear him as he had a towel over the lower half of his face. When she picked up the basin, she saw the soapy water and the whiskers in it, but even then she didn't register what Alex had done. Eli and Mr. Grady shaved every morning, so she was used to whiskery water.

With the basin in her hands, she turned away, but after two steps, she halted, and turned back to look at him.

Alex still had the towel over his face, and he was looking at her shyly, as though he was almost afraid to let her see that part of him naked. If they hadn't been surrounded by other people, she would have made jokes about what parts of him she had seen unclothed. "Let's see what you look like."

He didn't move, just kept looking at her, the towel held closely about his face.

Cay smiled reassuringly. "Don't worry,

I won't be shocked." Her voice softened, and she stepped closer to him.
"Even if you have scars under there, I
won't mind." She'd meant her words to
make him laugh, but she stopped smiling when she remembered that he'd
been in prison. She hadn't thought
about what they may have done to him
while he was there, but she did now.
Tortures that she'd read about in her
history studies—all of which Tally had
gleefully read aloud to her—ran through
her mind. She held on to the rim of the
basin until her knuckles were white.
"Please take the towel down," she said
softly as she prepared herself for what
she'd see.

Slowly and with reluctance, Alex removed the towel from his face and
looked at her.

Nothing could have prepared Cay for
what she saw when Alex's face was exposed. He was beautiful. Not just handsome, but as lovely, as perfect, as an
angel. His blue eyes, so familiar to her,
were set above a nose that was perfectly
formed. His lips, which she'd kissed so
many times but had never really seen,

were full and shaped like those in classical paintings. What was more was that Alex was young, less than thirty was her guess, and there wasn't a line or a flaw on his face. Compared to Alex, Mr. Grady was a plain-faced old man.

She stared at him in silence for a moment, unable to speak for her astonishment, then all the times she'd called him an old man, and all the things she'd said about the handsomeness of other men, came back to her—and anger began to run through her. He had lied to her by omission. She remembered how he'd laughed at her so many times, about so many things, but it looked as if that hadn't been enough for him. Since the day they'd met, he'd given himself the pleasure of knowing he was making a fool of her. How he must have enjoyed the thought of her humiliation when she found out the truth about him! And the worst was that even when they'd been making love, he was laughing at her.

Without a thought of what she was doing, Cay threw the dirty shaving water into his face, dropped the basin to the ground, and marched off. She didn't know where she was going, but she never wanted to see Alexander Mc-Dowell ever again.

He caught her by the time she reached the river and put his hand on her arm.

She jerked away, refusing to look at him. Cay stood there with her arms folded over her flattened chest and stared straight ahead at the water.

"What's wrong?" he asked.

"You know very well what's wrong." Her jaw was clenched so tightly she could hardly speak.

"Am I too ugly for you to look at?" He put his hand out to touch her shoulder, but she moved away.

She tightened her arms and her lips, but she still wouldn't look at him. "You are beautiful!" she said in a way that made the word sound like an accusation.

For a moment he was silent, then he said, "Am I better than Adam?"

That he was again—still—laughing at her, ridiculing her even now, made her want to hit him, to at least shout at him, but she wouldn't give him that satisfaction. If he could make jokes, so could she. "Of course not. And you're not better-looking than my father, either."

"How about Ethan?"

"Not even close."

"Nate?"

"Yes."

"I'm better-looking than Nate?"

"Yes." Her jaw was still clenched, and she hated that he was enjoying himself so very much.

"What about Tally?"

"Tally has horns and a forked tail."

"I'd better look."

"Look at what?" she snapped, and made the mistake of glancing at him. He was better-looking than her first sight told her he was. She turned back to the river. "No! Don't tell me. You mean to look to see if *you* have a tail. For your information, I've seen your bare behind, and it's completely ordinary."

"Is it?" There was laughter just under his voice.

"Stop laughing at me!"

"Sorry, lass, but this is the best conversation I've ever had in my life. When I was nine and a boy told me how babies were made, I liked that conversation, but this time is better."

"Well, I don't like it! I feel like . . . like Eve in the Garden of Eden."

"You mean you feel naked?"

"No! I mean that I can now see the truth. I thought you were older. I thought maybe you were Uncle T.C.'s age."

"I'm the *son* of his friend."

"I can see that now, but forgive me if I got a little mixed up. What with people shooting at me when I met you, and being near a murderer, my thoughts were a tad bit confused."

The laughter left Alex's voice and he moved closer to her, but he didn't touch her. "Lass, you must have known that I wasn't old. An old man can't . . ."

"Can't what?" She spun around to glare at him and blinked at the sight of his beautiful face. "Forgive me for not having your experience in seeing the naked bodies of so many men that I can compare them. Or your experience with the abilities of old men versus young men as lovers. I—"

"What about Eli?" he asked, his face solemn.

Cay didn't smile. "I hate you." She turned away from him, her body still held rigidly.

"Do you?"

"Yes! And stop looking at me like that."

"Since you won't look at me, how can you know how I'm looking at you?"

"I can feel it. You're looking at me in the same way that Ethan looks at girls."

"I am honored by the comparison."

"My brother is a good person. You, Alexander Lachlan McDowell, are *not.*" Without another glance at him, she went back to the campsite.

Twenty-one

❧

When Alex was fourteen, he had lusted after a girl who lived a few miles from them, but she wouldn't so much as look at him. One day he'd hidden in the bushes and jumped out at her. When she still would have nothing to do with him, he'd asked her why not. She told him that he was too pretty, that he'd never be faithful to a woman, so she wanted nothing to do with him. Despondent and angry at the unfairness of her accusation, Alex had gone home to his father and told him everything. Mac listened in sympathy, then said that women had ways of hurting a man that were worse than anything a sword or a pistol could do. At the time, Alex had thought that was absurd, but in the last three days with Cay, he'd found out what his father had been talking about.

For days now, Cay hadn't spoken to Alex or touched him. The day that he'd shaved, Alex had been sent away to hunt, so he hadn't seen Cay until that evening. While he'd been following deer trail through the thick vegetation on the shore, half running the whole way so he'd get to where the boat docked as early as possible, he'd planned what he'd say to her. He imagined conversations, all of them ending with Cay's falling into his arms and "forgiving" him for being handsome. The thought of what their argument was about always made him smile.

Sometimes his imagined conversations were angry. He thought of telling her how unfair and unjust what she'd said to him was. She would then agree with him and run to him.

Other times he thought of apologizing to her, saying he was sorry for not having revealed to her . . . And that's where he got stumped. What was he sorry about? When they were in old man Yates's barn, should he have told her that, by the way, under his mess of itchy hair he wasn't ugly? Or should he have told her when they were dancing in the store they'd broken into? Or on the night they first made love?

The truth—and Alex knew it well—was that he had purposefully let her think he was ugly and old. In fact, there had been more than once when he'd said something like, "Your young eyes can see better than mine." Or "You're younger, you do it."

And then there was Grady. If Alex were honest with himself, he'd been jealous of all the things Cay had said about Grady being so very good to look at. According to her, angels were jealous of Grady's looks. Or, in her words, "Jamie's beauty." It had been all Alex could do to keep his mouth shut when she said those things. Five minutes after they met Grady, Alex had wanted to shave. He knew he was better-looking and younger than Grady, and his impulse was to show her that, but something had held him back.

He knew what it was. He wanted to be sure that she liked him even though she thought the worst of him. Since Alex was a baby he'd had people speak of his looks. Women said what a pretty child he was, and men said to his father, "Handsome lad you have there." When Alex was older, his looks had caused problems with females. They seemed to either throw themselves at him or, as the girl he liked did, want nothing to do with him.

It was in the new country of America that his looks had brought him luck. He'd always believed that it was his good looks, combined with his skill with horses, that had let him into the rich society of the upper class of Charleston. And it was because he was there that he'd met Lilith. He knew that she would never have looked at him if he'd been ugly. That a woman of her extreme beauty was attracted to someone like him had always shocked him. Later, when they were in love and had been able to spend time alone together, she'd confided in him that she was poor, and little more than a servant to a rich old woman. She'd also explained that she couldn't accept one of the proposals from a plantation boy, because his family would expect her to have a fortune, but she had none. And she'd even admitted that, yes, Alex's good looks had been what first attracted her to him.

Alex had been so in love with her, so dazzled by her beauty, that he said he understood. At the time, he felt that he did. It was only after he met Cay and realized that she saw him as old and ugly, and as a possible murderer, that he grew to like the idea of staying that way to her. Whether she did or did not like him was based solely on *him,* on Alex, not on what she assumed about him based on how he looked. That she'd come to . . . like, if not love, him without ever seeing his face, had been wonderful.

Yes, great for him, but the problem was that it didn't seem to have been so good for *her.* So maybe it was true that he'd smiled a bit when she'd mentioned his age. And maybe he'd even laughed—inside, certainly not where she could see him—when she talked endlessly about how handsome Grady was.

And, true, maybe Alex had been so interested in his own side of it all, that he hadn't given a real thought to how Cay was going to react when she found out that he hadn't, well, been honest with her. The question now was how to lie his way out of it all.

All day long he thought of everything he could imagine to get back into her good graces. There were even a few minutes when he considered telling her the truth, that he'd made a big mistake and would she please forgive him. But he soon put that idea out of his head. Women liked men to be strong, and groveling and begging for forgiveness would never work. Although . . . he remembered that he'd apologized to her before and it had worked. But this was more serious than that time—and back then he'd not had the ultimate solution: kisses.

At the end of the day, when he saw the camp, he breathed a sigh of relief. Soon he'd be in the tent with her, and he'd pull her into his arms and make such sweet love to her that he'd never have to say a word. He'd *show* her he was sorry for anything he'd done to her, and that would solve everything. He'd make love to her with such tenderness that she'd forget all about what had happened between them. There would be no need for words, and certainly not for apologies.

By the time he got to the camp and had tied the deer carcass into a tree, he was smiling. No doubt Cay would be just as glad to make up the argument as he was. In fact, he'd learned a long time ago that he could use his looks to get 'round women. All he had to do was kiss the back of a woman's hand while looking up at her with half-closed eyes, and she'd forgive him anything. If he left her waiting for two hours while he ran a race, what did it matter? She'd forgive him. If he didn't show up for dinner with her family because he was arranging the next day's races, she forgave him. The most he'd had to do was kiss a woman's neck a few times. Neck kisses always made a woman forgive him for anything.

Except Lilith, he thought as he tied the rope holding the carcass up. Lilith didn't put up with anything from Alex. He'd stood her up only once, and the next day he saw her on the arm of another man, laughing at whatever he said, and she smiled happily at Alex when she saw him. That she hadn't been upset, hadn't even seemed to care that he'd missed their date, had made him never be late again.

So now he knew that Cay would be angry. He knew her temper, so he expected some unpleasantness, but he'd kiss her back into a good mood.

Feeling confident in his thoughts, he removed his sweaty shirt and crawled into the tent. He could see Cay's form asleep on the far side. She'd put a roll of canvas between the two blanket beds, and even a small crate, but Alex silently moved them away, and snuggled down beside her. He reached his hand out, lightly touched her shoulder, and put his face to her neck to start kissing.

Everything happened at once! Alex realized that the hairy neck he put his lips to was not Cay's, and the recipient awakened with a scream of horror. It was Tim who was in the tent with Alex, not Cay.

The boy yelled, "What the hell do you think you're doing?" and nearly knocked the tent down as he fought his way out.

The others were awakened by the noise and came out of their tents. Grady had a loaded pistol in his hand, and Eli had a big butcher knife. When Cay came out of Eli's tent, she looked at Alex with an expression of amusement.

"He tried to kiss me!" Tim yelled, stepping away from Alex and looking at him in disgust.

"I did no such thing," Alex said as he grabbed his shirt and put it back on. "I was pulling a blanket over myself and I fell forward. If Tim wants to think that I was kissing him, that's his own fantasy. Maybe he's been alone too long."

Alex refused to meet Cay's eyes while he made up this lie.

"Tim, I think you should get back in the tent and let us sleep," Mr. Grady said.

"I don't want to sleep with *him,*" the boy said. "And I don't see why I have to change tents anyway. I was fine with Eli."

"You need to let *me* get some sleep," Eli said. "Your snoring is enough to scare the gators. Young Cay here sleeps like a baby, and I need the peace he gives me. Let Alex take on your noises for a few nights."

If Alex'd had any doubts that Eli and Grady knew Cay was female, Eli's words would have ended it. Alex looked at Grady, but he wouldn't meet his eyes. It was obvious that they knew of the fight—maybe not the cause—but they knew of Cay's anger, and Eli had given her an excuse to get away from Alex.

For a moment, Alex debated whether he should admit the truth. If they all— except Tim, of course—knew what was going on, why couldn't he say it out loud? But he couldn't do that to Cay. He couldn't admit that the two of them had been lovers. It wasn't good for people to know that for sure, with all doubt re-moved. And, also, there was self-pres-ervation. If they knew about Cay, they must know who Alex was. He didn't want to have to sit around a campfire and answer questions about what had happened to him in Charleston.

"You keep your hands off of me!" Tim ordered Alex while looking from him to Cay, as though he wanted to say that there was something "not right" between the two of them. Grady wouldn't meet the boy's eyes.

"I think we should all get some rest," Mr. Grady said. "And, Tim, if you want to sleep outside with the mosquitoes, that's all right with me." Turning, he went back into his tent.

Cay was smiling. She seemed to be enjoying Tim's anger and the look of consternation on Alex's too-handsome face. She gave an exaggerated yawn and looked at Eli. "Shall we go back in and get some sleep?" She smiled at Alex. "Good night, brother. I hope some bug doesn't eat away that pretty face of yours. It would be a shame to mar such pulchritude."

"Huh?" Tim asked when Cay was inside the tent. "What did he say?"

Eli was chuckling. "Nothing that was meant for you. Now go to bed, boy, and try not to keep Alex awake." He went into the tent after Cay.

When they were alone, Tim looked at Alex in warning. "You touch me again and I'll . . . I'll . . ."

Alex gave him such a hard look that Tim didn't finish his sentence.

With one more suspicious look, Tim went inside the tent.

Alex was tempted to stay outside the rest of the night, but a mosquito bit him on the neck and as he slapped at it, he entered the tent. Tim was already asleep, and Alex heard what Eli meant when he referred to Tim's snoring. The boy made a wheezing sound when he drew breath in, and it came out in a high-pitched whistle. At first, the sound made Alex smile. He'd been hearing it since they'd started the trip, but he'd thought it was a night bird. Now that he knew what poor Eli'd had to put up with for the entire trip, he wondered how the man had managed.

The next morning, when Alex got up as tired as when he'd gone to bed, he was no longer smiling.

"Best night's sleep I've had since

we started on this trip," Eli said as he poured coffee into tin mugs and handed them around. "Not once did I wake up from hearing whistles and wheezes." He slapped Cay on the shoulder so hard she nearly fell off the log she was sitting on. "I tell you, boy, you're the quietest sleeper I ever met. If I could just find a woman that quiet, I'd marry her in a minute."

Alex was sitting across from them and glowering at Cay, but she was ignoring him.

"Are you looking for a wife?" Cay asked Eli.

"I told Mr. Grady before we left that this is my last time on one of his gadabouts. In fact, I said I didn't want to go on this one, but he begged me. 'I can't go without you, Eli,' he said. 'Especially not on *this* trip.'"

Alex looked at Cay to make sure she understood the significance of what Eli was saying. It was as though he was admitting that Grady, somehow, knew about Cay, and about Alex, too. They were to reach the trading post in just three days, and there they'd get horses and go riding south rather than on the flatboat. Alex couldn't help but wonder what would be waiting for them at the post. A sheriff with handcuffs?

But Cay wouldn't look at Alex, didn't acknowledge his hint to her. Her attention was on Eli. "I think I have the perfect wife for you."

"Do you?" Eli asked, his voice interested.

"I don't think that now is the time—" Alex began, meaning to cut her off. If, by chance, they didn't know she was female, her matchmaking would give her away for sure.

Again, Cay paid no attention to him. "She's Uncle T.C.'s goddaughter."

"Miss Hope?" Eli asked, his eyes wide in wonder.

"Then you know her?"

"I had the pleasure of her company on one instance when I was with Mr. Grady. A very handsome young woman."

"Then you know about . . ." Cay hesitated.

"Her leg? I do. But have you tasted that woman's apple pie?" Eli was dousing the breakfast fire. "I always wondered why a fine lady like her wasn't married."

"Then I take it you haven't met her father."

"T.C.?"

"Ah," Cay said, "I see that gossip travels well. No, I meant the man who was married to Hope's mother, Bathsheba."

"You mean Isaac Chapman." There was no mistaking the dislike in Eli's voice. "He once cheated me out of nearly a hundred dollars. When he dies, the devil will be richer."

"What did you do when you found out that he'd stolen money from you?" Cay's voice was curious.

"I'm ashamed to say that I hit him in the face, but then I took him to court, where I defended myself, and I won. The judge made him pay me back the money, pay the lawyer's fee, plus give me another ten pounds for all my trouble."

"Well done!" Cay stood up. "I think you'll do nicely. Hope asked me to bring her back a husband who could stand up to her father, and it looks like you can."

"Isaac Chapman won't let me marry his daughter," Eli said.

"Yes, he will. After I tell Hope about you, she'll make him agree," Cay said. "Oh, but there's something special she asked for."

Eli snorted, as though to say he knew there'd be a catch. "She'll want a young, handsome man like Alex here, not an old duffer like me."

"Hope asked for a man who wouldn't fall asleep on his wedding night."

At first, Eli showed his shock at those words, then he laughed loud and hard. "I can guarantee that I won't do that. You can bet money on it that I'd never fall asleep while I'm in the bed with a strong, young woman like Miss Hope."

For the first time that morning, Cay looked at Alex and gave a malicious little smile to remind him that *he* had fallen asleep on *his* wedding night.

Alex's eyes widened at what she'd done, how she'd set up Eli just so she could end the conversation with a jab at Alex. That she'd use the night his wife was murdered was beyond what he thought her capable of.

When Alex saw Eli and Grady looking at him with an expression of both
amusement and sympathy, he was pos-
itive that they knew everything.

Since they had enough food for a
couple of days, Alex was allowed to stay
on the flatboat that day, but he couldn't
get Cay away from the others to talk
to her. His lack of sleep hadn't put him
in the best of moods, so when he did
catch her sitting at the end of the boat
with a sketchpad on her lap, he could
hardly speak.

"You're endangering my life," he said
through clenched teeth.

"By trying to find Hope a husband?"

"Only girls matchmake."

"My brother Ethan has introduced
three couples to each other and they
got married. You have odd ideas of
what male and female can and cannot
do." She hadn't so much as glanced at
him.

"What did he do? Find husbands for
the girls who had latched on to him?
Was that his way of getting rid of them?"

"Yes."

Alex had thought he was being sar-

castic, but the fact that he was right
startled him. "Cay . . ." He reached out
to touch her arm, but she moved it away.

"If you don't want anyone to know I'm
female, then I suggest you stop touching me. And you definitely should stop
kissing Tim's neck."

"I miss you," he said, and there was
genuine agony in his voice.

"And I miss the man I thought I knew!
The liar with the pretty face is someone
I've never met."

"Cay!"

She turned to look at Mr. Grady, who
was pointing at a bird with a long bill
walking along the shore. "Yes, sir?"

"Did you paint him?"

"Yes, sir. I have four drawings of that
bird."

"Do you know its name?"

"No, sir, I don't. I plan to give all the
artwork to Uncle T.C. and let him figure
out the names of everything. His goddaughter Hope has a fine hand for pen-
manship, so she can write the names
on the drawings."

"It seems that you've thought of everything," Mr. Grady said with a smile before he turned away.

"He's going to ask you to marry him," Alex said from beside her.

"You're ridiculous! He thinks I'm a boy." When Alex said nothing, she glanced at him. "All right, so maybe they've guessed, but Eli and Jamie are too gentlemanly to say anything. Tim still thinks I'm a boy."

Alex sat down on the end of the boat beside her. "That boy whistles all night."

"That's what Eli said." Cay hadn't let up in her drawing. She was quickly doing a watercolor of the curve in the river ahead of them, trying to capture it before the boat rounded the corner and the scene was gone.

"A person could squeeze that boy's ribs in time to music and make an instrument of him. You could dance to his whistles." He looked at Cay to see if there was any sign that she'd laughed at his joke, but he saw nothing. It wasn't fair, he thought, that she could make him smile no matter how bad the situation was, but he didn't seem to have the same effect on her.

"Lass," he said softly, and his accent became very heavy, "I didn't mean to make you feel bad. I didn't shave while I was in jail because I couldn't. And I'm not the kind of man to brag that I'm not so bad to look at. There was nothing I could say that wouldn't have sounded vain, and I didn't want you to think that of me."

"No," she said calmly. "You wanted to see if I'd like you even when I thought you were an older man, and so ugly you had to hide your face."

He smiled at her perception. "Aye, I did. Is that so bad?"

"Actually, it is." She turned to glare at him. "You judged me to be so shallow that I could only care about a man if he looked a certain way. *I* was put on trial even though *I* had risked my life to save you. *You* were a convicted murderer, but I judged *you* for what I saw, not what I'd been told. Now will you go away so I can do my work?"

Alex got up, and when he turned away, he caught a glimpse of Eli looking at him with sympathy.

❧❧

Cay punished him for the entire three days it took them to get to the trading post. She would hardly look at him, rarely spoke to him, and, more or less, acted like he didn't exist. She even pretended she couldn't understand his accent. Alex hadn't realized it, but for the entire trip he'd talked in his Scottish accent and she had translated for him— until the others had come to understand him. Even Tim, who was no great shakes in the brain area, had started saying, "Och aye, an' dornt Ah ken it."

But when Cay was angry at Alex, she coolly said that she had no idea what he was saying, could he please speak English?

It was Eli who stopped the fight that seemed to have no end. He caught Alex alone, away from the others. "Tell Cay you were wrong."

"What?" Alex said, looking up from the rifle he was cleaning.

"Your brother. Tell him you were *wrong.*"

"But I did."

"Tell him you were wrong on the day you were born and have been wrong every day since."

"But—" Alex began.

Eli shrugged. "It's up to you, lad. But to be wrong and to have always have been wrong is the only way to solve this. Take it from a man who used to want to be right at all costs. And look where I am today. Alone. Traveling with a bunch of men. My three brothers have eighteen kids." Turning, a load of firewood in his arms, Eli went back to the camp.

Not that Alex had any more doubt that the men knew Cay was a girl, but Eli's words cinched it. Alex's first thought was to go to Cay and warn her, but his next thought was that he was past caring what the men on this trip knew. If it would make Cay stop being angry at him, he'd go to her on bended knee in front of them and beg. "And tell her I'm wrong," he said aloud. He still felt that he wasn't fully wrong. Not totally, but maybe . . . On the other hand, maybe he hadn't been 100 percent in the right, either.

He felt bad for doing it, but he followed her when she left the camp to take a privacy break and waited in the shrubs until she was on her way back. When he stepped out of the bushes, she gasped.

"I didn't mean to startle you," he said as contritely as he could manage. "I just wanted to tell you that . . . that . . ." He drew his shoulders up. "That I was wrong."

"About what?"

"All of it. Everything."

Cay narrowed her eyes at him. "Is this a trick?"

"This is a plea to get you to forgive me," he said. "I lied to you, I admit it. It won't happen again. And I misjudged you. I did think you were a frivolous girl who'd never had anything bad happen to her. But I've known women who wanted me only for the way I looked, so it was nice to see you start to, well, to *like* me even though you thought I was old and ugly. But it was all selfish of me, and I was wrong. From beginning to end, I was wrong. Totally and completely and absolutely *wrong*. Please say you'll forgive me."

"All right," she said, and started to walk back toward the camp.

Alex caught her arm and pulled her to face him. "All right? Is that it?"

"Do you want more? You did a truly bad thing to me and I—" Alex cut her off as he pulled her into his arms and kissed her.

She had missed him horribly, more than she would ever tell him. She'd missed the smell of him, the feel of his skin on hers, his actions, his habits. All of it was part of her, and she'd had to keep away from him for so long that she felt as though she was missing half of her body.

She kissed his beautiful face and felt the sharp prickle of his whiskers on her cheeks. There was a trickle of sweat running down one cheek, and she couldn't help it, but she licked it away. The sweat and the very male whiskers on her tongue sent waves of desire through her.

"Cay, I've missed you," Alex said. "Don't leave me again. Please don't leave me. I need you so very much."

She put her head back, and he ran his

lips down her neck. She'd thought that she'd feel differently when he touched her because now she knew what he looked like. It was as though he'd always worn a mask before, but now he was at last fully naked, and she thought he would be a different man to her. But he wasn't. With her eyes closed, he was the same man she'd spent many hours with. They'd laughed and loved together, and now they'd fought together. They'd come full circle.

Twenty-two

❧

"It's sweeter now," Alex said. One hand was on Cay's bare shoulder, and the other was just touching the water of the stream.

"What is?"

"Us. You and me. What's between us is better now."

Lifting up, she looked into his eyes. Their bodies were naked, and they were snuggled together in the tall grasses about a mile from the camp. Tomorrow they'd reach the trading post, and a new portion of their journey would begin. "What if we never went back?"

"You mean never leave this paradise and never return to people and noise?"

Around them the birds and the ever-present alligators were nearly deafening. Smiling, she put her head back down on his shoulder. "I just have a feeling that something is going to happen."

Alex started to say some words to quieten her worries but decided instead to tell the truth. "Me, too. But maybe I feel that way because of what went on before. Just when I thought I had everything, it was all taken from me." What he wasn't telling her was that he had that indefinable feeling that he'd inherited from his mother. Something was about to change. Whether it was for good or bad, he didn't know. It had always puzzled him that he hadn't had a premonition about his wife's death.

Cay was silent for a moment. "Do you wish you hadn't been through all this?"

"Of course! The stench of that jail cell will haunt me for the rest of my life. What was said about me at the trial, no man should have to hear, and—" He stopped talking when Cay sat up. "What's wrong?"

"Nothing. It's just getting cool is all." She began to wrap the cloth about her breasts.

"I wish you didn't have to wear that thing." Alex helped her fasten it. "If it weren't for Tim, I think you could wear your ball gown and the others wouldn't be surprised." When Cay still didn't say anything, he turned her to look at him. "Something's bothering you, so out with it."

She wouldn't meet his eyes. "It's just that if all of . . . of what happened, hadn't, you and I wouldn't have met."

When she looked at him, he knew what she was saying. She was asking him if he wished he had Lilith back rather than her. But how could Alex answer that? Lilith had been his wife. True, it was for a very short time, but they had loved each other from the first moment they saw one another. There was something about that initial feeling of love that overshadowed the more realistic relationship that he and Cay had.

Pulling away from him, Cay slipped her arms into her shirt. "She was your wife and you loved her. I understand. Would you please hand me my shoes?"

"We aren't going to have another fight, are we? You aren't going to stop speaking to me again, are you?"

"No," she said as she kissed him

softly on the lips. "In fact, I don't think
I'm ever going to do that again. The
next time you do something I don't like,
I think I'll punch you in your old, ugly
face."

Alex smiled as he lowered his eyelids
and looked up at her in the way that
had made many women forgive him for
whatever he'd done. "Is that so? Old
and ugly, am I?"

"Warthogs are prettier than you. And
if you don't quit looking at me like that,
I'll put that yellow flower under Tim's
pillow, the one that makes him sneeze.
He'll be wheezing all night long."

Alex stopped his seductive looks and
lay back on the grass, groaning. Since
he and Cay had made up from their argument, she'd not moved back into his
tent. Eli had said to Alex, "I think it's
your turn to sleep with the boy," and his
eyes said that he wasn't going to give
in.

Alex didn't tell Cay, but he thought
Eli's stance had something to do with the
fact that Alex and Cay had made love in
the tent next to Eli's. To hide his embar-
rassment, Alex had turned away. "You

win," he said to Cay. "I can't stand the boy's whistles, much less his sneezes." Twice, Tim's very loud sneezes had frightened flocks of birds out of overhead trees—and the people below had been cascaded by a rain of feathers and other not-so-pleasant droppings. "I hope we never fight again."

"So do I," Cay responded, but her voice was less hopeful. She wasn't sure why, but she was dreading tomorrow. It wouldn't be their little group of people, but there would be strangers at the trading post—and strangers carried news. She worried that fellow explorers had been to the settlement where Thankfull lived and asked questions. If law enforcement people knew Alex had gone into the swamps, maybe they'd do whatever was necessary to get there ahead of him, and they'd be waiting for him.

"Don't look so glum," Alex said as he put his arm around her. "You could always go back to those men who asked you to marry them. Now what were their names?" Laughing, he walked ahead of her.

"Alex," she whispered. "They were all named Alex."

❧❧

"I know him," Alex said, and his breath was so tight that Cay could hardly hear him. They'd arrived at the trading post two hours before, but both Cay and Alex had hesitated. They'd taken a long time to adjust the moorings of the boat, and Cay had made the excuse that she wanted to see to her drawings. Tim ran off the second the boat touched land. After where they'd been, the trading post, with its half a dozen small houses nearby, looked like a big city. Mr. Grady and Eli had also paused, but after a while, they went ahead, but they walked slowly and looked closely at everyone who passed them.

After a couple of hours and no one had run toward them with guns and handcuffs, Alex and Cay decided to go into the long, low building that was the center of the tiny settlement. It was where men came to take the furs they'd collected to exchange for goods and cash from the trader. He would then sell the trappings to the men who came down the river, and eventually, the furs would end up on the back of some rich woman in New York.

But when Alex and Cay cautiously entered the post, Alex had turned pale, whispered, "I know him," and quickly left. The young man behind the counter looked up from the bird feathers he was counting—to be used on ladies' hats— and saw only Cay. He looked her up and down, as though trying to remember if he'd seen her before, then went back to the feathers. Mr. Grady and Eli stood to one side, mugs of cider held to their lips, watching what was going on around them.

Cay slipped back out the door and began running, looking frantically for Alex. She found him sitting on a log not far from the boat.

"Who is he?" she asked as she sat down beside him. She was trying to remain calm, but her heart was beating in her throat.

"Believe it or not, he's one of the rich boys from the race track."

"Did you take much money from him?"

"What does that mean? You sound like I robbed him."

"Some gamblers feel that way. I want to know what we're up against, that's all."

Alex looked up at a tree full of white birds and sighed. "No, he wasn't like that. His name is George Campbell, and at one time I would have said he was my friend. He was invited to my wedding, but he was out of town."

Cay didn't like to think about Alex's wedding. "Maybe he hasn't heard about what happened to you, or maybe he was your true friend and won't say anything when he sees you."

"Is there anyone in this country who hasn't heard about me?"

"To be safe, I think we should assume there aren't," she said. Her mind was swirling with things that they'd need to do if the man could identify Alex. First of all, they needed to stay away from him. They couldn't let the man see Alex for fear of what he'd say or do. If he did see Alex, or even heard he was here, even though no one was here now to arrest him, how long would it be before the trader, this George Campbell, told someone who was going north? It could be just a matter of days before they were found.

"I want you to talk to him," Alex said.

"*Talk* to him? To the storekeeper? Are you insane?"

"Probably. After I married Lilith, everything I heard and saw is a blur to me, but maybe if George wasn't there he won't . . . won't hate me so much." Alex took a breath. "When George left town, he told me he was going to miss the way I stole everything he owned."

"Nice man," Cay muttered.

"It was a man's joke."

"Then I guess I couldn't possibly understand, could I?" she asked belligerently.

"You aren't going to start a fight, are you?"

"How can you ask that of me? All I'm trying to do is—" She stopped because she realized she *was* trying to get into an argument. Better that than to face what was going through her mind. "What do you want me to talk to him about?"

"I want you to find out what he knows."

"You mean find out what he's heard about people searching for you?"

"Yes," Alex said.

"I don't know if I'm any good at lying."

"What would you be lying about?" Alex asked. "Tell him you know of me through my father. Isn't that the truth?"

"And do you think that Mr. Grady and Eli won't know who I'm talking about? Even Tim will be able to figure this one out."

"Don't worry, I'll get them to come outside. You just talk to George and find out what you can. And I'll be right there with you."

"Making sure that he doesn't attack me at the mention of your name?"

"Aye, lass, that's just what I mean."

Cay swallowed. "All right," she said, but she didn't like the idea of being a spy. She slowly walked back to the trading post and stayed outside the door until she heard what sounded like an explosion in the direction of the boat.

Immediately, Mr. Grady and Eli came running outside, and Cay stepped into the shadows.

"What's that fool boy done now?" Eli said.

She gave only a second to wondering if he meant her or Tim before she went into the cool, dark trading post where the young man was counting a pile of furs. "Did I hear that your name is George Campbell?"

"As far as I know, I'm the only one in Florida."

Cay started to smile at him in a way that she knew appealed to men, but she stopped herself. She was supposed to be a boy. "My father has a friend named McDowell and he has a son who—"

"Alex?"

"Right," Cay said, her face lighting up. "Alex mentioned a George Campbell, and I wondered if you might be the same man."

"That I am." When George bent down behind the deep counter to pull up more furs, Cay saw Alex slip in through the door to hide behind a cabinet full of men's shirts. "How is Alex?"

Cay had to hide her astonishment at his question. "Fine. When did you see him last?"

"The day before I left Charleston. We got so drunk they had to carry me out and put me on the boat. When I woke up, I was in New Orleans, and I had a headache that lasted a week."

"New Orleans? Is that where you wanted to be?"

"Yeah," he said, smiling. "That's where I wanted to be. So where'd you go to school?"

"William and Mary," Cay lied quickly. It looked like she'd yet again given away too much about herself. "So you knew Alex well?"

"Knew? You sound like he's dead. He isn't, is he?"

"No," Cay said cautiously. "Last I heard, he was alive."

"Glad to hear it. I had some good times with Alex, even though I lost to him in about a hundred races. He brought in this horse . . ." George gave a whistle and shook his head. "That animal must have been bred on another planet. It was faster than anything I'd ever seen before. But then Alex is a great horse-man."

"Is he?" There was a stool by the counter and Cay slipped onto it. It was nice to hear about Alex from someone who knew him before he'd been called a murderer.

"What he can get a horse to do, no-body else can." George looked up from the furs. "What happened to him?"

"What do you mean?" Cay tried to keep her voice calm.

"I thought he was going to marry old Mrs. Underwood's niece, but, obviously, he didn't."

It took all of Cay's will power not to turn around and look in Alex's direction. "Why do you say that?" she asked as calmly as she could.

"Because I saw Lilith in New Orleans two weeks ago."

"You what?"

"I had to make a quick trip there and back because—" He waved his hand in dismissal. "Anyway, while I was there, I saw Lilith." George bent down again and came back up. "I could have sworn she saw me, but she turned away. I ran after her because I wanted to ask her about Alex, but Lilith slipped into a building and I didn't see her again. I even asked people about her, but no one knew her." He shrugged. "Maybe it wasn't her. Maybe it was someone who just looked like her. Except . . ."

"Except what?"

"Lilith had this little mole on the side of her neck, just where it meets her shoulder, and it was heart shaped. You're too young to know what I mean, but I can tell you that all of us men used to fantasize about that mole."

"And this woman in New Orleans had this mole?"

"She sure did. It's what made me notice her. Everything else about her seemed to be different. Her hair was pulled back, and she wasn't as pretty as she had been. Don't get me wrong, she was still beautiful, but she looked, well, almost frightened. When she saw me, I thought she was going to scream. Her eyes looked like some wild animal's.

I felt sorry for her. Why didn't she marry Alex? They have a fight?"

"I don't know," Cay said, and her voice was little more than a whisper. "I don't know anything about anything anymore."

"I thought I was the only one who felt like that. I came out here hoping that if my father didn't see me for a while he'd forget about what I did in New Orleans, but from what he said in his last letter, I may have to spend the rest of my life here."

Feeling as though she were in a daze, Cay slid off the stool. She couldn't help but look at Alex in the shadows behind the cabinet. When he motioned to her with his hand, it took her a moment to figure out what he meant. He wanted her to get George to leave the store. She looked back at the trader. "Was that someone at the back door?"

"I didn't hear anything."

"Oh. Maybe it was just some alligators. You know how they are. Tim nearly had his leg bitten off by one of them, but I hit the thing on the head with a paddle and killed it with one blow. I tell you, if I hadn't been there, that boy would have died. I think Mr. Grady is glad of the day when he hired *me*."

George looked Cay's slim form up and down in disbelief.

"What's more, I—"

"I think I better check that door," George said as he hurried out.

Alex slipped out from behind the cabinet. "And you said you weren't good at being a liar."

She ignored his remark. "What do we do now?"

"*You* don't do anything different. You're to stay here with the others and go south, just as planned." Turning, he left the store. Cay was about two inches away from his heels.

"And what do *you* plan to do?" she asked him.

"Go to New Orleans, of course."

Cay wasn't sure, but there seemed to be a different step to his walk, a quickness that hadn't been there before. "I'm going with you." She had to nearly run to keep up with him.

"No you're not."

She stopped walking and glared at the back of him. "Good! Then I'll have weeks and weeks alone with Jamie Armitage."

Alex halted in his tracks, stood still for a moment, then turned around to glare at her.

She smiled sweetly at him.

"Meet me back here in one hour." He walked ahead too fast for her to catch up with him.

"You leave without me and I'll send you an invitation to my wedding," she called after him. He raised his hand, but he didn't look back at her.

Cay stood still for a moment. Lilith might still be alive. Alex's *wife* might be alive and living in New Orleans. The woman he loved more than life itself could possibly be waiting for him just a few days' hard ride from where they were.

Cay's hands made into fists. "I hope she's not too big," she said under her breath. "I don't want to have to take too much trouble to kill her." That said, she felt better, and in the next second, she was running. She had to get ready to travel, this time on horseback, and alone with Alex. She'd heard of worse ideas.

Twenty-three

❧

New Orleans, 1799

"How in the world are we going to find your brother?" Alex asked. The two of them were dirty, sweaty, and tired beyond imagining. But as he looked across his horse at her, he couldn't help but give a one-sided grin.

"I'm glad you see something amusing because I don't. I want to take a bath and sleep for about three days."

"I was just remembering the first trip we took together. You were exhausted after just a couple of hours on a horse."

"Couple of hours?" She rubbed her itchy nose with her sleeve. "You mean when you made me ride without stopping for a day and a half, and you left

me under a tree at the mercy of whatever scalawags came by? *That* trip?"

"Aye," Alex said. "That's the one I
mean. You've ridden much harder this
time."

"Had to, didn't I?" Cay mumbled as
she followed him into the outskirts of
the city. Even though it was well after
midnight, she could see lights and hear
music in the distance.

"What was that?"

"Nothing. I didn't say anything." What
she'd meant was that he was so determined to find the woman he loved,
that he would have ridden all the way
without sleep if it were possible. As it
was, that's nearly what they'd done.
From the trading post, they'd hitched a
ride upriver on a boat, but it went too
slow for Alex's taste, so they'd stopped
at a plantation and used the last of the
money T.C. had given them to pay an
exorbitant price for two horses. Alex
had ridden hard along the shore of the
river, always heading north, and Cay was
right behind him. They'd only stopped
every other night, and one time they'd
had what Alex called an "unfortunate"

encounter with a bunch of alligators that were hiding in the sand.

Cay would have loved to have climbed a tree to safety, but that would have left Alex alone. He shot one with a rifle, tossed a loaded pistol to her, and Cay shot another one. There was no time to reload, so they'd had to use knives. Running, they did what they could to escape the creatures that were chasing them. In one of Eli's stories he'd said that alligators couldn't run in a zigzag pattern, so Alex and Cay went back and forth as they sought higher ground.

When they reached safety, Cay looked at Alex, and in the next minute she was in his arms and crying from fear. He held her so tightly she thought her ribs might break, but she didn't care. She clung to him just as hard.

They didn't sleep much that night, and the next morning, Alex had to find their horses. Cay didn't think he'd be able to, but he did. When he returned, she ran to him and kissed his face in such relief that they ended up taking a hour to make love, then they were off again, this time staying farther from the shore.

That evening they'd had to stop early because both of them were asleep on their horses, and their animals were too tired to go any farther. Alex built a fire, so they could eat and drink before bedding down together. Cay had been thinking about her brother Nate all day, wondering what he'd found out about the murder accusation. As she and Alex snuggled together after making love, and just as they were going to sleep, she told him the story of her brother Nate corresponding with someone in Scotland for most of his life. "My brother thinks we don't know anything about it, but we all know. We're pretty sure it's our cousin Lachlan. He's only a few years older than Nate and they get along well when we visit. Want to hear a big secret?"

Alex hoped she wasn't feeling how hard his heart was beating. "Aye, lass, I would like to hear a secret. Just so it's something good."

"It is to us, but I doubt if you'll think so. Nate calls his pen pal Merlin."

"Does he?" Alex asked, trying to sound disinterested and sleepy. "And why does he call him that?"

"I don't know. If anyone were called by a magician's name, I'd think it would be Nate." She could feel herself drifting into sleep. "I wonder what Merlin calls my scientific brother?"

When Alex felt Cay's breath calm and knew she was asleep, he whispered, "Archimedes."

Two days later, when they reached the settlement and saw Thankfull, Cay said, "*Now* I know why she's named that. I've never been so thankful to see anyone in my life."

"I have been," Alex said. "When we got away from those gators and I saw that you had all your beautiful body parts, I was the most thankful person on earth."

Cay could only sit on her horse and stare at him. It was the closest he'd come to saying he loved her.

"If you cry you'll make streaks in the dirt on your face," he said.

"Why would I cry? Over something *you* said? Not likely!" She went past him with her nose in the air, but she heard Alex's laughter.

Thankfull ran out to meet them. "He was here looking for you both," she said breathlessly as she took the reins of Cay's horse. "He got here two days after you left, and he would have gone after you, but a messenger came with a letter and that made him leave for New Orleans."

"Who was he?" Alex asked, his voice tight and strained.

"Tally," said the twins in unison. They had come out of the boardinghouse and were looking as though they'd been through some heavenly experience. "Tally."

"He's the most handsome man I've ever seen in my life," one twin said.

"Me, too," said the other one.

Thankfull was watching Alex dismount. "You look somewhat better now that you've shaved."

"Is he really your brother?" a twin asked Cay without so much as a glance at Alex.

"He's so much more . . . well, manly than you are." Where once the girls had thought Cay was beautiful, now they were nearly sneering at her.

But then, Cay knew she was horrible-looking—and smelling. Her embroidered vest, once so lovely, was torn and encrusted with the blood of the alligators. Her stockings were so dirty you couldn't see what color they were, as was her shirt.

"Come in," Thankfull said, "and eat. Would you like me to get you some new clothes? I have a feeling that you won't stay here long enough to be able to wash and dry what's left of those garments."

"Tally had on the most beautiful coat," a twin said dreamily. "It was embroidered at the pockets with sunflowers entwined with vines."

"I liked the honeybees best."

"Tally said his sister embroidered it for him."

Alex looked at Cay in question and she gave a quick nod. It was hard to remember a time when her life was so calm that she could sit in a chair by the fire and embroider pockets for her brothers' coats.

"Food sounds good," Alex said. "And new clothes. As for the cost—"

"Mr. Harcourt left money for you," Thankfull said as she glanced at Cay.

She knows, Cay thought. Tally told her that I'm a girl and she's kept the secret. "Did he tell you of Uncle T.C.?"

Thankfull's face lit up. "Yes, he did. In fact, he spent both his evenings here telling me all the stories he could remember about Mr. Connor. Your brother is a very kind and thoughtful young man." Opening the door, she let them go ahead of her. "I have soft soap for your hair," she whispered as Cay walked past her. "And jasmine oil for a bath."

Alex heard her, and turning, he looked at Cay. All the stress and hardship, all the fear of the last few days fell away, and they began to laugh. One second they were standing, almost too tired to move, and the next they were hanging on to each other's arms and laughing so loud the twins came in from outside to see what was going on.

Thankfull shooed the girls out the door and closed it. Cay and Alex were still holding on to each other, howling with laughter, and saying incomprehensible things like "downwind of you" and "robbers with their smell" and "my hair never smelled so good."

Smiling, Thankfull went into the kitchen to prepare them a huge meal.

For Cay, that night at Thankfull's boardinghouse had been lovely. She got to bathe, sleep in a clean bed—Alex secretly beside her—eat cooked food, and in the morning she'd put on new, clean clothes. That Alex had made her get up at 4 A.M. had been difficult, but Thankfull had been there with a packet of hot corn cakes to eat on the way.

"He must want something very much," Thankfull said softly to Cay just before she mounted her horse.

"Yes, he does." She didn't intend it, but there was anger in her voice. Now that they were getting closer, the reality of Alex's urgency was beginning to get through to her.

"I heard some things about him," Thankfull said, her voice so low Cay could hardly hear her. "But I don't believe them. I don't think he could do what people say he's done."

"He didn't, and we're going to prove it."

"Your brother—" Thankfull began, then stopped because she was giving away the secret.

"It's all right. Alex says I'm the worst at being a boy he's ever seen."

"That's not true. When you were here before, I thought you were male."

"Thank you," Cay said. "I think." On impulse, she kissed Thankfull's cheek. "I'll do what I can to plead your case with Uncle T.C., but he's a stubborn man. Mother says he'd rather mourn a woman than have to deal with a real one."

"Your mother sounds like a wise woman."

"She is, and I miss her very much."

"You'd better go," Thankfull said. "Alex is giving us hard looks." She leaned toward Cay. "Who would have thought he was so handsome under all that hair?"

"I didn't guess."

"But you seem to have made up for lost time."

"We, uh . . . ," Cay stammered.

"The walls in this place are very thin. Now go, so you can do what you need to. And tell Mr. Connor that . . . that . . ."

Cay swung up onto her horse. "I'll get you two together and let *you* tell him." She looked at Alex. "Are you going to stand there all day?"

Alex reined his horse away. "So are you matchmaking again? First Eli and T.C.'s daughter, and now you're finding a wife for T.C. himself. Did it ever occur to you that those people can find their own mates?"

"No, I can't say that it did. Think one of the twins would do for Tally?"

Alex set his horse to a trot.

It was days before they reached New Orleans, and by that time they were exhausted, but reaching their destination made new energy run through them.

"So where do you think your brother would be? Asleep in some rich hotel?" Alex raised an eyebrow at her. "Alone or with someone?"

"I'm sure Tally is a virgin. Adam and Father keep a close watch on him."

"As they do you?"

Cay grimaced. "I was allowed out by

myself because I was believed to be the sane and sensible one."

"I proved them wrong," Alex said, and there was such pride in his voice that she laughed.

"I've never been in this city before, so I don't know where the best hotels are."

Alex looked at her. Her thick auburn hair had grown in some during the last weeks, and it had escaped the tie at the back. It was curling about her shoulders in a way that made him want to pull her off her horse and onto his saddle.

"We don't have time for that now," Cay said at his look, but she was smiling. "I think you've corrupted me."

"I did my best." His eyes were blinking innocently.

"I'm glad it's only Tally here, because if Adam saw you looking at me like that . . ."

"What would he do?" Alex asked, amusement in his voice. "Slap me with one of his gloves and challenge me to a duel at dawn? Do you think he brought his father's dueling pistols?"

Cay gave him a smug little smile. "Obviously, you don't have the right impression of Adam. But I'm glad he's not here."

"Then who sent the letter to your little brother?"

"Nate," Cay said quickly. "I think Nate might be here, but he's no problem. If I told him I'd spent the whole time in bed with you, Nate would just ask me to explain why I had wasted my time in such an unproductive manner when I could have been learning something."

Alex couldn't laugh too hard at what she said for fear she'd figure out that he knew more than he was telling. But she'd sounded exactly like his friend. "Bourbon Street," he said. "Let's try there first."

"You've been here before?"

"Cay, my sweet, I've won thousands upon thousands of dollars in this city. Follow me."

All the way through the old, twisted streets of the city, she smiled at his endearment. They went through the sleepy outskirts toward the light and noise that she could hear from far away. As the noise became music and grew louder, she found herself sitting straighter on the horse and her tiredness falling away. Through the entire journey she'd not allowed herself to think about what it would mean if they found Alex's wife alive. In a second he'd go from being an available bachelor to a married man. No, she liked to think about the fact that if they found his wife alive, that meant Alex's conviction for murder could be overturned. He'd at last be free. He could . . . What? she thought. What would he want to do? Settle down? Travel more? Explore more unknown places? They hadn't really gone into the part of Florida that hadn't been explored, so maybe Alex would want to go back there.

Or would he want to stay with his wife and raise their children?

If that were the case, what would Cay do? The idea of returning to Edilean to the three men she'd contemplated marrying was now so absurd that all she could do was laugh at it. Right now she couldn't imagine that she'd ever been that young, naive, and innocent. A couple of times on the trip, she'd thought about what her life would have been like if she really had married one of those men. Dull, duller, and dullest, she'd concluded.

Alex had told her that she needed passion to marry someone, and now she knew what he meant. It was true that he'd done a bad thing in falsifying his appearance, and that he'd laughed at her for weeks. He'd even encouraged her to think of him in a way that wasn't true, but she'd forgiven him. She knew without a doubt that if Micah, Ephraim, or Ben had done something half as bad, she'd never have forgiven them.

She well remembered what he'd told her once. *"You should look at a man and feel that you'll die if you don't spend the rest of your life with him. Your heart needs to leap into your throat and stay there."* At the time, she'd thought she could never feel that way about anyone.

And, too, now she knew about making love. Even the thought of it made her warm all over. Who could have imagined that something so basic could be so exciting, so fulfilling? Alex's hands all over her! She thought of the positions that the two of them sometimes got into and her face turned red. If someone had told her she'd someday be stark naked with her ankles wrapped around a man's neck, she would have told them that was impossible. *She* would never do such a vulgar, disgusting, primitive thing! Never!

But she had, and she'd loved it. She had to suppress a giggle when she thought of doing something like that with Micah. Alex had told her that some couples only did one position, and she'd laughed. Now that she thought about it, Micah would probably have done only one way and that one very quickly.

"If you don't get that look off your face, we'll have to stop and rent one of these hotel rooms," Alex said from beside her, his voice low and husky.

"Actually, I was thinking about Micah."

"You have more brothers? Or is he one of your cousins?"

"As if you don't remember! There! Look at that hotel. It looks like a place Tally would stay." She was pointing to a conservative, well-kept smaller hotel just on the outskirts of the noise ahead of them.

"That place for a rich young man alone in New Orleans? I don't think so. From what you've told me, I think it's more likely that he'd stay there." Alex pointed down the street to the three-story building that seemed to be the source of the noise. The windows and open doors blazed with light that fell out into the street. Men with garishly dressed women on their arms strolled about, their laughter drifting on the night breeze.

"You're wrong," Cay said. "For all that Tally sometimes lacks mature judgment, he is a good boy. He would never go to such a place."

"How about if we ride around the back and take a look in a window? If we don't see him, I vote that we get a hotel room, and tomorrow we'll get cleaned up and look for him. Or for both of them if your other brother is here, too." Alex had to work to keep the enthusiasm out of his voice when he thought of at last getting to meet his childhood friend. Other than his father, Nate had been the most important person in Alex's life. The frequent letters they'd exchanged had helped him through everything.

"All right," Cay said. "But we just look through the window. We do *not* go inside. I'll walk through a swamp full of alligators with you, Alexander McDowell, but I'll not go into a disgusting, immoral place like that one."

"Me, neither," he said seriously. "Never have been in one and never will be." He turned his horse away.

"Is it me, or are you getting worse at lying?"

Alex's laugh came back to her, and she shook her head at him.

Twenty minutes later, they were at the back of the big building, and the music from inside covered any sounds that they made. The high-pitched, excited laughter of women was underscored by the throaty, suggestive sounds from the men. Cay gave Alex a look that told him she'd been right about the place.

"He's not in there!" she hissed at Alex as they moved under the tall windows. Alex had to half crouch to keep his head from being seen.

When they got close to the front, he stopped and stood upright. "I'll look and save your delicate sensibilities."

"Having morals doesn't mean I'm delicate. I've had enough strength to save your ungrateful life about a dozen times now."

Alex didn't bother to answer her as he looked in the tall, brightly lit window.

When several minutes passed and he said nothing, Cay looked up at him. The bottom of the window was above her eye level, so she was leaning against the wall. "What do you see?"

"Several old friends. How do you think you'd look in a red dress?"

"Will you keep your mind on the business at hand? Do you see my brother?"

Alex pulled himself away from the window to look down at her. "How would I know? I've never seen your brother before."

"Why didn't you say—?" She cut herself off from saying what she should have thought of herself. "Lift me up."

Alex made no expression, but she knew he was laughing at her. "I don't think that's a good idea. A sweet, innocent boy-girl like you would be shocked by what's in there. Why, there's one young man with a woman on his lap and he has his face buried in her . . ." Alex made a gesture to indicate a pro-digious bosom. "Someone who is as in-nocent as you are couldn't possibly see something as immoral as— Ouch!"

Alex held his arm where she'd hit him.

"Lift me up so I can see, and stop making fun of me."

"If I did that, I'd have to give up talk-ing. All right, lass, just don't hit me again. With all the alligators you've been wrestling, your punches are beginning to hurt."

She narrowed her eyes at him as he put his hands about her waist and lifted her. She put her feet on his bent thigh and stood still to get her bearings.

The first thing she saw—the only thing she saw—was her brother Tally sitting at a gaming table, one hand full of cards, the other around the waist of a woman who Cay thought was fat. Or she would be when she removed her corset. The middle of her was pulled into a small circle while the top and bottom bulged out in a truly vulgar way.

"Anybody you recognize?" Alex asked, his arms around her, his face pressed against her side.

She could tell by the laughter in his voice that, somehow, he knew exactly who the young man was. "I don't know anyone in that place," she said firmly.

"Are you sure? I could swear that I saw a resemblance between you and one of the young men in there. But I guess it was my imagination."

"Let me down!" she hissed, but he still held her up. Bending, she tried to get below the level of the window, but Alex's strong hands on her waist kept her standing on his thigh. "So help me, if you don't let me get down, I'll make you sorry."

"And what would you plan to do to me?" he asked suggestively.

"Not whatever it is you have in your tiny brain. Let go of me!" She struggled against him for a moment, then realized she was still standing in front of the window. When she glanced back inside, Tally was staring at her. At first she thought he couldn't possibly see her, but when he unceremoniously dumped the woman off his lap, put down the cards, and got up, all while his eyes were glued to Cay's, she knew he'd seen her and recognized her.

She bent down so she was out of the window. "Tally saw me, and he's coming out here."

Alex immediately put her down. "What do you want to do? We could hide tonight and see him tomorrow."

"Hide? From Tally? Not in this lifetime. I want you to . . ." She looked around. "I want you to help me get on top of that roof."

"You want what?" He looked to the small building that ran along half of the back of the hotel. It was low, only one story, and the roof slanted sharply. "If you're afraid of him, I'll talk to him first."

"I'm not afraid of him and I don't want to hide from him. If you won't help me up, I'll have to do it myself." She threw her leg up to get on top of a rain barrel, but it was too tall and her legs were too short.

Alex had no idea what she was up

to, but curiosity overcame his common sense. She shouldn't be walking on a roof in the middle of the night, but he wanted to see what was going to happen. Putting one hand under her round little fanny, he pushed her upward. He had to climb onto the barrel to help her up to the roof, then he went back to the ground just in time to see her brother come out the back door.

Standing in the shadows, Alex watched. Since he'd met Cay, she'd complained incessantly about this brother, and he wanted to see them together.

Tally was a tall young man, with dark hair that had a reddish tint. He was handsome in a mischievous way that Alex thought women would like, and he looked as though laughter was never far from him. Silently, Tally left the lighted hotel doorway and walked into the dark back alley. Alex wondered why Tally wasn't calling to his sister. Instead, the young man walked slowly, looking about him cautiously.

When Cay stepped to the edge of the roof and looked like she was about to jump, Alex left the shadows. What in the world was she doing?

Tally stopped walking when he saw Alex, and his eyes widened. In the next second, Cay emitted a sound that was a combination of Indian war cry and an alligator roar, and she leaped from the roof onto Tally.

Alex ran forward to try to catch her, but she hit Tally hard. He staggered backward but didn't fall. And Alex could see the way he was holding her, protecting her, so that not even a strand of her hair was hurt.

Alex stepped back and watched. Obviously, this was something that had happened between them many times. But, still, just in case, Alex stood nearby, ready to step in if he was needed.

"What the hell are you wearing?" Tally asked as he struggled against her.

It was Alex's guess that Tally wasn't used to the muscle his sister had developed in the last weeks, so he was unprepared when she slipped her ankle about his foot and pulled. Tally hit the ground hard, but as he fell, he held Cay in a way that kept her from being injured.

"I'm going to tell Mother that you were cursing and Alex made me into a boy."

Tally looked up from the ground at Alex; Cay was on top of him. "Is this the man that kidnapped you and put you in mortal danger?" When he started to get up, Alex braced himself.

Cay put all her weight on Tally's left arm, and it looked like she was going to break it. "Who! Who, you idiot!"

Tally stopped struggling and looked at her in consternation. "What?"

"It's 'who' not 'that.' Alex is the bastard *who* stole me and took me into the wilds of the Florida jungle. I can see that you haven't been studying while I was away."

"I was traipsing all over the country looking for you, so how was I to read anything?" He twisted his arm out from under her and tried to get up, but Cay threw her body over the top of his.

"You touch him and I'll make *you* into a girl," Cay said as she pushed him down.

Out of the shadows came another

young man, one Alex had not seen inside. He had dark blond hair, very serious eyes, and he was handsome, but in a calm way, very unlike Tally's fiery good looks. In an instant, Alex knew who he was, and for a moment the two of them stood there in the dim light and stared at each other. They'd been corresponding since they were children and they knew more about each other than anyone else did. They had confided things in their letters that they had never told another person.

"No one is castrating anyone," Nate said calmly as he put his body in front of Alex and looked down at his brother and sister wrestling on the ground.

Cay didn't hesitate as she got off of Tally and threw her arms around Nate. There was no wrestling, no falling to the ground, and no raucous remarks, just a quiet embrace.

"You're all right?" Nate asked. "Not hurt in any way?"

"Not at all," Cay said, standing on tiptoe, her arms around her brother's neck.

"Did you learn anything on your journey?"

"Everything. And more than that, I drew pictures of it all."

Nate's eyebrows rose. "Did you? Where are they?"

"Jamie Armitage has them."

"What?" Tally asked as he got up from the ground and dusted himself off. "An Armitage is involved in all this?"

"He calls himself Mr. Grady, and he led the trek."

"How many of there were you?" Nate asked. "And where did you go? Down the St. Johns? What wildlife did you encounter? What—?"

Cay kissed Nate's cheek. "I think you should talk to Alex about all that. He studied the books and knows the names of everything. I'm going to give the drawings to Uncle T.C. and let him identify the plants."

"And I guess this is Alex?" Tally asked, still looking as though he'd like to hit him.

"Yes." Cay moved away from her brothers to stand near Alex. It was all she could do not to slip her hand into his, but she thought that would be too much for Tally to handle. With his hotheaded temper, touching Alex might make Tally start hitting. "Alex and I—"

She broke off when she saw Tally look to his right, down the side of the building, and draw in his breath. Cay looked at Nate, and he gave a brief nod. She didn't see that he gave another look to Alex.

"He's here?" Cay asked in a whisper.

"Who's here?" Alex asked, speaking for the first time in minutes. Only Nate saw the way Alex stepped closer to Cay, as though to protect her from whatever, whomever, Tally was looking at.

But when Cay looked at Alex and shook her head, he stepped back. Nate noted that it had been a silent communication between them, saying that she was safe and he didn't need to protect her.

Slowly, Cay walked around the side of the building, Alex close behind her. Walking toward them was a big man, as tall as Alex, but with several more pounds on him, and from the way he moved, it was all muscle. Alex instantly knew he was the brother Cay talked about so often: Adam. From what Alex had gathered, her eldest brother was a stern and formidable character, and Alex braced himself. He didn't care if Adam was her brother or not, if he said even one unkind word to her, if he started to bawl her out, Alex was going to take him on. After all Cay had been through, no one, not even a brother, had the right to hurt her in any way.

Alex watched as Cay stood still and her brother stopped several feet away from them. Alex looked to see if she was so still because she was afraid of him, but he couldn't read her expression. Alex's hands made into fists. He might lose a fight with the man, but he'd die protecting her.

When Adam went down on the ground on one knee, Alex wasn't sure what was happening, but in the next second Adam opened his arms, and Cay went running. With his kneeling, she was almost the same height as he was. She threw her arms around him and buried her face in his neck. And in the next

second, the air was full of the sobs of
both of them.

Embarrassed at such a display of raw
emotion, Alex turned to look at Nate and
Tally. Their eyes were on their siblings,
who were locked together, their heads
bent in a position of surrender, their
quiet sobs coming to them on the hot
night air. There were tears running down
the cheeks of both Nate and Tally, but
they didn't bother to wipe them away.

Alex stepped away from them and
into the shadows. It was as though he'd
already lost Cay, as though their time
together had never been, and she was
now going back to where she belonged.
Alex had never felt more superfluous or
unneeded in his life than he did at that
moment. What was going on was between her and her brothers, and he had
no place in it.

Quietly, he turned and started to
walk away, but Nate's hand on his arm
stopped him.

"Don't leave. They'll calm down in a
moment, Adam will start telling her how
she scared all of us, and how she's
never going to be allowed out of the

house alone again. When it gets back to normal, you and I can go somewhere and talk. You look different than I imagined."

Alex knew what Nate meant. Both of them had been very modest in their letters about what they looked like. Alex had said he looked like a horse, and Nate had said he was as plain faced as all scientists. But Alex had the dark good looks of a Renaissance angel, and Nate had the chiseled features of a Greek sculpture.

"I'd hoped you were better-looking," Alex said with a straight face.

"It's evident that you've spent a great deal of time in the company of my sister," Nate said just as seriously. "There is no situation about which she doesn't make a jest. Ah! I see that the two of them have stopped crying. Perhaps we can get some dinner out of them. I have a lot to tell you, and I'll be able to think better if I have some sustenance inside me."

Alex couldn't resist a grin. Nate talked as formally as he wrote. And oh! how wonderfully familiar he sounded. After months of everyone and everything being new and different, it was very good to hear something that was known to him.

"Will you need a handkerchief?" Nate asked, one eyebrow raised.

"I leave the crying to your family," Alex answered, and was glad to see Nate give a small smile.

"You must show me what you do with the horses."

"And you have to solve the mystery that condemned me to be hanged," Alex answered.

"Even Tally figured that one out." Nate sounded as though a trained dog had done an extraordinary trick, and the two of them shared their first laugh, in person, together.

"Who is it that's made my very serious little brother laugh?" came a deep voice that was unfamiliar to Alex.

Nate and Alex turned to see Adam, his arm around Cay in such a way that if she tried to escape, she wouldn't be able to. Alex couldn't keep his hands from clenching. He didn't care if that

was her brother, he didn't want someone else touching her.

"I think we should all talk," Adam said
and Alex nodded.

⚜

Adam had arranged for a restaurant
to remain open, and they had it all to
themselves. Once they were seated at
a round table, Tally and Adam began to
speak at once, but Adam let his young
brother tell what they'd been through to
find Cay. "And Mac's son," he added as
an afterthought, obviously as yet unde-
cided as to whether Alex was friend or
foe.

When the waiters started filling the
table with plates of food, Alex had a
momentary fear of their being heard.
Maybe they'd forgotten that he was a
wanted man, but Alex would never forget. It wasn't until he saw a confused
look on the face of a waiter that he realized the entire family had slipped into a
Scottish accent so thick they sounded
as though they'd left the Highlands just
yesterday.

Tally told of going to the trading post and meeting Thankfull and her twin sisters. "I got there two days after you left." For a moment he stared into space and shook his head. "Those girls! They followed me wherever I went. I've never seen anything like them."

"Then not all girls are as aggressive as they are?" Cay asked. When Tally said no, she looked at Alex with an I-told-you-so expression.

"But I wish they were!" Tally said enthusiastically. "I wouldn't have to work so hard if all girls were like them."

Adam gave Tally a look that told him to keep his mouth shut, but Cay and Alex couldn't suppress their laughter.

"I told you we men liked that," Alex said.

"And I told you we women weren't all like them," Cay responded, laughing.

"Yet again, we're both right." Alex was laughing with her.

Adam looked at Tally, and the younger man shrugged. They had no idea what Cay and Alex were talking about.

"Nate stayed in Charleston, while I

went to New Orleans," Adam said over the laughter.

"But you didn't tell Uncle T.C. where you were going." Cay's voice was stern with disapproval.

"At the time, I was a bit vexed with him." Adam took a sip of his wine.

"He was ready to tear Uncle T.C.'s head off," Tally said to Cay. "I was wishing you were there so you could draw a picture of the fight. Wouldn't that have been something to see?"

"I hardly think such a thing would have happened," Adam said.

Tally went on telling of all his trials and tribulations of getting down to Florida to try and reach Cay before she took off on the boat. "Uncle T.C. didn't tell us you were with one of the Armitage boys."

"I doubt if it was important to him," Adam said. "Unless the man sprouts leaves and blooms on schedule, I don't think T.C. would think he was interesting."

"Was Grady warned about me, about us?" Alex asked.

Adam answered. "Not that I know of,

but the last time I saw Jamie, he asked if my little sister had grown up yet. I don't think it would have taken much for him to add things up."

Throughout all the talk, Nate sat in silence and watched. He liked to observe whatever was going on around him, whether it was people, animals, or even the changes of the landscape. He had a formidable memory and remembered all that he saw and heard.

He now watched Alex and Cay with all the concentration of observing them under a magnifying glass. He saw the way his sister had changed, both physically and mentally. He knew that all her life she'd been protected. He'd even told his father that the way Cay was treated wasn't necessarily good for her. If she married and moved to someone else's house, she was going to have a difficult time adjusting. She was used to only the best and the finest; no bad parts of life had been allowed to touch her.

But Nate saw that now his young sister was different. The fact that she was sitting next to a man who'd been tried for murder, but of whom she didn't seem in the least afraid, was a big change. On the walk to the restaurant, two men, obviously drunk, had nearly run into her. Adam had instantly reached out to push them away, but Cay had already sidestepped them. And she'd done it in such a deft way it was as though she'd done the same thing a hundred times. More unusual, she hadn't seemed to notice the men. Her eyes were on Alex. *Always* on Alex.

Now, in the restaurant, Adam was seated across from Cay, Tally and Nate on either side of him, and Alex was beside Cay. Adam had been telling what they'd done to track them down, while Tally was adding as much drama as he could to the story.

"When I was at Thankfull's I even saw an alligator," Tally said. "Really, I did. It was no more than fifty feet from me, but I stood still and let it pass."

"Did you?" Cay asked as she glanced at Alex, their eyes registering mutual merriment.

Tally looked from one to the other and frowned. He and Adam were too polite to comment on the fact that Cay and Alex were eating off each other's plates. They seemed to know every food the other liked, and without so much as a look at each other, they traded vegetables. The whole family knew that Cay didn't like green beans, so when they saw her eat them and share them with Alex, even Adam paused with the fork halfway to his mouth.

"I can't get over how you look," Tally said to his sister. "You've changed."

"My hair will grow back," she said. "Although maybe I don't want it to. I can ride better without fifty pounds of hair trailing behind me."

"Bad for your neck," Alex said, and Cay laughed, as though it was the funniest thing she'd ever heard.

Tally looked at Nate, but he was staring at Cay and Alex so hard that he didn't seem to be aware of what was going on. But Tally knew his brother was doing what they'd come to call "conjuring," meaning that he was studying something to figure out what it meant. He knew that later, Nate would tell them in one concise sentence what had actually taken place.

"After we eat," Adam said to his sister, "we'll go to the hotel I've arranged for us, and tomorrow morning I'll have some proper clothes brought to you. You won't need to dress like a boy anymore. I have enough brothers, I don't need any more."

Alex glanced up from his food. "No. The corset hurts her. Let her have as much time of freedom as possible. When she sees her mother, that will be soon enough to strap her back into that cage." His voice was quiet, but it held command in it, and Adam looked straight into Alex's eyes.

Nate had seen few men stand up to his oldest brother, and he'd never seen anyone except their father win against Adam, but Alex's unblinking stare and his immovable jaw said that he wasn't going to back down.

"Well, then," Adam said at last. "I guess that tomorrow we'll be five men moving about New Orleans. But Cay, you can't—" He broke off at a look from Alex.

"She can't what?" Alex asked, and his voice was that of a man who was ready to fight.

All three brothers looked at their sister, but she had her nose nearly on her plate.

"What do *you* think she should do?" Nate asked Alex.

"I think she should—" He cut himself off, and the challenging look left his face. He turned to Cay. "I think she should do whatever *she* wants to do."

The change in Alex's tone was dramatic. He'd been ready to fight all two-hundred-plus pounds of Adam, but when it came to telling Cay what to do, he blanched. In a second, his voice went from confrontational to conceding.

The men looked at one another, all of them over six feet tall, then looked at tiny Cay, and suddenly, they all burst into laughter. Cay tried to remain aloof, as though she had no idea what they were laughing about, but then she, too, joined in the merriment. When she slipped her hand to Alex's side and withdrew his big knife from its sheath and waved it around, the laughter grew louder.

Nate watched as Cay looked at Alex with eyes that seemed to melt. She's in love with him, Nate thought, and he had to repress a smile. How convenient it was that his sister was in love with his best friend.

But when he remembered that Alex had a wife who was alive and well and living not two miles from where they were sitting, Nate's smile left him. Alex was going to have to make a choice, and if he hurt Cay, Nate wondered if he'd have to choose between his sister and his best friend.

Twenty-four

❧

Cay was in bed asleep, dreaming about being on the flatboat and floating down the calm, peaceful Florida river. Mr. Grady and Eli were there, and Alex was sitting close beside her. Tim was by the side of the boat, his hand trailing in the water, and there was a little alligator following his fingers, its mouth open. She was just about to warn him when a sound woke her.

"Hey! Sleepyhead," Alex said softly as he slid into bed next to her.

She kept her eyes closed and snuggled against him. "You smell wonderful."

"That's not what I can say about you. You haven't had a bath, and you smell like a swamp."

"Mmmm. I thought you liked the

swamps." She put her leg over his and moved, as though to get on top of him.

Reluctantly, Alex pushed her thigh off his stomach. "Your brother is in the room next door, and with the noise you make, I don't dare do anything with you."

She put her leg back over him. "Since when are you afraid of Tally?"

"It's Adam who's next door."

Cay removed her leg, opened her eyes, and lowered her voice. "In that case, what are you doing in here, and when did you take a bath?"

He put her head back on his shoulder. "I've been up all night talking to Nate."

"Nate? My brother Nate?"

"Of course. Why not?"

"It's just that Nate doesn't talk to any-one. He'd rather watch and learn than give out information. So what did he tell you?"

"I wanted to know what Grady was told or figured out, but we can't ask him until he gets back from the jungle."

Cay knew Alex was stalling and waited for him to get to the important news. But she knew what he was go-ing to say before he spoke because Alex's arm tightened around her so she couldn't move.

"Nate told me about Lilith." When Cay started to roll away, Alex held her in place. "You're going to have to hear this sooner or later, so you can let one of your brothers tell you, or you can hear it from me. Your choice."

She knew that Alex would tell the story with more diplomacy than three of her brothers would. If Ethan had been there, she would have asked him to explain it all to her, but he wasn't. Cay took a breath. "All right, tell me. But if we hear anyone at the door and we think it might be Adam, you have to go out the window."

Alex smiled. "You do know that we're on the fourth floor, don't you?"

"If we were on the twelfth floor, you'd still have to go out that way. Neither your life nor mine would be worth anything if Adam were to find you in here with me."

"Nate said almost the same thing, and that's why he's keeping Adam busy."

Cay lifted her head to look at him. He was clean and had shaved, and she thought he was by far the most handsome man she'd ever seen. She'd never tell him, but she thought he was even better-looking than her brother Ethan. "You've certainly become friends with my brother in a short time."

Alex put her head back down. "Do you want to hear the story or not? There's only so long Nate can occupy Adam before your eldest brother gets suspicious."

"Tell me," she said and felt her body stiffen. She didn't like to think about what she was going to hear. "Why is your . . ." She couldn't say the word *wife.* "Why is that woman alive when so many people saw her with her throat cut?"

"That's just it. Very few people saw her. On that night the only people who saw her were the judge, the doctor, and the two men who handcuffed me. After that, Lilith's body was taken to the doctor's office, where she was put in a coffin that was nailed shut, and she was buried three days later."

"I take it she wasn't inside the coffin,"

Cay said, and wanted to add "more's the pity."

"No. What Nate found out was that the doctor was in on the whole scheme. He provided the drugs that were used to put me to sleep, and he wrote the note that was careful *not* to say that I had murdered my bride, but just that I could be found with her. The doctor threw the note through the judge's window and woke him up. The doctor also got the policemen, and he led all of them to my room. But only the doctor actually looked closely at Lilith. The other three men were too busy throwing me to the floor and telling me that I was a first cousin to the devil. Even I only had a quick glimpse of Lilith. But what I saw has haunted me since that moment. That one look was enough."

"I guess I should ask why she did such a horrible thing to you."

"That part we don't know and won't know until I talk to her today."

"Today?" There was fear in Cay's voice.

Alex stroked her hair as he held her close. "Aye, today. Your brothers have three hired guards surrounding her now."

"She knows you're here?"

"No. She knows nothing. Since she's so good at slipping away from people, your brothers thought it would be better not to warn her. They just hired men to follow her and watch everything she did, but not to let her see them. Your brothers want me to 'surprise' her." Alex's tone told what he thought of that.

Cay's face lit up as she remembered something. "The doctor died. Didn't you tell me that the doctor died of a heart attack?"

"Aye," Alex said. "I like to think the man had enough of a conscience that the guilt over what he'd done to me killed him. Nate says he doesn't think Lilith meant for me to be accused of her murder. He thinks she meant for the doctor to declare her death a suicide."

Cay was aghast. "And that would have been better? All your life you would have been haunted by that. A woman killed herself rather than spend the night with you."

Alex put his hand under her chin and lifted her face. The kiss he gave her told how grateful he was for her understanding.

She put her leg back over him—and he pushed it off. She sighed. "So you're going to go see her today and ask her why she did such a rotten, horrible, devious thing to you and almost got you hanged?"

Alex chuckled. "I'm glad you're on my side. But, aye, that's just what I'm going to do."

"If her plan was to fake her suicide, please be sure to ask her why she didn't come to your rescue when she heard or read that you were about to be hanged for murdering her."

"That question is at the top of my list."

"Then what? You'll . . ." She hesitated. "After you settle this, you can go back to Virginia with us."

"No," he said softly, "I can't. I have to clear my name."

"That's easy. Just get someone to verify that she's alive, have a lawyer present the paper to a judge in Charleston, and you're free. My family will help you. My father knows lots of people, so you should have your sentence removed in no time at all. You . . ." She could tell by the way Alex was saying nothing that there was more. "All right, tell me all of it, even the part you're hiding." Her voice was heavy, dreading what she was going to hear.

"I can get the charges dropped, true, but I need for my name to be *cleared.*"

"You keep saying that, but exactly what do you mean?"

"I hope you never know what it's like to go from thinking that you have many friends to finding out you have none. Before the day of my wedding, I would have sworn that I had some truly good friends. George told you how he and I used to go out drinking. I . . ." He paused for a moment. "The truth is, I thought I'd done some good things. I can't tell you the number of betting debts that I forgave. If a man couldn't afford what he'd lost, if he had a wife and children to support, I often said that I didn't get his bet in time to post it and gave him his money back. There were many times when men slapped me on the back and told me I was a truly *good* person. It's the way I conducted my life. And as for the women, I received many offers, but I never took up *any* of them. I didn't want a husband chasing me with a gun, or have a father or brother angry at me for what I'd done to an innocent girl."

Cay kissed his chest through his clean white shirt.

"I did what I could to earn friendship and respect," Alex said. "But after Lilith was found dead in my bed, not one person, not *one*! stood up for me."

"Except Uncle T.C."

"Aye, except for him."

Cay was trying to put together what he'd told her, and when she understood, she wanted to cry. "You want to go back to Charleston with . . . with *her* and show all those people that she's still alive. A piece of paper and a quiet settlement aren't enough for you."

He gave her shoulder a hug. "You understand."

"No. I just know you well enough to know that's what you want to do." She lifted up to put her head on her hand and looked at him. "I don't want you to go."

"I have to."

"No, you don't, and I'm asking you not to. At least don't go alone. Adam will go with you."

"Nate is going with me."

"Nate?" She narrowed her eyes at him. "Why is he talking to you so much? Nate doesn't make friends easily."

"There's more to this than just the murder. Did you forget that?"

Cay was well aware that Alex hadn't answered her question about Nate and had changed the subject. She knew what Alex meant. She fell back onto the pillow. "Marriage. If she's alive, then you're still married."

"Exactly. Nate and I think that if a judge is told what Lilith did to me, he'll declare the marriage invalid right there."

"An annulment."

"Aye, a legal decree that says the marriage never existed. The whole country knows it wasn't consummated."

She turned to look at him. "I *am* going with you."

"No, you're *not*! You're going back to Edilean with Adam and Tally. It's already been settled."

"And who did the 'settling'?"

"Don't look at me like that. Nate and I talked about everything all night long, and we decided that this is the best way. You're to go to Virginia and wait for me there."

"Wait, am I?" Her voice was rising. "I guess I'm supposed to strap on a corset, put on a pretty dress, get into a carriage, and go back to my mother in Virginia."

"That's exactly what you're going to do," Alex said firmly. "And I'm not going to argue with you about this. You can-*not* go with me to Charleston."

"'Her eyes met mine, and I was hers,'" she quoted.

"What?"

"That's what you said. I asked you if you loved her and you said, 'With all my heart and soul.' Then you said that you loved her in the first moment you saw her, and that when your eyes met, you were hers."

Alex snorted. "I'm sure I never said

such a ridiculous thing in my life. A man doesn't talk that way. It's too . . . too flowery. Now, if I had jasmine in my hair . . ." His eyes darkened and he rolled toward her, obviously meaning to kiss her.

She put her hands on his chest and pushed. "If you think you're going to distract me, Alexander McDowell, you have another think coming. So help me, if you don't answer my questions, I'll scream, and you can bet my brother will come through that door—or through the wall if he has to."

With a sigh, Alex lay back on the pillow and looked at the ceiling. "I'm not going to fall back in love with her, if that's what you're worried about. This is about justice and trying to make myself whole again. I'll never get rid of the stench of that prison from my mind, but I'm going to do the best I can. Did I tell you that they threw rocks at me on the way to the courtroom?"

"At least fifty times. What I want to know about is your stupid plan of going back to Charleston and *living* with a woman you are madly in love with."

"I'm not going to live with her, and I'm no longer in love with her." Turning, he looked at Cay. "I'm in love with someone else."

She glared at him. "Don't even consider saying what I think you're about to. You're a married man."

Alex sat up in bed and glared down at her. "That's what I've been saying! It's what I'm trying to explain to you! I have to get myself cleared of murder charges, and I have to get out of being married to her. Are you daft, girl, that you can't hear the simplest thing?"

"I can hear you and so can half the people in this hotel."

Alex fell back onto the pillow, shaking his head in frustration. "If any man in the world actually knew what it was like to be married, he'd never do it." Turning, he looked at her, his eyes pleading with her to understand. "You can't go with me because I don't want your name tainted. If I show up in Charleston with you on one arm and Lilith on the other, no matter what the truth is, people will say that *you* are the reason she had to fake her own death.

People will look for something to prove that they weren't the fools and morons that they were. When they find out that they condemned an innocent man to death, they're going to search for a reason to forgive themselves. If they see another woman with me they'll blame her—you."

"But I didn't meet you until after the verdict came in."

"Do you think they're going to believe that? You were in Charleston and your godfather was my only visitor. And are you forgetting that you were seen helping me escape? I know your family cleared your name legally, but no one will believe that anyone was innocently gullible enough to agree to help an escaped convict who she'd never even met. That's more than enough ammunition for them to make up stories about my having another woman. They said that the only reason I married Lilith was for the money she was supposed to inherit. They even wrote that in the newspapers. Nate has proof that Lilith isn't old lady Underwood's niece, but do you think people will *believe* that?"

"They'll see you had no ulterior motive for marrying her. Besides, *I* am the rich one," Cay said. "She's poor, but I'm rich, so if you were after any woman for her money, it would be *me.*"

Alex lifted his hands in frustration. "That's perfect. They'll say that when I found out Lilith wasn't rich, I looked for a woman who was. They'll say that I made Lilith's life so miserable she had to fake her own death to get away from me."

Cay frowned. "And no doubt people will look at that woman and at me, and they'll decide that the only possible reason you'd chosen *me* was because of my family's money."

"Aye, they will," Alex said. "They'll take one look at that dirty hair of yours, and your face, which is usually streaked with swamp mud, and they'll never understand why I prefer you over a renown beauty like Lilith."

"Is that supposed to make me feel *better*?"

"I think you should feel so certain of me that you know I could walk into a room full of naked women and all I'd think about was you."

"Even I know that in New Orleans that's possible, so I'd better not hear from Nate that you decided to test that theory."

When Alex was silent, Cay tried to come up with a logical reason of why she must go with him, but she couldn't think of one. All she felt was blinding, heart-piercing emotion. "You *are* in love with her. You're deeply and passionately in love with her. I know you are."

"No, I'm not. I hardly know her."

"You told me a person doesn't have to know everything about someone to be in love with her or him. You even made fun of my lists. That woman makes your blood boil! You said so yourself."

"And may I cut out my tongue for having done so," Alex said. "Cay, lass, don't you know what I've learned in these last weeks? What *you* have taught me? I've learned that love is more than just passion. It's caring about someone, knowing her, and overlooking her faults because you love her so very much. It's more than just looking at a beautiful woman with a glorious bosom and thinking that you'll die if you don't go to bed with her. It's—" One glance at Cay's face told him that he'd made a mistake.

Cay got out of the bed and stood by it, looking down at him. She was wearing her dirty boy's clothes, and she could feel the grime in her hair, but Alex was fresh and clean. "So you're saying that *I* have faults while *she* has a . . . What did you say? A 'glorious bosom.' And she's beautiful, is she? Always well dressed, is she?"

Alex put his hands behind his head and looked up at the ceiling. He knew he was in for a bout of Cay's anger and he'd just have to wait it out.

"I'll have you know that when I met you *I* was well dressed. I had on a silk gown that cost more than some houses, and I had diamonds in my hair. Does your *wife*"—she sneered the word—"have diamonds to wear in her hair? And the reason I've had to wear boy's clothing and bind my not so 'glorious' bosom has been to save *your* worthless, ungrateful neck. Maybe you think all women should prance around in silk and ribbons, but I couldn't because *you* needed my help. Did your precious Lilith ever *help* you? No, she did not. *She* was the reason people threw rocks at you. Might I remind you that if it hadn't been for *me,* you would be dead now."

Alex sighed, his eyes still on the ceiling. "You're not going with me and that's final."

Cay flopped down on the bed beside him, all her anger gone. "I could wear boy's clothes that you've now decided you despise. I won't be the great beauty that that woman is, but I'd be there with you."

"No," Alex said as he swung off the bed and stood up. "You're going to go back to Virginia and stay there. When this mess is finished, I'll . . ." He looked at her.

"You'll what? Come for me? Did you ever think that while you're with *her* I might meet a man who also has some glorious body parts, and I'll run off to a plantation in Florida with him?"

Alex gave an amused half smile. "And which body parts would that be, lass?"

"The one you love the best," she shot back at him.

Alex frowned. He'd thought she meant a man's face, but she was talking about going to bed with other men. "You must do what you think is right," he said tightly.

Cay went up to her knees and threw her arms around his neck. "Alex, don't leave me behind. You and I have been through so much together, and we've stood it all. This is just one of those times."

Alex held her tightly. "Do you think I *want* to go without you? I can't imagine waking up without you there. In those days when you were in Eli's tent, I thought I was going to go mad."

"That was just Tim's snores driving you crazy," she said, her face nuzzled in his neck.

"No," he said softly. "It was more than that. You make me whole."

"You mean because you lost so much in the trial? I know I make you laugh."

"You make me . . ." He pulled her

arms from around his neck so he could look at her. "You're correct when you say that now I have no right to tell you what I feel about you and what I hope will happen between us. Right now I'm a married man and I'm still hunted by the law. Until I can come to you pure, and clean, I can't allow myself to say all the things I want to, to tell you what you mean to me."

He glanced down at her stomach. "Is it possible that you're . . . ?"

"No, I'm not," she said, and there were tears in her voice. She'd started her monthly flow yesterday. She would like nothing more than to tell him she was carrying his child, so he had to return to *her.*

Alex's face showed as much disappointment as hers did. Bending, he looked into her eyes. "What is it that you're really afraid of?"

"That you'll see her great beauty and realize that you've loved her forever."

He smiled. "I find that highly unlikely. What if an alligator runs through the dining room? Who's going to help me get rid of it? And what about large, poisonous vipers? You're the snake charmer."

Cay didn't smile. "You married the most poisonous serpent of all, and I'm better at jokes than you are."

"Aye, lass, I did and you are. You're better at a lot of things than I am. When I think back on it, I marvel at my arrogance when I thought I could best you at drawing. Beat you at anything, for that matter."

"You can ride better than I can," she said. Her lower lip was quivering. She was so very afraid that when Alex saw his wife that he'd fall in love with her all over again, and Cay would never again see him.

"I can what?"

Cay didn't answer him.

"Please repeat it, lass. I want to hear you say that you know there's anything in the entire world that I can do better than you can."

She put her arms back around his neck. "I hate you and you can't go without me. I'll stay in a hotel all day long. I won't leave our room."

He kissed her earlobe, but when she

turned her lips to his, he pulled her arms from around his neck. "I have to go. Nate is waiting for me."

Cay sat back on her heels on the bed. "You're going to see her now, aren't you?"

"Aye, I am. But not because I want to. If it were up to me, I'd never see her again, but I must."

"After you see her, you'll go back with her to Charleston. And you two will be alone."

"No, I told you that Nate will be with us."

"I don't understand why Nate is going with you. He doesn't do things with other people. Certainly not strangers. He—"

"I'm Merlin."

Cay sat there blinking at Alex in disbelief. "You're Nate's Merlin?"

"Aye, I am. Until you told me so, I didn't know that your family knew anything about me, except your mother, of course. She's the one who got the correspondence between Nate and me started back when we were children, just after my mother died. My father's grief was bad, and he dealt with it in silence. I needed someone to talk to. During that first year, I wrote to Nate every day, and he wrote back every day. I used to get his letters in big packets. They saved me. I owe him and your mother a great deal."

"Merlin." Cay wasn't sure whether she felt betrayed or happy that Alex had such a firm connection to her family.

"That's what Nate called me after your cousin said I was a 'magician' with animals."

"Why didn't you come to visit us when we were in Scotland?"

"I wanted to, but my dad said that all the riches of your family made him nervous. Lairds and former lairds living in a castle wasn't what we were used to."

"Nate never told us anything about you," Cay said, still looking at him in wonder.

"It seems he told me even less about *you.* My first question was why he didn't tell me you were an artist."

"He didn't think it was important," Cay said.

"That's exactly what he said. Years

ago, he told me he wanted something private that he didn't have to share with his family and I was it. Was it Tally who found out about us?"

"Of course. You can't keep a secret from Tally. He probably snooped through Nate's things. They share a bedroom." She took Alex's hand and looked up into his eyes, pleading. "Please let me go with you. I'm Nate's sister, so I have a reason for being there."

Alex smiled at her, but she could see that he wasn't going to relent. "I have to go now, lass. Nate is waiting and we're going to go see Lilith. I'll come back to-night and tell you what happened."

"What kind of perfume does she wear?"

"I have no idea."

"If you come back smelling like a woman's perfume, I'll—"

"I know. Make me sorry. But, lass, don't you see that right now I already am sorry? Now, come and give me a kiss, then I have to leave. Nate is—"

"Waiting. Yes, I know. You don't have to worry about him. He takes care of himself. By now he's probably read three books about some obscure sub- ject no one can pronounce, much less understand. If you want to help Nate, introduce him to a woman he can love."

"A lady scientist?" Alex asked, smil- ing.

"No, a lady alligator wrestler. If any- one needs to be taught what passion is, it's my brother."

"Like I taught you about it?" Alex's eyes turned warm.

"Ha! I'm the creative one. I taught you most of what you know about ev- erything."

"Aye, that you did, my love," Alex said softly as his arms tightened around her. "I'm going to miss you. No matter how long I'm gone, even if it's just ten min- utes, I'm going to miss you every sec- ond of that time." Gently, he kissed her, and when she tried to turn it into more, he drew back and took her arms from around his neck. "I must go." He kissed her forehead. "I'll be back as soon as I can." He kissed her nose. "Tonight I'll have a story to tell you about why a woman faked her own death." He kissed her chin. "And I'll hold you in my arms and tell you all of it."

"You promise?"

"On my honor." He went to the door. "And when this is all over, I'll tell you in detail what I feel about you."

"Swear it?"

"I swear it." Smiling, he opened the door and looked out into the hall. "I'm surprised that one of your brothers isn't here watching your door." When he looked back at her, there was such longing in his eyes that for a moment she thought he was going to change his mind. But in the next second he stepped into the hallway and closed the door behind him.

Cay collapsed on the pillow and began to cry. But five minutes later, she sat up. She was going to follow him. She was going to see for herself that Alex was no longer in love with the woman he'd married. If she saw that that was true, then she knew she could return to Virginia and wait forever for him. She thought about calling for a bath to be brought to her, but there wasn't time.

She was going as the dirty boy people thought she was.

Silently, she slipped out of the room and went down the hall.

Twenty-five

❧

"What the hell are you doing here?" Tally asked as he pulled Cay in through the hotel window. "And how the hell did you get up here to the third floor?"

"If you don't stop cursing I'm going to tell Father about that fat woman you had on your lap. Did you know that the whole family thinks you're a virgin?" She stood up in the room, noting its elegant furnishings. "This place costs a lot. Who's paying for it?"

"What do you know about virginity?" Tally asked. "And since when have you cared anything about money except how much of it you could spend?"

"As we go through life, we learn things." She dusted off the seat of her pants. To get into the room, she'd had to scoot along an iron balcony so the people in the room next door wouldn't see her.

"You sound like you're on a pulpit. And when are you going to put on some clean clothes?"

"When I feel like it, Mr. Priss." She gave Tally a look up and down and saw that he was dressed in his finest. She was glad to see that he was wearing the jacket she'd embroidered. "The twins liked your coat."

"They kept putting their hands in my pockets. Why can't other girls be like them?"

"The rest of us have brains. So where are they now?" On a marble-topped table was a bowl of fruit and a basket of bread. There was also a pot of luke-warm tea. "I'm starving."

"After what you ate last night, I'd think you wouldn't want to eat for the rest of the week." Sitting down across from her, Tally stretched his long legs out. "How did you find us?"

Cay gave a one-shouldered shrug. "It wasn't difficult. I want to go to Charleston with Alex."

"It seems to me that you want to be

with that man every minute of every day."

Cay motioned that her mouth was full so she couldn't answer him.

"They won't let you stay here in this room, you know. Adam will send you away."

"Not if he doesn't know I'm here." She gave a look around the pretty sitting room. On the far side was a tall cabinet set about a foot from the corner wall. There was just enough space beside it for her to hide. She looked at Tally.

"Oh, no, you don't. If you hide and you're found out, Adam will blame *me.*"

Cay broke a piece of bread in half and buttered it. "Might I remind you of all the things I know about you that I could use for blackmail?"

"I think I know some things about you, too," he said slyly.

"I'm so glad. I do hope you tell Father that I've been sleeping with Alex Mc-Dowell for weeks now so he'll make us get married."

Tally's eyes widened. "When did you get so coarse?"

"When I found out what real life is like. Are you going to help me or not?"

"Of course I am. I always do, don't I? But just remember that if you see something you don't like, you'll get hurt."

Cay finished the last of the bread. "So what's she like?"

"Who?"

She narrowed her eyes at him.

"Pretty, but not the great beauty that I'd heard she was."

"Are you just saying that?"

"Yeah," Tally said. His little sister always knew when he was lying. "She isn't dressing like we'd heard she did in Charleston, but even in her drab clothes, she's a beauty. Eyes like a cat's, lips like ripe cherries, and her body is—"

"I get the idea. You do know what she did to Alex, don't you?"

"Sure. But couldn't he have done something to stop her?"

Cay felt the hairs on the back of her neck rise. "What do you mean by that? That he should have figured out that the woman he loved was a low-down, lying skunk? Should he have seen that she was using him in some devious plot she'd come up with? That she couldn't have cared less that Alex was hanged, as long as *she* got what *she* wanted?" By the time Cay finished, she was standing up and glaring down at Tally.

He was looking at her with interest. "If this is what love does to a person, I hope it never happens to me."

Cay sat back down. "No woman would be insane enough to fall in love with you."

"There, my dear little sister, you're wrong. Half of the women in New Orleans have fallen for me. The other half want Adam."

"That's because Ethan isn't here." She heard noises outside the door. "They're here."

Tally grabbed her arm and pulled her upright. "If I had any sense, I'd push you back out the window." He half dragged her across the room to the cabinet, and when she tried to trip him, he sidestepped her.

"Let me go! I can walk."

"Walking isn't the problem," he said as he pushed her into the little space beside the cabinet. "If you'd never been taught to ride, you wouldn't be in the mess you're in now. Stay there and don't make a sound."

Cay started to make a retort to that, but she thought better of it. Tally might tell her brothers and Alex she was there, and they'd send her away. To find out where Alex was going, she'd had to follow him through the streets of New Orleans. She'd hidden behind a big palm tree in the lobby of a hotel, and when Alex went up the stairs, she'd told the clerk she had a package to deliver to the man's fiancée. She hinted that it was a ring.

The man had been repulsed by Cay's dirty clothes, but that kept him from looking at her too hard. She was told that Nathaniel Harcourt had taken two rooms in their hotel, one of them the bridal suite on the top floor. Cay asked the man for the key to the room so she could surprise him, but he'd given her a look to let her know she wasn't going to get it. She knew that if she were a pretty, well-dressed young lady, he would have given her anything she asked for. It looked like there were advantages and disadvantages to being of either sex.

In the end, Cay'd had to climb the balconies at the back of the hotel, over-looking the garden, to get into the room. Twice she'd nearly fallen, and it had taken sheer muscle power to haul her-self up to safety. "Thank you, Florida," she'd whispered when she reached the top balcony. All those boxes she'd had to carry, the pole she'd had to use to help get the boat unstuck, not to men-tion energetic evenings spent with Alex, had made her much stronger.

To hide her, Tally opened all four doors on the cabinet and set a decora-tive wooden box at the bottom to cover her feet. You'd have to look hard to see her behind the open doors, but Cay was just the right height to look out through the gap between the doors.

Once she was hidden, she thought about what she was doing. She was waiting to see this woman she'd heard so much about. The great love of Alex's life. The woman he'd merely looked at and known he loved.

Tally was barely two feet away when the door opened. It was Nate.

"If you'll step into here," Nate said in his cool voice, as though he felt nothing about what was going on. But Cay knew him, and she heard the underlying distaste. Nate didn't like injustice. In college, he'd written several papers against slavery, and he'd petitioned President Adams, asking if he, Nathaniel Harcourt, could help reform the entire judicial system of the United States.

Cay could now tell that her brother thoroughly disliked the woman whom Alex had married in passion.

Cay held her breath as she heard the light footsteps of a woman, then saw the back of her. She was tall, and her thick, black hair was dressed high on her head. From the back, Cay could see that she was firmly corseted inside a blue silk dress that had obviously been made for her. She wore a tiny jacket that Cay knew was the height of fashion. When the woman started to turn around, Cay's heart almost stopped beating.

Lilith Grey was indeed beautiful. She

had chiseled cheekbones, eyes shaped like almonds, and perfect red lips— which Cay thought had to have some artificial color on them.

Cay tried to be sensible and think of her from a man's standpoint. Tally was staring at her with a stupid expression on his face, as though he was seeing a star that had landed on this planet. At least Nate wasn't enamored of her, Cay thought. He was looking toward the open door as though he saw some- thing a great deal more interesting than the woman.

In the next moment, Nate looked about the room, and when he saw the table with its empty bowl, which had contained fruit, and the empty bread basket, his eyes opened wider. Cay wanted to kick herself for not remem- bering that Nate would be there. He saw everything.

Nate instantly looked from the ta- ble to the rest of the room and within a second he saw Cay's eyes peeping through the gap between the open cab- inet doors. He even took a step toward her, but then Alex entered and Nate looked back at his friend.

Cay hadn't thought about what she'd expected from the woman Alex had almost been hanged for, but she would have imagined that contrition would be her main emotion. She would apologize and beg his forgiveness, wouldn't she?

But Lilith just stood there, looking at what Cay assumed was Alex approaching her, and her beautiful face went into a smile—and she became even more lovely. To Cay's disbelief, the woman seemed to be looking at someone she loved very much.

When Alex got within a few feet of her, his back to Cay so she couldn't see his face, the woman took two steps forward, and she slipped her arms around Alex.

"How very, very much I've missed you, my darling," Lilith said in a low, throaty voice. "And how glad I am that you're going to remain my husband."

Cay saw Alex put his arms around her waist, and when Lilith kissed him, he kissed her back.

Cay fainted. The blood left her head,

her body became light, and she lost consciousness. Both Tally and Nate had surreptitiously been watching her, and they were able to catch her before she hit the floor.

When Alex ran to her, Tally put up his arms and blocked him. "Go to your wife, and if you get near my sister again, I'll kill you."

Twenty-six

🍀

Before Adam answered the knock on his hotel door, he felt sure he knew who it was. This morning Tally had told him about Cay fainting and nearly hitting her head on the hard floor. Tally had been so angry that he'd wanted to challenge Alex to a duel. At the very least, he wanted to press charges against him.

"Don't you think he's had enough trouble from the law?" Nate asked, calm as always.

Adam turned to Nate and asked what had happened.

"Our sister wanted to see Alex with his wife. She did, and it was too much for her."

Tally glared at Nate. "Tell him why you aren't concerned about this. Tell Adam why you couldn't care less about what's been done to our little sister, including dragging her into uncharted territory where even the plants have teeth."

"I have yet to see proof of plants that devour human flesh, no matter that Mr. Connor loves to tell stories of them."

"Proof? You don't need proof for what happened this morning. Just because *you* think McDowell can do no wrong doesn't mean—"

"Tally!" Adam said. "Am I right that our sister is unhurt?"

"If you call crying hard enough to break a man's heart to hear her, and refusing to eat or speak to anyone 'unhurt,' then yes she is."

"Interesting observation," Nate said calmly, "since it's usually you who makes her cry."

"Why you—" Tally made a lunge for Nate, who put up his fists. Nate had had boxing lessons from a professional.

Adam's long arm reached out and stopped Tally. "Sit! I want to know what happened, and since you, Tally, seem to be incapable of coherent thought, I'll let Nate tell me. First of all, why does our angry brother think you aren't concerned about our little sister?"

"Tell him!" Tally said as he slumped down on to a chair.

"Alexander McDowell is Merlin."

Adam stared at Nate for a few moments before he spoke. "Now I understand. It's why you've been so involved in this hunt for the truth."

"Yes, it is," Nate answered. "With both my sister and my friend involved, I could do no less than my best."

"So what happened after Cay fainted?" Adam asked.

Tally answered. "I carried her to Nate's room."

Adam nodded. Last night, he and Cay had stayed in one hotel, while Nate, Tally, and Alex went to another one. It was at Nate's hotel that they had arranged for Alex to meet with his wife. "What did Alex do that so upset Cay?"

"He kissed the woman," Tally said angrily.

"If by 'the woman' you mean his wife, then he had a right to, didn't he?" Nate said.

"In front of Cay?" Tally shot back.

"If you had kept proper vigilance, she wouldn't have been concealing herself behind some cabinet doors and seen it all."

"Since when am I her sitter?"

"Stop it!" Adam said. "I want to know what happened between Alex and that woman."

Tally and Nate looked at each other, then at Adam.

"We don't know," Nate said. "We were more concerned about Cay. We got her to my room, I revived her with smelling salts, and she . . ." Nate didn't like great emotion and he especially didn't like to see his sister crying in such pain.

Tally continued. "When I got back to the room where McDowell was to meet his wife, they were gone. Think they're on their honeymoon by now?"

"If they're in this city, I can find them," Nate said.

"No," Adam answered. "What's between them is none of our business. Tally, I want you to take Cay home. Let Mother deal with her tears. She'll know how to handle them."

"Our father will be very angry," Nate said.

"Yeah, won't he?" Tally said, grinning. "He'll skin McDowell alive and nail his hide to the barn door."

"Tally," Nate said, "I really don't think there's a need for your bloodthirsty declarations."

"I'd like you to take care of our sister," Adam said to his youngest brother.

"Gladly!" Tally stood up. "I want her as far away from McDowell as possible."

Nate remained seated, looking at Adam. "What are you going to do?"

"I'm going to wait here for Alex to come to me."

Nate couldn't repress a smile. "He will come."

"Yes," Adam said, "I'm sure he will. My fear is that after we talk, he'll go to Cay, and she'll forgive him everything, then we'll have a war on our hands. Now, while she's angry at him, I want to get her out of here."

"You're going to talk to the bastard?" Tally asked.

"I'm going to listen to every word he

has to say. I think it's time that someone listened to him. Now go and get Cay while she's still upset. When she comes to her senses, I want her to be in Edilean and under Father's care."

"I like this plan," Tally said as he headed for the door, but he stopped and looked back at Nate. "And what do *you* plan to do?"

"After Merlin . . . Alex talks to Adam, I am going to help him however he needs me."

"You're going to choose that bastard over your own family?"

"No," Nate said calmly. "I'm going to—"

"Tally," Adam said, "would you please see to Cay and do what you can to calm down? And Nate—"

But Nate was already on his feet and ready to leave with Tally. "I'll give you time alone with him. I hope that you'll . . ."

"I'll be fair and I'll listen," Adam said. "The man was falsely accused and convicted of murder. I can't imagine what that must have done to him."

After giving a quick nod, Nate left Adam's hotel room.

❧❧

It was late, and someone was knocking on Adam's door, and he felt sure it was Alexander McDowell.

"Is she gone?" Alex asked as he stepped inside Adam's room.

"Yes. Cay left for Edilean with Tally this morning. Nate is waiting to help you in whatever needs to be done. Cay wanted to stay, but we all think it's better that she be with our family now." Adam did his best to think and act in a rational manner, but he couldn't help himself. "What in the hell were you thinking when you kissed that woman in front of Cay?"

Alex sat down heavily on a chair. He looked as though he'd aged twenty years in one day. "First of all, I didn't know Cay was hiding in the room. I told her—" He ran his hand over his eyes. "That I'd told her she couldn't go should have made me know that she'd be there."

Some of Adam's anger left him; that was exactly like his sister. "So why did you kiss a woman who'd done what she did to you?"

"I don't know. I think it was relief that she was alive and not dead, which meant that the nightmare of my life was going to end. A thousand things went through my mind."

"Cay . . ." Adam was torn between wanting to shout at the man and feeling sympathy for him. But if there was one thing he knew, it was that Alex loved Cay. He'd seen it. Their love for each other was so strong a person could almost touch it. "Are you in love with your wife?"

Shaking his head, Alex gave a derogatory little laugh. "I'd never spent a whole day with her, and after today, I don't know how I ever believed I was in love with her. Cay told me I was a fool for marrying someone I didn't know, and she was right."

"I saw her, and her beauty dazzles a man."

"Aye, it does. That she wanted *me* made me feel that I had been given some great honor. But she also made me feel that I needed to earn masses of money so I could give her everything, houses, carriages, beautiful clothes. I wanted to give all that I could to her."

"She isn't like my little sister?" There was curiosity in Adam's voice.

Alex smiled. "Cay couldn't be more different. I think that if I told her I wanted to set up housekeeping on the moon, Cay would start packing."

"I always knew that if she fell in love, it would be hard."

"So she wasn't in love with her three men?"

Smiling, Adam sat down on a chair across from Alex. "It was me who persuaded our father to let her go to Charleston to have some time to think about her three marriage proposals. I wanted her to meet some other people, to see new places. I hoped that time and distance would make her forget those men she was thinking about marrying." Adam got up and poured two glasses full of single malt MacTarvit Scotch and handed one to Alex. "Did she tell you about the Daisies?"

"Never heard of them."

"Several of my father's friends, your father's friends, too, settled in Edilean, and got married. By chance, there were five baby girls born in the same year as Cay, and as they grew up, they became fast friends. When they were eight, they announced that they were going to call themselves The Chain because their friendship was as strong as steel. I think the idea came from Jess, the daughter of Naps and Tabitha who . . ." Adam waved his hand in dismissal. "If you knew them, you'd understand. Anyway, Tally heard this decree and said they were more like a chain of daisies than of steel. The name stuck. The five girls are still the best of friends, and we all call them the Daisies."

"All Cay talked about was her brothers," Alex said. "Night and day, it was all about the four of you. I didn't hear anything about her friends, except about one of them having ten brothers and sisters, and parents with a bad marriage. She said the daughter stayed at her house all the time to escape her home." Alex also remembered what

Cay had told him about a girl named Jessica and her tongue, but he didn't say that.

"That would be Jess. Yes, her parents fight a lot, but Jess stays at our house because my sister rolls out the red carpet for her. Dresses, riding, schooling. Whatever Jess wants, Cay gives it to her."

"That sounds like her." Alex was smiling.

"Are you hungry? I haven't had dinner. I could order something to be brought up. I figure you have a lot to tell me, and we can do it just as well over dinner."

"That sounds good," Alex said. He got up to look out the window as Adam pulled a cord on the wall and a white-coated steward appeared. Alex knew he was being given time to relax because Adam wanted all the information he could get, and he felt sure that Adam had some decrees of his own to make. Alex suspected that Adam was going to tell him that he couldn't see Cay again until the mess about Lilith was finished. Marriage, murder, all of it had to be done with and behind him before Alex could see Cay again. That was all right, because that was the same decision Alex had reached.

The two men didn't talk much until the food arrived, and they sat down to eat. Adam held out a plate of brussels sprouts and his eyes told Alex that it was time for him to start talking.

There was so much to tell that Alex wasn't sure where to start. "I'm not married."

"Oh?" Adam asked.

"The woman who walked down the aisle to me has a husband living in England. It seems that she murdered her husband's nephew, his heir, and I was used as a way for her to get out of being arrested. When she was living in Charleston, she discovered that some men were searching for her, so she came up with the plan to fake her own death in a very public way. She thought the men would report back to the English authorities that she was dead, then she'd be free to change her name again and . . ." He waved his hand. "I have no idea what she planned to do."

Alex took a few bites. "As soon as she told me she had a living husband, I took her to a judge here in New Orleans. I can tell you that that was no mean feat to get her there." Alex took a bite of food and chewed slowly. It was difficult to tell all that he'd learned in the last day. "The judge told us that if all two people had to do was swear that one of them was still married to someone else and thereby their marriage would be dissolved, there wouldn't be even one marriage left in this country. He said, 'I need *proof*! If she was married in England, then go to England and get me some documents. I want papers with seals on them. Gold seals. Just so I believe all of it.'"

"So you have to go back to England with her?"

"If I want all this horror taken from my life, yes I do." Alex took a deep breath. "I think that all I've been through because of that woman has taken away my ability to feel pity—at least for her." Alex took a bite of his steak and waited before speaking again. He was determined to get his anger under control.

"Even Nate didn't find any of this out . . . Merlin."

Alex smiled. "Merlin. All that seems like a lifetime ago. I wish I could walk away from here today and go to Cay a free man, but it's going to take me a long time to get all this settled legally. I've already told Cay that I need to go to Charleston with . . ." Alex looked down at his food. "Legal papers saying that I didn't kill her aren't enough for me. Does that make sense?"

"Perfectly. If I were in your situation . . . Actually, I can't imagine what I'd do."

"But then, you wouldn't have to, would you?" Alex said quickly. "You have family and friends. I had only T.C."

"I think you could add my sister and Nate to that list of people who've helped you and believed in you. And Tally and I have done a bit. By the way, Nate has already let me know that wherever you go, he's going with you. My brother is a very loyal person."

Smiling, Alex began to relax. "You'll have to forgive me. I've had a harrowing day."

"Take your time, I'm not going anywhere."

Alex pushed his half-eaten plate away
and stood up. "First, I need to go to
Charleston to clear my name. I need to
walk through the streets with . . ." He
looked at Adam. "Her name isn't Lilith Grey, it's Margaret Miller. She was
called Megs as a girl. You see, everything about her is a lie. Would you like to
hear her story, the one that she seemed
to think would make me forgive her for
everything?"

"I can't think of anything that I'd like
more than to hear why she did such an
abominable thing. We'll have cigars and
brandy."

Adam pulled the cord on the wall, and
the steward came so quickly that Alex
was sure the man had been waiting outside. It wasn't long before the table was
cleared, and when he and Adam were
alone again, Alex spoke.

"That kiss! What a great lot of trouble it caused! Megs thought that kiss
meant I'd forgiven her, so she tried to
flutter her lashes at me and lean over
me in a way that used to drive me wild

with desire. Now, it just repulsed me. It took hours to get the truth out of her, but she finally told me the whole story, and every word was told with loud sobs and pleas for sympathy." Alex calmed himself. "It seems that she was raised in great poverty, with a father who beat her. Again, I apologize for my lack of sympathy, but after what the woman did to me, I can feel nothing for her."

"I understand completely," Adam said, smoking his cigar and watching Alex as he paced the floor. "What did she say when you asked her why she stayed hidden while you were on trial?"

"She swears that she didn't know that I'd been accused of her murder, and she says that if she'd known she would have returned to Charleston immediately. I don't believe her." He paused. "After she found out that men were in town searching for her, she came up with her diabolical plan to make them think she was dead. She'd seen the way the doctor looked at her, so she cried and made up some sad, pathetic story. I don't know what it was, but it must have been a good one, because the doctor agreed to do whatever she wanted him to. She said that if he hadn't died, it would have worked perfectly, but . . ." Alex took a breath. "Anyway, after I was arrested and taken away to jail, the doctor had her 'body' taken to his office, where she washed the blood off her neck and got into a waiting carriage that was loaded with her luggage."

"And what was her plan for *you*?"

Alex had to take a breath before he could speak. "Nate figured that one out, too. The doctor was to declare her death to be a suicide, and that would get me released from jail."

"The town would have said that she killed herself rather than spend her life with you." Adam's voice showed his disgust.

"Aye, they would have. I think I might have preferred hanging. Even now, after people see that I didn't murder my wife, what I can't abide is if Cay's name is associated with this ugly mess. If she's there in Charleston with me—as she wants to be—people would say that she had something to do with all of it."

"Where there's smoke, there's fire."

"Exactly. That old adage. No," Alex said with a grimace, "I want all the gossip put where it belongs: on to Megs's head."

"What did she do after she left the doctor's?"

"She says she went to a tiny town in Georgia and stayed there. She even told me she did the best she could to look plain so no one would notice her."

"And how'd that work?" Adam asked, taking a long draw on his cigar.

"As always, she had some trouble with men. She presented herself as a young, beautiful widow living alone in a small town, so of course she had problems."

"Where'd she get the money to live?"

"She didn't say and I didn't ask, but I think she stole it from old lady Underwood. Do you know about her?"

"I don't think there was anything Nate didn't uncover about your trial, so, yes, we were told about the rich old woman. But since she lied under oath about your wife being her niece, I don't think she's going to prosecute for thievery."

"No. Lilith . . . Megs has a way of turning bad situations to her advantage."

"I take it the 'man problems' were what sent her packing to New Orleans."

"Aye, they did. She said she thought she could get lost in a city easier than in a small town. My opinion is that she was looking for her next husband to dupe. But who knows the truth? Maybe she just got bored and wanted excitement. If it hadn't been for George Campbell seeing her . . ."

Adam spoke. "When we were in Charleston, Nate questioned someone who mentioned New Orleans, so he made one of his 'educated guesses' as to where she was heading. Our plan was that I'd go to New Orleans and Tally would go into the swamps to find you two. Anyway, Tally was dying to go."

"I think he'd like being an explorer."

"Did you?" Adam asked.

"I enjoyed the company," Alex said with a smile as he remembered times with Cay.

"I think I'll skip that part, if you don't

mind. After all, we are talking about my little sister. Did you find out why the woman, Megs, chose *you* to pull this trick on?"

"It was one of the first things I asked her. She said that there were many men in Charleston who looked at her with eyes glazed in lust—those were her exact words: 'glazed in lust.' But I was different in that I had no family there, and the only people I knew hadn't known me for long. She said that after her faked suicide, she figured I'd leave town and never see any of them again."

"I take it that means she was only thinking about your welfare, not her own."

"According to her."

"So what was the story this woman gave you to explain her perfidy?"

Alex sat down. "I don't know if it's true or not, but I'll repeat what she told me. She said her father wanted to prostitute her out. He said her beauty could make them a great deal of money, but Megs had other plans for her life. When she was sixteen, she saw her chance to run away and took it. About twenty miles from where she grew up, she saw a carriage that had overturned, and the driver and the passenger, a young lady, were lying on the side of the road, both of them dead. I have to give it to Megs that she can think fast—and she seems to have no conscience about what she does to people. Anyway, she traded clothes with the dead girl and rolled her corpse into a river. When the bloated body was found weeks later, her father identified it as his daughter."

"So she got rid of him by faking her own death," Adam said. "Since it worked that time, I guess that's why she decided to use the same ploy again years later. What did she do when she was dressed in her fine clothing?"

"She went to the nearest rich estate and presented herself as a young lady who had lost her memory." Alex grimaced. "When I knew her, she said she couldn't understand my accent, but today I found out that she's good at mimicking. She showed me her original, impossible-to-understand London accent, then switched to the sounds of the English aristocracy. She even imitated my Scottish brogue. She should have gone on stage."

"I give it to her that she has courage."

"That's not what I would call it." Alex lit his cigar. "To make a long story short, a few years later, she married the rich widower who owned the house. He was forty-five and she was nineteen."

"Were they in love?"

"Megs said they were, but who knows? She used to tell me that she loved me more than life itself."

"Maybe she wasn't lying," Adam said, and Alex gave a guffaw.

"With her, I'll never know. It seems that her entire life has been a lie."

"Maybe a necessary one."

"If that's supposed to make me have sympathy for her, I ask you to go through what I did and see if you can make yourself care about her unhappy life."

"But then, she was the reason you met my sister," Adam added.

Alex smiled. "Even evil sometimes has good inside it."

"Was the murder what made her come to America?"

"Aye, it was. Her husband's nephew, who was to inherit, showed up, and he didn't take kindly to his rich uncle marrying a young, fertile woman. He hired some men to search and found out who she actually was."

"Ah, blackmail."

"At first, but she says it became something much worse. When he persisted in trying to blackmail her, molest her, all of it, Megs picked up a candlestick, hit the nephew over the head, and killed him."

Adam sat there, looking at Alex for a moment. "For her to go back to get a certificate declaring your marriage to be invalid would mean she'd have to stand trial for murder."

"Aye, she would," Alex said quietly. "I told her that I hope she can escape that, so I've promised to help her in any way that I can, but I'm not going to give up my life for her."

"And she's willing to return to England to face this?"

"Not at all. In fact, she threatened to

hit *me* with a candlestick." Alex looked at Adam. "I don't trust her. Right now I have those guards Nate hired *in* the room with her. I know that if she were given half a chance, she'd flee. Any woman who could do what she did to me, I don't trust. I'm going with her, first to Charleston, then to England. Whatever I have to do to get the proof that an American judge needs, I'll do it. If she has to stand trial for murder, so be it. I've sworn to her that I'll stay with her out of . . . of respect for another human being, but that's all. Maybe I'll change, but right now, I feel that if they hang her, she deserves it."

Alex rubbed his hand over his face. "How could I have thought I loved a woman I didn't really know? I should have been like Cay and made a list of the woman's good and bad points."

"I think my sister would disagree with you on that. I think that if you asked her now, she'd tell you that you should let passion carry you away." He was looking hard at Alex.

"What woman treats a man convicted

of murder with all the kindness and consideration that she would a guest in her own home?"

"My sister," Adam said. "Since the day she was born, she's been nothing but loving to us. Tally's done some truly awful things to her, but Cay's always managed to stand up to him."

"And what did you do to Tally when you caught him?"

Adam gave a one-sided grin. "I'd rather not say, but by the time he was eight, he knew better than to torture his sister." Adam's eyes turned serious. "What do you plan to do about my sister?"

For a moment, Alex couldn't speak. He walked to the far side of the room. "I think I'm going to need at least a year to clear all of this up."

"I take it you mean that during that time you won't see my sister?"

When Alex took a breath, it caught in his throat. "I want to give her a chance to make up her own mind. I want her to know what she really and truly wants. She was put with me in a live-

or-die situation, and I worry that maybe she thinks she loves me because of what we went through together." Alex straightened his shoulders. "And there's the subject of class. I'm just a poor man from the Highlands. I'm good with horses and not much else, but Cay is beautiful, educated, and used to a life that I'll never be able to give her." He looked at Adam. "Unless I used her father's money, and I won't do that. I know Cay's been sheltered, and she's had little exposure to life. Those men she wanted to marry—"

"Horrible!" Adam said. "They were all half my sister's intelligence, a quarter of her education, with not an ounce of her talent. Cay wants to please our parents, and she thinks to do that by making a suitable marriage."

Alex didn't smile at Adam's words. "And I'm not 'suitable.' If she chooses me, I want it to be of her own free will, not because of . . . of memories."

"That's very noble of you. If I were in your place and had found a woman I could love, I'd never let her go. If I had to, I'd lock her in a room and hide the key."

"That's a good idea. I'll—" Adam's look cut him off, and Alex laughed.

"You want something from me, don't you?" Adam said.

"Yes. While I'm away settling this horror, I want you to see that Cay is exposed to more of life. She found our foray into the wilds exciting, and I fear that that's what she likes about me. Wild rides across the countryside, sleeping in tents, hacking at alligators with a knife."

"I don't think I know the girl you're talking about. My little sister likes silk dresses and tea parties with French porcelain."

"She also likes—" Alex didn't finish that sentence because he'd been about to say that she liked making love in the moonlight. "I saw a different side of her, one that she's just beginning to discover."

"And you want her to see more of that?"

"Yes, I do."

Adam looked at Alex for a long moment. "She's young, beautiful, and rich. Are you sure you want to put her out there so other men can see her?"

"Of course I don't. If I'd never met Megs . . ." Alex paused, then looked back at Adam. "The truth is that I would never have looked at Cay if it hadn't been for all I've been through. If I'd met her under normal circumstances, I think I would have seen her as Nate's little sister, and I would have ignored her. I've always been attracted to the tall, beautiful, mysterious type."

Adam smiled. "Aren't we all? But in this case, the mystery had an evil core to it. I think that what you ask has some sound reasoning behind it, but in the same circumstances, I don't know that I'd be as generous as you are. I'll talk to Mother and she'll see that Cay is introduced to men outside of Edilean."

"Outside of Virginia. Outside of this country. Take her to Italy and get her an Italian drawing master. I don't think she knows how talented she is. I can see Charles Albert Yates paintings hanging in museums around the world."

"I see. *C.A.Y.* Yet another thing you know about her that her family doesn't."

"I have to go and get some sleep," Alex said. "Do I still have the hotel room?"

"I kept Cay's room open for you. I believe you know where it is."

Alex grinned. "Aye, that I do." He stopped at the door. "I don't know how I'm going to get through all this without Cay's humor. No matter how bad things were, she made me smile."

"She does that to all of us. As soon as she learned to talk, she made jokes."

"And drew."

"Yes. She drew and painted everything. You should ask Mother about the time she painted the drawing room wall."

"I would love to. There's something I wanted to ask you. Cay often talks about her mother's great beauty. Is she as pretty as Cay says?"

"Better. She's older now, but she still stops men in their tracks—much to my father's annoyance."

"Cay thinks she isn't as pretty as her mother is."

"And what do you think?" Adam asked.

"I think God was smiling when He made Cay."

"That's what we all think. Will you write her?"

Alex's hand tightened on the door handle. "I don't think so. I want to give her time to make up her own mind. The idea of a bad marriage scares her, so I want her to be sure of what she decides to do."

"I'll tell her the truth of what happened and where you went and why."

"Thank you," Alex said. "You know, I thought you were going to be different than what you are. Or maybe it was just jealousy at hearing your name morning, noon, and night. I'm beginning to think that you're worthy of being Cay's brother." With a smile, Alex left the room, closing the door behind him.

Adam stared at the door for a few minutes, then went to the desk to start writing a letter to his mother. He planned to comply with Alex's wishes about exposing Cay to other things, and to other people in her life, but Adam knew who he wanted for his brother-in-law, and he was going to work to see that it happened.

He began the letter.

Twenty-seven

❧

ONE YEAR LATER
Edilean, Virginia, 1800

Cay was sitting by the pond not far from the house, an easel in front of her, a watercolor tablet on her lap. She was idly painting the pretty little ducks on the water, the cattails growing along the edge, and the—

The smell of jasmine reached her, and she couldn't help but close her eyes in delicious memory. The scent brought to mind nights full of hot, humid air and making love for hours.

When she opened her eyes, she saw the form of a man reflected in the water and instantly knew who he was. She tried to still her heart, which had started pounding, and worked to control her urge to leap up and throw her arms around him. It had been so very, very long since she'd seen him.

"I saw Tim," she said and tried not to stop painting.

"Did you?"

The sound of his voice, so very familiar yet at the same time sounding like something from the faraway past, made her pulse race. His accent had mellowed, and that made her want to cry. She'd missed that change. Had his *wife* taught him how to speak like an English gentleman?

"I did," she said. "He didn't recognize me, so I flirted outrageously with him, and I asked about his trip into the wilds of Florida."

Alex put a large bouquet of jasmine by her easel where she could see it. Pinned to the stems were the three diamond stars and her pearl earrings that she'd left behind when they went to New Orleans. Alex knelt on the grass beside her, but she still didn't look at him. "And what did he say about that trip?"

"According to Tim, he saved my life half a dozen times."

When Alex spoke, there was laughter in his voice. "And what did you do to that poor lad for saying that?"

Cay didn't look at him but kept painting, as though his presence meant nothing to her. She didn't realize that she was painting the pond pink. "I did nothing whatever. However, later, he did have a most unfortunate accident with a rowboat. It seems that a poor little snake—well, not so little—had crawled inside the boat with him. Tim was so agitated that he fell into the pond. I had no idea he couldn't swim, so Tally had to dive in and save him."

Alex sat down on the grass. "He must have been glad Tally was there."

"Tim said he was saving Tally." She took a breath and began to fill in the sky with pale green paint. "Hope and Eli got married two months after they met."

"Nate told me. You were right about that match."

"Thankfull came to visit me, and Uncle T.C. happened to be here at the same time."

"That was a stroke of good luck. Did the twins come with her?"

"Aye, they did," Cay said, realizing she was slipping into the Scottish brogue that they'd always used between them. "And my mother found husbands for them."

"Did she?" Alex picked up one of the brushes from the wooden box on the ground and handed it to her.

Turning her head just slightly, Cay took the brush and looked at Alex's hand, but not at his face. It was a hand that she knew so very well, and it had touched every inch of her body.

"I hear that Armitage came to visit." Alex's voice was serious.

"Yes, he did, and we had a long talk. He told me that he knew who I was on the trip. Not at first, but after he saw my drawing, he said he remembered me. He said he also figured out who you were."

"I thought he did. I was afraid he'd have me locked up when we got to the trading post."

"Jamie said he thought about it, but

that he'd watched us and knew that you weren't hurting me. Adam told him everything about what happened."

"Your brother's been a good friend to me."

"He's like that." Cay used the brush that Alex handed her to paint the ducks purple. "Jamie asked me to marry him."

"Adam wrote that to Nate and he told me," Alex said. "When he read that to me, I went out and got drunk for three days, and I had to wait for nearly a month before a letter got to us saying that you'd turned him down."

"My mother was glad, but my father thinks I'm an idiot."

"And what do you think?" Alex asked softly.

"That I haven't a brain in my head."

Alex laughed. "I never loved you for your brain, anyway."

His words made Cay's heart pound so hard that her corset stays were straining. She wanted so much to look at him, but she'd had a year to think about her life and her future, and there were things that bothered her. "I heard that you and she spent a lot of time together in Charleston. I was told that you two make a beautiful couple."

"And I heard that your mother introduced you to a thousand young men."

"She did," Cay said, smiling as she put a blue bill on a duck. "She took me to London, Paris, and Rome for eight whole months, and I met everyone. My father's distant cousin married an earl's daughter, so that makes their son an earl. They have little money and no estate, but he does have the title. My mother used every connection she could get to introduce me to every eligible bachelor in three countries. She wanted to take me to Vienna, too, but by that time she was so miserable from missing my father that I couldn't take it anymore."

"What did you do?"

"I got sick. None of the doctors were clever enough to figure out what was wrong with me until I finally *told* one of them. We conspired, and he informed my mother that I was suffering from such a severe case of homesickness that she had to take me home immediately. My mother packed and had us on a ship within twenty-four hours. The funny thing was . . ."

"Was what?"

"That when she got home, she was so ill that she had to stay in bed for four whole days—and my father was so worried about her health that he stayed in there with her."

Alex laughed, and when he did, he reached out to take the hem of her skirt in his hands. He wasn't sure, but he didn't think he'd laughed even once in the last year. Between the hell that he'd been through and the seriousness of Nate's company, there hadn't been much to laugh about. "And what about the young men you met?"

"Some of them were wonderful," Cay said enthusiastically. "But some of them were horrible. I met a duke's son who told me that if I asked him to marry me, he would consider it. I think he believed I should be flattered by his offer."

"But you weren't?"

"Not in the least. I went on enough picnics that I nearly turned into a basket. Opera, ballet, concerts. And dances! I must have worn out a hundred pairs of shoes with dancing."

"And the result was?"

"What my mother wanted: marriage proposals, of course. My family is rich, thanks to what my mother came into the marriage with, and my father increased the money. Add that to the fact that I'm not difficult to look at, and that even the Englishmen admitted my manners didn't embarrass them, and I had dozens of men on their knees before me."

"And did you accept any of their proposals?"

She took a moment before answering. "I was so angry at you for leaving me behind that I wanted to. I fantasized about writing a letter telling you that I was very happy, madly in love, and going to marry a fabulous man."

"But you didn't," Alex said, and there was the beginning of relief in his voice.

"No, I didn't. But then none of the men knew *me*. They looked at me to see whether or not I'd fit into their lives. How many children could I bear? Was I capable of taking care of their estates? And my favorite was whether or not I would put up with their affairs. You know who was the only man I was truly attracted to?"

Alex tried to hold his frown back, but he couldn't. "No, who?"

"One of the horse trainers on the huge estate of an Englishman who wanted to marry my dowry. He was a tall man, with broad shoulders, and lots of dark hair. The English called him a 'wizard' with horses."

"A wizard?"

"I called him Merlin, and when we went out riding, I kissed him."

"Did you?" Alex's hands clenched into fists.

"Yes." Cay's voice changed to anger. "Yes! While you were kissing your *wife*"—she sneered—"*sleeping* with her, for all I know, I kissed a man."

Alex's hands unclenched. He was glad to hear her anger and her jealousy. "I kissed her just that once, when you were hiding behind the cupboard and saw it. Other than that, I didn't touch her, and I can assure you that I didn't sleep with her. Thanks to you, I was able to look past what had attracted me to her and saw the person. She never quit swearing that she didn't know I was put on trial for her murder, but there's no way she could not have known. Nate went to that little town in Georgia where she ran to right after what she did to me, and the newspapers there were full of the trial. The editor even had a record that she, under the false name she used there, had subscribed to the paper." He took a breath. "I could hardly bear to be near a woman who was capable of what she did to me."

"I know," Cay said. "Nate wrote us about how much you disliked her. But my brain and my heart don't seem to be connected. One hears and understands, but the other feels."

When Cay slid her foot toward him, he touched her ankle, encased in a silk stocking. When she didn't move away, he put his hand on her foot.

"Did Nate tell you that her husband's nephew is alive? She hadn't killed him, just knocked him unconscious. The men in Charleston who'd been searching for her were from her husband. He wanted her back."

"Nate wrote me everything." There was emphasis in her voice, letting him know that *he,* Alex, had never written her even once. But, through Nate, they had communicated. "So she's back with her husband?"

"Aye, she is." Alex removed her shoe and began to caress her foot. He knew that Nate had been writing and telling Cay what was going on, but there were some things that Alex had saved to tell her himself. "I talked to her husband in private and told him all that the woman had done to me. I even made Megs tell him the truth about her early life and how she lied to meet him. But he already knew it. She hadn't told me, but she'd worked in his kitchen when she was a girl, and he remembered her. He knew who she was when she showed up at his house wearing the clothes of his cousin's daughter. It didn't take much for him to figure out what had happened."

"And he forgave her?"

"More than that, he loved her. He told me that he'd married the first time to please his father and he'd hated his rich, aristocratic wife, but the second time he married to please himself."

"So they're happy?"

"When Nate and I left, Megs was carrying his child."

"Nate's child? Father won't like that at all!"

For a moment, Alex was confused, then he began to laugh—*really* laugh. It started inside him, rumbled up like a volcano erupting. He had forgotten her way of constantly making jokes about everything. He'd had a year of nothing but seriousness, of little laughter, as he cleared his name and dealt with judges and lawyers and Megs. He'd soon found that her beauty was a poor replacement for someone who wanted to make him feel good.

His laughter relaxed him, and Alex'd had all he could take of Cay's refusal to look at him. Her painting of the pond looked like something a color-blind child had drawn, what with its purple ducks with their blue beaks swimming in a pink pond. His hand went up her leg, and in the next second he pulled her down onto the grass beside him, and he began to kiss her face and neck.

"I've missed you," he said. "Every second of every day, I thought about you and wanted to be with you. Nate read me the letters you and your mother wrote to him, about every party and every dance you went to. Your mother even wrote about your damned shoes wearing out from so much dancing."

"I told her to put that in," Cay said, her eyes smiling as she looked up at him. Her hands were on his cheeks, feeling the smoothness of his face. She knew she'd probably show him the hundred or so pictures she'd drawn of him from memory in the last year. No matter how many men she met or how handsome they were, all she ever saw was Alex.

"I thought maybe you did, but I told myself, no, that my darling Cay could never be that cruel."

"Me cruel? You invented cruelty. The Spanish Inquisition could take lessons from you. My horrible brother wrote every word that you two found out about that . . . that woman and her stupid husband. He should have *hated* her!

Are you sure she didn't murder that girl in the carriage? Maybe she—"

When Alex kissed her, she stopped what she was saying. He moved his lips from hers, and looked at her, his eyes searching her face, memorizing it, as he smoothed her hair back. "I thought of that, too, but her husband knew about the accident. One of his workmen had already seen it, and the husband was on his way there when Megs showed up at his door, saying she was the dead girl. He was amused by her audacity, and it wasn't long before he was in love with her." Alex's voice lowered. "Who can understand love?" He ran his thumbs over her eyebrows, smoothing them. "I agree with your father, and if you had any sense at all, you'd take Armitage up on his offer to marry him. He's much more your class and—"

"My mother told me the truth."

He looked at her curiously. They were lying on the ground, and he was half on top of her, but he was too heavy for her to move. "The truth about what?"

"About her and my father."

"And what truth would that be?" His voice showed his amusement.

Cay pushed at him to get him off of her. "If you're going to lie to me and act like you didn't know the true story, you can just go back to wherever you were and stay there! You said, 'They were the most ill-matched couple in all of Christendom,' so I know that you know the whole story."

"How in the world do you remember every word of a sentence that was spoken over a year ago?"

She ignored his question. "I'm not going to be treated like a little girl anymore. Not by you or anyone else!"

Alex began to kiss her neck. "You mean your mother told you about your father being dirt poor and your mother wallowing in gold? That truth?"

"By all that's holy, but I think you're already laughing at me. I'd think that you'd at least put that ring you bought on my finger before you began making fun of me."

"I couldn't wait." He put his leg over her thighs.

She turned to look at him, taking in the

sweet familiarity of his face and thinking how very much she loved him—and always would. On the ship home, her mother had told her in detail all that she and Cay's father had been through before they married. All her life, Cay had been told sweet, perfect stories—lies, actually—about their courtship. But the truth had been very different, and Cay had been shocked to hear about the many similarities between what her mother and she had been through. When her mother told her about shaving Angus and seeing that he was handsome under all that hair, Cay told about throwing shaving water in Alex's face.

"Just dirty water?" her mother asked. "I shot at your father and nearly killed him."

Wide-eyed, Cay had listened to every word of her mother's story.

"Why are you looking at me like that?" Alex asked.

She started to tell him what she'd been told, but now was not the time. Instead, she glared at him. "If you think you're going to use me before marriage, you have another think coming."

"Use you? I remember a time when—"

With a hard shove, she rolled out from under him and held out her left hand. Her expression told him what she wanted.

With a sigh of defeat, Alex sat up. "What makes you think I have a ring? Ah, yes, Nate. He'd see no reason to keep the fact that I bought you a ring a secret."

"Of course my brother told me what you were up to, even to your trips to London jewelry stores. And he told me about that woman's husband giving you horses, and that you purchased the farm from my father. Nate said you wanted to rename it McDowell's, but it's going to be called Merlin's Farm or I'm not going to live there. Did my brother tell you that Uncle T.C. took my paintings from the Florida trip to London to present to the African Association, but they said a female couldn't have painted such pictures, much less have traveled into the inner reaches of Florida, so they want nothing to do with my drawings?"

"I know, love," Alex said softly. "He did tell me. But don't worry, we'll figure out something. And you can call the farm anything you want. I brought a dozen horses from England with me, and I got Tarka back." For all that Nate had seemed to tell "everything," Alex was well aware that his friend had told no one that in England Nate had met a woman very much like himself. But then, Alex had seen that Nate had no idea how affected he was by her.

"And I hear that your father came to America with you," Cay said, bringing Alex back to the present.

"Aye, he did, and my prize money from Charleston was returned to me, and I added to it with a few races while I was in England."

"So now you're rich," Cay said, sitting on the grass a few feet from him, her eyes looking as though she meant to devour him.

"Not by the standards of your father, but I can support a wife." He smiled. "And a child or two."

"I'm going to have nothing but girls."

"A wise choice. I've met your brothers."

"What's wrong with my brothers?"

she shot back, but when she realized he was teasing her, she glared at him. "I'm going to get you for that."

"Please do," he said, and when he opened his arms to her, just as he'd once imagined, she fell into them.

Enjoy a preview of Jude Deveraux's newest novel in the Edilean Series
Scarlet Nights

FORT LAUDERDALE, FLORIDA

"I think we've found her," Captain Erickson said. His voice was forced, showing that he was working hard to control his jubilation.

They were sitting at a picnic table at the Hugh Taylor Birch State Park, just off A1A in Fort Lauderdale. It was a September morning, and South Florida was beginning to cool off. By next month the weather would be divine.

"I guess you mean Mitzi," Mike Newland said, for just yesterday the captain had given him a thick file on the family. Mizelli Vandlo was a woman several police departments, including the fraud squad of Fort Lauderdale, plus the Secret Service—for financial crimes—and the FBI—for violence—had been searching for for years. As far as anyone knew, the only photo of her had been taken in 1973, when she was sixteen and about to marry a fifty-one-year-old man. Even then, she was no beauty and her face was easily remembered for its large nose and lipless mouth.

When the captain didn't answer, Mike knew that a Big Job was coming and he worked to keep his temper from rising to the surface. He'd just finished an undercover case that had taken three years and for a while there had been contracts out on his life.

Although Mike had never worked on the Vandlo case, he'd heard that a few years ago there had been major arrests in the family, all of it happening on one day, but in several cities. But Mitzi, her son Stefan, and some other family members had somehow been tipped off and had quietly slipped away. Until recently, no one had known where they went.

Mike poured green tea from a thermos into a cup and offered it to the captain.

"No thanks," the captain said, shaking his head. "I'll stick with this." He held up a can of something that was full of additives and caffeine.

"So where is she?" Mike asked, his voice even more raspy than usual. He often had to answer questions about his voice, and his standard half-lie was that it was caused by a childhood accident. Sometimes he even elaborated and made up stories about tricycles or car wrecks, whatever appealed to him that day. No matter what the story, Mike's voice was as intimidating as his body was when he went into action.

"Ever hear of . . . ?" As the captain fumbled in his shirt pocket for a piece of paper, Mike could tell that he was excited about something other than finding Mitzi. After all, this was at least the sixth time they'd heard she'd been found. "Ah, here it is." The captain's eyes were dancing about. "Let's see if I can pronounce the name of this place."

"Czechoslovakia no longer exists," Mike said, deadpan.

"No, no, this town is in the U.S. Somewhere up north."

"Jacksonville is 'up north.'"

"Found it," the captain said. "Eddy something. Eddy . . . Lean."

"Eddy Lean is a person's name, not a place."

"Maybe I'm saying it wrong. Say it faster."

A muscle worked in Mike's jaw. He didn't like whatever game the captain was trying to play. "Eddylean. Never heard of it. So where—?" Halting, Mike took in a breath. "Ed-uh-lean," he said softly, his voice so low the captain could hardly hear him. "Edilean."

"That's it." The captain put the paper back into his pocket. "Ever hear of the place?"

Mike's hands began to shake so much he couldn't lift his cup. He willed them to be still while he tried to relax his face so his panic wouldn't show. He'd told only one man about Edilean and that had been a long time ago. If that man was involved, there was danger. "I'm sure you've found out that my sister lives there," Mike said quietly.

The captain's face lost its smile. He'd meant to tease Mike, but he didn't like seeing such raw emotion in one of the men under his command. "So I was told, but this case has nothing to do with her. And before you ask, no one but me and the attorney general know about her being there."

Mike worked on controlling his heart rate. Many times before he'd been in situations where he'd had to make people believe he was who he wasn't, so he'd learned to keep calm at all costs. But in those times, it had been his own life in danger. If there was something going on in tiny Edilean, Virginia, then the life of the only person who mattered to him, his sister Tess, was in jeopardy.

"Mike!" the captain said loudly, then lowered his voice. "Come back to earth. No one knows about you or your hometown or your sister, and she's perfectly safe." He hesitated. "I take it you two are close?"

Mike gave a one-shoulder shrug. Experience had taught him to reveal as little about himself as possible.

"Okay, so don't tell me anything. But you do know the place, right?"

"Never been there in my life." Mike forced a grin. He was back to being himself and was glad to see the frown that ran across the captain's face. Mike liked to be the one in charge of a situation. "You want to tell me what this is about? I can't imagine that anything bad has happened in little Edilean." Not since 1941, he thought as about a hundred images ran through his mind—and not one of them was good. While it was true that he'd never actually been to Edilean, the town and its inhabitants had ruled his childhood. He couldn't help it as he put his hand to his throat and remembered *that* day and his angry, hate-filled grandmother.

"Nothing has happened, at least not yet," the captain said, "but we do know that Stefan is there."

"In Edilean? What's he after?"

"We don't know, but he's about to marry some hometown girl." The captain took a drink of his cola. "Poor thing. She grew up in a place that sells tractors, then Stefan comes along with his big-city razzle-dazzle and sweeps her off her feet. She never had a chance."

Mike bent his head to hide a smile. The captain was a native of South Florida where there were stores on every corner. He felt sorry for anyone who'd ever had to shovel snow.

"Her name's Susie. Or something with an S." He picked up a file folder from beside him on the bench. "It's Sara—"

"Shaw," Mike said. "She's to marry Greg Anders. Although I take it Greg Anders is actually Mitzi's son, Stefan?"

"You sure know a lot about the place for someone who's never been there." The captain paused, giving Mike room to explain himself, but he said nothing. "Yeah, he's Stefan, and we have reason to believe that Mitzi is also living in that town."

"And no one would pay attention to a middle-aged woman."

"Right." The captain slid the folder across the table to Mike. "We don't know what's going on or why two major criminals are there, so we need someone to find out. Since you have a connection to the place, you're the winner."

"And here I'd never considered myself a lucky man." When Mike opened the folder, he saw that the first page was from the Decatur, Illinois, police department. He looked at the captain questioningly.

"It's all in there about how Stefan was found. An off-duty cop was on vacation in Richmond, Virginia, with his wife, and he saw Stefan and the girl in a dress shop. The cop found out where they lived. As for you, a guy you worked with a long time ago knew about Edilean and your sister." When Mike frowned at that, the captain couldn't help grinning. Mike's secrecy—or "privacy" as he called it—could be maddening. Everybody in the fraud squad would go out for a few beers and afterward the captain would know whose wife had walked out, who was getting it on with a "badge bunny," and who was having trouble with a case. But not Mike. He'd talk as much as the other guys as he told about his training sessions, his food, and even about his car. It seemed like he'd told a lot about himself, but the next day the captain would realize that he'd learned absolutely nothing personal about Mike.

When the Assistant U.S. Attorney General for the Southern District of Florida called and said they thought one of the most notorious criminals in the U.S. might be in Edilean, Virginia, and that Mike Newland's sister lived there, the captain nearly choked on his coffee. He would have put money on it that Mike didn't have a relative in the world. In fact, the captain wasn't sure Mike had ever had a girlfriend outside a case. He never brought one to the squad functions, and as far as the captain knew, Mike had never invited anyone to his apartment—which changed every six months. But then, Mike was the best undercover cop they'd ever had. After every assignment, he'd had to hide until all of the people he'd exposed were in prison.

Mike closed the folder. "When do I go and what do I do?"

"We want you to save her."

"Mitzi?" Mike asked in genuine horror. "So she can stand trial?"

"No, not her. The girl. Of course we want you to find Mitzi, but we also want you to save this Sara Shaw. Once the Vandlos get whatever it is they want from her, no one will ever see her again." He paused. "Mike?"

Mike looked at the captain.

"If your sister really is there and if they find out about you . . ."

"Don't worry," Mike said. "Right now Tess is in Europe on her honeymoon. I'll tell her to keep her new husband out of town until this is solved one way or the other."

The captain opened another folder and withdrew an 8 x 10 glossy of a woman with dark hair and eyes. She was stunningly beautiful. She was standing on a street corner waiting for the light to change, and a slight wind had blown her clothes close to her body. She had a figure that made a man draw in his breath. "Does your sister really look like this?"

Mike barely glanced at the photo. "Only on her worst days."

The captain blinked a few times. "Okay." He put a picture of Sara Shaw on the table. The young woman had an oval face, light hair, and was wearing a white dress that made her look as sweet as Mike's sister looked, well, tempting. "She's not Vandlo's usual type."

Mike picked up the photo and studied it. He wasn't about to tell the captain that he knew quite a bit about Sara Shaw. She was one of his sister's two best friends, which said a lot, since Tess's sharp tongue didn't win over many people. But from their first meeting Sara had seen past Tess's biting words and extraordinary looks to the person beneath.

"Do you know her?"

"Never met Miss Shaw, but I've heard some about her." He put the picture down. "So no one has any idea what the Vandlos want in Edilean?"

"There's been a lot of research both from a distance and locally, but everybody who tried drew a blank. Whatever it is, Miss Shaw seems to be at the center of it. Is she rich but no one knows about it? Is she about to inherit millions?"

"Not that I've heard. She just opened a shop with . . . ." His sister kept him up-to-date on the gossip in Edilean but it wasn't easy to remember it all. Now it seemed that every word she'd told him was of vital importance. "With her fiancé, Greg Anders. Tess hates the man, says he snubs everyone who isn't buying something from him. But Tess does all of Sara's accounting so she's made sure Sara hasn't been put into debt by him."

"That sounds like a Vandlo." The captain hesitated. "Your sister manages people's finances?" His tone said that he couldn't believe a woman who looked like Tess could also have a brain.

Mike had no intention of answering that. He well knew the captain's curiosity about his private life and he wasn't going to reveal anything. "So you want me to catch these criminals, but I'm also to get the lovely Miss Shaw away from Stefan Vandlo? Is my assignment to follow and watch? Or am I to do more than that?"

"You have to do whatever you must to keep her alive. We think Stefan will murder Sara the minute he gets what he wants from her—and what he seems to want most is marriage."

"My hunch is that since the dresses

in the shop are expensive, Sara must get into a lot of rich houses. Maybe the Vandlos want to see what's in them."

"That's what we thought, too, but as her boyfriend, Vandlo already has access to the houses and no robberies have been reported. It's bigger than that and no one has a clue what it is." The captain tapped the folder. "After you read what's in here, I think you'll see that this scam of theirs is much more than just stealing a few necklaces. It's got to be if both mother and son are there." He lowered his voice. "We think Stefan divorced his wife of nineteen years just so his marriage to Miss Shaw will be legal—which means he'll inherit whatever she owns after she dies in some so-called 'accident.'" He looked at Mike expectantly. "You're sure you have no idea what's connected to Miss Shaw that's so valuable that two of the most evil conners in the world have prepared so well for this?"

"None whatever," Mike said honestly. "The McDowells are rich and Luke Adams lives there, but—"

"The author of the Thomas Canon

books? I've read every one of them! Hey! Maybe you can get me an autographed copy."

"Sure. I'll be a tourist who's lost his way."

The captain became serious again. "Too distant. You're going to have to use your connections to your sister, to the town, anything you can find, to get close enough to this girl to talk her out of marrying Stefan. We do *not* want it set up that he can inherit what is hers. And you have to do this right away because the wedding is in three weeks."

Mike looked at him in disbelief. "What am I supposed to do? Seduce her?"

"No one would ask you to do this if we didn't think you could. And, besides, I seem to remember that you've succeeded with several women. There was that girl in Lake Worth. What was her name?"

"Tracy, and she got ten to twenty. This one is a *good_*girl. How do I deal with her?"

"I don't know. Treat her like a lady. Cook for her. Pull out her chair. Girls like her fall for gentlemen. I'm sure that's how Vandlo got her. And before you ask, no, you can't kidnap her and you can't shoot Stefan. This young woman, Sara Shaw, has to stay there to help you find out what those two want." The captain grinned in a malicious way. "We've arranged for Stefan to be away for the whole time before the wedding. We gave him some family troubles that he can't ignore."

"Such as?"

"Even though he divorced his wife, we know he's still attached to her, so we arrested her on a DUI charge—which was easy. She's done a lot of drinking since Stefan left her, so we just picked her up one night, and now she's facing jail. We let her call him in the wee hours, and just as we'd hoped, he came immediately. If he gives us any trouble, we'll lock him up until he cools off." The captain smiled. "I wonder what he told his fiancée to explain why he went running off to his ex-wife?"

Mike was closing his thermos, his mind still on how to accomplish this mission. "I doubt if a liar like Vandlo had told her about his ex-wife."

"Eventually, you'll have to tell Miss Shaw the truth, so that should be a point in your favor. Whatever you do, you just have to do it *fast,*" the captain said. "And never forget that this young woman would be the fourth one to disappear after she got attached to Stefan Vandlo. He used a fake name and took those girls for everything they had. Then the girls 'disappeared' and the boyfriend, Vandlo, couldn't be found."

"Yeah, I read that," Mike said. "And if it weren't for some vague eyewitness reports, we wouldn't know who he was."

"Right, because Stefan left nothing behind, not so much as a fingerprint. And you know the rule: no evidence; no conviction. Personally, I'd like to arrest the man right now, but the higher ups want an undercover operation so we can get the mother. We take away her son and she'd just start using her nieces and nephews. She's the brains so we have to get *her* out of action. Permanently."

Mike looked at his watch. "I just need to stop by my apartment to get some things, then I can leave—"

"Uh, Mike," the captain said in a tone of apology, "it looks like you haven't seen the news in the last couple of hours. There's something else you need to know."

"What happened?"

The captain took the last documents from the bench and handed them to him. "I'm really sorry about this."

When Mike opened the folder, he saw a computer printout of a news story. *Apartment Burned,* the headline read. *Cigarettes to Blame, Say the Authorities.*

Mike's anger flared as he looked at the photo. It was his six-story apartment building and flames were coming out of the corner of the fourth floor—*his* apartment.

He put the papers with the others before he looked up at the captain. "Who did it?"

"The Feds say it must have been . . . Let me check. I don't want to misquote anyone." His voice was sarcastic as he flipped a paper over. "'A fortuitous accident' is what they called it. Lucky for them, that is." The captain's eyes were sympathetic. "I'm sorry about this, Mike, but they want you to go there clean. Your story is that your apartment burned down, so you decided to take a much-needed vacation from police work. It makes sense that you'd stay at your sister's apartment since it's empty. It's supposed to be a coincidence that her place is on the same property as Miss Shaw's. We—they—want you to lie as little as possible. Oh, yeah, I nearly forgot." He reached into his pocket, pulled out a new BlackBerry, and handed it to Mike. "Stefan cut his teeth on pickpocketing so when you do meet with him he'll take your phone. We don't want him to find any numbers on it that would give you away. While you're in Edilean you're to contact us *only* through your sister. Will that be all right with her?"

"Sure," Mike said, and renewed his vow to tell Tess to stay away. The case must be really serious if they'd burned down his apartment. He'd never tell anyone, but Tess had been sending him baked goods from her friend Sara Shaw for years now, and it was Mike's opinion that anyone who could bake like she could deserved to be saved.

When Mike was silent, the captain said, "Sorry about your clothes." They all knew Mike was a "dresser." "What did you lose?"

"Nothing important. Tess keeps whatever means anything to me in a storage bin in—" He hesitated. "In Edilean."

"My advice is that you don't visit it." The captain wanted to lighten the mood. "Again, too bad about the apartment. I was going to volunteer to look after your goldfish."

Mike snorted as he stood up. He didn't have goldfish or a dog or even a permanent home. He'd lived in furnished, rented apartments since he left his grandparents' home at seventeen.

Mike glanced at the roadway that wound through the park. He'd take a run—he needed it—then go. "I'll leave in two hours," he said. "I should be in Edilean about ten hours after that—if I use the siren now and then, that is."

The captain smiled. "I knew you'd do it."

"Want to go for a run with me?"

The captain grimaced. "I leave that torture to you. Mike?"

"Yeah?"

"Be careful, will you? Stefan has a bit of a conscience—or at least a fear of reprisals—but his mother . . ."

"Yeah, I know. Could you put together more info for me on mother and son?"

"How about if you jog over to my car right now and I give you three boxes full of material?"

Mike gave one of his rare laughs, making the captain look at him in question.

"You have something in mind, don't you?"

"I was thinking of how to introduce myself to Miss Shaw and I remembered a story my sister told me about a very old tunnel. It just happens to open right into the floor of my sister's bedroom. All I have to do is move Miss Shaw in there."

The captain waited, but Mike didn't elaborate. "You've only got three weeks. Think you can entice Miss Shaw away from a big-city charmer like Stefan in that time?"

Mike gave a sigh. "Usually, I'd say yes, but now . . ." He shrugged. "In my experience, the only way to get a woman is to find out what she wants, then give it to her. It's just that I have no idea what a woman like Sara Shaw could possibly want." He looked at the captain. "So where are these boxes of info? I need to get out of here." Mike followed him to his car.